THE SORCERESS OF THE STRAND AND OTHER STORIES

broadview editions
series editor: Martin R. Boyne

THE SORCERESS OF THE STRAND AND OTHER STORIES

L.T. Meade

edited by Janis Dawson

broadview editions

BROADVIEW PRESS – www.broadviewpress.com
Peterborough, Ontario, Canada

Founded in 1985, Broadview Press remains a wholly independent publishing house. Broadview's focus is on academic publishing; our titles are accessible to university and college students as well as scholars and general readers. With over 600 titles in print, Broadview has become a leading international publisher in the humanities, with world-wide distribution. Broadview is committed to environmentally responsible publishing and fair business practices.

The interior of this book is printed on 100% recycled paper.

Library and Archives Canada Cataloguing in Publication

Meade, L.T., 1844-1914
[Short stories. Selections]
The sorceress of the Strand and other stories / L.T. Meade ; edited by Janis Dawson.

(Broadview editions)
Includes bibliographical references.
ISBN 978-1-55481-148-9 (paperback)

I. Dawson, Janis, editor II. Title. III. Title: Short stories. Selections IV. Series: Broadview editions

PR4990.M34A6 2016 823'.8 C2015-908177-7

Broadview Editions
The Broadview Editions series is an effort to represent the ever-evolving canon of texts in the disciplines of literary studies, history, philosophy, and political theory. A distinguishing feature of the series is the inclusion of primary source documents contemporaneous with the work.

Advisory editor for this volume: Michel Pharand

Broadview Press handles its own distribution in North America
PO Box 1243, Peterborough, Ontario K9J 7H5, Canada
555 Riverwalk Parkway, Tonawanda, NY 14150, USA
Tel: (705) 743-8990; Fax: (705) 743-8353
email: customerservice@broadviewpress.com

Distribution is handled by Eurospan Group in the UK, Europe, Central Asia, Middle East, Africa, India, Southeast Asia, Central America, South America, and the Caribbean. Distribution is handled by Footprint Books in Australia and New Zealand.

Broadview Press acknowledges the financial support of the Government of Canada through the Canada Book Fund for our publishing activities.

Typesetting by Aldo Fierro
Cover design by Lisa Brawn

PRINTED IN CANADA

For Wayne

Contents

List of Illustrations

Illustrators and Illustrations

Stories from the Diary of a Doctor, *Strand Magazine* (1893–94). Illustrated by Alfred Pearse.
Stories from the Diary of a Doctor, *Strand Magazine* (1895). Illustrated by Gordon Browne.
The Brotherhood of the Seven Kings, *Strand Magazine* (1898). Illustrated by Sidney Paget.
The Sorceress of the Strand, *Strand Magazine* (1902–03). Illustrated by Gordon Browne.
The Heart of a Mystery, *Windsor Magazine* (1901). Illustrated by Adolf Thiede.

Alfred Pearse (1855–1933) was an illustrator and cartoonist whose work appeared in numerous newspapers and magazines including the *Strand*, *Illustrated London News*, *Boy's Own Paper*, and *Punch*. He also designed campaign posters for women's suffrage.

Gordon Browne (1858–1932), the son of Dickens's famous illustrator Hablot K. Browne ("Phiz"), was one of Britain's most prolific illustrators. Although closely associated with the *Strand*, his work also appeared in many newspapers, magazines, and popular children's books.

Sidney Paget (1860–1908) gained popular recognition through his definitive illustrations of Sherlock Holmes for Arthur Conan Doyle's popular *Strand* series. Paget's illustrations also appeared in the *Sphere*, *Graphic*, *Illustrated London News*, *Pall Mall Gazette*, and *Pictorial World*.

The work of Adolf Thiede (active 1882–1908) appeared in many leading magazines, including the *Queen*, *Illustrated London News*, *Ludgate Monthly*, *Temple Magazine*, and *Windsor Magazine*. He also illustrated children's books, including a number published by the RTS (Religious Tract Society) and the SPCK (Society for Promoting Christian Knowledge).

Acknowledgements

I would like to thank Lisa Surridge and Mary Elizabeth Leighton at the University of Victoria for their advice and encouragement in the introductory stages of this project. I would also like to thank Sally Mitchell at Temple University for her inspiration and professional generosity. Thanks are also due to Marjorie Mather at Broadview Press for her early and continuing interest in this project, and to Martin Boyne and Michel Pharand for their editorial assistance. To Wayne Meckle who has supported me in this work and in all things—a very special thank you. This one is for you.

Portions of the Introduction were included in "Rivaling Conan Doyle: L.T. Meade's Medical Mysteries, New Woman Criminals, and Literary Celebrity at the Victorian *Fin de Siècle*," *English Literature in Transition* 58.1 (2015): 54–72; the material is reprinted here by permission of the editor, Robert Langenfeld. The picture postcard "We Want the Vote" is reproduced by permission of the Museum of London (UK).

Introduction

L.T. Meade: A Portrait of a Literary Celebrity

In December 1898, readers of the popular *Strand Magazine* (1891–1950) who were fond of tidbits and gossip turned to the long-running illustrated feature "Portraits of Celebrities at Different Times of their Lives" for "a closer acquaintance" with Mrs. L.T. Meade (see Appendix A1, p. 251).[1] Meade, described by the magazine as one of its most popular contributors, was praised for her early literary successes with her girls' books and commended for her industry. Most readers would have recognized her as the author of trendsetting girls' school stories and the former editor of the highly regarded middle-class girls' literary magazine *Atalanta* (1887–98), but as her stories began to appear in the *Strand* in the summer of 1893, she gained additional recognition as the creator of compelling scientific and medical mysteries. Her series *Stories from the Diary of a Doctor* (1893–95) competed directly with Arthur Conan Doyle's celebrated *The Adventures of Sherlock Holmes* (1891–93); her latest series, *The Brotherhood of the Seven Kings* (1898), featuring the criminal schemes of the sinister female gang leader Madame Koluchy, had just concluded. Meade's elevated status in the most successful middle-class magazine of the period expanded her public image from popular girls' writer to include celebrity author of adult crime fiction. As a professional woman writer, she must have been pleased with the *Strand*'s recognition. "Portraits of Celebrities" included not only literary celebrities, but also artists, musicians, scientists, statesmen, bishops, generals, aristocrats, and crowned heads of state. It conferred status and significant market advantage upon an ambitious writer and signaled to Meade that she had achieved her youthful ambition to win "a niche in the temple of fame" (Meade, "How I Began" 62; see Appendix A2, p. 252).

But Meade's celebrity was short-lived. Although she authored

1 Meade was positioned as the leading celebrity in the feature that also included H.G. Wells (1866–1946), most famous for *The Time Machine* (1895) and *The War of the Worlds* (1898).

close to 300 books and countless stories in a variety of genres for readers of all ages, like many nineteenth-century women writers of popular literature her name is now little known. In the decades following her death, she was remembered (if at all) as the author of formulaic girls' fiction judged to have little merit. More recently, however, critics have looked beyond her girls' fiction to consider a wider range of her professional activity in the literary and cultural contexts of her time.[1] *The Sorceress of the Strand and Other Stories* draws attention to Meade's important contribution to the development of crime fiction at the Victorian *fin de siècle*[2] through a selection of some of her most significant stories published in popular magazines. It includes the complete six-part series *The Sorceress of the Strand* (*Strand*, 1902–03) along with selections from *The Brotherhood of the Seven Kings* (*Strand*, 1898), *Stories from the Diary of a Doctor* (*Strand*, 1893–95), and *The Heart of a Mystery* (*Windsor Magazine*, 1901). Each story focuses on the machinations of a fascinating, dangerous woman.

The Making of a Professional Woman Writer

Elizabeth ("Lillie") Thomasina Meade was born on 5 June 1844 in a rural rectory near Cork in southern Ireland. Although she was later famous for her girls' school and college stories and known for her support of women's higher education, her own educational experience was more traditional. Like most girls of her class in the mid-nineteenth century, Meade was educated at home by a governess. According to her accounts of her childhood, she began to write at an early age, but her literary inclinations were not encouraged. She claimed that her father denied her writing paper (she overcame this difficulty by writing on the margins of the local newspaper) and initially disapproved of her desire to earn money as an author (Meade, "How I Began" 58–59; Tooley 191 [see Appendix A3, p. 254]). Nevertheless she persevered, and in 1866 she published her first book, *Ashton Morton*.

Following her mother's death in 1874 and her father's remar-

1 Examples include Standlee; Pittard, *Purity*; Miller, *Framed*; and Hughes.

2 End of the century (French); generally used in reference to the latter decades of the nineteenth century. The period is often characterized as a time of social and cultural anxiety, political and economic uncertainty, decadence, and self-doubt. See Showalter.

riage shortly thereafter, Meade moved to London and began to prepare herself for a literary career by working daily in the Reading Room of the British Museum (Meade, "How I Began" 62; see Appendix A2, p. 252). The Reading Room, the heart of the nation's copyright library, was widely known as the Mecca of writers and literary researchers and the place where critical personal and professional connections were forged (Harris 24). Here Meade set herself the task of learning how to write marketable stories. She became particularly adept at following literary trends, frequently crafting her narratives by borrowing freely from her competitors' work. She also became proficient at exploiting sensational incidents and topical issues to construct bestselling novels about child abandonment and abuse, slum landlords, workhouse conditions, medical clinics for the poor, temperance issues, and mine disasters. With *Lettie's Last Home* (1875), the story of a London slum girl murdered by her alcoholic baby-farmer mother, Meade took advantage of public outrage over shocking details about baby-farming exposed by James Greenwood (1832–1929) and other investigative journalists.[1] Baby-farming, a practice whereby parents unable or unwilling to care for an infant consigned it to a guardian for a fee (many infants did not survive), was not new, but aggressive reporting combined with the sensationalized murder trials of two baby-farmers between 1865 and 1870 raised it from a tolerated activity to a national scandal (Knelman 145–80).[2] As the first novel of Meade's professional career, *Lettie* was well received by critics. A reviewer for the children's magazine *Aunt Judy* (1866–85) even suggested that the work might be read by "those who need enlightenment on the subject" (59).

Lettie was followed by a series of popular "street arab" tales modelled after the work of bestselling evangelical author Hesba Stretton (1832–1911), and within two years of her arrival in London, Meade secured a place in the juvenile market. She considered her professional career established with the publication

1 As a journalist with the *Pall Mall Gazette* (1865–1923), Greenwood had been foremost among the investigators who brought the appalling details of the practice before the public in the 1860s. He ranked baby-farming among the first of London's "curses" in his *Seven Curses of London* (1869). Greenwood was Meade's primary source for *Lettie* ("How I Began" 62).

2 Both women were found guilty of murder; one was executed while the other languished in prison for three decades (a wax figure of her was installed in Madame Tussaud's Chamber of Horrors until 1891).

of *Great St. Benedict's* (1876), a novel about the treatment of the poor in the out-patient system of London's hospitals, and *Scamp and I: A Story of London By-Ways* (1877), a sentimental novel about a faithful dog and an endearing orphan who earns a scanty living by cobbling old boots in a dank cellar in a London slum. As she later wrote, "From that day till now I have never been obliged to ask for orders—orders have come to me" ("How I Began" 64; see Appendix A2, p. 253). Her marriage to London solicitor Alfred Toulmin Smith in 1879 and the birth of four children in the next decade did not alter her determination to pursue a very active and public professional career as L.T. Meade.

Intense public interest in girls' education provided Meade with a new market opportunity in the 1880s. *A World of Girls* (1886), one of the most successful books of her career, established her as the founding author in the developing genre of the girls' school story. More school stories followed, and in 1891 Meade extended her range with her first college girl novel, *A Sweet Girl Graduate*. It was an immediate bestseller and (along with her other college stories) widely credited with popularizing the idea of higher education for women (Mitchell, "Elizabeth Thomasina Meade" 643; Sims and Clare 368; Reimer [14]).

Meade's reputation as a bestselling girls' author secured her the editorship of the newly founded girls' magazine *Atalanta* in 1887. The position brought her considerable prestige and opportunities to take leadership roles in women's literary and professional associations such as the feminist Pioneer Club and the Literary Ladies' Dining Club (Mitchell, *New Girl* 10; Hughes 244–48). Under Meade's editorship, *Atalanta* published progressive articles on girls' schooling, careers, and women's contributions to literature and national culture. It also mentored girls with scholarly and literary aspirations through its "Scholarship and Reading Union" and "School of Fiction" features. The magazine was known for its celebrity contributors—including Christina Rossetti (1830–94), Charlotte Yonge (1823–1901), Frances Hodgson Burnett (1849–1924), H. Rider Haggard (1856–1925), Andrew Lang (1844–1912), Grant Allen (1848–99), and Walter Besant (1836–1901)—and for the high calibre of its literary content, qualities clearly linked to Meade's reputation as a popular author.

By 1893, however, Meade was ready for a change. Following *Atalanta*'s amalgamation with the *Victorian Magazine* (1891–92), she resigned her position. The new arrangements may have precipitated her decision, but as she admitted in a celebrity interview in 1892, *Atalanta* took up "a great deal" of time: "more than half my days are occupied with it" ("How I Write My Books" 122–23). Given the direction of her career following her resignation, it seems likely that she wanted to devote her energies to a new genre: mystery and crime fiction, a genre closely identified with George Newnes's new *Strand Magazine*. In July 1893, two months before she left *Atalanta*, Meade's medical mystery series *Stories from the Diary of a Doctor* began to appear regularly in the *Strand*.

Meade's movement into new literary markets and genres marked an important period in the trajectory of her professional career, but she had no interest in abandoning the devoted girl readers who had helped her secure her niche in the temple of fame. She continued to publish bestselling girls' fiction alongside her crime fiction. In February 1899, two months after her *Strand* recognition, Meade topped the *Girl's Realm*'s list of the "most popular living writers of stories for girls" ("The Six Most Popular Living Writers for Girls" 431).

Meade and the *Strand Magazine*: New Markets

Popular taste for mystery and crime fiction was driven by the phenomenal success of Conan Doyle's Sherlock Holmes series introduced in the *Strand* in July 1891. That success clearly inspired Meade, and by the time he sent his detective hero to a presumed untimely and much lamented death in December 1893, Meade was on her way to earning recognition as one of the *Strand*'s most popular contributors of crime fiction.

But it was not only Conan Doyle's success that interested Meade. *The Strand*'s rapid domination of the periodical market within a short time of its launch in December 1890 (its first issue was dated January 1891) must have indicated to her that the magazine was a publishing phenomenon to be taken seriously. Close to 300,000 copies of the initial six-penny issue were printed and sold—a "staggering number for the time" (Adrian, *Strange Tales* xv). Circulation figures remained high throughout its first decade. *The Strand* was a trendsetting magazine poised to have a profound effect on the form and content of the middle-class periodical in particular, and on the literary market generally.

The Strand represented a distinct departure from the family literary magazine, the periodical format that had dominated the middle-class market for three decades. Family literary magazines such as the *Cornhill* (1860–1975) typically offered a variety of informational articles, reviews, and critical essays, but their mainstay was serial fiction. As a literary magazine for girls, Meade's *Atalanta* followed this model, relying on serials by popular writers (including the editor herself) to attract and retain readers. However, the *Strand* employed a different strategy: it presented itself as a middle-class miscellany offering readers entertaining and accessible information on a variety of subjects, from trivia and human-interest pieces to articles on natural history, science, travel, history, health, education, the arts, and current events. Romance, espionage, adventure, fantasy, mystery, detective, and children's fiction were well represented, but Newnes's preference for short pieces ("tit-bits") meant that each narrative had to be complete in itself, prompting a new interest in the short-story sequence involving a recurrent hero.[1]

The shift in the market contributed to the decline of many literary magazines, including *Atalanta*. A number of new *Strand*-inspired magazines were launched in the 1890s, including the *Ludgate* (1891–1901), *Idler* (1892–1911), *Windsor* (1895–1939), *Pearson*'s (1896–1939), *Royal* (1898–1930), *Harmsworth* (later the *London Magazine*) (1898–1930), and a refashioned *Cassell*'s (1897–1912). Meade's status as a *Strand* celebrity did not prevent her from taking advantage of publishing opportunities offered by its competitors.

[Readers are advised that plot details are revealed in the following sections.]

Meade's Medical and Scientific Mysteries

Even before Meade made her *Strand* debut, she turned to medical fiction with *The Medicine Lady* (1892), an ambitious adult novel about a woman who acquires a vaccine for tuberculosis and administers it with fatal consequences. Prompted by new medical discoveries by German physician Robert Koch (1843–1910) and written with Metropolitan Police surgeon Edgar Beaumont (1860–1921) using the pseudonym Clifford Halifax, M.D., the work marked the beginning of a new market interest for Meade—one that later earned her recognition as the inventor of the subgenre of the medical mystery (Mitchell, *New Girl* 11). It was also the first of two highly productive collaborative relationships that Meade formed with medical doctors. Beaumont, Meade's

1 Newnes introduced his formula for "time-saving reading which represents the scattered wisdom and opinion of the civilized world" in his highly successful lower-class miscellany *Tit-Bits*, launched in 1881 (Pound 2).

collaborator for *Stories from the Diary of a Doctor*, was succeeded by Robert Eustace Barton (1868–1943). Barton, using the pseudonym Robert Eustace, contributed to *The Brotherhood of the Seven Kings*, *The Sorceress of the Strand*, and *The Heart of a Mystery*. Beaumont and Barton provided Meade with medical and scientific information for a number of novels and stories while she did the actual writing (Greene ix; Mitchell, *New Girl* 11; Adrian, *Detective Stories* xxi; Hall 71–96).[1]

Meade's partnerships produced a compelling series of mysteries with a medical or scientific angle. Plots typically turn on manifestations of insanity, addiction, mesmerism, and new scientific discoveries ("impossible" discoveries are presented as "a forecast of an early realization").[2] Conventions common to gothic and sensation fiction are freely employed in these collaborations,[3] but Meade–Eustace narratives are particularly inclined toward "scientific gimmicks and gadgets," "bizarre medical information," and generous infusions of the supernatural and the occult (Greene ix; Mitchell, *New Girl* 11).

Stories from the Diary of a Doctor (1893–95)

Although Meade has been credited with inventing the medical mystery, she was not the first to introduce a medical doctor as

1 Barton also supplied scientific information (some of it inaccurate) to the celebrated crime writer Dorothy Sayers (1893–1957). See Hall 72–73.

2 *Stories from the Diary of a Doctor*, second series. Each story in the second series is prefaced with a declaration that "Those stories which may convey an idea of the impossible are only a forecast of an early realization." The defensive tone indicates that the medical and scientific accuracy of the authors' work had been questioned (Pittard, *Purity* 157–58).

3 Conventions include a menacing or foreboding atmosphere and a sense of decay; settings are characteristically gloomy, often involving prisons, asylums, and isolated or remote dwellings, while plots frequently focus on family secrets, disputed legacies, insanity, bigamy, abduction, and murder. Sensation fiction, an enormously popular genre in the 1860s and onward, drew on many of the conventions of gothic fiction, an earlier (eighteenth-century) literary form. Sensation novels, however, were "up to the minute in their topicality" and commonly inspired by current criminal cases reported in the press (Sutherland 563). As discussed later in the Introduction, gothic fiction itself underwent a revival in the latter decades of the nineteenth century.

the narrator and protagonist in a tale of mystery and suspense. Six decades earlier, Samuel Warren (1807–77) created such a character for *Passages from the Diary of a Late Physician* (1830–37), a long-running series published in *Blackwood's Magazine* (1817–1980). Warren specialized in deathbed scenes embellished with intimate (sometimes criminal) confessions and memorable incidents of insanity attended by a wordy moralizing physician whose character was often overshadowed by his more interesting patients. Warren's popular work (republished in volume form several times in the nineteenth century) was probably known to Meade, but it seems likely, given Conan Doyle's growing fame, that her initial inspiration came from the latter's early medical stories. Conan Doyle's fame now rests on his contribution to the detective genre through his celebrated detective, but prior to his *Strand* series he published a number of stories with medical themes or settings (many were reprinted in a collection titled *Round the Red Lamp* [1894]). The success of Conan Doyle's rational detective may have prevented him from exploiting the full potential of these medical stories, but Meade quickly saw the marketability of the material. Her medical mysteries are significant because they participate directly in the expanding discourse on crime as disease promulgated by criminal anthropologists such as Cesare Lombroso (1835–1909) and Havelock Ellis (1859–1939), who proposed a medical model of crime that situated criminal tendencies in the body, thus fuelling fears of degeneration or reverse evolution.[1] In *fin-de-siècle* medical mysteries like Meade's *Stories from the Diary of a Doctor*, crime became a "degenerative social disease," with the medical practitioner taking the part of the detective.[2]

Meade's series, which appeared in twelve parts beginning in July 1893, "excited considerable interest," according to contemporary sources (Black 228). This was no small achievement for Meade and Halifax, given that for six months they competed with the final episodes of Conan Doyle's series. There is no clear evidence that interest in Meade's series rose following the "death" of Sherlock Holmes as devoted fans sought compensation for their literary loss (Holmes was famously resurrected eight years later

1 See the Introduction to Lombroso's *Criminal Man* by Gibson and Rafter 2; Thomas 659; Pittard, "Victorian Detective Fiction" [6–7]).

2 See Pittard, "Victorian Detective Fiction" [7]; Pittard, *Purity* 145; Parrett 99–103.

in another *Strand* series, *The Hound of the Baskervilles*). However, Meade and other writers including Grant Allen,[1] Arthur Morrison (1863–1945),[2] and Dick Donovan (1842–1934),[3] profited from the success of Conan Doyle's series. The popularity of Meade's medical mysteries prompted a second twelve-part series that began in January 1895.

Although it never achieved the fame of *The Adventures of Sherlock Holmes*, Meade's *Stories from the Diary of a Doctor* is compelling. As in Conan Doyle's series, Meade's stories are presented by a medical man. However, Dr. Halifax, unlike Conan Doyle's Dr. Watson, is no admiring amanuensis; Halifax narrates his own adventures. Because he can focus on the problem at hand rather than on the ratiocinations of his clever associate, Halifax injects greater urgency and immediacy into his accounts. By giving Halifax the primary role in the narrative, Meade sets her series firmly within contemporary discussions of crime, disease, and degeneration.

Halifax and Holmes have much in common. Both are gentlemen who engage in amateur detective work from their London homes. Both are bachelors, and though Halifax seems more susceptible to the charms of beautiful women than Holmes—he is attracted to a number of fascinating but dangerous women—like Holmes he avoids serious romantic attachments. Halifax and Holmes also pursue similar cases involving property crime, fraud, forgery, blackmail, theft, and disputed inheritances, and their intervention generally (though not always) ensures a reassuring restoration of the status quo. Their cases are also replete with imperial allusions and artifacts, including exotic characters and creatures, mysterious drugs and poisons, fabulous jewels,

---

1 Allen's contributions to detective fiction in the *Strand* include numerous short stories and three series: *An African Millionaire* (1896–97), *Miss Cayley's Adventures* (1898–99), and *Hilda Wade* (1899–1900).

2 Morrison, now best known for his naturalistic fiction about London's slums, wrote a series of popular detective stories for the *Strand* and *Windsor* magazines between 1894 and 1896 featuring private investigator Martin Hewitt. Hewitt also appears in *The Red Triangle*, published in the *London Magazine* (1903).

3 Dick Donovan, the pseudonym of Joyce Emerson Preston Muddock, wrote dozens of detective stories and thrillers. His four-part series *A Romance from a Detective's Casebook* was published in the *Strand* in 1892 in the interval between the first and second Sherlock Holmes series.

and references to England's interests in India, Asia, the West Indies, and the Americas.

Although all of Meade's stories have medical settings or incidents, not all involve detection or mystery. For example, "The Heir of Chartlepool" (October 1893) focuses on Halifax's remarkable ability to perform successful brain surgery in his sleep. Other stories involve miracle cures by means yet unknown to science but, according to the authors, "within the region of practical medical science" (Preface, *Stories from the Diary of a Doctor*, Second Series). For example, in "Creating a Mind" (January 1895), Halifax cures an "idiot" child by performing a life-threatening operation to expand its skull (the medical procedure is now regularly performed by specialists to prevent brain damage). Drug abuse and various criminal activities also underpin many of the cases that require Halifax's medical intervention. In "My First Patient," the opening story in the first *Strand* series (July 1893), Halifax attends a woman dying from an opium overdose. Halifax discovers that her husband, a physician with a secret past, has poisoned the unsuspecting woman and attempted to take his own life in order to escape exposure. Using the latest medical procedures, Halifax revives both patients, but the story ends on a morally ambiguous note because Halifax preserves his colleague's secret, thus allowing the extortionist to escape. As in a number of Conan Doyle's stories, such as "The Adventure of the Copper Beeches" (1892) and "The Adventure of Charles Augustus Milverton" (1904), crimes are committed but no one is brought to justice because the investigating protagonists suppress critical information from the police or other legal authorities. Halifax's last word on the case is that the doctor's wife "was never told the real story of that night."[1]

Three stories in the series feature a *femme fatale*: "Very Far West" (September 1893), "With the Eternal Fires" (October 1895), and "The Seventh Step" (February 1895; reprinted in this collection, pp. 47–70). The dangerous female characters in these stories are early examples of the deadly women at the centre of Meade's later series, *The Brotherhood of the Seven Kings*, *The Sorceress of the Strand*, and *The Heart of a Mystery*. Though not unique to the nineteenth century, the *femme fatale* figures prominently in *fin-de-siècle* fiction as a recurring expression of social and cultural anxiety. As Rebecca Stott observes, "she is fabricated, reconstructed in, and apparently necessary to, the cultural expressions of the closing years of the century":

1 "My First Patient," *Diary* (July 1893): 102.

> [T]here is a variety of names for her, from the 'wild woman' of Eliza Lynn Linton, to the vampires of Bram Stoker. She appears time and time again in art, poetry and fiction either in her mythical forms or in contemporary guise: she can be prostitute, man-hunting aristocrat, vampire, African queen ... or murderess. She crosses boundaries of class and race. (viii)

In "Very Far West," a beautiful young woman named Leonora lures Halifax to a strange house in a deserted square outside central London on the pretext of providing medical assistance to her father. It is clear from Halifax's description of the woman's physical charms that his interest in the case is more than professional. Halifax places himself in grave danger by following the woman home, and before the night is over, he is locked in a secret room, rendered unconscious by a deadly gas, robbed, and dumped in a hansom cab bound for an unknown London address. Halifax recovers, but, confused by the gas, he is unable to lead the police to the deadly house. The story thus concludes with a sense of profound unease; the location of the crime cannot be fixed and the criminals disappear, presumably to strike again.

In "With the Eternal Fires," Halifax pursues a Creole woman named Thora who has abducted the son of a wealthy patient. Like all of Meade's dangerous women, Thora is strikingly beautiful and capable of exerting unbounded influence over her victims. She is also "quite the cleverest woman," expert in the art of disguise, capable of "outwitting twenty detectives," and impossible to contain.[1] Halifax eventually locates the child in a remote Russian town known for its kerosene works ("eternal fires") and its cult of Hindu fire worshippers, but Thora disappears and is never brought to justice.

In "The Seventh Step," Halifax meets beautiful Olga Krestofsky—a dangerous political terrorist in disguise—while on a holiday cruise to Russia. When the boat docks in St. Petersburg, Olga lures Halifax to a nearby palace where her associates plan to kill him. At the last minute, however, she helps him escape through a secret passage, and, like the other dangerous women Halifax encounters, she disappears and is never seen again.

"The Seventh Step" is an interesting contribution to "dynamite narratives," a popular fiction genre inspired by *fin-de-siècle* political unrest at home and abroad and fuelled by "the public's

1 "With the Eternal Fires," *Diary* (October 1895): 381.

appetite for espionage, conspiracies, and explosions" (Agathocleous 12).[1] Significant examples of dynamite fiction include Henry James's *The Princess Casamassima* (1886), Grant Allen's *For Maimie's Sake* (1886), Isabel Meredith's *A Girl among the Anarchists* (1903), and Joseph Conrad's *The Secret Agent* (1907). Although bombings and terrorist events in Britain in the 1880s and 1890s were largely the work of Irish revolutionaries (including Irish Americans) determined to abolish British control of Ireland and establish an independent Irish republic, English *fin-de-siècle* authors apparently preferred their dynamite narratives to have a more international flavour. Apart from some notable exceptions, such as *The Dynamiter* (1885) by Robert Louis Stevenson and Fanny Van de Grift Stevenson, and "A Service to the State" (1897) by Guy Boothby, Irish political agitation and extremism were too immediate to be highly marketable as leisure reading. Female terrorists and operatives were common in dynamite fiction from the 1880s on; Meade introduced more female terrorists in *The Siren* (1898) and *The Heart of a Mystery*. However, as Elizabeth Carolyn Miller observes, "there were no women assassins, bombers, or dynamiters in late-Victorian Britain" (*Framed* 190). Miller links the popularity of fictional female terrorists to emerging feminism, gender anxiety prompted by women's increasing visibility in the public sphere, and fears of "degenerative masculinity and unruly femininity" (*Framed* 159). Fictional female terrorists rebel against established political and patriarchal structures of authority, typically eluding capture by ineffective male detectives, policemen, and secret agents (some escape through suicide). Meade's Olga reflects these gender anxieties; significantly, she disappears after arranging Halifax's escape, leaving him stranded and alone on a dark St. Petersburg street, his vulnerability and ineffectiveness all too apparent.

Leonora, Thora, and Olga are exceptional characters in *Stories from the Diary of a Doctor.* The leading female characters in the series are generally melodramatic or relatively conventional, although there are examples of female strength and courage. But Meade's most skilful and compelling creations are her dangerous women. Leonora, Thora, and Olga are prototypes for her arch-villainesses, Madame Koluchy, Madame Sara, and Mademoiselle Delacourt—fictional women who seem to prove Lombroso's theory that the female criminal is more monstrous, diabolical, and terrible than the male (see Appendix C3, pp. 289–93).

1 See Appendix D, pp. 297–302.

The Brotherhood of the Seven Kings (1898) and *The Sorceress of the Strand* (1902–03)

Dangerous and Deadly New Women: Madame Koluchy and Madame Sara

In her article on Meade's *The Sorceress of the Strand*, Jennifer Halloran suggests that contemporary readers would have been struck by the "oddity" of the central character, Madame Sara, "a female and foreign manifestation of the arch-villain, so diabolically clever that ... she 'made [traditional] rogues look like sissies'" (176). With her occult powers and her mastery of the latest scientific knowledge Madame Sara is indeed a formidable force, but she is a remake of the deadly Madame Koluchy introduced four years earlier in *The Brotherhood of the Seven Kings*.

Although Madame Sara deserves her dangerous reputation, in the creation of Madame Koluchy, Meade establishes the character of the beautiful female criminal who is skilled in witchcraft and the occult, well versed in the administration of mysterious drugs and lethal poisons, experienced in the use of explosives, and expert in the modern sciences to which few women had access. As the "chief and queen" of the sinister "Brotherhood of the Seven Kings" (see "At the Edge of the Crater" pp. 73–94),[1] Koluchy is considered the first female gang leader in literature (Mitchell, *New Girl* 11). She is a fictional example of the real female gang leaders ("Napoleon[s] in petticoats") described in Lombroso's *The Female Offender* (see Appendix C3, p. 292). Koluchy and Sara, archetypal *femmes fatales*, represent a serious danger to the established order. Both traverse gender boundaries, foil established patriarchal networks of power and influence, and repeatedly use their wealthy female clients to gain entry into domestic spaces where they commit heinous crimes and vanish before they can be brought to justice.

Significantly, at a time when imperial interests and the emerging science of criminal anthropology linked criminality to foreignness in the public imagination (Thomas 658–59), these women are not English: Koluchy is Italian; Sara is an exotic mixture of Italian and Indian (South Asian or South American). Foreign nationalities were long associated with criminality in literature—perhaps most famously in Conan Doyle's *The Sign of Four* (1890) and Wilkie Collins's *The Woman in White* (1860) and *The Moonstone* (1868)—but Sara's hybrid identity is particularly threatening. As Clare Clarke notes in her

1 All parenthetical page references to "The Seventh Step," "At the Edge of the Crater," "A Little Smoke," and *The Sorceress of the Strand* are to this Broadview edition.

discussion of Boothby's *A Prince of Swindlers* (1897), set in London and Calcutta, "for readers in the late 1800s, hybrid national identity [was] a well-known and often-employed signifier of potential danger" (533). Sara's foreignness is highlighted by her relationship with other "exotic" characters who assist her with her criminal schemes: José Aranjo, "partly Indian, partly Italian," reputedly "as cruel as he [is] clever" and known to possess "wonderful secrets of poisoning unknown to the West" ("Madame Sara," p. 137); and Achmed, an Arabian servant described as "one of the most dangerous men ... ever seen, with the subtlety of a serpent, and legerdemain in every one of his ten fingers" ("The Blood-Red Cross," p. 148). The women's origins are otherwise obscure, although both appear to be wealthy (presumably though the proceeds of crime) and well informed about the manners and customs of the English upper classes.

Meade exploits widespread fears of anarchist organizations and concerns about foreign-based criminal societies by introducing *The Brotherhood of the Seven Kings* as an account of "real" incidents that began in London only a few years earlier (1894 and 1895). In a brief introduction appended to the first story ("At the Edge of the Crater," reprinted here), the authors frame the series and present its narrator and protagonist, Norman Head, a scientist, former member of the Brotherhood, and Koluchy's one-time lover (pp. 73–74). Throughout the series, Head struggles to apprehend Koluchy with the help of his friend and legal advisor Colin Dufrayer and a team of Scotland Yard detectives. Dufrayer is murdered by Koluchy in the final episode.

Head's counterpart in *The Sorceress of the Strand*, set in 1899, is the narrator Dixon Druce, the manager of a solvency inquiry agency and an amateur scientist. Druce and his police surgeon colleague Eric Vandeleur combine forces to capture Sara, but they are unsuccessful. In both series, the authorities' inability to bring the women to justice draws attention to the villainesses' cleverness, emphasizes their fascinating powers, and heightens their appeal; Koluchy and Sara are "at once so appalling *and* so appealing" (Miller, *Framed* 67).[1] Contributing to the tension is the awareness that the world in which the women commit their nefarious crimes is disturbingly recognizable. They operate—apparently unchecked—in a landscape firmly anchored in the real world of *fin-de-siècle* London with its familiar streets, busy railway stations, fashionable neighbourhoods, theatres, clubs, and famous public monuments.

1 The phrase refers to the female criminal in Conan Doyle's "The Adventure of Charles Augustus Milverton," but it is an apt description of Meade's characters.

Fig. 1. The fascinating Madame Sara. "The Teeth of the Wolf," *The Sorceress of the Strand, Strand Magazine* (March 1903): 281

Meade's stories are unsettling because Koluchy and Sara challenge many of the conventions of nineteenth-century detective fiction by subverting "traditional portrayals of the relationship between detective and criminal" in which the detective defeats the criminal and restores order and control (Halloran 176). By contrast, her stories present a "dystopic view of a society in which the aberrant criminal can be contained only provisionally" (Halloran 176). Her characters are modelled after Lady Audley and Lydia Gwilt, well-known villainesses in Mary Elizabeth Braddon's *Lady Audley's Secret* (1862) and Collins's *Armadale* (1866) respectively.[1] Seductive, scheming, and treacherous, Lady Audley and Lydia Gwilt possess snakelike abilities to hypnotize their victims and a willingness to commit murder to achieve their ends. Interestingly, the "ageless" Sara also resembles the "childish" Lady Audley; both characters

1 Both novels were bestsellers in the 1860s and remained popular and controversial for decades.

have blue eyes, "quantities of rippling gold hair," beautiful complexions, and "innocent," "childlike" manners.[1]

The crimes committed by Koluchy and Sara include fraud, blackmail, gambling, robbery, kidnapping, torture, murder, and (in Koluchy's case) acts too "ghastly," "grotesque," and "horrible" to describe ("At the Edge of the Crater," p. 74). But Meade's characters are more than criminals; they are entirely evil. Koluchy has "eyes of terrible power and Satanic beauty"—"she is a devil not a woman," a "fiend in human guise";[2] while Sara, described as "uncanny and terrible" by one of her clients ("Madame Sara," p. 123), is no less fiendish ("Madame Sara," p. 141; "The Blood-Red Cross," p.157). She casts "spells" over vulnerable women who seek her advice, sapping their vitality and leaving them nervous, depressed, and fearful.[3] Both women haunt the dreams of the men who fail to catch them.[4] Additionally, as beautiful fiends with occult powers of fascination, Koluchy and Sara draw on the character of the female vampire represented in nineteenth-century gothic fictions such as Florence Marryat's *The Blood of the Vampire* (1897) and Bram Stoker's *Dracula* (1897). This association is significant; as Jamieson Ridenhour observes, "psychological, religious, sexual, ethnic, and nationalist fears [are] crystallized in the vampire" (x).

Koluchy and Sara are more threatening than their sensational sisters of the 1860s because they are modern women—bold, ambitious, transgressive, vampiric *femmes fatales* aligned with the controversial New Woman[5]—who operate successful businesses in the public sphere and use the latest scientific and medical techniques

---

1 "Madame Sara," p. 120; Braddon 52, 90.

2 "The Iron Circlet," *Brotherhood* (July 1898): 13; "The Strong Room," *Brotherhood* (August 1898): 128, 130.

3 ("Madame Sara," pp. 125, 128-29). Sara has this effect on most of her female clients.

4 "The Talk of the Town," p. 186; "The Doom," *Brotherhood* (October 1898): 416.

5 The term "New Woman" emerged in the 1890s to describe women who sought opportunities for self-development and independence beyond the traditional domestic sphere (marriage and devotion to the family). New Women were often portrayed in the press and in literature as mannish, unnatural, dangerous, and grotesque. Because they agitated for educational and employment opportunities, greater personal and economic freedom, and even the vote, New Women were often represented as a threat to the political and social status quo. See Appendix C, pp. 279-96.

to serve their crimes. Koluchy, who "has science at her finger ends" and the ability to perform "wonderful cures," calls herself a medical professional and a beauty therapist and advertises that "she is able to restore youth and beauty by her arts."[1] Koluchy is known as "the great lady doctor," while the narrator confirms, "The medical world agitated itself about her to an extraordinary degree.... Under her influence and treatment weak people became strong again. Those who stood at the door of the Shadow of Death returned to their intercourse with the busy world. Beneath her spell pain vanished."[2]

Sara is also called a doctor as well as a "professional beautifier" ("Madame Sara," pp. 120, 122, 127). As the elaborate arrangements of her business premises in the Strand indicate, she is accustomed to providing not only beauty treatments but also surgeries in her sophisticated modern laboratory *cum* operating room or "sanctum sanctorum" ("Madame Sara," pp. 126–27). Apparently "Madame's dentistry is renowned" ("Madame Sara," p. 130); indeed, her proficiency enables her to administer a deadly poison to two wealthy heiresses by secreting it in cavities in their teeth ("Madame Sara," pp. 140–41). The furnishings of Madame's *sanctum sanctorum* and the secrecy surrounding her premises recall Collins's description of Mother Oldershaw's establishment in *Armadale*.

Madame Rachel: The Sorceress of Bond Street

As beauty therapists, Koluchy and, to an even greater extent, Sara draw on the career of a real female criminal, Madame Rachel (Sara Rachel Leverson; also Levinson or Levison), a self-styled professional beautifier who flourished in the 1860s and 1870s. Little is known about Rachel's origins; according to various accounts she began her career by telling fortunes and selling old clothes and fried fish in a London slum market before publishing (with her daughter's assistance) a successful beauty manual (*Beautiful For Ever!*) and establishing herself in an expensive shop in Bond street in one of the most fashionable parts of London. She managed to amass a considerable fortune that bought her a handsome carriage and pair, a fine house, a £400 box at the opera, and costly educations for her children (Chesney 281–82; Rappaport 59, 87–88).

Because of the notoriety of her activities, contemporary

1 "The Winged Assassin," *Brotherhood* (February 1898): 146; "At the Edge of the Crater," pp. 76–77.

2 "The Star-Shaped Marks," *Brotherhood* (June 1898): 656; "The Luck of Pitsey Hall," *Brotherhood* (April 1898): 379.

readers would have connected Rachel with Meade's Madame Sara despite the passage of time. Rachel's very public trials for fraud, blackmail, and theft attracted enormous attention in the press and inspired ballads, vaudeville productions, and wax effigies. She was displayed in numerous travelling exhibitions and in the permanent exhibition of Madame Marie Tussaud (1761–1850), the most celebrated wax modeller of the period.[1] Rachel's activities also inspired countless references in topical novels, including Margaret Harkness's *In Darkest London* (1889), a social-realist work about the activities of the Salvation Army's "slum saviours" in London's poorest neighbourhoods.[2] However, the most memorable literary allusions occur in *Lady Audley's Secret* (she is named several times) and *Armadale*. Most critics concede that Rachel, who may have been "a 'madam' in more ways than one," was the model for Collins's Mother Oldershaw, a beautician, procuress, and abortionist's agent, as well as Lydia Gwilt's confidante (Miller, "Shrewd Women" 313).[3] Other examples of Rachel's notoriety include a New Zealand hot spring known in the 1880s as "Madame Rachel's Bath" (Boase 323; McDonnell 645) and a shade of face-powder called "Rachel" marketed well into the twentieth century (Miller, "Shrewd Women" 313).

---

1 Tussaud's work included the heads of well-known philosophers and statesmen as well as the death masks of prominent victims of the guillotine during the French Revolution. Tussaud brought her collection to Britain from France in the early nineteenth century and staged exhibitions throughout the country before establishing herself in London in the 1830s. One of the main attractions of Tussaud's museum was the Chamber of Horrors, which incorporated some of her original victims of the Revolution in addition to new figures of murderers and other criminals. Her successful business expanded after her death and it is now a major London tourist attraction.

2 "Madame Rachel, the beautifier of London" is described as one of the main attractions at the "East London Palace of Royal Waxworks," where she is exhibited along with likenesses of Queen Victoria, Napoleon the Third, the Shah of Persia, Joan of Arc, Henry the Eighth and his wives, Moses in the bulrushes, and Jesus with his Apostles at the Last Supper (107–08).

3 Collins's description of Oldershaw's "Ladies' Toilette Repository," flanked by the premises of the dubious Doctor Downward (presumably an abortionist), suggests a less prosperous version of Sara's shop in the Strand.

Fig. 2. "Madame Rachel." *Illustrated Police News* 2 March 1878 (cover page)[1]

Contemporary reports indicate that Rachel's crimes were less disconcerting to the authorities and the general public than was her transgressiveness; she was an illiterate Jewish woman of obscure origins who challenged gender, ethnic, and class boundaries by operating a successful business in an upscale part of London, where she gained the trust of wealthy women customers (Miller, "Shrewd Women" 313–15; Rappaport 106–08). Rachel, like Meade's Koluchy and Sara, specialized in swindling money, jewellery, and family heirlooms from her clients. Although "magnetic influence" and "witchcraft" were attributed to Rachel by at least one of her victims (*Extraordinary Life and Trial of Madame Rachel* 78–79), unlike her fictional counterparts she was not strikingly

1 The portrait of Madame Rachel in the centre of the cover page was copied from an 1868 photograph used for her *carte de visite*, a small photographic calling card. *The Illustrated Police News* (1864–1938) was a weekly penny tabloid specializing in sensational accounts of crimes, disasters, and society scandals. The paper was particularly popular with working-class readers.

beautiful (though as her *carte de visite* indicates [Fig. 2 above], she was not as hideous as anti-Semitic cartoons in the *Illustrated Police News* suggest [Fig. 3]). Nor did she escape justice or commit the ultimate crime of murder. She died in prison in 1880.

Fig. 3. "Madame Rachel or Beautiful For Ever." *Illustrated Police News* 9 March 1878 (cover page)

"Is this a civilized country ...?": Meade's Sorceresses and *Fin-de-Siècle* Anxieties

Meade's Koluchy and Sara stories also exploit popular invasion narratives such as G.T. Chesney's *The Battle of Dorking* (1871) and H.G. Wells's *The War of the Worlds* (1898)[1] that depict England overrun by foreigners and aliens (Germans and Martians), as well as unsettling fantasies such as Richard Marsh's *The Beetle* (1897) and Stoker's *Dracula* that portray the nation penetrated by ageless, unwholesome, atavistic beings. Meade directly references Stoker's bestseller in "The Star-Shaped Marks" (June 1898), in which a young boy is kidnapped by one of Koluchy's victims and held in a remote Scottish castle. The name of the fortress, Bram Castle, recognizes the author of the famous vampire narrative, while the child's penchant for calling his captor "pitty lady" evokes Stoker's account of the "bloofer lady" who lures young children from their homes and leaves them with mysterious throat wounds (*Dracula* 214–15). Koluchy's victim also has peculiar wounds—"star-shaped marks"—on his neck and face, but they are caused by the discharge of powerful cathode and X-rays rather than the bite of an infernal creature.

While acknowledging a "common font of cultural anxiety,"

1 First published in *Pearson's Magazine* in 1897.

Stephen Arata distinguishes between *The Battle of Dorking* and similar fictions that express concerns about threats to British political and economic interests presented by Germany and other industrialized nations, and fantasies such as *The Beetle* and *Dracula* in which "the 'civilized' world is on the point of being overrun by 'primitive' forces" ("Occidental Tourist" 622–24; *Fictions of Loss* 108). The latter are examples of what Arata calls "narratives of reverse colonization" or expressions of *fin-de-siècle* imperial anxiety and cultural guilt; in his words, these are "products of the geopolitical fears of a troubled imperial society.... In the marauding, invasive Other, British culture sees its own imperial practices mirrored back in monstrous forms" (*Fictions of Loss* 108).[1]

Meade's series, like the phenomenally popular works by Marsh and Stoker, play on contemporary anxieties about race, crime, gender, and degeneration that underlay the resurgence of gothic fiction at the end of the nineteenth century. *The Beetle* and *Dracula* are "exemplary texts" not only of the gothic revival but also of the *fin de siècle* itself (Luckhurst 159); the former introduces a "man-woman-goddess-beetle-Thing" (Luckhurst 160) that stalks an English politician through London seeking revenge for the defilement of an Egyptian tomb, while the latter depicts a vampire (a prime signifier of imperial decline and cultural decay[2]) that attempts to colonize England with boxes of infected Transylvanian grave dirt. Like the terrifying creations in *The Beetle* and *Dracula*, Koluchy and Sara are foreigners—Others—with mesmeric occult powers, who circumvent English laws and institutions and baffle the authorities that would control or expel them. Physically attractive, charismatic, and accomplished, Koluchy and Sara are potentially more threatening to "Englishness" and the welfare of the nation than are the repulsive Egyptian creature and the foul Transylvanian count who manifest significant physical signs of Lombrosian degeneration and criminality (see Appendix B, pp. 263–78). Through their personal charms and professional relationships with the impressionable daughters and wives of

---

1 According to Arata, *The War of the Worlds* was inspired by a discussion between Wells and his brother about the extermination of the native population of Tasmania under British rule ("Occidental Tourist" 623).

2 Dr. Van Helsing, Dracula's tireless opponent and an expert on the subject of the "Un-Dead," links the vampire to the rise and fall of empires and the invasion of "barbarian" hordes (278).

the nation's most affluent bankers, businessmen, politicians, and clergymen, these so-called arch-fiends Koluchy and Sara easily penetrate the heart of the English family and the nation; in Koluchy's case, "even Royalty are among her patients" ("At the Edge of the Crater," p. 77). As Halloran writes, "through [their] attack on the family, [Koluchy and Sara] strik[e] at the secret locus of British power, the vulnerable place in which the future leaders of the nation are raised" (180). Indeed, as the husband of one of Sara's victims exclaims: "Is this a civilized country when death can walk abroad like this, invisible, not to be avoided?" ("Madame Sara," p. 134).

In her Koluchy–Sara narratives, Meade, like the author of *The Beetle*, portrays England as a nation "without a stable center ... in which the very possibility of agency, whether individually or collectively on the part of the English is called into question" (Wolfreys 25). As Julian Wolfreys writes in his discussion of Marsh's text, "Faced with what is perceived as the irrational, the Englishmen ... respond in a concerted fashion, calling to their aid the police and modern technologies of telegraph and public transport" (25). In Meade's stories, the Englishmen also call upon their old school networks and professional alliances, yet their best efforts are repeatedly thwarted. Although Meade's villainesses are destroyed in the final episode of each series, the end does not come about through the direct action of the Englishmen.[1]

Koluchy chooses her own end when she lures the detectives to her laboratory and then immolates herself (and one of the detectives) by releasing a trap door and dropping into a 2,400°C gas furnace—a fitting end for one so closely associated with infernal forces. Once the room cools sufficiently for Head and the detectives to inspect the scene, they find Koluchy's remains (or so they believe)[2] in the form of a small heap of smouldering ashes: "These were all the earthly remains of the brain that had conceived and the body that had executed some of the most malignant designs against mankind

1 Koluchy and Sara escape the fates of Sheridan Le Fanu's Carmilla and Stoker's Lucy, who are staked and beheaded in their tombs by their male opponents. Showalter has described Lucy's violent end as a "gang-rape" (181). Critics generally consider that Le Fanu's vampire novella *Carmilla* (1871–72) "helped to shape *Dracula*" (Tracy xxi).

2 As Chris Willis suggests, there is "no way of proving that the 'smouldering ashes' are those of Mme Koluchy, who has made supposedly impossible escapes in previous episodes" (64).

that the history of the world has ever shown."[1] The moment evokes (no doubt deliberately) the apparent death of the African sorceress queen Ayesha in Rider Haggard's best-selling *She* (1886–87).[2]

Fig. 4. "HANDS UP, OR I FIRE!" Madame Koluchy confronts Norman Head and detectives. "The Doom," *The Brotherhood of the Seven Kings*, *Strand Magazine* (October 1898): 429

Sara meets a less dramatic end through the agency of a woman she has double-crossed. The woman, a wolf-tamer,

1 "The Doom" 429.

2 Despite her great age (2,000 years old), Ayesha, like Meade's characters, appears ageless until the pillar of fire returns her to her true age and she dies a shriveled monkey. She is resurrected in Haggard's "Ayesha: The Return of She," *Windsor* (1904–05).

plans to murder Sara with a set of steel teeth fashioned after the bite of one of the wolves in her menagerie, but in the end the false teeth are unnecessary; Sara's throat is ripped out by the real animal when she enters its cage ("The Teeth of the Wolf," pp. 246–47). Even in death, Meade's characters elude the authorities and the Englishmen who would control them. Although both women are dispatched by the end of their respective series, neither is brought to justice nor made accountable for her crimes in the conventional way, and neither is destroyed nor contained by male agency—circumstances hardly conducive to easing existing fears about degenerative masculinity. Despite evidence of their deaths, these dangerous women continue to threaten *fin-de-siècle* English society as examples of female transgressiveness and unruliness.

Mademoiselle Delacourt and *The Heart of a Mystery* (1901)

The Second Boer War (1899–1902)[1] between the British Empire and the Boer republics in South Africa prompted an outpouring of patriotic sentiment in popular magazines and weekly papers, but it also aggravated anxieties about Britain's status as an imperial power as British forces failed to achieve an easy victory over a smaller force of guerilla fighters. The high number of men who were rejected for military service because of physical inadequacies heightened fears about national degeneracy, raising questions about the superiority of the British "race" and the safety of the nation and the Empire. These concerns form the background of Meade's six-part series *The Heart of a Mystery* published in the *Windsor Magazine*, a periodical known for its conservative stance on gender and class issues and its support for the British Empire. The series is interesting not only as an example of Meade's contribution to spy fiction but also for its portrayal of Mademoiselle Francesca Delacourt, a ruthless *femme fatale* who knows more than a little about explosives, poisons, and deadly micro-organisms. Delacourt is the head of a "most dreadful gang of spies"[2]—perhaps the first female character in literature to hold such a position.

The Heart of a Mystery is set in 1898 as governments in

1 An earlier, less well-known conflict occurred in 1880–81.
2 "A Conjuring Trick," *Heart of a Mystery* (September 1901): 462.

Britain, Europe, and South Africa position themselves for a formal declaration of war. It begins as the narrator Rupert Phenays, a London gentleman of independent means, is summoned to Paris to the bedside of a dying friend. The latter, a British Secret Service agent, attempts to confide critical information about a secret meeting between the French and Russian governments regarding Britain's imperial interests in South Africa. However, Delacourt's sudden intrusion precipitates the agent's death and the secret passes with him. Nonetheless, Delacourt believes Phenays has the information she seeks, and when he attempts to dismiss her, she plots his destruction. After two attempts on his life (the second occurs in "A Little Smoke," pp. 97-114), Phenays enlists the help of Senhor José Pinheiro, a Portuguese detective who specializes in diplomatic affairs and international intrigues. Despite Pinheiro's best efforts, Delacourt remains a threat to Phenays and British interests until the final episode.

Although she is not a professional beautifier or a self-proclaimed doctor like Koluchy and Sara, Delacourt shares many of their characteristics. She is beautiful, seductive, "devilish[ly] clever," "fiendish," and "uses as her weapon the most deadly scientific knowledge."[1] She also has the ability to fascinate her victims; according to Pinheiro, "Mademoiselle's great power lies in the fact that she can turn men, and women too, round her finger."[2] At one point Phenays confirms, "the more I think of that woman, the more she overpowers me"; and later, "I could no more have resisted her than the paralysed bird resists the cobra."[3] Even Pinheiro finds that he "can't help admiring her sometimes."[4] Delacourt demonstrates her influence over women when she involves them in schemes to murder Phenays in "A Little Smoke" (July 1901) and "The Tiger's Claw" (August 1901). In "A Conjuring Trick" (September 1901), Delacourt befriends the daughter of a member of the British War Office with predictable results; the naïve girl becomes a conduit for the transfer of state secrets to Britain's enemies in the Transvaal.

---

1 "The Tiger's Claw," *Heart of a Mystery* (August 1901): 288; "A Gallop with the Storm," *Heart of a Mystery* (October 1901): 587, 590.

2 "The Tiger's Claw" 292.

3 "A Conjuring Trick" 459; "The Lost Square," *Heart of a Mystery* (November 1901): 706.

4 "The Tiger's Claw" 288.

Fig. 5. Mademoiselle Delacourt. "Mademoiselle Delacourt," *The Heart of a Mystery, Windsor Magazine* (June 1901): 55

Despite their similarities, there are significant differences between Delacourt and the criminous Koluchy and Sara. Like the latter, Delacourt has extensive social connections, but with an English mother and a father related to "one of the best old French families," her origins are neither obscure nor threatening. "She goes everywhere," one of her acquaintances declares; "her beauty and position give her the *entrée* wherever she wills."[1] Thus Delacourt's family connections rather than her ability to perform miraculous cures ensure her welcome in places of power and influence. Although their crimes are similarly heinous, Delacourt's actions are (for the most part) politically motivated; she is reported to have "considerable political influence" and numerous friends in the Diplomatic Corps.[2] Interestingly, while there is no suggestion that Koluchy and Sara are mentally unbalanced,

1 "Mademoiselle Delacourt," *Heart of a Mystery* (June 1901): 54.
2 "Mademoiselle Delacourt" 56.

Delacourt's criminality is linked to a mental disorder: "She is ... mad," Pinheiro asserts; "no one who was not mad could be so devilish clever."[1] Pinheiro's statement associates Delacourt's behaviour with mattoidism, a category created by Lombroso to describe a form of insanity he associated with political criminals.[2] But the most important difference between Delacourt and the Koluchy-Sara characters relates to their respective fates. While the latter are never contained by male authorities or brought to justice in the usual way, Pinheiro arrests Delacourt in the final episode of the series. Phenays is assured that "clever as she is, she cannot escape from her prison walls."[3] Presumably the current political situation as well as the *Windsor*'s imperial orientation dictated Delacourt's capture and detention.

⋆ ⋆ ⋆

Given Meade's active promotion of women's culture and New Woman ideals through her literary magazine and professional associations, it seems curious that her most innovative, interesting, and memorable literary characters should be female villains who reinforce negative gender stereotypes about women's involvement with witchcraft and the occult and whose influence is so closely tied to their physical attractiveness and powers of fascination. Her characters' much celebrated intelligence and scientific knowledge might be read as a celebration of women's intellectual abilities and contributions to the national culture but for their penchant for preying on other women—most frequently young and vulnerable women of the class Meade targeted in her girls' fiction.

Clearly Meade's criminal women were literary commodities engendered by her professional and market interests, yet their transgressiveness—the characteristic that made them both appalling and appealing—aligned them with the New Woman. Koluchy, Sara, and Delacourt are what Miller calls "New Woman Criminals," "figure[s] of fantasy" who had "little to do with (most) real, historical female criminals of the period" who tended to commit domestic crimes and were generally poorly educated, destitute, desperate, desolate, and often the victims of abuse (*Framed* 3–4).

---

1 "The Tiger's Claw" 288.

2 According to Lombroso, mattoids, who generally "display few signs of physical degeneration," can be "crafty and capable in daily life" (*Criminal Man* 284).

3 "The Lost Square" 710.

Meade's female villains were popular because they were attractive, clever, and successful. Apart from their foreignness (and unlike other criminal characters in the series), they show no outward physical evidence of the so-called telltale signs of criminality—"nature's danger-signals"—outlined in popular Lombrosian theory (see Appendix B, pp. 266–72). True, they embodied existing social and cultural anxieties about women's movement out of the domestic sphere and into public spaces, while their foreignness exploited widespread concerns about international and domestic crime, degeneration, and cultural contamination, but these characteristics only made them more dangerous, exciting, and current (even if fantastic).

Although Meade's dangerous women bear little resemblance to real nineteenth-century women criminals, their transgressiveness associates them with New Woman ideals in a number of important ways. Koluchy and Sara are professional women who operate lucrative (albeit criminal) businesses. All three women use the most modern scientific techniques to achieve their ends. They are women who live not just by their wits but also by their intellects; whatever their evil machinations, they excel in science and medicine, disciplines dominated by men. Their operations in these male preserves reflect women's recent movement into the professions. And their terrible crimes notwithstanding, Koluchy and Sara—and Delacourt for a time—consistently and effectively challenge, baffle, and resist the attempts of the patriarchal authorities to control them.

Meade's emergence as a *Strand* celebrity through her popular crime fiction, a developing genre inspired by the magazine itself, demonstrates her market savvy, versatility, and determination to succeed as a professional woman writer. Her magazine fiction showcases her talent in identifying literary trends and packaging her work for popular consumption using skills she developed early in her career. Beyond market considerations, however, her contributions to the genre were significant, and include the creation of the subgenre of the medical mystery, the first medical detective, and the first female gang leaders.

L.T. Meade: A Brief Chronology

[Over the course of her professional career, Meade published close to 300 books as well as countless short stories and articles. A limited number of titles are included here.]

1844 Elizabeth ("Lillie") Thomasina Meade born 5 June in Bandon, County Cork, Ireland, the eldest daughter of Reverend Richard Thomas Meade (1815–88) and his wife Sarah Lane (c. 1814–74).

1856 Family moves to Templetrine rectory near Bandon.

1866 First full-length novel, *Ashton Morton; or Memories of My Life*, is published anonymously in a limited run.

1874 Death of Meade's mother. Meade submits an early version of *Lettie's Last Home* to London publisher John Shaw.

1875 Father's remarriage. Meade moves to London. Revises and publishes *Lettie's Last Home.*

1877 Professional career is established with the publication of *Great St. Benedict's* (1876) and *Scamp and I* (1877).

1879 Marries solicitor Alfred Toulmin Smith in September and moves to the London suburb of Dulwich, where she resides for more than three decades. Four children are born to Meade and her husband in the next decade (one dies in infancy). Maintains her professional persona as L.T. Meade.

1886 Publishes her first school story, *A World of Girls*, widely considered the first successful girls' school story.

1887 Assumes the editorship of *Atalanta* (1887–98), a new middle-class girls' literary magazine.

1891 Publishes her first college girl novel, *A Sweet Girl Graduate.*

1892 Publishes *The Medicine Lady*, her first adult novel written with Metropolitan Police surgeon Dr. Edgar Beaumont writing as "Clifford Halifax, M.D."

1893 *This Troublesome World* by Meade and Halifax; *Stories From the Diary of a Doctor* by Meade and Halifax begins in the July number of the *Strand Magazine* and runs concurrently with the final installments of Arthur Conan Doyle's *The Adventures of Sherlock Holmes.* Meade resigns her editorship of *Atalanta* in September but continues to publish popular short stories and novels for girls (up to twelve novels a year over the next two decades).

1895 *Stories from the Diary of a Doctor* (Second Series) by Meade and Halifax begins in the *Strand Magazine* in January.

1896 *The Adventures of a Man of Science* by Meade and Halifax begins in the *Strand Magazine* in July.

1897 Publishes *Under the Dragon Throne* with Robert Kennaway Douglas, Keeper of Oriental Printed Books and Manuscripts at the British Museum. Meade begins to publish with a second medical collaborator, Dr. Robert Eustace Barton writing as "Robert Eustace"; *A Master of Mysteries: The Adventures of John Bell—Ghost-Exposer* by Meade and Eustace begins in *Cassell's Magazine* in June.

1898 Publishes *The Siren*; *The Brotherhood of the Seven Kings* by Meade and Eustace begins in the *Strand Magazine* in January; *Stories of the Gold Star Line* by Meade and Eustace begins in the *Windsor Magazine* in December. Meade is featured in the *Strand Magazine*'s "Portraits of Celebrities" in December.

1899 The first two stories in a six-part series by Meade and Eustace featuring lady detective Florence Cusack is published in the *Harmsworth Magazine* in April and July (the remaining stories are published over the next two years); *Stories of the Sanctuary Club* by Meade and Eustace begins in the *Strand Magazine* in July.

1901 *The Heart of a Mystery* by Meade and Eustace begins in the *Windsor* in June.

1902 *The Experiences of the Oracle of Maddox Street* by Meade and Eustace begins in *Pearson's Magazine* in February; *The Sorceress of the Strand* by Meade and Eustace begins in the *Strand Magazine* in October.

1907 "The Invisible Enemy," Meade's last known collaboration with Eustace, is published in Cassell's *Storyteller.*

1914 Dies at her home in Oxford on 26 October.

A Note on the Text

The text and selected illustrations used in this edition have been reproduced from the stories as they first appeared in the *Strand* and *Windsor* magazines. The original spelling and punctuation have been retained. Obvious typographical errors in the original have been corrected.

STORIES FROM THE DIARY OF A DOCTOR (SECOND SERIES)

Stories from the Diary of a Doctor (Second Series)

From L.T. Meade and Clifford Halifax, M.D., *Stories from the Diary of a Doctor*, Second Series, *Strand Magazine* 9 (January–June 1895).

[These stories are written in collaboration with a medical man of large experience. Many are founded on fact, and all are within the region of practical medical science. Those stories which may convey an idea of the impossible are only a forecast of an early realization.][1]

II. —THE SEVENTH STEP. [152–65]

A pleasure yacht, of the name of *Ariadne*, was about to start upon a six-weeks' cruise. The time of the year was September—a golden, typical September—in the year of grace 1893. The *Ariadne* was to touch at several of the great northern ports: Christiania, St. Petersburg, and others. I had just gone through a period of hard and anxious work. I found it necessary to take a brief holiday, and resolved to secure a berth on board the *Ariadne*, and so give myself a time of absolute rest. We commenced our voyage on the second of the month; the day was a lovely one, and every berth on board had secured an occupant.

We were all in high spirits, and the weather was so fine that scarcely anyone suffered from sea-sickness. In consequence, the young ship's doctor, Maurice Curwen, had scarcely anything to do.

The passengers on board the *Ariadne* were, with one exception, of the most ordinary and conventional type, but a girl who was carried on board just before the yacht commenced her voyage aroused my professional sympathies from the first. She was a tall, dark-eyed girl of about eighteen or nineteen years of age—her lower limbs were evidently paralyzed, and she was accompanied by a nurse who wore the picturesque uniform of the Charing Cross Hospital.

The young girl was taken almost immediately to a deck cabin which had been specially arranged for her, and during the first two or three days of our voyage I had not an opportunity

---

1 Authors' declaration.

of seeing her again. When we reached the smooth waters of the Norwegian fiords, however, she was carried almost every day on deck. Here she lay under an awning, speaking to no one, and apparently taking little interest either in her fellow-passengers or in the marvellous beauties of Nature which surrounded her.

Her nurse usually sat by her side—she was a reserved-looking, middle-aged woman, with a freckly face and thin, sandy hair. Her lips were perfectly straight in outline and very thin, her eyebrows were high and faintly marked—altogether, she had a disagreeable and thoroughly unsympathetic appearance.

I was not long on board the *Ariadne* before I was informed that the sick girl's name was Dagmar Sorensen—that she was the daughter of a rich city merchant, and was going to St. Petersburg to see her father's brother, who was a celebrated physician there.

One morning, on passing Miss Sorensen's cabin, my footsteps were arrested by hearing the noise of something falling within the room. There came to my ears the crash of broken glass. This was immediately followed by the sound of rapid footsteps which as suddenly stopped, as though the inmate of the room was listening intently. Miss Sorensen's nurse, who went by the name of Sister Hagar, was probably doing something for her patient, and was annoyed at anyone pausing near the door. I passed on quickly, but the next moment, to my astonishment, came face to face with Sister Hagar on the stairs. I could not help looking at her in surprise. I was even about to speak, but she hurried past me, wearing her most disagreeable and repellent expression.

What could the noise have been? Who could have moved in the cabin? Miss Sorensen's lower limbs were, Curwen, our ship's doctor, had assured me, hopelessly paralyzed. She was intimate with no one on board the *Ariadne*. What footsteps had I listened to?

I thought the matter over for a short time, then made up my mind that the stewardess must have been in Miss Sorensen's cabin, and having come to this conclusion, I forgot all about the circumstance.

That afternoon I happened to be standing in the neighbourhood of the young lady's deck chair; to my surprise, for she had not hitherto taken the least notice of me, she suddenly raised her full, brilliant dark eyes, and fixed them on my face.

"May I speak to you?" she said.

I came up to her side immediately.

"Certainly," I answered. "Can I do anything for you?"

"You can do a great deal if you will," she answered. "I have heard your name: you are a well-known London physician."

"I have a large practice in London," I replied to her.

"Yes," she continued, "I have often heard of you—you have doubtless come on board the *Ariadne* to take a holiday?"

"That is true," I answered.

"Then it is unfair——" She turned her head aside, breaking off her speech abruptly.

"What is unfair?" I asked.

"I have a wish to consult you professionally, but if you are taking a holiday, it is unfair to expect you to give up your time to me."

"Not at all," I replied. "If I can be of the slightest use to you, pray command me; but are you not under Curwen's care?"

"Yes, oh, yes; but that doesn't matter." She stopped speaking abruptly; her manner, which had been anxious and excited, became suddenly guarded—I looked up and saw the nurse approaching us. She carried a book and shawl in her hands.

"Thank you, Sister Hagar," said Miss Sorensen. "I shall not require your services any more for the present."

The nurse laid the shawl over the young lady's feet, placed the book within reach, and, bestowing an inquisitive glance on me, walked slowly away.

When she was quite out of sight, Miss Sorensen resumed her conversation.

"You see that I am paralyzed," she said.

I bowed an acknowledgment of this all-patent fact.

"I suffer a good deal," she continued. "I am on my way to St. Petersburg to see my uncle who is a very great physician. My father is most anxious that I should consult him. Perhaps you know my uncle's name—Professor Sorensen? He is one of the doctors of the Court."

"I cannot recall the name just now," I said; "but that is of no consequence. I have no doubt he is all that you say."

"Yes, he is wonderfully clever, and holds a high position. It will be some days before we get to Russia, however, and—I am ill. I did not know when I came on board the *Ariadne* that a doctor of your professional eminence would be one of the passengers. Perhaps Mr. Curwen will not object——" She paused.

"I am sure he will not object to having a consultation with me over your case," I answered. "If you wish it, I can arrange the matter with him."

"Thank you—but—I don't want a consultation. My wish is to see you—alone."

I looked at her in surprise.

"Don't refuse me," she said, in a voice of entreaty.

"I will see you with pleasure with Curwen," I said.

"But I want to consult you independently."

"I am sorry," I answered; "under the circumstances, that is impossible."

She coloured vividly.

"Why so?" she asked.

"Because professional etiquette makes it necessary for the doctor whom you have already consulted to be present," I replied.

Her eyes flashed angrily.

"How unkind and queer you doctors are," she said. "I cordially hate that sentence for ever on your lips, 'Professional etiquette.' Why should a girl suffer and be ill, because of anything so unreasonable?"

"You must forgive me," I said. "I would gladly do anything for you; I will see you with pleasure with Curwen."

"Must he be present?"

"Yes."

"I cannot stand this. If he consents to your seeing me alone, have you any objection to make?"

At that moment Curwen suddenly appeared. He was talking to one of the ship's crew, and they were both slowly advancing in Miss Sorensen's direction.

"Mr. Curwen, can I speak to you?" called out Miss Sorensen.

He came to her at once.

I withdrew in some annoyance, feeling pretty well convinced that the young lady was highly hysterical and required to be carefully looked after.

By-and-by, as I was standing by the deck rail, Curwen came up to me.

"I have talked to Miss Sorensen," he said. "She is most anxious to consult you, Dr. Halifax, but says that you will not see her except in consultation with me. I beg of you not to consider me for a moment. I take an interest in her, poor girl, and will be only too glad to get your opinion of her case. Pray humour her in this matter."

"Of course, if you have no objection, I have none," I answered. "I can talk to you about her afterwards. She is evidently highly nervous."

"I fear that is the case," replied Curwen. "But," he added, "there is little doubt as to her ailment. The lower limbs are paralyzed; she is quite incapable of using them."

"Did you examine her carefully when she came on board?" I asked.

"I went into the case, certainly," replied Curwen; "but if you mean that I took every step to complete the diagnosis of the patient's condition, I did not consider it necessary. The usual symptoms were present. In short, Miss Sorensen's case was, to my mind, very clearly defined to be that of spastic paralysis, and I did not want to worry her by useless experiments."

"Well, I will see her, as she wishes for my opinion," I replied, slowly.

"I am very pleased that you should do so," said Curwen.

"Do you happen to have an electric battery on board?" I asked.

"Yes, a small one, but doubtless sufficient for your purpose. Will you arrange to see Miss Sorensen to-morrow morning?"

"Yes," I answered. "If I am to do her any good, there is no use in delay."

Curwen and I talked the matter over a little further, then he was obliged to leave me to attend to some of his multifarious duties.

The nightly dance had begun—awnings had been pulled down all round the deck, and the electric light made the place as bright as day. The ship's band was playing a merry air, and several couples were already revolving round in the mazes of the waltz.

I looked to see if Miss Sorensen had come on deck. Yes, she was there; she was lying as usual on her own special couch. The captain's wife, Mrs. Ross, was seated near her, and Captain Ross stood at the foot of her couch. She was dressed in dark rose-coloured silk, worn high to the throat, and with long sleeves. The whiteness of her complexion and the gloomy depths of her big, dark eyes were thus thrown into strong relief. She looked strikingly handsome.

On seeing me, Captain Ross called me up, and introduced me to Miss Sorensen. She smiled at me in quite a bright way.

"Dr. Halifax and I have already made each other's acquaintance," she said. She motioned me to seat myself by her side. The conversation, which had been animated before I joined the little party, was now continued with *verve*. Miss Sorensen, quite contrary to her wont, was the most lively of the group. I observed that she had considerable powers of repartee, and that her conversational talent was much above the average. Her words were extremely well chosen, and her grammar was invariably correct. She had, in short, the bearing of a very accomplished woman. I further judged that she was a remarkably clever one, for I was not five minutes in her society before I observed that she was watching me with as close attention as I was giving to her.

After a time Captain and Mrs. Ross withdrew, and I found myself alone with the young lady.

"Don't go," she said, eagerly, as I was preparing to rise from my chair. "I spoke to Mr. Curwen," she continued, dropping her voice; "he has not the slightest objection to your seeing me alone. Have you arranged the matter with him?"

"I have seen him," I replied, gravely. "He kindly consents to waive all ceremony. I can make an appointment to see you at any hour you wish."

"Pray let it be to-morrow morning—I am anxious to have relief as soon as possible."

"I am sorry that you suffer," I replied, giving her a sudden, keen glance—"you don't look ill, at least not now."

"I am excited now," she answered. "I am pleased at the thought——"

She broke off abruptly.

"Is Sister Hagar on deck?" she asked.

"I do not see her," I replied.

"But look, pray, look. Dr. Halifax—I *fear* Sister Hagar."

There was unquestionable and most genuine terror in the words. Miss Sorensen laid her hand on mine—it trembled.

I was about to reply, when a thin voice, almost in our ears, startled us both.

"Miss Sorensen, I must take you to bed now," said Nurse Hagar.

"Allow me to help you, nurse," I said, starting up.

"No, thank you, sir," she answered, in her most disagreeable way; "I can manage my young lady quite well alone."

She went behind the deck-chair, and propelled it forward. When she got close to the little deck cabin, she lifted Miss Sorensen up bodily in her strong arms, and conveyed her within the cabin.

During the night I could not help giving several thoughts to my new patient—she repelled me quite as much as she attracted me. She was without doubt a very handsome girl. There was something pathetic, too, in her dark eyes and in the lines round her beautifully curved mouth; but now and then I detected a ring of insincerity in her voice, and there were moments when her eyes, in spite of themselves, took a shifty glance. Was she feigning paralysis? What was her motive in so anxiously desiring an interview with me alone?

Immediately after breakfast, on the following morning, Sister Hagar approached my side.

"Miss Sorensen would be glad to know when it would be convenient for you to see her, Dr. Halifax," she said.

"Pray tell her that I can be with her in about ten minutes," I replied.

The nurse withdrew and I went to find Curwen.

"Is your electric battery in order?" I asked.

"Come with me to my cabin," he replied.

I went with him at once. We examined the battery together, put it into order, and then tested it. I took it with me to Miss Sorensen's cabin. Sister Hagar stood near the door. She came up to me at once, took the battery from my hands, and laid it on a small table near the patient. She then, to my astonishment, withdrew, closing the door noiselessly behind her.

I turned to look at Miss Sorensen, and saw at a glance that she was intensely nervous. There was not a trace of colour on her face; even her lips were white as death.

"Pray get your examination over as quickly as you can," she said, speaking in an almost fretful voice.

"I am waiting for the nurse to return," I replied. "I have several questions to ask her."

"Oh, she is not coming back. I have asked her to leave us together."

"That is nonsense," I said; "she must be present. I cannot apply the electric battery without her assistance. If you will permit me, I will call her."

"No, no, don't go—don't go!"

I looked fixedly at my patient. Suddenly an idea occurred to me.

I pushed the table aside on which the battery had been placed, and stood at the foot of Miss Sorensen's bed.

"The usual examination need not take place," I said, "because——"

"Why?" she asked. She half started up on her couch; her colour changed from white to red.

"Because you are not paralyzed!" I said, giving her a sudden, quick glance, and speaking with firmness.

"My God, how do you know?" she exclaimed. Her face grew so colourless that I thought she would faint. She covered her eyes with one trembling hand. "Oh, Sister Hagar was right," she continued, after a moment. "I did not believe her—I assured her that it was nothing more than her fancy."

"I have guessed the truth?" I said, in a stern voice.

"Alas, yes, you have guessed the truth." As she spoke, she sprang with a light movement from her couch and stood before me.

Fig. 6. "SHE SPRANG FROM HER COUCH AND STOOD BEFORE ME."

"I am no more paralyzed than you are," she said; "but how, *how* do you know?"

"Sit down and I will tell you," I replied.

She did not sit—she was far too much excited. She stood near the door of her little cabin. "Did you really hear the bottle fall and break, yesterday morning?"

"I heard a noise which might be accounted for in that way," I answered.

"And did you hear my footsteps?"

"I heard footsteps."

"Sister Hagar said that you knew—I hoped, I hoped—I earnestly trusted that she was wrong."

"How could she possibly tell?" I replied. "I met her on the stairs coming towards the cabin. I certainly said nothing—how was it possible for her to read my secret thoughts?"

"It was quite possible. She saw the knowledge in your eyes; she gave you one glance—that was sufficient. Oh! I hoped she was mistaken."

"Mine is not a tell-tale face," I said.

"Not to most people, but it is to her. You don't know her. She is the most wonderful, extraordinary woman that ever breathed. She can read people through and through. She can stand behind you and know when your eyes flash and your lips smile. Her knowledge is terrible. She can almost see through stone walls. I told you last night that I dreaded her—I do more than that—I fear her horribly—she makes my life a daily purgatory!"

"Sit down," I said, in a voice which I made on purpose both cold and stern: "it is very bad for you to excite yourself in this way. If you dislike Sister Hagar, why is she your nurse? In short, what can be your possible motive for going through this extraordinary act of deception? Are you not aware that you are acting in a most reprehensible manner? Why do you wish the passengers of the *Ariadne* to suppose you to be paralyzed, when you are in reality in perfect health?"

"In perfect health?" she repeated, with a shudder. "Yes, I am doubtless in perfect bodily health, but I am in—oh, in such bitter anguish of soul."

"What do you mean?"

"I can no more tell you that, than I can tell you why I am in Sister Hagar's power. Pray forget my wild words. I know you think badly of me, but your feelings would be changed to profound pity if you could guess the truth. Now listen to me—I have only a moment or two left, for Sister Hagar will be back almost directly. She found out yesterday that you had guessed my secret. I hoped that this was not the case, but, as usual she was right and I was wrong. The moment my eyes met yours, when I first came on deck, I thought it likely that you might see through my deception. Sister Hagar also feared that such would be the case. It was on that account that I avoided speaking to you, and also that I remained so silent and apparently uninterested in everyone when I went on deck. I asked for this interview yesterday for the express purpose of finding out whether you really knew about the deception which I was practising on everyone on board. If I discovered that you had pierced through my disguise, there was nothing for it but for me to throw myself on your mercy. Now you know why I was so desirous of seeing you without Mr. Curwen."

"I understand," I answered. "The whole matter is most strange, wrong, and incomprehensible. Before I leave you, may I ask what motive influences you? There must be some secret reason for such deception as you practise."

Miss Sorensen coloured, and for the first time since she began to make her confession, her voice grew weak and faltering—her eyes took a shifty glance, and refused to meet mine.

"The motive may seem slight enough to you," she said; "but to me it is, and was, sufficiently powerful to make me go through with this sham. My home is not a happy one; I have a step-mother, who treats me cruelly. I longed to get away from home and to see something of life. My father's brother, Professor Sorensen, of St. Petersburg, is a very celebrated Court physician—my father is proud of him, and has often mentioned his name and the luxurious palace in which he lives. I have never met him, but I took a curious longing to pay him a visit, and thought of this way of obtaining my desires. Professor Sorensen has made a special study of nervous diseases such as paralysis. Sister Hagar and I talked the matter over, and I resolved to feign this disease in order to get away from home and to pay my uncle a visit. All went well without hitch of any sort until yesterday morning."

"But it is impossible for you to suppose," I said, "that you can take in a specialist like Professor Sorensen."

"I don't mean to try—he'll forgive me when I tell him the truth, and throw myself on his mercy."

"And is Sister Hagar a real nurse?" I asked, after a pause.

"No, but she has studied the part a little, and is far too clever to commit herself."

Miss Sorensen's face was no longer pale—a rich colour flamed in her cheeks, her eyes blazed—she looked wonderfully handsome.

"And now that you have confided in me," I said, "what do you expect me to do with my knowledge?"

"To respect my secret, and to keep it absolutely and strictly to yourself."

"That is impossible—I cannot deceive Curwen."

"You must—you shall. Why should two—two be sacrificed? And he is so young, and he knows nothing now—nothing. Oh, have mercy on him! Oh, my God, what wild words am I saying? What must you think of me?"

She paused abruptly, her blazing eyes were fixed on my face.

"What must you think of me?" she repeated.

"That you are in a very excitable and over-strained condition, and perhaps not quite answerable for your actions," I replied.

"Yes, yes," she continued; "I am over-strained—over-anxious—not quite accountable—yes—that is it—that is it—but you will not tell Mr. Curwen—Oh, be merciful to me, I beg of you. We shall soon reach St. Petersburg. Wait, at least, until we get there before you tell him—promise me that. Tell him then if you like—tell all the world, then, if you choose to do so, but respect my secret until we reach Russia."

As Miss Sorensen spoke, she laid her hand on my arm—she looked at me with a passion which seemed absolutely inadequate to her very poor reason for going through this extra-ordinary deception.

"Promise me," she said—"there's Sister Hagar's knock at the door—let her in—but promise me first."

"I will think the whole case over carefully before I speak to anyone about it," I replied. I threw the door open as I spoke, and went out of the little cabin as Sister Hagar came in.

That afternoon Curwen asked me about Miss Sorensen—I replied to him briefly.

"I will tell you all about the case," I said, "in a short time—there is a mystery which the young lady has divulged, and which she has earnestly implored of me to respect until we reach St. Petersburg."

"Then you believe she can be cured?" said Curwen.

"Unquestionably—but it is a strange story, and it is impossible for me to discuss it until I can give you my full confidence. In the meantime, there is nothing to be done in the medical way for Miss Sorensen—I should recommend her to keep on deck as much as possible—she is in a highly hysterical state, and the more fresh air she gets, the better."

Curwen was obliged to be satisfied with this very lame summary of the case, and the next time I saw Miss Sorensen, I bent over her and told her that I intended to respect her secret until after we arrived at St. Petersburg.

"I don't know how to thank you enough," she said—her eyes flashed with joy, and she became instantly the most animated and fascinating woman on board.

At last we reached the great northern port, and first amongst those to come on board the *Ariadne* was the tall and aristocratic form of Professor Sorensen. I happened to witness the meeting between him and his beautiful niece. He stooped down and kissed her on her white brow. A flush of scarlet spread all over her face as he did so. They spoke a few words together—then Sister Hagar came up and touched Miss Sorensen on her arm. The next moment I was requested to come and speak to the young lady.

"May I introduce you to my uncle, Dr. Halifax?" she said. "Professor Sorensen—Dr. Halifax. I can scarcely tell you, Uncle Oscar," continued the young lady, looking full in his face, "how good Dr. Halifax has been to me during my voyage."

Professor Sorensen made a polite rejoinder to this, and immediately invited me to come to see him at his palace in the Nevski Prospect.[1]

I was about to refuse with all the politeness I could muster, when Miss Sorensen gave me a glance of such terrible entreaty that it staggered me, and almost threw me off my balance.

"You will come; you must come," she said.

"I can take no refusal," exclaimed the Professor. "I am delighted to welcome you as a brother in the great world of medical science. I have no doubt that we shall have much of interest to talk over together. My laboratory has the good fortune to be somewhat celebrated, and I have made experiments in the cultivation of microbes which I should like to talk over with you. You will do me the felicity of dining with me this evening, Dr. Halifax?"

I considered the situation briefly—I glanced again at Miss Sorensen.

"I will come," I said—she gave a sigh of relief, and lowered her eyes.

Professor Sorensen moved away, and Sister Hagar went into the young lady's cabin to fetch something. For a moment Miss Sorensen and I were alone. She gave me an imperious gesture to come close to her.

"Sit on that chair—stoop down, I don't want others to know," she said.

I obeyed her in some surprise.

"You have been good, more than good," she said, "and I respect you. I thank you from my heart. Do one last thing for me."

"What is that?"

"Don't tell our secret to Maurice Curwen until you have returned from dining with my uncle. Promise me this; I have a very grave reason for asking it of you."

"I shall probably not have time to tell him between now and this evening," I said, "as I mean immediately to land and occupy myself looking over the place."

At this moment Sister Hagar appeared, carrying all kinds of rugs and parcels—amongst them was a small, brass-bound box, which seemed to be of considerable weight. As she approached us, the nurse knocked her foot against a partition in the deck, stumbled, and would have fallen had I not rushed

1 A famous street named for Alexander Nevsky, a thirteenth-century military hero. It is known for its palaces, opulent houses, churches, museums, monuments, shops, and restaurants.

to her assistance. At the same time the heavy, brass-bound box fell with some force to the ground. The shock must have touched some secret spring, for the cover immediately bounced open and several packets of papers were strewn on the deck. I stooped to pick them up, but Nurse Hagar wrenched them from my hands with such force that I could not help glancing at her in astonishment. One packet had been thrown to a greater distance than the others. I reached back my hand to pick it up, and, as I did so, my eyes lighted on a name in small black characters on the cover. The name was Olga Krestofski. Below it was something which looked like hieroglyphics, but I knew enough of the Russian tongue to ascertain that it was the same name in Russ—with the figure 7 below it.

I returned the packet to the nurse—she gave me a glance which I was destined to remember afterwards—and Miss Sorensen uttered a faint cry and turned suddenly white to her lips.

Professor Sorensen came hastily up—he administered a restorative to his niece, and said that the excitement of seeing him had evidently been too much for her in her weak state. A moment later the entire party had left the yacht.

It was night when I got to the magnificent palace in the Nevski Prospect where Professor Sorensen resided.

I was received with ceremony by several servants in handsome livery, and conducted immediately to a bedroom on the first floor of the building. The room was of colossal size and height, and, warm as the weather still was, was artificially heated by pipes which ran along the walls. The hangings and all the other appointments of this apartment were of the costliest, and as I looked around me, I could not help coming to the conclusion that a Court physician at St. Petersburg must hold a very lucrative position.

Having already made my toilet, I was about to leave the room to find my way as best I could to the reception-rooms on the ground floor, when, to my unbounded amazement, I saw the massive oak door of the chamber quickly and silently open, and Miss Sorensen, magnificently dressed, with diamonds in her black hair and flashing round her slim white throat, came in. She had not made the slightest sound in opening the door, and now she put her finger to her lips to enjoin silence on my part. She closed the door gently behind her, and, coming up to my side, pressed a note into my hand. She then turned to go.

"What is the meaning of this?" I began.

"The note will tell you," she replied. "Oh, yes, I am well, quite well—I have told my uncle all about my deception on board the

Ariadne. For God's sake don't keep me now. If I am discovered, all is lost."

She reached the door as she spoke, opened it with a deft, swift, absolutely silent movement, and disappeared.

I could not tell why, but when I was left once more alone, I felt a chill running through me. I went deliberately up to the oak door and turned the key in the heavy lock. The splendid bedroom was bright as day with electric light. Standing by the door, I opened Miss Sorensen's note. My horrified eyes fell on the following words:—

"We receive no mercy, and we give none. Your doom was nearly fixed when you found out the secret of my false paralysis on board the *Ariadne*. It was absolutely and irrevocably sealed when you saw my real name on the packet of letters which fell out of the brass-bound box to-day. The secret of my return to Russia is death to those who discover it unbidden.

"It is decreed by those who never alter or change that you do not leave this palace alive. It is utterly hopeless for you to try to escape, for on all hands the doors are guarded; and even if you did succeed in reaching the streets, we have plenty of emissaries there to do our work for us. You know enough of our secrets to make your death desirable—it is therefore arranged that *you are to die*. I like you and pity you. I have a heart, and you have touched it. If I can, I will save you. I do this at the risk of my life, but that does not matter—we hold our lives cheap—we always carry them in our hands, and are ready to lay them down at any instant. I may not succeed in saving you, but I will try. I am not quite certain how your death is to be accomplished, but I have a very shrewd suspicion of the manner in which the final attack on your life will be made. Your only chance—remember, your only chance of escape—is to appear to know absolutely nothing—to show not the ghost of a suspicion of any underhand practices; to put forth all your powers to fascinate and please Professor Sorensen and the guests who will dine with us to-night. Show no surprise at anything you see—ask no impertinent questions. I have watched you, and I believe you are clever enough and have sufficient nerve to act as I suggest. Pay me all the attention in your power—make love to me even a little, if you like—that will not matter, for we shall never meet again after to-night. After dinner you will be invited to accompany Professor Sorensen to his laboratory—he will ask no other guest to do this. On no account refuse—go with him and I will go with you. Where he goes and where I go, follow without flinching. If you feel astonishment, do not show it. And now, all that I have said leads up to this final remark. *Avoïd the seventh step.* Bear this in your mind—it is your last chance. —DAGMAR."

I read this note over twice. The terrible feeling of horror left me after the second reading. I felt braced and resolute. I suspected, what was indeed the case, that I had fallen unwittingly into a hornet's nest of Nihilists.[1] How mad I had been to come to Professor Sorensen's palace! I had fully made up my mind that Miss Sorensen had told me lies, when she gave me her feeble reasons for acting as she had done on board the *Ariadne*. No matter that now, however. She spoke the truth at last. The letter I crushed in my hand was not a lie. I resolved to be wary, guarded—and when the final moment came, to sell my life dearly.

I had a box of matches in my pocket. I burnt the note to white ash, and then crushed the ashes to powder under my foot. I then went downstairs.

Servants were standing about, who quickly directed me to the reception-rooms. A powdered footman[2] flung the door of the great drawing-room open and called my name in a ringing voice. Professor Sorensen came forward to meet me. A lady came up at the same moment and held out her hand. She was dressed in black velvet, with rich lace and many magnificent diamonds. They shone in her sandy hair and glistened round her thin throat. I started back in amazement. Here was Sister Hagar metamorphosed.

"Allow me to introduce my wife, Madame Sorensen," said the Professor.

Madame Sorensen raised a playful finger and smiled into my face.

"You look astonished, and no wonder, Dr. Halifax," she said. "But, ah, how naughty you have been to read our secrets." She turned away to speak to another guest. The next moment dinner was announced.

As we sat round the dinner table, we made a large party. Men and women of many nationalities were present, but I quickly perceived, to my own surprise, that I was the guest of the evening. To me was given the terribly doubtful honour of escorting Madame Sorensen to

---

1 Nihilism (Latin *nihil*, nothing) is a philosophy or doctrine that rejects established social conventions and beliefs, and argues that existence is without objective meaning, purpose, or intrinsic value. As a political movement, Nihilism was associated with a diffuse revolutionary movement in Russia that believed that the established political and social institutions were corrupt and needed to be destroyed through acts of terrorism and assassination.

2 A servant wearing a powdered wig as part of his household uniform.

the head of her table, and in honour of me also, English—by common consent—was the language spoken at dinner.

Miss Sorensen sat a little to my left—she spoke gaily to her neighbour, and her ringing, silvery laugh floated often to my ears. There had been some little excitement caused by the bursting of a large bomb in one of the principal streets that evening. Inadvertently I alluded to it to my hostess. She bent towards me and said, in a low voice:—

"Excuse me, Dr. Halifax, but we never talk politics in Petersburg."

She had scarcely said this before she began to rattle off some brilliant opinions with regard to a novel which was just then attracting public attention in England. Her remarks were terse, cynical, and intensely to the point. From one subject of interest to another she leaped, showing discernment, discrimination, and a wide and exhaustive knowledge of everything she touched upon.

As I listened to her and replied as pertinently as possible, a sudden idea came to me which brought considerable comfort with it. I began to feel more and more assured that Miss Sorensen's letter was but the ugly result of a mind thrown slightly off its balance. The brilliant company in which I found myself, the splendid room, the gracefully appointed table, the viands and the wines of the best and the choicest, my cultivated and gracious hostess—Professor Sorensen's worn, noble, strictly intellectual face—surely all these things had nothing whatever to do with treachery and assassination! Miss Sorensen's mind was off its balance. This fact accounted for everything—for the malingering which had taken place on board the *Ariadne*—for the queer letter which she had given to me before dinner. "*When you saw my real name to-day, your doom was irrevocably sealed,*" she said. "*Avoid the seventh step,*" she had continued. Could anything be more utterly absurd? Miss Sorensen was the acknowledged niece of my courtly host—what did she mean by attributing another name to herself?—what did she mean by asking me to avoid the seventh step? In short, her words were exactly like the ravings of a lunatic.

My heart, which had been beating uncomfortably high and strong, calmed down under these reflections, but presently a queer, cold, uncomfortable recollection touched it into fresh action as if with the edge of bare steel.

It was all very well to dispose of Miss Sorensen by treating her wild words as the emanations of a diseased brain; but what about Madame Sorensen? How was I possibly to account for her queer change of identity? I recalled her attitude on board the *Ariadne*. The malevolent glances she had often cast at me. The look on her face that very morning when I had saved her from falling, and picked up the papers which had fallen out of the brass-bound box. She had seen my eyes rest upon the name "Olga Krestofski." I could not soon forget the expression in her cold eyes when I returned her that packet. A thrill ran through me even now, as I recalled the vengeance of that glance.

The ladies withdrew, and the men of the party did not stay long over wine. We went to the drawing-rooms, where music and light conversation were indulged in.

As soon as we came in, Miss Sorensen, who was standing alone in a distant part of the inner drawing-room, gave me a look which brought me to her side. There was an imperious sort of command in her full, dark eyes. She held herself very erect. Her carriage was queenly—the lovely carnation of excitement bloomed on her cheeks and gave the finishing touch to her remarkable beauty. She made way for me to sit on the sofa beside her, and bending her head slightly in my direction, seemed to invite me to make love to her.

There was something in her eyes which revived me like a tonic.

I felt suddenly capable of rising to my terrible position, and resolved to play the game out to the bitter end.

I began to talk to Miss Sorensen in a gay tone of light badinage, to which she responded with spirit.

Suddenly, as the conversation arose full and animated around us, she dropped her voice, gave me a look which thrilled me, and said, with slow distinctness:—

"You Englishmen have pluck—I—I admire you!"

I answered, with a laugh, "We like to think of ourselves as a plucky race."

"You are! you are! I felt sure you would be capable of doing what you are now doing. Let us continue our conversation—nothing could be better for my purpose—don't you observe that Hagar is watching us?"

"Is not Madame Sorensen your aunt?" I asked.

"In reality she is no relation; but, hush, you are treading on dangerous ground."

"It is time for me to say farewell," I said, rising suddenly to my feet—I held out my hand to her as I spoke.

"No, you must not go yet," she said—she rose also—a certain nervous hesitation was observable for a moment in her manner, but she quickly steadied herself.

"Uncle Oscar, come here," she called out. Professor Sorensen happened to be approaching us across the drawing-room—he came up hastily at her summons. She stood in such a position that he could not see her face, and then gave me a look of intense warning.

When she did this, I knew that the gleam of hope which had given me false courage for a moment during dinner was at an end. There was no insanity in those lovely eyes. Her look braced me, however. I determined to take example by her marvellous coolness. In short, I resolved to do what she asked me, and to place my life in her hands.

"Uncle Oscar," said the young lady, "Dr. Halifax insists upon leaving us early; that is scarcely fair, is it?"

"It must not be permitted, Dr. Halifax," said the Professor, in his most courteous tone. "I am looking forward with great interest to getting your opinion on several points of scientific moment." Here he drew me a little aside. I glanced at Miss Sorensen: she came a step or two nearer.

"You will permit me to say that your name is already known to me," continued my host, "and I esteem it an honour to have the privilege of your acquaintance. I should like to get your opinion with regard to the bacterial theory of research. As I told you on board the *Ariadne* to-day, I have made many experiments in the isolation of microbes."

"In short, the isolation of those little horrors is my uncle's favourite occupation," interrupted Miss Sorensen, with a light laugh. "Suppose, Uncle Oscar," she continued, laying her lovely white hand on the Professor's arm—"suppose we take Dr. Halifax to the laboratory? He can then see some of your experiments."

"The cultivation of the cancer microbe for instance," said Sorensen. "Ah, that we could discover something to destroy it in the human body, without also destroying life! Well, doubtless, the time will come." He sighed as he spoke. His thoughtful face assumed an expression of keen intellectuality. It would be difficult to see anyone whose expression showed more noble interest in science.

"I see all my guests happily engaged," he continued. "Shall we follow Dagmar's suggestion, then, and come to the laboratory, Dr. Halifax?"

"I shall be interested to see what you have done," I said.

We left the drawing-rooms. As we passed Madame Sorensen, she called out to me to know if I were leaving.

"No," I replied; "I am going with your husband to his laboratory. He has kindly promised to show me some of his experiments."

"Ah, then, I will say good-night, and farewell. When Oscar goes to the laboratory he forgets the existence of time. Farewell, Dr. Halifax." She touched my hand with her thin fingers; her light eyes gave a queer, vindictive flash. "Farewell, or, *au revoir*, if you prefer it," she said, with a laugh. She turned abruptly to speak to another guest.

To reach the laboratory we had to walk down more than one long corridor—it was in a wing at some little distance from the rest of the house. Professor Sorensen explained the reason briefly.

"I make experiments," he said; "it is more convenient, therefore, to have the laboratory as distant from the dwelling-house as possible."

We finally passed through a narrow covered passage.

"Beneath here flows the Neva,"[1] said the Professor; "but here," he continued, "did you ever see a more spacious and serviceable room for real hard work than this?"

He flung open the door of the laboratory as he spoke, and touching a button in the wall, flooded the place on the instant with a blaze of electric light. The laboratory was warmed with hot pipes, and contained, in addition to the usual appliances, a couple of easy chairs and one or two small tables; also a long and particularly inviting-looking couch.

"I spend the night here occasionally," said Dr Sorensen. "When I am engaged in an important experiment, I often do not care to leave the place until the early hours of the morning."

We wandered about the laboratory, which was truly a splendid room and full of many objects which would, on another occasion, have aroused all my scientific enthusiasm, but I was too intensely on my guard just now to pay much attention to the Professor's carefully worded and elaborate descriptions. My quick eyes had taken in the whole situation as far as it was at present revealed to me: the iron bands of the strong door by which we had entered; the isolation of the laboratory. I was young and strong, however, and Professor Sorensen was old. If it came to a hand-to-hand fight, he would have no chance against me. Miss Sorensen, too, was my friend.

We spent some time examining various objects of interest, then finding the torture of suspense unendurable, I said, abruptly: "I should greatly like to see your process of cultivation of the cancer microbes before I take my leave."

"I will show it to you," said Dr. Sorensen. "Dagmar, my love, light the lantern."

"Is it not here?" I asked.

"No; I keep it in an oven in a small laboratory, which we will now visit."

Miss Sorensen took up a silver-mounted lantern, applied a match to the candle within, and taking it in her hand, preceded

---

1 The main waterway of St. Petersburg connecting the city to the Baltic Sea.

us up the whole length of the laboratory to a door which I had not before noticed, and which was situated just behind Dr. Sorensen's couch. She opened it and waited for us to come up to her.

"Take the lantern and go first, Uncle Oscar," said the young lady. She spoke in an imperious voice, and I saw the Professor give her a glance of slight surprise.

"Won't you go first, Dagmar?" he said. "Dr. Halifax can follow you, and I will come up in the rear."

She put the lantern into his hand.

"No, go first," she said, with a laugh which was a little unsteady. "No one knows your private haunts as well as you do yourself. Dr. Halifax will follow me."

The Professor took the lantern without another word. He began to descend some narrow and steep stairs. They were carpeted, and appeared, as far as I could see through the gloom, to lead into another passage farther down. Miss Sorensen followed her uncle immediately. As she did so, she threw her head back and gave me a warning glance.

Fig. 7. "THE PROFESSOR TOOK THE LANTERN."

"Take care, the stairs are steep," she said. "Count them; I will count them for you. I wish, Uncle Oscar, you would have this passage properly lighted."

"Come on, Dagmar: what are you lingering for?" called the Professor.

"Follow me, Dr. Halifax," she said. Her hand just touched mine—it burnt like coal. "These horrid stairs," she said. "I really must count them, or I'll fall." She began to count immediately in a sing-song, monotonous voice, throwing her words back at me, so that I doubt if the Professor heard them.

"One," she began, "two—three—four—five—six." When she had counted to six, she made an abrupt pause. We stood side by side on the sixth step.

"Seven is the perfect number," she said, in my ear—as she spoke, she pushed back her arm and thrust me forcibly back as I was about to advance. At the same instant, the dim light of the lantern went out, and I distinctly heard the door by which we had entered this narrow passage close behind us. We were in the dark. I was about to call out: "Miss Sorensen—Professor Sorensen," when a horrid noise fell upon my ears. It was the heavy sound as of a falling body. It went down, down, making fearful echoes as it banged against the sides of what must have been a deep well. Presently there was a splash, as if it had dropped into water.

That splash was a revelation. The body, whatever it was, had doubtless fallen into the Neva. At the same instant, Miss Sorensen's mysterious words returned to my memory: "Avoid the seventh step." I remembered that we had gone down six steps, and that as we descended, she had counted them one by one. On the edge of the sixth step she had paused, had pushed me back, and then had disappeared. The Professor had also vanished. What body was that which had fallen through space into a deep and watery grave? Miss Sorensen's mysterious remark was at last abundantly plain. *There was no seventh step*—by this trap, therefore, but for her interference, I was to be hurled into eternity.

I sank back, trembling in every limb. The horror of my situation can scarcely be described. At any moment the Professor might return, and by a push from above, send me into my watery grave. In my present position, I had no chance of fighting for my life. I retraced my steps to the door of the upper laboratory and felt vainly all along its smooth, hard surface. No chance of escape came from there. I sat down presently on the edge of the first step, and waited for the end with what patience I could. I still believed in Miss Sorensen, but would it be possible for her to come to my rescue? The silence and darkness of the grave surrounded me. Was I never to see daylight again? I recalled Madame Sorensen's face when she said "farewell"—I recalled the passion of despair in Miss Sorensen's young voice. I had touched secrets inadvertently with which I had no right to meddle. My death was desired by the Invincible and the Merciless—of course, I must die. As I grew accustomed to the darkness and stillness—the stillness itself was broken by the gurgling, distant sound of running water—I could hear the flow of the Neva as it rushed past my dark grave.

At the same moment the sound of voices fell on my ear. They were just below me—I felt my heart beating almost to suffocation. I clenched my hands tightly together—surely the crucial moment had come—could I fight for my life?

The Professor's thin, polished tones fell like ice on my heart.

"We had better come back and see that all is safe," he said. "Of course, he must have fallen over, but it is best to be certain.

"No, no, Uncle Oscar, it is not necessary," I heard Miss Sorensen say. "Did you not hear the sound—the awful sound—of his falling body? I did. I heard a splash as it fell into the Neva."

"Yes, I fancy I did hear it," answered the Professor, in a reflective voice.

"Then don't come back—why should we? It is all so horrible—let us return to the drawing-rooms as quickly as possible."

"You are excited, my dear—your voice trembles—what is the matter with you?"

"Only joy," she replied, "at having got rid of a dangerous enemy—now let us go."

Their voices died away—I could even hear the faint echo of their footsteps as they departed. I wondered how much longer I was to remain in my fearful grave. Had I the faintest chance of escaping the doom for which I was intended? Would Miss Sorensen be true to the end? She, doubtless, was a Nihilist, and as she said herself, they received no mercy and gave none. My head began to whirl—queer and desperate thoughts visited me. I felt my nerves tottering, and trembled, for a brief moment, for my reason. Suddenly a hand touched my arm, and a voice, clear, distinct, but intensely low, spoke to me.

"Thank God, you are here—come with me at once—don't ask a question—come noiselessly, and at once." I rose to my feet—Miss Sorensen's hot fingers clasped mine—she did not speak—she drew me forward. Once again I felt myself descending the steps. We came to the bottom of the sixth step. "This way," she said, in a muffled tone. She felt with her hands against the wall—a panel immediately gave way, and we found ourselves in a narrow passage, with a very faint light at the farther end. Miss Sorensen hurried me along. We went round a sort of semi-circular building, until at last we reached a small postern door in the wall. When we came to it she opened it a few inches, and pushed me out.

"Farewell," she said then. "I have saved your life. Farewell, brave Englishman."

She was about to shut the door in my face, but I pushed it back forcibly.

"I will not go until you tell me the meaning of this," I said.

"You are mad to linger," she replied, "but I will tell you in a few words. Professor Sorensen and his wife are no relations of mine. I am Olga Krestofski, suspected by the police, the owner of important secrets: in short, the head of a branch of the Nihilists. I shammed illness, and assumed the name under which I travelled, in order to convey papers of vast importance to our cause, to Petersburg. Professor Sorensen, as Court physician, has not yet incurred the faintest breath of suspicion—nevertheless, he is one of the leaders of our party, and every individual with whom you dined to-night belongs to us. It was decreed that you were to die. I decided otherwise. There was, as you doubtless have discovered, *no* seventh step. I warned you, and you had presence of mind sufficient not to continue your perilous downward course beyond the edge of the sixth step."

"But I heard a body fall," I said.

"Precisely," she replied; "I placed a bag of sand on the edge of the sixth step shortly after my arrival this morning, and just as I was following Professor Sorensen through the secret panel in the wall into the passage beyond, I pushed the bag over. This was necessary in order to deceive the Professor. He heard it splash into the water, and I was able to assure him that it was your body. Otherwise he would inevitably have returned to complete his deadly work. Now, good-bye—forgive me, if you can."

"Why did you bring me here at all?" I asked.

"It was your only chance. Madame Sorensen had resolved that you were to die. You would have been followed to the ends of the earth—now you are safe, because Professor and Madame Sorensen think you are dead."

"And you?" I said, suddenly. "If by any chance this is discovered, what will become of you?"

There was a passing gleam of light from a watery moon—it fell on Miss Sorensen's white face.

"I hold my life cheap," she said. "Farewell. Don't stay long in Petersburg."

She closed the postern door as she spoke.

THE BROTHERHOOD OF THE SEVEN KINGS

The Brotherhood of the Seven Kings

From L.T. Meade and Robert Eustace, *The Brotherhood of the Seven Kings*, *Strand Magazine* 15 (January–June 1898).

[Although the series featuring a criminal gang headed by the deadly Madame Koluchy exploited current anxieties about criminal gangs, secret societies, and terrorist organizations, the authors may have been inspired in part by earlier accounts of the Carbonari, one of a number of secret political societies that emerged in Europe in the eighteenth and nineteenth centuries. The Carbonari ("charcoal burners") developed an extensive international network promoting a "popular mix of revolution, mysticism and democracy" (Sweet 669). Wilkie Collins referred to the Carbonari as the "Brotherhood" in *The Woman in White* (Sweet 575); the buffoonish Professor Pesca and the villainous Count Fosco are both members of this powerful secret society whose real-life members included some of the founders of the modern Italian state. Additionally, Meade and Eustace may have been influenced by Mary Elizabeth Braddon's sensational series *The Black Band: Or, The Mysteries of Midnight* (1861–62; rpt. 1876–77), which featured a secret political organization engaged in robbery around the world. Braddon derived some of her information from newspaper accounts of Italian political societies that financed their activities through extortion, robbery, and murder (Carnell xv–xvi).]

I. —AT THE EDGE OF THE CRATER. Told by Norman Head. [86–98]

Introduction.—That a secret society, based upon the lines of similar institutions so notorious on the Continent during the last century, could ever have existed in the London of our day may seem impossible. Such a society, however, not only did exist, but through the instrumentality of a woman of unparalleled capacity and genius, obtained a firm footing. A century ago the Brotherhood of the Seven Kings was a name hardly whispered without horror and fear in Italy, and now, by the fascinations and influence of one woman, it began to accomplish fresh deeds of unparalleled daring and subtlety in London. By the wide extent of its scientific resources, and the impregnable secrecy of its organizations, it threatened to become a formidable menace to society, as well as a source of serious anxiety to the authorities of the law. It is to the courtesy of Mr. Norman Head that we are indebted for the subject-matter of the following hitherto unpublished revelations.

It was in the year 1895 that the first of the remarkable events which I am about to give to the world occurred. They found me something of a philosopher and a recluse, having, as I thought, lived my life and done with the active part of existence. It is true that I was young, not more than thirty-five years of age, but in the ghastly past I had committed a supreme error, and because of that paralyzing experience, I had left the bustling world and found my solace in the scientist's laboratory and the philosopher's study.

Ten years before these stories begin, when in Naples studying biology, I fell a victim to the wiles and fascinations of a beautiful Italian. A scientist of no mean attainments herself, with beauty beyond that of ordinary mortals, she had appealed not only to my head, but also to my heart. Dazzled by her beauty and intellect, she led me where she would. Her aims and ambitions, which in the false glamour she threw over them I thought the loftiest in the world, became also mine. She introduced me to the men of her set—I was quickly in the toils,[1] and on a night never to be forgotten, I took part in a grotesque and horrible ceremony, and became a member of her Brotherhood.

It was called the Brotherhood of the Seven Kings, and dated its origin from one of the secret societies of the Middle Ages. In my first enthusiasm it seemed to me to embrace all the principles of true liberty. Katherine was its chief and queen. Almost immediately after my initiation, however, I made an appalling discovery. Suspicion pointed to the beautiful Italian as the instigator, if not the author, of a most terrible crime. None of the details could be brought home to her, but there was little doubt that she was its moving spring. Loving her passionately as I then did, I tried to close my intellect against the all too conclusive evidence of her guilt. For a time I succeeded, but when I was ordered myself to take part in a transaction both dishonourable and treacherous, my eyes were opened. Horror seized me, and I fled to England to place myself under the protection of its laws.

---

1 Snare or trap.

Ten years went by, and the past was beginning to fade. It was destined to be recalled to me with startling vividness.

When a young man at Cambridge I had studied physiology, but never qualified myself as a doctor, having independent means; but in my laboratory in the vicinity of Regent's Park,[1] I worked at biology and physiology for the pure love of these absorbing sciences.

I was busily engaged on the afternoon of the 3rd of August, 1894, when Mrs. Kenyon, an old friend, called to see me. She was shown into my study, and I went to her there. Mrs. Kenyon was a widow, but her son, a lad of about twelve years of age, had, owing to the unexpected death of a relative, just come in for a large fortune and a title. She took the seat I offered her.

"It is too bad of you, Norman," she said; "it is months since you have been near me. Do you intend to forget your old friends?"

"I hope you will forgive me," I answered; "you know how busy I always am."

"You work too hard," she replied. "Why a man with your brains and opportunities for enjoying life wishes to shut himself up in the way you do, I cannot imagine."

"I am quite happy as I am, Mrs. Kenyon," I replied; "why, therefore, should I change? By the way, how is Cecil?"

"I have come here to speak about him. You know, of course, the wonderful change in his fortunes?"

"Yes," I answered.

"He has succeeded to the Kairn property, and is now Lord Kairn. There is a large rent-roll and considerable estates. You know, Norman, that Cecil has always been a most delicate boy."

"I hoped you were about to tell me that he was stronger," I replied.

"He is, and I will explain how in a moment. His life is a most important one. As Lord Kairn, much is expected of him. He has not only, under the providence of God, to live, but by that one little life he has to keep a man of exceedingly bad character out of a great property. I allude to Hugh Doncaster. Were Cecil to die, Hugh would be Lord Kairn. You have already doubtless heard of his character?"

"I know the man well by repute," I said.

"I thought you did. His disappointment and rage at Cecil succeeding to the title are almost beyond bounds. Rumours of his

1 One of London's largest parks. A number of elegant villas and upscale terraced houses are located in the Park and surrounding area.

malevolent feelings towards the child have already reached me. I am told that he is now in London, but his life, like yours, is more or less mysterious. I thought it just possible, Norman, that you, as an old friend, might be able to get me some particulars with regard to his whereabouts."

"Why do you want to know?" I asked.

"I feel a strange uneasiness about him; something which I cannot account for. Of course, in these enlightened days he would not attempt the child's life, but I should be more comfortable if I were assured that he was nowhere in Cecil's vicinity."

"But the man can do nothing to your boy!" I said. "Of course, I will find out what I can, but—"

Mrs. Kenyon interrupted me.

"Thank you. It is a relief to know that you will help me. Of course, there is no real danger; but I am a widow, and Cecil is only a child. Now, I must tell you about his health. He is almost quite well. The most marvellous recuperation has taken place. For the last two months he has been under the care of that extraordinary woman, Mme. Koluchy. She has worked miracles in his case, and now to complete the cure she is sending him to the Mediterranean. He sails to-morrow night under the care of Dr. Fietta. I cannot bear parting with him, but it is for his good, and Mme. Koluchy insists that a sea voyage is indispensable."

"But won't you accompany him?" I asked.

"I am sorry to say that is impossible. My eldest girl, Ethel, is about to be married, and I cannot leave her on the eve of her wedding; but Cecil will be in good hands. Dr. Fietta is a capital fellow—I have every faith in him."

"Where are they going?"

"To Cairo. They sail to-morrow night in the *Hydaspes*."

"Cairo is terribly hot at this time of year. Are you quite sure that it is wise to send a delicate lad like Cecil there in August?"

"Oh, he will not stay. He sails for the sake of the voyage, and will come back by the return-boat. The voyage is, according to Mme. Koluchy, to complete the cure. That marvellous woman has succeeded where the medical profession gave little hope. You have heard of her, of course?"

"I am sick of her very name," I replied; "one hears it everywhere. She has bewitched London with her impostures and quackery."

"There is no quackery about her, Norman. I believe her to be the cleverest woman in England. There are authentic accounts of her wonderful cures which cannot be contradicted. There are even rumours that she is able to restore youth and beauty by her arts. The whole of society is at her feet, and it is whispered that even Royalty are among her patients. Of course, her fees are enormous, but look at the results! Have you ever met her?"

"Never. Where does she come from? Who is she?"

"She is an Italian, but she speaks English perfectly. She has taken a house which is a perfect palace in Welbeck Street."[1]

"And who is Dr. Fietta?"

"A medical man who assists madame in her treatments. I have just seen him. He is charming, and devoted to Cecil. Five o'clock! I had no idea it was so late. I must be going. You will let me know when you hear any news of Mr. Doncaster? Come and see me soon."

I accompanied my visitor to the door, and then, returning to my study, sat down to resume the work I had been engaged in when I was interrupted.

But Mrs. Kenyon's visit had made me restless. I knew Hugh Doncaster's character well. Reports of his evil ways now and then agitated society, but the man had hitherto escaped the stern arm of justice. Of course, there could be no real foundation for Mrs. Kenyon's fears, but I felt that I could sympathize with her. The child was young and delicate; if Doncaster could injure him without discovery, he would not scruple to do so. As I thought over these things, a vague sensation of coming trouble possessed me. I hastily got into my evening dress, and having dined at my club, found myself at half-past ten in a drawing-room in Grosvenor Square.[2] As I passed on into the reception-rooms, having exchanged a few words with my hostess, I came across Dufrayer, a lawyer, and a special friend of mine. We got into conversation. As we talked, I noticed where a crowd of men were clustering round and paying homage to a stately woman at the farther end of the room. The marked intelligence and power of her face could not fail to arrest attention, even in the most casual observer. At the first glance I felt that I had seen her before, but could not tell when or where.

"Who is that woman?" I asked of my companion.

"My dear fellow," he replied, with amused smile, "don't you know? That is the great Mme. Koluchy, the rage of the season, the great specialist, the great consultant. London is mad about

---

1 A street in London's affluent West End associated with the medical profession.

2 Located in the West End in the exclusive Mayfair district.

her. She has only been here ten minutes, and look, she is going already. They say she has a dozen engagements every night."

Fig. 8. "HER EYES MET MINE."

Mme. Koluchy began to move towards the door, and, anxious to get a nearer view, I also passed rapidly through the throng. I reached the head of the stairs before she did, and as she went by looked her full in the face. Her eyes met mine. Their dark depths seemed to read me through. She half smiled, half paused as if to speak, changed her mind, made a stately inclination of her queenly head, and went slowly down stairs. For a moment I stood still, there was a ringing in my ears, and my heart was beating to suffocation. Then I hastily followed her. When I reached the pavement Mme. Koluchy's carriage stopped the way. She did not notice me, but I was able to observe her. She was bending out and talking eagerly to someone. The following words fell on my ear:—

"It is all right. They sail to-morrow evening."

The man to whom she spoke made a reply which I could not catch, but I had seen his face. He was Hugh Doncaster.

Mme. Koluchy's carriage rolled away, and I hailed a hansom.[1] In supreme moments we think rapidly. I thought quickly then.

"Where to?" asked the driver.

"No. 140, Earl's Terrace, Kensington,"[2] I called out. I sat back as I spoke. The horror of past memories was almost paralyzing me, but I quickly pulled myself together. I knew that I must act, and act quickly. I had just seen the Head of the Brotherhood of the Seven Kings. Mme. Koluchy, changed in much since I last saw her, was the woman who had wrecked my heart and life ten years before in Naples.

With my knowledge of the past, I was well aware that where this woman appeared victims fell. Her present victim was a child. I must save that child, even if my own life were the penalty. She had ordered the boy abroad. He was to sail to-morrow with an emissary of hers. She was in league with Doncaster. If she could get rid of the boy, Doncaster would doubtless pay her a fabulous sum. For the working of her schemes she above all things wanted money. Yes, without doubt, the lad's life was in the gravest danger, and I had not a moment to lose. The first thing was to communicate with the mother, and if possible put a stop to the intended voyage.

I arrived at the house, flung open the doors of the hansom, and ran up the steps. Here unexpected news awaited me. The servant who answered my summons said that Mrs. Kenyon had started for Scotland by the night mail[3]—she had received a telegram announcing the serious illness of her eldest girl. On getting it she had started for the north, but would not reach her destination until the following evening.

"Is Lord Kairn in?" I asked.

"No, sir," was the reply. "My mistress did not like to leave him

1 A two-wheeled carriage for one or two passengers, with the driver seated behind. Hansom cabs were popular in London because they were light enough to be pulled by a single horse and able to move quickly around larger vehicles.

2 One of London's most expensive streets in a very affluent area of London. Kensington contains some of London's most significant buildings and monuments, including Kensington Palace.

3 A regular evening train service carrying mail in addition to passengers.

here alone, and he has been sent over to Mme. Koluchy's, 100, Welbeck Street. Perhaps you are not aware, sir, that his lordship sails to-morrow evening for Cairo?"

"Yes, I know all about that," I replied; "and now, if you will give me your mistress's address, I shall be much obliged to you."

The man supplied it. I entered my hansom again. For a moment it occurred to me that I would send a telegram to intercept Mrs. Kenyon on her rapid journey north, but I finally made up my mind not to do so. The boy was already in the enemy's hands, and I felt sure that I could now only rescue him by guile. I returned home, having already made up my mind how to act. I would accompany Cecil and Dr. Fietta to Cairo.

At eleven o'clock on the following morning I had taken my berth in the *Hydaspes*, and at nine that evening was on board. I caught a momentary glimpse of young Lord Kairn and his attendant, but in order to avoid explanations kept out of their way. It was not until the following morning, when the steamer was well down Channel, that I made my appearance on deck, where I at once saw the boy sitting at the stern in a chair. Beside him was a lean, middle-aged man wearing a pair of *pince-nez*. He looked every inch a foreigner, with his pointed beard, waxed moustache, and deep-set, beady eyes. As I sauntered across the deck to where they were sitting, Lord Kairn looked up and instantly recognised me.

"Mr. Head!" he exclaimed, jumping from his chair, "you here? I am very glad to see you."

"I am on my way to Cairo, on business," I said, shaking the boy warmly by the hand.

"To Cairo? Why, that is where we are going; but you never told mother you were coming, and she saw you the day before yesterday. It was such a pity that mother had to rush off to Scotland so suddenly; but last night, just before we sailed, there came a telegram telling us that Ethel was better. As mother had to go away, I went to Mme. Koluchy's for the night. I like going there. She has a lovely house, and she is so delightful herself. And this is Dr. Fietta, who has come with me." As the boy added these words Dr. Fietta came forward and peered at me through his *pince-nez*. I bowed, and he returned my salutation.

"This is an extraordinary coincidence, Dr. Fietta!" I exclaimed. "Cecil Kenyon happens to be the son of one of my greatest friends. I am glad to see him looking so well. I am fortunate in having the honour of meeting so distinguished a savant as yourself. I have heard much about Mme. Koluchy's marvellous occult powers, but I suppose the secrets of her success are very jealously guarded. The profession, of course, pooh-pooh her, I know, but if one may credit all one hears, she possesses remedies undreamt-of in their philosophy."

"It is quite true, Mr. Head. As a medical man myself, I can vouch for her capacity, and unfettered by English professional scrupulousness, I appreciate it. Mme. Koluchy and I are proud of our young friend here, and hope that the voyage will complete his cure, and fit him for the high position he is destined to occupy."

The voyage flew by. Fietta was an intelligent man, and his scientific attainments were considerable. But for my knowledge of the terrible past my fears might have slumbered, but as it was they were always present with me, and the moment all too quickly arrived when suspicion was to be plunged into certainty. On the day before we were due at Malta,[1] the wind sprang up and we got into a choppy sea. When I had finished breakfast I went to Cecil's cabin to see how he was. He was just getting up, and looked pale and unwell.

"There is a nasty sea on," I said, "but the captain says we shall be out of it in an hour or so."

"I hope we shall," he answered, "for it makes me feel squeamish, but I dare say I shall be all right when I get on deck. Dr. Fietta gave me something to stop the sickness, but it has not had much effect."

"I do not know anything that really stops sea-sickness," I answered; "but what has he done?"

"Oh, a curious thing, Mr. Head. He pricked my arm with a needle on a syringe, and squirted something in. He says it is a certain cure for sea-sickness. Look," said the child, baring his arm, "that is where he did it."

I examined the mark closely. It had evidently been made with a hypodermic injection needle.

"Did Dr. Fietta tell you what he put into your arm?" I asked.

"Yes, he said it was morphia."[2]

"Where does he keep his needle?"

"In his trunk there under his bunk. I shall be dressed directly,

---

1 Located south of Sicily in the Mediterranean, Malta became part of the British Empire in 1814 and was an important naval base and shipping station on the way to Egypt and India.

2 Morphine, a drug derived from opium and used in medicine to alleviate pain.

and will come on deck."

I left the cabin and went up the companion.[1] The doctor was pacing to and fro on the hurricane-deck.[2] I approached him.

"Your charge has not been well," I said, "I have just seen him. He tells me you have given him a hypodermic of morphia."

He turned round and gave me a quick glance of uneasy fear.

"Did Lord Kairn tell you so?"

"Yes."

"Well, Mr. Head, it is the very best cure for sea-sickness. I have found it most efficacious."

"Do you think it wise to give a child morphia?" I asked.

"I do not discuss my treatment with an unqualified man," he replied, brusquely, turning away as he spoke. I looked after him, and as he disappeared down the deck my fears became certainties. I determined, come what would, to find out what he had given the boy. I knew only too well the infinite possibilities of that dangerous little instrument, a hypodermic syringe.

As the day wore on the sea moderated, and at five o'clock it was quite calm again, a welcome change to the passengers, who, with the permission of the captain, had arranged to give a dance that evening on deck. The occasion was one when ordinary scruples must fade out of sight. Honour in such a mission as I had set myself must give place to the watchful zeal of the detective. I was determined to take advantage of the dance to explore Dr. Fietta's cabin. The doctor was fond of dancing, and as soon as I saw that he and Lord Kairn were well engaged, I descended the companion, and went to their cabin. I switched on the electric light, and, dragging the trunk from beneath the bunk, hastily opened it. It was unlocked and only secured by straps. I ran my hand rapidly through the contents, which were chiefly clothes, but tucked in one corner I found a case, and, pulling it out, opened it. Inside lay the delicate little hypodermic syringe which I had come in search of.

I hurried up to the light and examined it. Smeared round the inside of the glass, and adhering to the bottom of the little plunger, was a whitish, gelatinous-looking substance. This was no ordinary hypodermic solution. It was half-liquefied gelatine such as I knew so well as the medium for the cultivation of micro-organisms. For a moment I felt half-stunned. What infernal

---

1 A stairway or ladder between decks on a boat or ship (leading to cabins).

2 Upper deck.

culture might it not contain?

Time was flying, and at any moment I might be discovered. I hastily slipped the syringe into my pocket, and closing the trunk, replaced it, and, switching off the electric light, returned to the deck. My temples were throbbing, and it was with difficulty I could keep my self-control. I made up my mind quickly. Fietta would of course miss the syringe, but the chances were that he would not do so that night. As yet there was nothing apparently the matter with the boy, but might there not be flowing through his veins some poisonous germs of disease, which only required a period of incubation for their development?

At daybreak the boat would arrive at Malta. I would go on shore at once, call upon some medical man, and lay the case before him in confidence, in the hope of his having the things I should need in order to examine the contents of the syringe. If I found any organisms, I would take the law into my own hands, and carry the boy back to England by the next boat.

No sleep visited me that night, and I lay tossing to and fro in my bunk longing for daylight. At 6 a.m. I heard the engine-bell ring, and the screw[1] suddenly slow down to half-speed. I leapt up and went on deck. I could see the outline of the rock-bound fortress and the lighthouse of St. Elmo looming more vividly every moment. As soon as we were at anchor and the gangway down, I hailed one of the little green boats and told the men to row me to the shore. I drove at once to the Grand Hotel in the Strada Reale, and asked the Italian guide the address of a medical man. He gave me the address of an English doctor who lived close by, and I went there at once to see him. It was now seven o'clock, and I found him up. I made my apologies for the early hour of my visit, put the whole matter before him, and produced the syringe. For a moment he was inclined to treat my story with incredulity, but by degrees he became interested, and ended by inviting me to breakfast with him. After the meal we repaired to his consulting-room to make our investigations. He brought out his microscope, which I saw, to my delight, was of the latest design, and I set to work at once, while he watched me with evident interest. At last the crucial moment came, and I bent over the instrument and adjusted the focus on my preparation. My suspicions were only too well confirmed by what I saw. The substance which I had extracted from the syringe was a mass of micro-organisms, but of what nature I did not know. I had never seen any quite like

1 Propeller.

them before. I drew back.

"I wish you would look at this," I said. "You tell me you have devoted considerable attention to bacteriology. Please tell me what you see."

Dr. Benson applied his eye to the instrument, regulating the focus for a few moments, in silence; then he raised his head, and looked at me with a curious expression.

"Where did this culture come from?" he asked.

"From London, I presume," I answered.

"It is extraordinary," he said, with emphasis, "but there is no doubt whatever that these organisms are the specific germs of the very disease I have studied here so assiduously; they are the micrococci of Mediterranean fever, the minute round or oval bacteria. They are absolutely characteristic."

I jumped to my feet.

"Is that so?" I cried. The diabolical nature of the plot was only too plain. These germs injected into a patient would produce a fever which only occurs in the Mediterranean. The fact that the boy had been in the Mediterranean even for a short time would be a complete blind as to the way in which they obtained access to the body, as everyone would think the disease occurred from natural causes.

"How long is the period of incubation?" I asked.

"About ten days," replied Dr. Benson.

I extended my hand.

"You have done me an invaluable service," I said.

"I may possibly be able to do you a still further service," was his reply. "I have made Mediterranean fever the study of my life and have, I believe, discovered an antitoxin for it. I have tried my discovery on the patients of the naval hospital with excellent results. The local disturbance is slight, and I have never found bad symptoms follow the treatment. If you will bring the boy to me I will administer the antidote without delay."

I considered for a moment, then I said: "My position is a terrible one, and I am inclined to accept your proposition. Under the circumstances it is the only chance."

"It is," repeated Dr. Benson. "I shall be at your service whenever you need me."

I bade him good-bye and quickly left the house.

It was now ten o'clock. My first object was to find Dr. Fietta, to speak to him boldly, and take the boy away by main force if necessary. I rushed back to the Grand Hotel, where I learned that a boy and a man, answering to the description of Dr. Fietta and Cecil, had breakfasted there, but had gone out again immediately afterwards. The *Hydaspes* I knew was to coal, and would not leave Malta before one o'clock. My only chance, therefore, was to catch them as they came on board. Until then I could do nothing. At twelve o'clock I went down to the quay and took a boat to the *Hydaspes*. Seeing no sign of Fietta and the boy on deck, I made my way at once to Lord Kairn's cabin. The door was open and the place in confusion—every vestige of baggage had disappeared. Absolutely at a loss to divine the cause of this unexpected discovery, I pressed the electric bell. In a moment a steward appeared.

"Has Lord Kairn left the ship?" I asked, my heart beating fast.

"I believe so, sir," replied the man. "I had orders to pack the luggage and send it on shore. It went about an hour ago."

I waited to hear no more. Rushing to my cabin, I began flinging my things pell-mell into my portmanteau. I was full of apprehension at this sudden move of Dr. Fietta's. Calling a steward who was passing to help me, I got my things on deck, and in a few moments had them in a boat and was making rapidly for the shore. I drove back at once to the Grand Hotel in the Strada Reale.

"Did the gentleman who came here to-day from the *Hydaspes*, accompanied by a little boy, engage rooms for the night?" I asked of the proprietor in the bureau at the top of the stairs.

"No, sir," answered the man; "they breakfasted here, but did not return. I think they said they were going to the gardens of San Antonio."

For a minute or two I paced the hall in uncontrollable excitement. I was completely at a loss what step to take next. Then suddenly an idea struck me. I hurried down the steps and made my way to Cook's office.[1]

"A gentleman of that description took two tickets for Naples by the *Spartivento*, a Rupertino boat,[2] two hours ago," said the clerk, in answer to my inquiries. "She has started by now," he

1 Thomas Cook and Son, England's leading travel agency, founded in the 1840s.

2 Most likely a reference to the Rubattino Line, a major Italian shipping company founded in 1838 by Raffaele Rubattino (1809–81) to operate between Genoa and the Mediterranean ports. It later merged with a Sicilian company to form the *Navigazione Generale Italiana*, which dominated Italian shipping in the Mediterranean for many years.

continued, glancing up at the clock.

"To Naples?" I cried. A sickening fear seized me. The very name of the hated place struck me like a poisoned weapon.

"Is it too late to catch her?" I asked.

"Yes, sir, she has gone."

"Then what is the quickest route by which I can reach Naples?"

"You can go by the *Gingra*, a P. and O. boat,[1] to-night to Brindisi,[2] and then overland. That is the quickest way now."

I at once took my passage and left the office. There was not the least doubt what had occurred. Dr. Fietta had missed his syringe, and in consequence had immediately altered his plans. He was now taking the lad to the very fountain-head of the Brotherhood, where other means if necessary would be employed to put an end to his life.

It was nine o'clock in the evening, three days later, when, from the window of the railway carriage, I caught my first glimpse of the glow on the summit of Vesuvius.[3] During the journey, I had decided on my line of action. Leaving my luggage in the cloak-room, I entered a carriage and began to visit hotel after hotel. For a long time I had no success. It was past eleven o'clock that night when, weary and heart-sick, I drew up at the Hotel Londres. I went to the concierge with my usual question, expecting the invariable reply, but a glow of relief swept over me when the man said:—

"Dr. Fietta is out, sir, but the young lord is in. He is in bed—will you call to-morrow? What name shall I say?"

"I shall stay here," I answered; "let me have a room at once, and have my bag taken to it. What is the number of Lord Kairn's room?"

"Number forty-six. But he will be asleep, sir; you cannot see him now."

I made no answer, but going quickly upstairs, I found the boy's room. I knocked; there was no reply, I turned the handle

---

1 The Peninsular and Oriental Steam Navigation Company operated ships between England, the Iberian Peninsula, Malta, Athens, and Egypt.

2 A major port on the Adriatic Sea for trade with Greece and the Middle East.

3 An active volcano located near Naples, famous for its eruption in 79 CE that destroyed the Roman cities of Pompeii and Herculaneum. Thomas Cook sold package tours to Vesuvius and operated the funicular railway that carried tourists to the summit.

and entered. All was dark. Striking a match I looked round. In a white bed at the further end lay the child. I went up and bent softly over him. He was lying with one hand beneath his cheek. He looked worn and tired, and now and then moaned as if in trouble. When I touched him lightly on the shoulder, he started up and opened his eyes. A dazed expression of surprise swept over his face; then with an eager cry he stretched out both his hands and clasped one of mine.

"I am so glad to see you," he said. "Dr. Fietta told me you were angry—that I had offended you. I very nearly cried when I missed you that morning at Malta, and Dr. Fietta said I should never see you any more. I don't like him—I am afraid of him. Have you come to take me home?" As he spoke he glanced eagerly round in the direction of the door, clutching my hand still tighter as he did so.

"Yes, I shall take you home, Cecil. I have come for the purpose," I answered; "but are you quite well?"

"That's just it; I am not. I have awful dreams at night. Oh, I am so glad you have come back, and you are not angry. Did you say you were really going to take me home?"

"To-morrow, if you like."

"Please do. I am—stoop down, I want to whisper to you—I am afraid of Dr. Fietta."

"What is your reason?" I asked.

"There is no reason," answered the child, "but somehow I dread him. I have done so ever since you left us at Malta. Once I woke in the middle of the night and he was bending over me—he had such a queer look on his face, and he used that syringe again. He was putting something into my arm—he told me it was morphia. I did not want him to do it, for I thought you would rather he didn't. I wish mother had sent me away with you. I am afraid of him."

"Now that I have come, everything will be right," I said.

"And you will take me home to-morrow?"

"Certainly."

"But I should like to see Vesuvius first. Now that we are here it seems a pity that I should not see it. Can you take me to Vesuvius to-morrow morning, and home in the evening, and will you explain to Dr. Fietta?"

"I will explain everything. Now go to sleep. I am in the house, and you have nothing whatever to fear."

"I am very glad you have come," he said, wearily. He flung himself back on his pillow; the exhausted look was very manifest on his small, childish face. I left the room, shutting the door, softly.

To say that my blood boiled can express but little the emotions which ran through my frame—the child was in the hands of a monster. He was in the very clutch of the Brotherhood, whose intention was to destroy his life. I thought for a moment. There was nothing now for it but to see Fietta, tell him that I had discovered his machinations, claim the boy, and take him away by force. I knew I was treading on dangerous ground. At any moment my own life might be the forfeit, for my supposed treachery to the cause whose vows I had so madly taken. Still, if I saved the boy nothing else really mattered.

I went downstairs into the great central hall, interviewed the concierge, who told me that Fietta had returned, asked for the number of his private sitting-room, and, going there, opened the door without knocking. At a writing-table at the farther end sat the doctor. He turned as I entered, and, recognising me, started up with a sudden exclamation. I noticed that his face changed colour, and that his beady eyes flashed an ugly fire. Then, recovering himself, he advanced quietly towards me.

"This is another of your unexpected surprises, Mr. Head," he said, with politeness. "You have not, then, gone on to Cairo? You change your plans rapidly."

"Not more so than you do, Dr. Fietta," I replied, watching him as I spoke.

"I was obliged to change my mind," he answered. "I heard in Malta that cholera had broken out in Cairo. I could not therefore take my patient there. May I inquire why I have the honour of this visit? You will excuse my saying so, but this action of yours forces me to suspect that you are following me. Have you a reason?"

He stood with his hands behind him, and a look of furtive vigilance crept into his small eyes.

"This is my reason," I replied. I boldly drew the hypodermic syringe from my pocket as I spoke.

With an inconceivably rapid movement he hurried past me, locked the door, and placed the key in his pocket. As he turned towards me again I saw the glint of a long, bright stiletto which he had drawn and was holding in his right hand, which he kept behind him.

"I see you are armed," I said, quietly, "but do not be too hasty. I have a few words to say to you." As I spoke I looked him full in the face, then I dropped my voice.

"*I am one of the Brotherhood of the Seven Kings!*"

When I uttered these magical words he started back and looked at me with dilated eyes.

"Your proofs, instantly, or you are a dead man," he cried, hoarsely. Beads of sweat gleamed upon his forehead.

Fig. 9. "'YOUR PROOFS, INSTANTLY, OR YOU ARE A DEAD MAN,' HE CRIED."

"Put that weapon on the table, give me your right hand, and you shall have the proofs you need," I answered.

He hesitated, then changed the stiletto to his left hand, and gave me his right. I grasped it in the peculiar manner which I had never forgotten, and bent my head close to his. The next moment I had uttered the pass-word of the Brotherhood.

"La Regina,"[1] I whispered.

"*E la regina*," he replied, flinging the stiletto on the carpet.

"Ah!" he continued, with an expression of the strongest relief, while he wiped the moisture from his forehead. "This is too wonderful. And now tell me, my friend, what your mission is? I knew you had stolen my syringe, but why did you do it? Why did you not reveal yourself to me before? You are, of course, under the Queen's orders?"

"I am," I answered, "and her orders to me now are to take Lord Kairn home to England overland to-morrow morning."

1 The Queen (Italian).

"Very well. Everything is finished—he will die in one month."

"From Mediterranean fever? But it is not necessarily fatal," I continued.

"That is true. It is not always fatal acquired in the ordinary way, but by our methods it is so."

"Then you have administered more of the micro-organisms since leaving Malta?"

"Yes; I had another syringe in my case, and now nothing can save him. The fever will commence in six days from now."

He paused for a moment or two.

"It is very odd," he went on, "that I should have had no communication. I cannot understand it." A sudden flash of suspicion shot across his dark face. My heart sank as I saw it. It passed, however, the next instant; the man's words were courteous and quiet.

"I of course accede to your proposition," he said: "everything is quite safe. This that I have done can never by any possibility be discovered. Madame is invincible. Have you yet seen Lord Kairn?"

"Yes, and I have told him to be prepared to accompany me home to-morrow."

"Very well."

Dr. Fietta walked across the room, unlocked the door and threw it open.

"Your plans will suit me admirably," he continued. "I shall stay on here for a few days more, as I have some private business to transact. To-night I shall sleep in peace. Your shadow has been haunting me for the last three days."

I went from Fietta's room to the boy's. He was wide awake and started up when he saw me.

"I have arranged everything, Cecil," I said, "and you are my charge now. I mean to take you to my room to sleep."

"Oh," he answered, "I am glad. Perhaps I shall sleep better in your room. I am not afraid of you—I love you." His eyes, bright with affection, looked into mine. I lifted him into my arms, wrapped his dressing-gown over his shoulders, and conveyed him through the folding-doors, down the corridor, into the room I had secured for myself. There were two beds in the room, and I placed him in one.

"I am so happy," he said, "I love you so much. Will you take me to Vesuvius in the morning, and then home in the evening?"

"I will see about that. Now go to sleep," I answered.

He closed his eyes with a sigh of pleasure. In ten minutes he was sound asleep. I was standing by him when there came a knock at the door. I went to open it. A waiter stood without.

He held a salver in his hand. It contained a letter, also a sheet of paper and an envelope stamped with the name of the hotel.

"From the doctor, to be delivered to the signor immediately," was the laconic remark.

Still standing in the doorway, I took the letter from the tray, opened it, and read the following words:—

"You have removed the boy, and that action arouses my mistrust. I doubt your having received any communication from madame. If you wish me to believe that you are a *bonâ-fide* member of the Brotherhood, return the boy to his own sleeping-room immediately."

I took a pencil out of my pocket and hastily wrote a few words on the sheet of paper, which had been sent for the purpose:—

"I retain the boy. You are welcome to draw your own conclusions."

Folding up the paper I slipped it into the envelope, and wetting the gum with my tongue, fastened it together, and handed it to the waiter, who withdrew. I re-entered my room and locked the door. To keep the boy was imperative, but there was little doubt that Fietta would now telegraph to Mme. Koluchy (the telegraphic office being open day and night) and find out the trick I was playing upon him. I considered whether I might not remove the boy there and then to another hotel, but decided that such a step would be useless. Once the emissaries of the Brotherhood were put upon my track, the case for the child and myself would be all but hopeless.

There was likely to be little sleep for me that night. I paced up and down my lofty room. My thoughts were keen and busy. After a time, however, a strange confusion seized me. One moment I thought of the child, the next of Mme. Koluchy, and then again I found myself pondering some abstruse and comparatively unimportant point in science, which I was perfecting at home. I shook myself free of these thoughts, to walk about again, to pause by the bedside of the child, to listen to his quiet breathing.

Perfect peace reigned over his little face. He had resigned himself to me, his terrors were things of the past, and he was absolutely happy. Then once again that queer confusion of brain returned. I wondered what I was I doing, and why I was anxious about the boy. Finally I sank upon the bed at the farther end of the room, for my limbs were tired and weighted with a heavy oppression. I would rest for a moment, but nothing would induce me to close my eyes. So I thought, and flung myself back on my pillow. But the next instant all present things were forgotten in dreamless and heavy slumber.

I awoke long hours afterwards, to find the sunshine flooding the room—the window which led on to the balcony wide open, and Cecil's bed empty. I sprang up with a cry; memory returned with a flash. What had happened? Had Fietta managed to get in by means of the window? I had noticed the balcony outside the window, on the previous night. The balcony of the next room was but a few feet distant from mine. It would be easy for anyone to enter there, spring from one balcony to the other, and so obtain access to my room. Doubtless this had been done. Why had I slept? I had firmly resolved to stay awake all night. In an instant I had found the solution. Fietta's letter had been a trap. The envelope which he sent me contained poison on the gum. I had licked it, and so received the fatal soporific.[1] My heart beat wildly. I knew I had not an instant to lose. With hasty strides I went into Fietta's sitting-room: there was no one there; into his bedroom, the door of which was open: it was also empty. I rushed into the hall.

"The gentleman and the little boy went out about half an hour ago," said the concierge, in answer to my inquiries. "They have gone to Vesuvius—a fine day for the trip." The man smiled as he spoke.

My heart almost stopped.

"How did they go?" I asked.

"A carriage, two horses—best way to go."

In a second I was out in the Piazza del Municipio. Hastily selecting a pair-horse carriage out of the group of importunate drivers, I jumped in.

"Vesuvius," I shouted, "as hard as you can go."

The man began to bargain. I thrust a roll of paper-money into his hand. On receiving it he waited no longer, and we were soon dashing at a furious speed along the crowded, ill-paved streets, scattering the pedestrians as we went. Down the Via Roma, and out on to the Santa Lucia Quay, away and away through endless labyrinths of noisome, narrow streets, till at length we got out into the more open country, at the base of the burning mountain. Should I be in time to prevent the catastrophe which I dreaded? For I had been up that mountain before, and knew well the horrible danger at the crater's mouth—a slip, a push, and one would never be seen again.

The ascent began, and the exhausted horses were beginning to fail. I leapt out, and giving the driver a sum which I did not wait to count, ran up the winding road of cinders and pumice, that curves round beneath the observatory. My breath had failed me, and my heart was beating so hard that I could scarcely speak, when I reached the station where one takes ponies to go over the new, rough lava. In answer to my inquiries, Cook's agent told me that Fietta and Cecil had gone on not a quarter of an hour ago.

1 A drug causing sleep.

I shouted my orders, and flinging money right and left, I soon obtained a fleet pony, and was galloping recklessly over the broken lava. Throwing the reins over the pony's head I presently jumped off, and ran up the little, narrow path to the funicular wire-laid railway, that takes passengers up the steep cone to the crater.

"Just gone on, sir," said a Cook's official, in answer to my question.

"But I must follow at once," I said, excitedly, hurrying towards the little shed.

The man stopped me.

"We don't take single passengers," he answered.

"I will, and must, go alone," I said. "I'll buy the car, and the railway, and you, and the mountain, if necessary, but go I will. How much do you want to take me alone?"

"One hundred francs,"[1] he answered, impertinently, little thinking that I would agree to the bargain.

"Done!" I replied.

In astonishment he counted out the notes which I handed to him, and hurried at once into the shed. Here he rang an electric bell to have the car at the top started back, and getting into the empty car, I began to ascend up, and up, and up. Soon I passed the empty car returning. How slowly we moved! My mouth was parched and dry, and I was in a fever of excitement. The smoke from the crater was close above me in great wreaths. At last we reached the top. I leapt out, and without waiting for a guide, made my way past, and rushed up the active cone, slipping in the shifting, loose, gritty soil. When I reached the top a gale was blowing, and the scenery below, with the Bay and Naples and Sorrento, lay before me, the most magnificent panorama in the world. I had no time to glance at it, but hurried forward, past crags of hot rock, from which steam and sulphur were escaping. The wind was taking the huge volumes of smoke over to the farther side of the crater, and I could just catch sight of two figures as the smoke cleared for a moment. The figures were those of Fietta and the boy. They were evidently making a *détour* of the crater, and had just entered the smoke. I heard a guide behind shout something to me in Italian, but I took no notice, and plunged at once into the blinding, suffocating smoke that came belching forth from the crater.

I was now close behind Fietta and the boy. They held their handkerchiefs up to their faces to keep off the choking, sulphurous fumes, and had evidently not seen me. Their guide was ahead of them. Fietta was walking slowly; he was farthest away from the

1 The franc was the basic monetary unit of several European countries including France, Switzerland, and Belgium.

crater's mouth. The boy's hand was within his; the boy was nearest to the yawning gulf. A hot and choking blast of smoke blinded me for a moment, and hid the pair from view; the next instant it passed. I saw Fietta suddenly turn, seize the boy, and push him towards the edge. Through the rumbling thunder that came from below I heard a sharp cry of terror, and bounding forward I just caught the lad as he reeled, and hurled him away into safety.

With a hoarse yell of baffled rage, Fietta dashed through the smoke and flung himself upon me. I moved nimbly aside, and the doctor, carried on by the impetus of his rush, missed his footing in the crumbling ashes and fell headlong down through the reeking smoke and steam into the fathomless, seething caldron below.

What followed may be told in a few words. That evening I sailed for Malta with the boy. Dr. Benson administered the antitoxin in time, and the child's life was saved. Within a fortnight I brought him back to his mother.

It was reported that Dr. Fietta had gone mad at the edge of the crater, and in an excess of maniacal fury, had first tried to destroy the boy, and then flung himself in. I kept my secret.

Fig. 10. "THE DOCTOR FELL HEADLONG DOWN."

THE HEART OF A MYSTERY

The Heart of a Mystery

From L.T. Meade and Robert Eustace, *The Heart of a Mystery*, *Windsor Magazine* 14 (June–November 1901).

[*The Strand*-inspired *Windsor Magazine* (1895–1939) was a high-quality, illustrated middle-class magazine that supported traditional views about women, the family, and social class. As its title suggests, the magazine was a staunch ally of the royal family, the British aristocracy, and British imperialism. Despite its conservative orientation (it was particularly opposed to feminism and socialism), the magazine published a variety of informative and educational articles as well as adventure and mystery fiction. Many of the *Strand*'s most popular writers, including Arthur Conan Doyle, also published fiction in the *Windsor Magazine*.

The following story, published in July 1901, is the second in the six-part series *The Heart of a Mystery*, set in 1898 on the eve of the Second Boer War (1899–1902). The previous story introduces the narrator Rupert Phenays and his foe, Mademoiselle Francesca Delacourt, the head of a "most dreadful gang of spies" plotting against Britain. Like Meade's other dangerous women, Delacourt is beautiful, clever, and fascinating. "A Little Smoke" begins as Phenays ponders his recent narrow escape from a horrific explosion arranged by the deadly Mademoiselle.]

II. —A LITTLE SMOKE. [225–35]

Looking back on my startling experience, I come to the conclusion that in the whole of England there were probably few men in a stranger position than I, Rupert Phenays, when, on a certain dull February morning, I found myself, after my brief visit to Paris, once more back in London. In that visit all my life had been changed. I had gone to Paris to see my greatest friend, who, in struggling to tell me a terrible and important secret, had died. Agents of the French Secret Service believed me to be in possession of this great secret, and in consequence my life was in danger. Such was the state of affairs. Already I had been within an ace of being hurled into eternity; what further dangers were in store for me it was impossible to tell.

When I arrived at my comfortable rooms in Half Moon Street[1] I owned to a momentary sensation of relief, but this was of short duration. My fears with regard to the future quickly returned, and I determined to put the whole matter before my lawyer, Mr. Charles Tempest, of Lincoln's Inn Fields,[2] and take his advice.

I called on Tempest soon after breakfast; he was within and saw me almost immediately. I told him of the curious position in which I found myself, and I could see that at first he was almost unable to take my communication seriously. It was not until I had driven home fact after fact that he assumed his normal professional attitude.

"Now for your advice, sir," I said. "I do not know anyone in such a deplorable position as I find myself in. All the British Government and Scotland Yard combined cannot prevent my assassination by desperadoes. Is it likely that the persecution will be continued?"

"It is certainly possible," replied Tempest. "The attempt already made on your life is sufficient to show you that these people are in earnest. Your position is, I take it, this. You are supposed by the agents of the French Secret Service to be in possession of a great secret, and nothing you can say will convince them to the contrary."

"That is so."

"In reality you have no secret whatever?"

"Precisely."

"It is the lady you call Mademoiselle Delacourt whom you principally fear?"

"Yes."

"You believe that she is one of the agents of the French Secret Service?"

"Yes."

"There is little doubt that you are in danger," continued Tempest. "The issues, you see, are considerable; they are international, and lives are cheap when these things hang in the balance. Well, you have two courses open to you. One, to take no notice at all and go on with your usual life—the other, to disappear. The first offers the greatest danger to yourself, and the second may

1 Located in the fashionable area of Mayfair in central London near Buckingham Palace.

2 A large public square in central London bordered by Lincoln's Inn, one of four Inns of Court in London. Members of the legal profession established chambers in and around Lincoln's Inn.

seem a trifle cowardly, but in your position and circumstances I should quietly drop out of sight. Go to some remote part of Europe, amuse yourself with your favourite occupation, sketching, and wait there until the thing blows over."

"I do not like the idea," I answered. "I should be, to all intents and purposes, a sort of escaped criminal, except that in my case the situation would be reversed, for the criminals would be hunting down the innocent man. Thank you for your advice, Tempest, but at present I like neither alternative which you have suggested, and yet I have no third plan to propose for myself. Is it possible that the law can do nothing to help me?"

"Nothing; yours is probably a unique situation in the annals of circumstance."

I could not help sighing in self-pity.

"I am only five-and-twenty," I said, "and at any moment my life may be taken by some low brute."

"I pity you, my dear fellow, but what is to be done?"

"I am like a man in a nightmare," I answered. "The whole thing is horrible."

"Take my advice, Phenays, and leave England. I can watch your case in this country, and will employ a good detective for the purpose. Now, think over what I have been saying and let me know when you have made your plans."

I left Tempest's office in profound depression. It was something, at any rate, to know the exact, crude, legal opinion of my position, which briefly amounted to this: I was liable at any moment to be assassinated.

Piccadilly and Pall Mall[1] looked bright and cheerful as usual, but as I passed through the familiar crowd I shuddered more than once; my assassin might turn up at any corner, he might lay his hand on me at any moment, anywhere. The thought was enough to upset the stoutest nerves.

I entered my club, ordered lunch, and sat down to eat. I had barely begun when I heard a voice behind me exclaim—

"My dear Phenays!"

A hand was laid on my shoulder. I swung round. Before me stood my old friend Jack Tracey, whom I had not seen for nearly

1 Two major thoroughfares in central London. Piccadilly was known for its fashionable residences, embassies, upscale shops, and department stores. It remains one of London's principal shopping streets. Pall Mall is known for its gentlemen's clubs, government offices, and palaces.

four years. He was a civil engineer, and had been abroad for some time, in Ceylon, laying some electric tramways.

"Just the very man I want," he cried. "I got home last week and found another billet[1] waiting for me. This time it is in Portugal. I am looking out for a mate to come with me. I know that you are a lazy sort of dog, also that you have nothing special to do—will you come? Lovely climate—beautiful scenery, and lots for you to paint; for my work will be in Cintra,[2] about the most lovely spot in Europe—just the place for you to sketch in. The Portuguese Government are going to run a new road alongside one of the mountains, and the work has been given to our firm, to the honour and glory of Cooper's Hill.[3] Just lunching? I will join you; I am as ravenous as a hawk."

He took a seat at my table. His bronzed, honest face and breezy heartiness cheered me, and I was genuinely glad to see him again.

"When do you want to start?" I asked.

"The day after to-morrow. Is that too early for you? If you really make up your mind to come, I dare say I can put off for a day or two to suit you."

"Give me a little time to consider, my dear fellow. I never saw such a chap as you, always just the same, bursting with energy, enthusiasm, and impatience."

"I do not care what you call me, provided you come, Phenays. I want a mate, and you and I have always got on well together. Now, make up your mind and be sensible."

I finished my lunch without further remark; but while I ate, my thoughts were busy. Here, indeed, was a chance. Why should I not go? I should have just the companion I liked best, I should escape the east winds of the spring, and have a good excuse for that flitting which Tempest had advised me to undertake.

As we chatted and talked together, Tracey recounted all his experiences, and while I listened to him I made up my mind. Yes, I would leave England the day after to-morrow, and, taking the

---

1 Assignment or position.

2 A popular tourist destination located in a mountainous region near Lisbon.

3 The Royal Indian Engineering College, commonly known as Cooper's Hill, was established in the 1870s at Cooper's Hill estate in southern England to train civil engineers for service in the Indian Public Works Department. The college extended its program in the 1880s to include non-Indian services. It closed in 1906.

Royal Mail[1] to Lisbon, escape from my persecutors—they surely would not follow me into Portugal. It had always been one of my greatest wishes to see Cintra, and here was the opportunity.

Two hours later I once more reached Tempest's office, and there told him that I had made my plans.

"The way of escape has come, and I have not sought for it," I remarked. "Such an opportunity ought not to be missed."

"It is the very thing," he replied, "and I am heartily glad, for your sake, Phenays. But now I will tell you what we had better do. It is most important that you and I should keep up a certain communication one with the other. I have already put a detective on your affairs. He is a capital fellow, and will watch things from this side of the water. By to-night's post[2] I will send you a key of a private cipher,[3] in which I can communicate with you if important news reaches me."

I agreed to this, and went back to my rooms to make necessary arrangements for my departure.

I had just settled down after dinner to write some letters when my servant entered.

"A lady to see you, sir," he said, handing me a card.

I started in surprise. What woman—unless, indeed, the terrible Mademoiselle Delacourt—took the slightest interest in me? I had neither mother nor sister, neither wife nor sweetheart. I glanced at the card which the man had given to me. The name I saw written upon it dispelled all thought of Mademoiselle. Miss Cecil Hamilton was a lady I had never heard of before.

"Show Miss Hamilton in," I said.

The next moment a slightly-built girl, with a dark face and beautiful eyes, entered the room. I rose and bowed; she bowed also to me. There was a deprecating, almost frightened look about her whole appearance which disarmed my anger.

"I am speaking to Mr. Phenays?" she said in a tentative voice.

"Yes." I answered. "Will you sit down?"

I pushed a chair towards her, but she did not take it. She continued to stand, laying one slender hand lightly on the back of the chair.

"I have much to apologise for," she said. "My errand is dis-

---

1 Vehicle (train or ship) used by the Royal Mail, Britain's national postal service.

2 There were numerous mail deliveries a day in London by the turn of the twentieth century.

3 Secret or disguised writing or code.

tasteful and unpleasant. I am the bearer of a message from a lady, Mademoiselle Delacourt, whom you met in Paris."

"I do not wish to have any further communication with that lady," I interrupted, speaking hotly.

She held up her hand, as if to entreat my patience.

"I must deliver my message," she said. "I am Miss Delacourt's greatest friend. I am an English girl by birth, but have spent most of my life in Paris. In order to prove my identity, it will be sufficient for me to say that I am fully acquainted with your position as regards the secret entrusted to you by your late friend Mr. Escott, and which secret should have been given to Mademoiselle Delacourt."

Here she stopped speaking and looked earnestly at me. Her eyes were kindly and compassionate. Her lips slightly trembled.

"I am sorry for you," she said. "You are so young, and unless you accede to my request your fate is so terrible."

"I can do without your pity, Miss Hamilton," I answered. "Please tell me at once why Mademoiselle has presumed to send you to visit me."

"Because she also is sorry for you, Mr. Phenays. Because it has occurred to us both that, although you have already refused to put yourself into a position of safety, yet on mature consideration you will be willing to discharge your duty to your friend's memory and so act as a man of honour."

It was with difficulty I could restrain a burst of indignation.

"Mademoiselle wishes you to communicate your secret to me. Will you do so?"

"I will not," I replied. "Forgive me if I speak frankly, but you have intruded on me in what I consider an unwarrantable manner, and this is no moment for courtesy. Tell Mademoiselle that I possess no secret, and am therefore incapable of communicating what I do not know. Tell her also that I could, if necessary, throw light on a recent occurrence, in the neighbourhood of Paris, which would be by no means to her credit. Tell her, further, that at any instant I could put her within the arm of the law. And finally tell her that there is a law in England, if not in France, by which redress can be claimed for personal annoyance."

At these words, to my amazement and distress, the girl fell on her knees.

"It is for your sake, believe me, it is for your sake," she pleaded. "I can understand your indignation, and forgive it. Please reconsider things. You will regret this—oh, terribly—if you do not. Please change your mind. Do you think I like forcing myself upon you? I beg of you to tell me your secret, because I have your true interest at heart."

"It is unpleasant to be rude to a lady," I replied, "but I must ask you, Miss Hamilton, to leave me. I have one answer to give to Mademoiselle, and that is, an emphatic 'No.' I have no secret; and if I had, she is the last person on earth to whom I would tell it."

As I spoke I rang the bell. My servant entered.

"Show this lady downstairs," I said.

She left me without a word. After she had gone I sent a line to Tempest to acquaint him with my interview. I received the following reply—

"Do nothing but get away," were his brief and emphatic words.

All the next day I was busy packing and settling my affairs, and the following morning, at eight o'clock, Tracey and I, with my large Newfoundland dog Zulu, had left Charing Cross[1] *en route* for Portugal. It was only at the last moment that I decided to take Zulu with me. He was a splendid animal, and had been my constant companion since his puppyhood. Our journey to Cintra took place without any adventure, and when we had put up at Lawrence's comfortable hotel I congratulated myself on having left England and France so far behind. I surely must be safe in this remote corner of the world. It was therefore with an elation of heart that I received my first impressions of the charming spot where Tracey's work lay.

The little village was situated close to the base of a range of granite mountains, the extreme continuation of the Estrella.[2] The mountains were clothed with verdure and trees of every variety and size. Towering above us, on twin peaks, stood an old ruined Moorish castle and the new royal castle of the Pena.[3]

We arrived at Cintra about midday, and immediately after lunch we started out to climb to the Moorish castle in company with the Portuguese overseer, who was anxious to show Tracey the site of the projected new road. While they were talking business I had time to take in the romantic loveliness and exquisite richness of the colouring around me. The trees were just bud-

---

1 Railway terminus in central London serving the south and east of the city and the coast.

2 The highest mountain range in continental Portugal.

3 Built as a royal summer residence on the site of a medieval chapel, the Pena Palace combines elements of Gothic, Renaissance, Rococo, and Moorish styles.

ding, birds were singing, and the air was full of the sweet scent of heliotrope that hung in clusters on the walls of the *quintas*[1] as we climbed past them. I felt light-hearted as I had not been since my terrible adventure in Paris. I saw before me months of undisturbed enjoyment, painting among these enchanting hills and dales, for surely the most inveterate enemy would scarcely follow an inoffensive and innocent man to this remote part of Portugal.

I recall my sensations on this first day very vividly, because of the darker recollections which were so soon to follow.

The next morning Tracey and I started off again to the site of his work. Already some Portuguese labourers were busy clearing timber and blasting rocks. The latter operation interested me considerably. A deep hole was drilled into the centre of a boulder, into this a handful of dynamite was poured—then a little moss was pushed on the top, and the fuse inserted. After it was lit we scrambled away to a safe spot. In a couple of minutes a terrific roar rent the air, and the great granite boulder lay split into half a dozen fragments.

I had spent over a week at Lawrence's Hotel, and a picture which I was painting was in full progress, my life was happy, my days fully occupied, when one evening, at a single blow, all sense of security was shattered.

Tracey and I were returning home, when we saw standing on the balcony of the little hotel the slight and graceful figure of Miss Hamilton.

"Good Heavens!" I could not help exclaiming; the blood rushed back to my heart and I felt my face turning cold.

My violent start and words of consternation caused Tracey to turn and glance at me in astonishment.

"What is the matter?" he asked.

"Do you see that lady standing there?"

"I see a remarkably pretty girl. Is she an old flame, Phenays? In the name of Fortune, what is the matter with you?"

"I saw her once before," I gasped. "I hoped never to meet her again. What has she come for?"

"How can I tell you? I presume visitors are allowed to stay at the hotel without our being consulted."

"If you knew all——" I began.

But I had scarcely spoken the words before Miss Hamilton, having seen us both, waved her hand to me with a gesture of recognition, and the next instant was tripping down the steps of the hotel to meet us.

---

1 Villas or farmsteads.

"Mr. Phenays," she exclaimed, "by what good fortune do we meet? How do you do? Pray introduce me to your friend."

Her manner was so frank and pleasant, the expression in her eyes so joyous and unshaded by embarrassment, that in spite of myself I began to think it a hideous dream that this pretty girl had ever come to me to plead for Mademoiselle Delacourt. I replied to her stiffly, however, and when she glanced in Tracey's direction gave the necessary introduction with marked unwillingness.

"Oh, what a lovely dog!" she said as Zulu came up.

The next moment she had dropped on her knees by the dog, clasped her arms round his neck, and printed a kiss on his broad forehead. To these blandishments Zulu immediately succumbed, although, as a rule, he was extremely distant to strangers; he licked Miss Hamilton's hand, wagged his bushy tail, and when she slowly returned to the hotel, to my still greater amazement, he left us to follow her.

"Your friend, or your enemy, or whatever you like to call her, seems to have considerable power over the dog world," said Tracey. "But what is up, Phenays? You look as if you had got a shock."

"So I have; and perhaps I'll tell you to-morrow, perhaps I'll keep it to myself. God help me! I do not know what to do."

"Your nerves are unstrung; you had better have some dinner and forget your trepidations," said Tracey, with a dash of impatience.

There was nothing for it but to follow his advice. At *table d'hôte*[1] Miss Hamilton dined with us. She said quite frankly that she had a passion for travelling, had come by sea to Lisbon, and was making a brief tour through Portugal *en route* for Spain.

"I shall stay here for two or three days," she remarked. "Cintra is the most lovely spot I have ever seen in my life."

Tracey was evidently much taken with her; he was quite enthusiastic when he and I paced up and down the terrace for our evening smoke. He now asked me in wonder what I knew about her.

"She visited me in London," I answered. "The purport of her visit I prefer not to talk about."

He shrugged his shoulders.

"Keep your secret, Phenays," he remarked. "Whatever you may know about her, I protest that Miss Hamilton is as charming a girl as I have often seen. I have promised her that she shall accompany us to-morrow to see some of the blasting operations; she is much interested in them."

1 Restaurant meal or menu offering a series of courses at a fixed price, generally at a set time.

Early the following morning I arose, and seeing Miss Hamilton up and walking in the direction of the shore, I resolved to follow her. Zulu, of course, accompanied me.

"Miss Hamilton," I cried as I drew near.

She stopped, turned, and looked me full in the face.

"How do you do, Mr. Phenays?" she remarked. "Oh, this lovely dog!"

Again all her attention was absorbed by the Newfoundland, who pressed close to her, wagged his tail, and licked her small hand.

"I want to ask you a direct question," was my next remark. "Why have you followed me here?"

"Our meeting at Lawrence's Hotel is a coincidence," she said. "Make what you like of it."

"Then you have not followed me?"

She glanced at me for a moment.

"No," she said.

"I do not believe you," I replied. "You are telling me a lie."

When I said this the colour swept into her face. She had been looking at me, now she turned away. The action was significant. I was certain now of what I was almost sure of before. She had come to Cintra because I was there, for what ghastly purpose Heaven only knew.

I would have questioned her further, but just then Tracey made his appearance. He was evidently more than attracted by Miss Hamilton. Her gentle words, her pretty, well-trained voice, her graceful actions, impressed this rough, good-hearted fellow in a way which amazed me.

"What are our plans for to-day?" he asked in a genial voice. "I, of course, shall be busy with my work, but if you would really like to see the blasting, Miss Hamilton, I will promise to look after you. You, Phenays, and I can lunch together just on the spot where Phenays is painting his celebrated picture."

"Oh, you are an artist, Mr. Phenays?" she asked, and she gave me a gentle and what looked like a beseeching glance. "Your plan is delightful, Mr. Tracey," she continued; "let us carry it out to the letter."

Tracey grew now almost boisterous. We interviewed our landlady, with the result that we were provided with an excellent luncheon-basket, and immediately after breakfast we started for our day's expedition.

I went to my accustomed place, sat down and made arrangements to continue my painting. I gazed right across the valley at the glorious scene which I was endeavouring to depict; my palette was in my hand, my brushes lay near. All of a sudden I missed the dog. Where was he? It was the habit of this faithful creature to lie at my feet during the long hours that I was employed over my work, and never for an instant to leave me. His absence puzzled me, until I remembered his extraordinary penchant for Miss Hamilton. Could it be possible that he was with her? At lunch time this turned out to be the case, for Miss Hamilton, Tracey, and the dog appeared together.

"Ah, Zulu," I cried, pretending to be angry with the handsome creature, "you have forsaken me for the first time in your life."

As I said the words I noticed a peculiar flash of satisfaction in Miss Hamilton's eyes. She was in high spirits and insisted on opening the luncheon-basket and acting as hostess. We two young men were as children in her hands. She was so gentle, bright, picturesque, and graceful that even I forgot my alarms and enjoyed myself thoroughly. After lunch Tracey rose.

"It is hard to tear myself away, but Duty calls," he exclaimed. "Are you coming back," he added, looking at Miss Hamilton, "or will you watch Phenays for a time?"

"I will follow you presently with Zulu," she answered, "but just now I should like to watch Mr. Phenays."

Tracey went off, and Miss Hamilton and I were alone. The dog lay at her feet. Now and then her pretty hand touched his black head, now and then she looked at me without speaking—her attitude was one of repose and contentment.

"How well you paint!" she said suddenly.

"This is the hobby of my life," I answered. "I should, indeed, think small beer of myself[1] if I did not do it fairly well."

"You are, perhaps, a professional artist, Mr. Phenays?"

"No," I replied, "I am an amateur. I have never earned my bread—I have enough money to live on."

"Ah, lucky you!" she replied.

"I do not agree with you," I answered shortly. "The man who has enough money to live on is deprived of the most powerful stimulus which can animate the human race. He need not work to live, therefore he scarcely works at all. But there," I added, reading a curious expression in her eyes, "I have done for to-day."

I put down my palette, collected my brushes, and, putting them back in their case, looked full at her.

"When are you going away?" I asked.

"Do not you like to have me here?"

"Frankly, no."

"That means that you are afraid of me."

---

1 A low opinion; "think little of myself."

I was silent.

"Mr. Phenays," she said gently, "I did not mean to say a word, but your question and your attitude towards me force me to speak. You dislike my presence at Cintra, you resent it. Cintra is your *hiding-place*, and I have come to it."

I shook my head when she said that Cintra was my hiding-place. She gazed back at me and laughed, then she said abruptly—

"You need not deny it. You say that I have followed you here, I say that you have come here to hide; that means that you are afraid. Now, Mr. Phenays, I am sorry for you. It is a pity that one so young and good-looking, and with enough money to live on, should needlessly endanger his life—yes, I repeat the word, his life. I will go to-morrow morning if you will confide to me that small secret which you refused to communicate to Mademoiselle Delacourt."

I rose now and bent over Miss Hamilton, who was still seated on the ground.

"You think me a coward," I said, "but I am not quite so bad as that. Listen. The subject to which you have alluded must be in the future a closed book between us. I decline to discuss it—you are not to allude to it. Now, what do you think of this view? Come and stand just here and see what I am making of it."

She rose and entered into a critical and very intelligent dissertation with regard to my picture. Soon afterwards we both wended our way in the direction where Tracey was busy superintending the making of the new road.

Notwithstanding my growing anxiety, the evening passed cheerfully. Miss Hamilton had brought her guitar, and she sang Spanish ditties, to her own accompaniment, with excellent taste. Tracey was in greater raptures with our visitor than ever.

"I tell you what it is, old fellow," I could not help exclaiming, when we found ourselves alone, "you had better look before you leap. The next thing I shall hear is that you have fallen in love with Cecil Hamilton."

"Is Cecil her Christian name?"

"Yes."

"How do you know?"

"I saw it on her card."

"In this hotel?"

"No, before I came to Portugal."

"Phenays, won't you explain this mystery?"

"I hope I may never need to," was my answer. "But, Tracey, one word of warning. Whoever you lose your heart to, do not let Cecil Hamilton be the girl."

He laughed, then he sighed.

"I never intend to marry; I would not tie myself to a woman for all creation, but I may as well own that if I could see myself conducted to the altar for the sake of any woman, it would be for that of the pretty girl who is now at the hotel."

A few days went by, and my sketch progressed. Miss Hamilton did not leave Cintra, and Zulu became more and more attached to her. We two young men and this dark-eyed, pretty girl now spent the greater part of our days together; in the evening she sang to us. Tracey was like a moth coming ever nearer and nearer to the candle. Beyond these small facts nothing happened in the least interesting.

Another week went by, and a morning dawned with bright sunshine and cloudless sky. I had got up rather earlier than usual, intending to continue my picture before the sun got too hot, when the waiter entered the dining-saloon and handed me a telegram. I tore it open, my heart quickened with a sense of alarm. It was in cipher and was signed "Tempest." I quickly took out my copy of the key and translated the words, which ran as follows:—

"You are in the utmost danger. Enemy has been close to you since you left England.—Tempest."

I sank into a chair and grasped the paper in my hand. It did not need Tempest's words to tell me where the danger lay. Even a pretty girl, if employed by your enemies, can be ruthless and desperate. I felt a sick sensation round my heart. The inability to know from what direction the blow would fall was the worst of my trial. Till now I had refrained from telling Tracey a word of my extraordinary position, but on receipt of the telegram I determined to take him into my confidence. Perhaps he might help me. I sought his room and found him dressing. As piece by piece I communicated all the facts of my strange story, I observed a succession of changes passing over his face. First of all surprise, then incredulity, and last, as I showed him the telegram, a grave expression.

"What am I to do?" I cried. "This is fact, remember."

"So it appears," he answered. "You are a nice sort of companion to go about with." Here he laid his hand on my shoulder. "Never mind, old man," he continued, "I will stick to you through thick and thin; but do for Heaven's sake get the idea, that poor little Cecil Hamilton is mixed up in this affair, out of your head."

"By her own showing she is in communication with Miss Delacourt," I answered.

"That may be; but for any vulgar violence, any danger to your life, she would be the last person employed. If I were you, I would try to keep up my pecker,[1] Phenays. We are not in fairyland or the realm of impossibilities; you cannot do any more than you are doing. Take my revolver with you this morning. I shall stay pretty near; and if there is the slightest sign of tricks, we will make it warm for the individual, whoever he may happen to be. Wait till I have had breakfast, and we will go up the mountain as usual. Of course, go on with your picture, it will help to take your mind off this nasty affair; and you have got Zulu, a bodyguard in himself. If it is any sort of vulgar violence, he will account for somebody."

After thinking for a moment or two I resolved to take Tracey's advice. There was, as he said, no help for the present situation, and to sit still with my hands before me meant madness.

Just as he and I were starting for the mountain, Miss Hamilton came into the hall to meet us. She was fully dressed, as if for a journey, and at that moment I saw the hall-porter conveying her luggage down-stairs.

"What!" I exclaimed, "are you off?"

"Yes," she answered. "I go to Lisbon by the next train. I have had a sudden message which obliges me to get to Paris as soon as possible."

Here she gave me a full and very penetrating stare.

"Then we shall not meet again?" I said.

There was unmistakable relief in my tones.

"We are not likely to meet any more," she answered gravely, almost solemnly. She held out her hand. I just touched it; as I did so I felt an extraordinary repugnance seizing me.

"I shall miss you both," she said, "and in especial shall I miss Zulu; but goodbye, don't let me keep you. *Au revoir*, gentlemen."

She waved her hand in the pretty way she had done when I had first seen her standing on the balcony, and the next instant Tracey, Zulu, and I started for our day's expedition.

"Well, that is a relief!" I could not help muttering.

Tracey shrugged his shoulders.

"I wish you would leave that unfortunate girl out of the thing," he said. "She is not what you think her, of that I am firmly convinced."

I did not reply. We went up the mountain by our usual path, and I soon settled myself in my accustomed nook to continue my sketch.

"There you are, old chap," said Tracey. "Paint away, and good luck to you! I shall be just above you, a hundred yards or so, and I will come down to have a smoke and a chat now and then. I do not wonder you feel capsized, but there is really no possible danger."

He started up the path and disappeared into a thicket of high

1 Courage; "keep my chin up."

laurels. I felt little inclined to work, and for half an hour scarcely touched my canvas; but by and by I became once more interested and then completely absorbed. Presently I rose from my stool and took a step back to view the picture, and then glanced up at the scenery. All Nature seemed to be dozing in the bright midday sunshine. The still air was laden with the perfume of thousands of flowers; a bright yellow butterfly, the first I had seen, passed close to me. Just at that moment I glanced around and perceived for the first time that Zulu was missing. I slightly wondered at his absence. Miss Hamilton was no longer in the neighbourhood to attract him. I resolved to give him a scolding when he reappeared, and then sat down to my work. I was busy just then trying exactly to fix the depth of the purple haze that hung on the distant mountains. I had just dipped my brush into my water-can, when I suddenly heard my name shouted from above in Tracey's deep tones. The voice came booming down over the rocks, and extreme excitement rang in the sharp-flung words.

"Phenays, run, quick! for God's sake get away from the dog!"

I started up, overturning my easel as I did so.

"What is it?" I shouted back, as a chill fear of a danger I could not see shook me.

But I had scarcely uttered the words when, turning swiftly, I saw Zulu coming along the path at an even canter towards me. What on earth was the matter with him? There was something queer on his back that bulged up above his great head. Good God, it was something smoking! What, I could not see—but it was enough. I knew what had happened. Miss Hamilton's interest in the blasting operations was explained. Miss Hamilton's visit to Cintra was made plain; the reason of her remarkable friendship for Zulu was all too manifest—the dog was to be the weapon used for my destruction. It was a fuse that towered above his big head. Any moment the fuse would reach the dynamite below and a terrific explosion would scatter his life and mine.[1] The very imminence of the peril cooled my blood. I crouched down on the ground and, as Zulu approached, made an effort to snatch the fuse from his head. In vain—he would not come near. He was excited and half mad with spirits. The poor brute gambolled round me, little knowing that there was but a step between him and a horrible death. Suddenly he made for me, as though to caress me, and I, possessed by an impulse which I could not restrain, nor fathom, nor overcome, fled from him. I fled down

1 Meade may have been inspired by an earlier incident on the Continent in which a dog carrying an explosive canister was reportedly "blown to smithereens" (Melchiori 51).

the mountain side like one possessed. Even in that mad flight my reason told me I had little chance of escape. The faster I went, the quicker did the dog pursue me; I could hear his hurried breath as he rushed after me. In less than a minute I had reached the top of a stony and steep descent to the little church of Santa Maria. On one side of the path was a stone wall, on the other a sheer drop of sixty feet. Scarcely knowing what I did, with one frantic leap I cleared the wall. I had hardly done so before an appalling explosion rent the air; the very earth seemed to shake; a huge fragment of stonework flew whistling by, and then the roar died away in echoes reverberating along the mountain side. Trembling and half stunned, I looked back over the wall. Not a vestige of the dog was to be seen, nothing but a huge ragged hole where the macadam[1] had been torn up. I sank down sick and giddy. After a time I vaguely wondered why Tracey did not appear. It was nearly an hour before he came running down the path. When we met he grasped my hand; his ruddy face was white and he was panting heavily.

Fig. 11. "WITH ONE FRANTIC LEAP I CLEARED THE WALL."

1 A smooth road surface made from successive compressed layers of broken stone. The method was promoted in the early nineteenth century by Scottish surveyor J.L. McAdam (1756–1836).

"By Jove! old man, that was a near thing!" he gasped.

"But how did it happen? Tell me, how was it done? What did you see?" I asked.

My teeth were chattering even in the hot sunshine. I looked at Tracey, who stood quiet now by my side.

"Why do you not speak?" I asked.

"What do you want to know?" he replied. "The dog is dead, poor brute, and you have escaped by the skin of your teeth."

"But how did it happen? Tell me what you know."

"I will," he said then. "I was standing close up alongside that tower under the pines, when I saw Zulu come round the corner just where the wall is low. He passed within two feet of me, wagging his tail. I spoke to him; he looked round, but did not stop. Suddenly, to my amazement, I saw that he had something fastened to his collar, something from which a little smoke was rising. The next instant I perceived that it was a fuse exactly like those my men use for blasting. Then the horror of the thing struck me. I remembered your telegram and I knew what it meant. I grabbed at the dog to tear it off, but he slipped by, making down to you, as was natural. Then I shouted, for I saw your danger. Thank God! you just escaped; but it was a near thing, a matter of seconds."

As he said the last words I saw that he was trembling horribly; something in his attitude and manner aroused my suspicions.

"The explosion took place nearly an hour ago," I said. "Why did you not come to me sooner? You are concealing something—what is the matter?"

He did not speak.

"You are concealing something?"

"Yes, oh, my God! yes."

"What, Tracey? Speak, in Heaven's name! It was not that girl—tell me—Miss Hamilton, had nothing to do with it?"

"Yes," said Tracey again—"yes."

He spoke in gasps, as though his breath failed him.

"I will tell you," he said. "You must know, and the sooner it is over the better. When the dog rushed to you I saw a girl crouching behind a boulder of rock. She was Miss Hamilton. She was straining her neck and bending forward to watch the movement of the dog. She never saw me. When the report came she clapped her hands to her ears, looked again as though her eyes would start from her head, uttered a shriek, and flew down the mountain in the opposite direction. I followed her like a madman. I called to her to stop. A sort of instinct told me what she was going to do. I knew that she was making for the cliff, just where there is a drop of five hundred feet. She had an advantage of me and she ran like the wind. She got to the edge of the cliff while I was still a good way behind her. How she stopped herself I do not know, but she did. She stood as rigid as a statue, pressed her hand to her heart, turned and shouted to me—

"'Your friend is alive,' were her words. 'I have failed. Those who belong to the French Secret Service *die* when they fail——'

"With that she was over the precipice. Phenays, old man—I—am—sick."

The great burly fellow fell like a lump of lead at my feet.

Tracey came to himself, and I brought him back to the hotel, and that evening I went with some workmen to discover the body of the miserable girl whose mission it had been to take my life. I found it mangled out of recognition. The next day we buried her on the side of the mountain. That evening Tracey spoke to me—

"I cannot stay here, Phenays; it is no use. I have wired to Cooper's Hill. They must send out another man to complete this job; I leave Cintra to-morrow morning."

"And I go with you," was my answer.

[Before he returns to England, Phenays travels to Lisbon to discuss his situation with the British Consul. The Consul directs Phenays to José da Fondeca Pinheiro, a Portuguese detective who specializes in international political intrigue. Pinheiro, as Phenays soon discovers, is an ideal confidant: he is well-informed about diplomatic affairs, in touch with governments and police forces in every European capital, and moves in the best Portuguese society. Pinheiro also has his own personal reasons (never fully revealed) for wanting to secure Mademoiselle Delacourt's arrest. In the remaining stories, Phenays and Pinheiro work together to achieve that end, but she continues to elude them. She makes further attempts on Phenays' life using deadly micro-organisms and explosives. In the final episode, she lures Phenays to a derelict house in Lisbon where she uses his skills with codes and ciphers to secure a cache of diamonds. Phenays faces certain death in the house but for the timely arrival of Pinheiro and his assistants. This time Delacourt does not escape; she is arrested and carried off to prison where she can pose no further threat.]

THE SORCERESS OF THE STRAND

The Sorceress of the Strand

L.T. Meade and Robert Eustace, *The Sorceress of the Strand, Strand Magazine* 24 (July–December 1902).

I. —MADAME SARA. [387–401]

Everyone in trade and a good many who are not have heard of Werner's Agency, the Solvency Inquiry Agency of all British trade. Its business is to know the financial condition of all wholesale and retail firms, from Rothschild's[1] to the smallest sweetstuff shop in Whitechapel.[2] I do not say that every firm figures on its books, but by methods of secret inquiry it can discover the status of any firm or individual. It is the great safeguard to British trade and prevents much fraudulent dealing.

Of this agency I, Dixon Druce, was appointed manager in 1890. Since then I have met queer people and seen strange sights, for men do curious things for money in this world.

It so happened that in June, 1899, my business took me to Madeira[3] on an inquiry of some importance. I left the island on the 14th of the month by the *Norham Castle* for Southampton. I got on board after dinner. It was a lovely night, and the strains of the band in the public gardens of Funchal came floating across the star-powdered bay through the warm, balmy air. Then the engine bells rang to "Full speed ahead," and, flinging a farewell to the fairest island on earth, I turned to the smoking-room in order to light my cheroot.

"Do you want a match, sir?" The voice came from a slender, young-looking man who stood near the taffrail.[4] Before I could reply he had struck one and held it out to me.

---

1 A wealthy and powerful family closely allied to European and British nobility, the Rothschilds attained their position through their international family-controlled banking empire.

2 A slum neighbourhood associated with Jack the Ripper's murders in the late 1880s.

3 An important wine-producing region situated off the coast of Portugal. Ships travelling to the New World and the East Indies regularly stopped here to pick up supplies of its celebrated wine. Funchal is Madeira's capital and principal city.

4 The rail around the stern of a vessel.

"Excuse me," he said, as he tossed it overboard, "but surely I am addressing Mr. Dixon Druce?"

"You are, sir," I said, glancing keenly back at him, "but you have the advantage of me."

"Don't you know me?" he responded. "Jack Selby, Hayward's House, Harrow,[1] 1879."

"By Jove! so it is," I cried.

Our hands met in a warm clasp, and a moment later I found myself sitting close to my old friend, who had fagged[2] for me in the bygone days, and whom I had not seen from the moment when I said good-bye to the "Hill" in the grey mist of a December morning twenty years ago. He was a boy of fourteen then, but nevertheless I recognised him. His face was bronzed and good-looking, his features refined. As a boy Selby had been noted for his grace, his well-shaped head, his clean-cut features; these characteristics still were his, and although he was now slightly past his first youth he was decidedly handsome. He gave me a quick sketch of his history.

"My father left me plenty of money," he said, "and The Meadows, our old family place, is now mine. I have a taste for natural history; that taste took me two years ago to South America. I have had my share of strange adventures, and have collected valuable specimens and trophies. I am now on my way home from Para, on the Amazon, having come by a Booth boat to Madeira and changed there to the Castle Line.[3] But why all this talk about myself?" he added, bringing his deck-chair a little nearer to mine. "What about your history, old chap? Are you settled down with a wife and kiddies of your own, or is that dream of your school days fulfilled, and are you the owner of the best private laboratory in London?"

"As to the laboratory," I said, with a smile, "you must come and see it. For the rest I am unmarried. Are you?"

"I was married the day before I left Para, and my wife is on board with me."

---

1 One of Britain's oldest and most prestigious boys' boarding schools, whose graduates have included statesmen and aristocrats.

2 A common practice at schools like Harrow whereby junior students were required to perform chores (fag) for senior students. A restricted version of fagging continues at some schools.

3 Booth and Castle were prominent steamship lines. The Booth Line provided services between Europe, the United States, and Northern Brazil including the Amazon, while the Castle Line had interests in India and South Africa.

"Capital," I answered. "Let me hear all about it."

"You shall. Her maiden name was Dallas; Beatrice Dallas. She is just twenty now. Her father was an Englishman and her mother a Spaniard; neither parent is living. She has an elder sister, Edith, nearly thirty years of age, unmarried, who is on board with us. There is also a step-brother, considerably older than either Edith or Beatrice. I met my wife last year in Para, and at once fell in love. I am the happiest man on earth. It goes without saying that I think her beautiful, and she is also very well off. The story of her wealth is a curious one. Her uncle on the mother's side was an extremely wealthy Spaniard, who made an enormous fortune in Brazil out of diamonds and minerals; he owned several mines. But it is supposed that his wealth turned his brain. At any rate, it seems to have done so as far as the disposal of his money went. He divided the yearly profits and interest between his nephew and his two nieces, but declared that the property itself should never be split up. He has left the whole of it to that one of the three who should survive the others. A perfectly insane arrangement, but not, I believe, unprecedented in Brazil."

"Very insane," I echoed. "What was he worth?"

"Over two million sterling."[1]

"By Jove!" I cried, "what a sum! But what about the half-brother?"

"He must be over forty years of age, and is evidently a bad lot. I have never seen him. His sisters won't speak to him or have anything to do with him. I understand that he is a great gambler; I am further told that he is at present in England, and, as there are certain technicalities to be gone through before the girls can fully enjoy their incomes, one of the first things I must do when I get home is to find him out. He has to sign certain papers, for we shan't be able to put things straight until we get his whereabouts. Some time ago my wife and Edith heard that he was ill, but dead or alive we must know all about him, and as quickly as possible."

I made no answer, and he continued:—

"I'll introduce you to my wife and sister-in-law to-morrow. Beatrice is quite a child compared to Edith, who acts towards her almost like a mother. Bee is a little beauty, so fresh and round and young-looking. But Edith is handsome, too, although I sometimes

1 In the range of £220 million or US $340 million (including inflation) at 2015 rates.

think she is as vain as a peacock. By the way, Druce, this brings me to another part of my story. The sisters have an acquaintance on board, one of the most remarkable women I have ever met. She goes by the name of Madame Sara, and knows London well. In fact, she confesses to having a shop in the Strand.[1] What she has been doing in Brazil I do not know, for she keeps all her affairs strictly private. But you will be amazed when I tell you what her calling is."

"What?" I asked.

"A professional beautifier. She claims the privilege of restoring youth to those who consult her. She also declares that she can make quite ugly people handsome. There is no doubt that she is very clever. She knows a little bit of everything, and has wonderful recipes with regard to medicines, surgery, and dentistry. She is a most lovely woman herself, very fair, with blue eyes, an innocent, childlike manner, and quantities of rippling gold hair. She openly confesses that she is very much older than she appears. She looks about five-and-twenty. She seems to have travelled all over the world, and says, that by birth she is a mixture of Indian and Italian, her father having been Italian and her mother Indian. Accompanying her is an Arab, a handsome, picturesque sort of fellow, who gives her the most absolute devotion, and she is also bringing back to England two Brazilians from Para. This woman deals in all sorts of curious, secrets, but principally in cosmetics. Her shop in the Strand could, I fancy, tell many a strange history. Her clients go to her there, and she does what is necessary for them. It is a fact that she occasionally performs small surgical operations, and there is not a dentist in London who can vie with her. She confesses quite naïvely that she holds some secrets for making false teeth cling to the palate that no one knows of. Edith Dallas is devoted to her—in fact, her adoration amounts to idolatry."

"You give a very brilliant account of this woman," I said. "You must introduce me tomorrow."

"I will," answered Jack, with a smile. "I should like your opinion of her. I am right glad I have met you, Druce, it is like old times. When we get to London I mean to put up at my town

---

1 The principal thoroughfare from London's West End to the City. It is part of a commercial area known for its shops, coffee houses and taverns, hotels, and publishing firms. Madame Rachel, Sara's real-life counterpart, established her shop in the more upscale Bond Street. See Introduction, p. 29.

house in Eaton Square[1] for the remainder of the season. The Meadows shall be re-furnished, and Bee and I will take up our quarters, some time in August; then you must come and see us. But I am afraid before I give myself up to mere pleasure I must find that precious brother-in-law, Henry Joachim Silva."

"If you have any difficulty apply to me," I said. "I can put at your disposal, in an unofficial way, of course, agents who would find almost any man in England, dead or alive."

I then proceeded to give Selby a short account of my own business.

"Thanks," he said, presently, "that is capital. You are the very man we want."

The next morning after breakfast Jack introduced me to his wife and sister-in-law. They were both foreign-looking, but very handsome, and the wife in particular had a graceful and uncommon appearance.

We had been chatting about five minutes when I saw coming down the deck a slight, rather small woman, wearing a big sun hat.

"Ah, Madame," cried Selby, "here you are. I had the luck to meet an old friend on board—Mr. Dixon Druce—and I have been telling him all about you. I should like you to know each other. Druce, this lady is Madame Sara, of whom I have spoken to you. Mr. Dixon Druce—Madame Sara."

She bowed gracefully and then looked at me earnestly. I had seldom seen a more lovely woman. By her side both Mrs. Selby and her sister seemed to fade into insignificance. Her complexion was almost dazzlingly fair, her face refined in expression, her eyes penetrating, clever, and yet with the innocent, frank gaze of a child. Her dress was very simple; she looked altogether like a young, fresh, and natural girl.

As we sat chatting lightly and about commonplace topics, I instinctively felt that she took an interest in me even greater than might be evinced from an ordinary introduction. By slow degrees she so turned the conversation as to leave Selby and his wife and sister out, and then as they moved away she came a little nearer, and said in a low voice:—

"I am very glad we have met, and yet how odd this meeting is! Was it really accidental?"

"I do not understand you," I answered.

"I know who you are," she said, lightly. "You are the manager

1 A large residential garden square in London's expensive Belgravia district.

of Werner's Agency; its business is to know the private affairs of those people who would rather keep their own secrets. Now, Mr. Druce, I am going to be absolutely frank with you. I own a small shop in the Strand—it is a perfumery shop—and behind those innocent-looking doors I conduct that business which brings me in gold of the realm. Have you, Mr. Druce, any objection to my continuing to make a livelihood in perfectly innocent ways?"

"None whatever," I answered. "You puzzle me by alluding to the subject."

"I want you to pay my shop a visit when you come to London. I have been away for three or four months. I do wonders for my clients, and they pay me largely for my services. I hold some perfectly innocent secrets which I cannot confide to anybody. I have obtained them partly from the Indians and partly from the natives of Brazil. I have lately been in Para to inquire into certain methods by which my trade can be improved."

"And your trade is——?" I said, looking at her with amusement and some surprise.

"I am a beautifier," she said, lightly. She looked at me with a smile. "You don't want me yet, Mr. Druce, but the time may come when even you will wish to keep back the infirmities of years. In the meantime can you guess my age?"

"I will not hazard a guess," I answered.

"And I will not tell you. Let it remain a secret. Meanwhile, understand that my calling is quite an open one, and I do hold secrets. I should advise you, Mr. Druce, even in your professional capacity, not to interfere with them."

The childlike expression faded from her face as she uttered the last words. There seemed to ring a sort of challenge in her tone. She turned away after a few moments and I rejoined my friends.

"You have been making acquaintance with Madame Sara, Mr. Druce," said Mrs. Selby. "Don't you think she is lovely?"

"She is one of the most beautiful women I have ever seen," I answered, "but there seems to be a mystery about her."

"Oh, indeed there is," said Edith Dallas, gravely.

"She asked me if I could guess her age," I continued. "I did not try, but surely she cannot be more than five-and-twenty."

"No one knows her age," said Mrs. Selby, "but I will tell you a curious fact, which, perhaps, you will not believe. She was bridesmaid at my mother's wedding thirty years ago. She declares that she never changes, and has no fear of old age."

"You mean that seriously?" I cried. "But surely it is impossible?"

Fig. 12. "'I AM A BEAUTIFIER,' SHE SAID."

"Her name is on the register, and my mother knew her well. She was mysterious then, and I think my mother got into her power, but of that I am not certain. Anyhow, Edith and I adore her, don't we, Edie?"

She laid her hand affectionately on her sister's arm. Edith Dallas did not speak, but her face was careworn. After a time she said, slowly:—

"Madame Sara is uncanny and terrible."

There is, perhaps, no business imaginable—not even a lawyer's—that engenders suspicions more than mine. I hate all mysteries—both in persons and things. Mysteries are my natural enemies; I felt now that this woman was a distinct mystery. That she was interested in me I did not doubt, perhaps because she was afraid of me.

The rest of our voyage passed pleasantly enough. The more I saw of Mrs. Selby and her sister the more I liked them. They were quiet, simple, and straightforward. I felt sure that they were both as good as gold.

We parted at Waterloo,[1] Jack and his wife and her sister going to Jack's house in Eaton Square, and I returning to my quarters in St. John's Wood.[2] I had a house there, with a long garden, at the bottom of which was my laboratory, the laboratory that was the pride of my life, it being, I fondly considered, the best private laboratory in London. There I spent all my spare time making experiments and trying this chemical combination and the other, living in hopes of doing great things some day, for Werner's Agency was not to be the end of my career. Nevertheless, it interested me thoroughly, and I was not sorry to get back to my commercial conundrums.

The next day, just before I started to go to my place of business, Jack Selby was announced.

"I want you to help me," he said. "I have been already trying in a sort of general way to get information about my brother-in-law, but all in vain. There is no such person in any of the directories. Can you put me on the road to discovery?"

I said I could and would if he would leave the matter in my hands.

"With pleasure," he replied. "You see how we are fixed up. Neither Edith nor Bee can get money with any regularity until the man is found. I cannot imagine why he hides himself."

"I will insert advertisements in the personal columns of the newspapers," I said, "and request anyone who can give information to communicate with me at my office. I will also give instructions to all the branches of my firm, as well as to my head assistants in London, to keep their eyes open for any news. You may be quite certain that in a week or two we shall know all about him."

Selby appeared cheered at this proposal, and, having begged of me to call upon his wife and her sister as soon as possible, took his leave.

On that very day advertisements were drawn up and sent to several newspapers and inquiry agents; but week after week passed without the slightest result. Selby got very fidgety at the delay. He was never happy except in my presence, and insisted on my coming, whenever I had time, to his house. I was glad to do so, for I took an interest both in him and his belongings, and as to Madame Sara I could not get her out of my head. One day Mrs. Selby said to me:—

"Have you ever been to see Madame? I know she would like to show you her shop and general surroundings."

"I did promise to call upon her," I answered, "but have not had time to do so yet."

---

1 A major railway terminus serving areas south and west of London.

2 An affluent area on the northwest side of Regent's Park known for its large secluded villas and quiet streets.

"Will you come with me tomorrow morning?" asked Edith Dallas, suddenly.

She turned red as she spoke, and the worried, uneasy expression became more marked on her face. I had noticed for some time that she had been looking both nervous and depressed. I had first observed this peculiarity about her on board the *Norham Castle*, but, as time went on, instead of lessening it grew worse. Her face for so young a woman was haggard; she started at each sound, and Madame Sara's name was never spoken in her presence without her evincing almost undue emotion.

"Will you come with me?" she said, with great eagerness.

I immediately promised, and the next day, about eleven o'clock, Edith Dallas and I found ourselves in a hansom driving to Madame Sara's shop. We reached it in a few minutes, and found an unpretentious little place wedged in between a hosier's on one side and a cheap print-seller's on the other. In the windows of the shop were pyramids of perfume bottles, with scintillating facet stoppers tied with coloured ribbons. We stepped out of the hansom and went indoors. Inside the shop were a couple of steps, which led to a door of solid mahogany.

"This is the entrance to her private house," said Edith, and she pointed to a small brass plate, on which was engraved the name—"Madame Sara, Parfumeuse."

Edith touched an electric bell and the door was immediately opened by a smartly-dressed page-boy. He looked at Miss Dallas as if he knew her very well, and said:—

"Madame is within, and is expecting you, miss."

He ushered us both into a quiet-looking room, soberly but handsomely furnished. He left us, closing the door. Edith turned to me.

"Do you know where we are?" she asked.

"We are standing at present in a small room just behind Madame Sara's shop," I answered. "Why are you so excited, Miss Dallas? What is the matter with you?"

"We are on the threshold of a magician's cave," she replied. "We shall soon be face to face with the most marvellous woman in the whole of London. There is no one like her."

"And you—fear her?" I said, dropping my voice to a whisper.

She started, stepped back, and with great difficulty recovered her composure. At that moment the page-boy returned to conduct us through a series of small waiting-rooms, and we soon found ourselves in the presence of Madame herself.

"Ah!" she said, with a smile. "This is delightful. You have kept your word, Edith, and I am greatly obliged to you. I will now show Mr. Druce some of the mysteries of my trade. But understand, sir," she added, "that I shall not tell you any of my real secrets, only as you would like to know something about me you shall."

"How can you tell I should like to know about you?" I asked.

She gave me an earnest glance which somewhat astonished me, and then she said:—

"Knowledge is power; don't refuse what I am willing to give. Edith, you will not object to waiting here while I show Mr. Druce through my rooms. First observe this room, Mr. Druce. It is lighted only from the roof. When the door shuts it automatically locks itself, so that any intrusion from without is impossible. This is my sanctum sanctorum[1]—a faint odour of perfumes pervades the room. This is a hot day, but the room itself is cool. What do you think of it all?"

Fig. 13. "THIS IS MY SANCTUM SANCTORUM."

1 Holy of holies (Latin), literally the inner chamber inside the Jewish Temple in Jerusalem where the Ark of the Covenant containing sacred texts was kept, but often used to refer to any place considered especially sacred or private.

I made no answer. She walked to the other end and motioned to me to accompany her. There stood a polished oak square table, on which lay an array of extraordinary-looking articles and implements—stoppered bottles full of strange medicaments, mirrors, plane and concave, brushes, sprays, sponges, delicate needle-pointed instruments of bright steel, tiny lancets, and forceps. Facing this table was a chair, like those used by dentists. Above the chair hung electric lights in powerful reflectors, and lenses like bull's-eye lanterns. Another chair, supported on a glass pedestal, was kept there, Madame Sara informed me, for administering static electricity. There were dry-cell batteries for the continuous currents and induction coils for Faradic currents.[1] There were also platinum needles for burning out the roots of hairs.

Madame took me from this room into another, where a still more formidable array of instruments were to be found. Here were a wooden operating-table and chloroform and ether apparatus. When I had looked at everything, she turned to me.

"Now you know," she said. "I am a doctor—perhaps a quack. These are my secrets. By means of these I live and flourish."

She turned her back on me and walked into the other room with the light, springy step of youth. Edith Dallas, white as a ghost, was waiting for us.

"You have done your duty, my child," said Madame. "Mr. Druce has seen just what I want him to see. I am very much obliged to you both. We shall meet to-night at Lady Farringdon's 'At-home.'[2] Until then, farewell."

When we got into the street and were driving back again to Eaton Square, I turned to Edith.

"Many things puzzle me about your friend," I said, "but perhaps none more than this. By what possible means can a woman who owns to being the possessor of a shop obtain the *entrée* to some of the best houses in London? Why does Society open her doors to this woman, Miss Dallas?"

---

1 Faradic or intermittent alternating electric currents were first described by British physicist Michael Faraday (1791–1867), credited with discovering the principle of electromagnetic induction. Faradic currents have been used on the face and body for medical and cosmetic treatments to tone the nerves and muscles, remove body hair, and destroy warts, moles, and tumours.

2 A social gathering held in the home of a host or hostess at designated hours.

"I cannot quite tell you," was her reply. "I only know the fact that wherever she goes she is welcomed and treated with consideration, and wherever she fails to appear there is a universally expressed feeling of regret."

I had also been invited to Lady Farringdon's reception that evening, and I went there in a state of great curiosity. There was no doubt that Madame interested me. I was not sure of her. Beyond doubt there was a mystery attached to her, and also, for some unaccountable reason, she wished both to propitiate and defy me. Why was this?

I arrived early, and was standing in the crush near the head of the staircase when Madame was announced. She wore the richest white satin and quantities of diamonds. I saw her hostess bend towards her and talk eagerly. I noticed Madame reply and the pleased expression that crossed Lady Farringdon's face. A few minutes later a man with a foreign-looking face and long beard sat down before the grand piano. He played a light prelude and Madame Sara began to sing. Her voice was sweet and low, with an extraordinary pathos in it. It was the sort of voice that penetrates to the heart. There was an instant pause in the gay chatter. She sang amidst perfect silence, and when the song had come to an end there followed a *furore* of applause. I was just turning to say something to my nearest neighbour when I observed Edith Dallas, who was standing close by. Her eyes met mine; she laid her hand on my sleeve.

"The room is hot," she said, half panting as she spoke. "Take me out on the balcony."

I did so. The atmosphere of the reception-rooms was almost intolerable, but it was comparatively cool in the open air.

"I must not lose sight of her," she said, suddenly.

"Of whom?" I asked, somewhat astonished at her words.

"Of Sara."

"She is there," I said. "You can see her from where you stand."

We happened to be alone. I came a little closer.

"Why are you afraid of her?" I asked.

"Are you sure that we shall not be heard?" was her answer.

"Certain."

"She terrifies me," were her next words.

"I will not betray your confidence, Miss Dallas. Will you not trust me? You ought to give me a reason for your fears."

"I cannot—I dare not; I have said far too much already. Don't keep me, Mr. Druce. She must not find us together."

As she spoke she pushed her way through the crowd, and before I could stop her was standing by Madame Sara's side.

The reception in Portland Place[1] was, I remember, on the 26th of July. Two days later the Selbys were to give their final 'At-home' before leaving for the country. I was, of course, invited to be present, and Madame was also there. She had never been dressed more splendidly, nor had she ever before looked younger or more beautiful. Wherever she went all eyes followed her. As a rule her dress was simple, almost like what a girl would wear, but to-night she chose rich Oriental stuffs made of many colours, and absolutely glittering with gems. Her golden hair was studded with diamonds. Round her neck she wore turquoise and diamonds mixed. There were many younger women in the room, but not the youngest nor the fairest had a chance beside Madame. It was not mere beauty of appearance, it was charm—charm which carries all before it.

I saw Miss Dallas, looking slim and tall and pale, standing at a little distance. I made my way to her side. Before I had time to speak she bent towards me.

"Is she not divine?" she whispered. "She bewilders and delights everyone. She is taking London by storm."

"Then you are not afraid of her to-night?" I said.

"I fear her more than ever. She has cast a spell over me. But listen, she is going to sing again."

I had not forgotten the song that Madame had given us at the Farringdons', and stood still to listen. There was a complete hush in the room. Her voice floated over the heads of the assembled guests in a dreamy Spanish song. Edith told me that it was a slumber song, and that Madame boasted of her power of putting almost anyone to sleep who listened to her rendering of it.

"She has many patients who suffer from insomnia," whispered the girl, "and she generally cures them with that song, and that alone. Ah! we must not talk; she will hear us."

Before I could reply Selby came hurrying up. He had not noticed Edith. He caught me by the arm.

"Come just for a minute into this window, Dixon," he said. "I must speak to you. I suppose you have no news with regard to my brother-in-law?"

"Not a word," I answered.

"To tell you the truth, I am getting terribly put out over the matter. We cannot settle any of our money affairs just because this man chooses to lose himself. My wife's lawyers wired to Brazil yesterday, but even his bankers do not know anything about him."

1 An upscale address in central London.

"The whole thing is a question of time," was my answer. "When are you off to Hampshire?"

"On Saturday."

As Selby said the last words he looked around him, then he dropped his voice.

"I want to say something else. The more I see"—he nodded towards Madame Sara—"the less I like her. Edith is getting into a very strange state. Have you not noticed it? And the worst of it is my wife is also infected. I suppose it is that dodge[1] of the woman's for patching people up and making them beautiful. Doubtless the temptation is overpowering in the case of a plain woman, but Beatrice is beautiful herself and young. What can she have to do with cosmetics and complexion pills?"

"You don't mean to tell me that your wife has consulted Madame Sara as a doctor?"

"Not exactly, but she has gone to her about her teeth. She complained of toothache lately, and Madame's dentistry is renowned. Edith is constantly going to her for one thing or another, but then Edith is infatuated."

As Jack said the last words he went over to speak to someone else, and before I could leave the seclusion of the window I perceived Edith Dallas and Madame Sara in earnest conversation together. I could not help overhearing the following words:—

"Don't come to me to-morrow. Get into the country as soon as you can. It is far and away the best thing to do."

As Madame spoke she turned swiftly and caught my eye. She bowed, and the peculiar look, the sort of challenge, she had before given me flashed over her face. It made me uncomfortable, and during the night that followed I could not get it out of my head. I remembered what Selby had said with regard to his wife and her money affairs. Beyond doubt he had married into a mystery—a mystery that Madame Sara knew all about. There was a very big money interest, and strange things happen when millions are concerned.

The next morning I had just risen and was sitting at breakfast when a note was handed to me. It came by special messenger, and was marked "Urgent." I tore it open. These were its contents:—

"My dear Druce, —A terrible blow has fallen on us. My sister-in-law, Edith, was taken suddenly ill this morning at breakfast. The nearest doctor was sent for, but he could do nothing, as she died half an hour ago. Do come and see me, and if you know

1 Clever trick.

any very clever specialist bring him with you. My wife is utterly stunned by the shock. —Yours, Jack Selby."

I read the note twice before I could realize what it meant. Then I rushed out and, hailing the first hansom I met, said to the man:—

"Drive to No. 192, Victoria Street,[1] as quickly as you can."

Here lived a certain Mr. Eric Vandeleur, an old friend of mine and the police surgeon for the Westminster district,[2] which included Eaton Square. No shrewder or sharper fellow existed than Vandeleur, and the present case was essentially in his province, both legally and professionally. He was not at his flat when I arrived, having already gone down to the court. Here I accordingly hurried, and was informed that he was in the mortuary.

For a man who, as it seemed to me, lived in a perpetual atmosphere of crime and violence, of death and coroners' courts, his habitual cheerfulness and brightness of manner were remarkable. Perhaps it was only the reaction from his work, for he had the reputation of being one of the most astute experts of the day in medical jurisprudence, and the most skilled analyst in toxicological cases on the Metropolitan Police staff. Before I could send him word that I wanted to see him I heard a door bang, and Vandeleur came hurrying down the passage, putting on his coat as he rushed along.

"Halloa!" he cried. "I haven't seen you for ages. Do you want me?"

"Yes, very urgently," I answered. "Are you busy?"

"Head over ears, my dear chap. I cannot give you a moment now, but perhaps later on."

"What is it? You look excited."

"I have got to go to Eaton Square like the wind, but come along, if you like, and tell me on the way."

"Capital," I cried. "The thing has been reported, then? You are going to Mr. Selby's, No. 34A; then I am going with you."

He looked at me in amazement.

"But the case has only just been reported. What can you possibly know about it?"

"Everything. Let us take this hansom, and I will tell you as we go along."

---

1 A street in central London connecting Westminster Abbey and Victoria Station, a major railway terminus serving areas south and east of London.

2 Located in central London. The district includes London's most significant historical and political landmarks.

As we drove to Eaton Square I quickly explained the situation, glancing now and then at Vandeleur's bright, clean-shaven face. He was no longer Eric Vandeleur, the man with the latest club story and the merry twinkle in his blue eyes: he was Vandeleur the medical jurist, with a face like a mask, his lower jaw slightly protruding and features very fixed.[1]

"This thing promises to be serious," he replied, as I finished, "but I can do nothing until after the autopsy. Here we are, and there is my man waiting for me; he has been smart."

On the steps stood an official-looking man in uniform, who saluted.

"Coroner's officer," explained Vandeleur.

We entered the silent, darkened house. Selby was standing in the hall. He came to meet us. I introduced him to Vandeleur, and he at once led us into the dining-room, where we found Dr. Osborne, whom Selby had called in when the alarm of Edith's illness had been first given. Dr. Osborne was a pale, under-sized, very young man. His face expressed considerable alarm. Vandeleur, however, managed to put him completely at his ease.

"I will have a chat with you in a few minutes, Dr. Osborne," he said; "but first I must get Mr. Selby's report. Will you please tell us, sir, exactly what occurred?"

"Certainly," he answered. "We had a reception here last night, and my sister-in-law did not go to bed until early morning; she was in bad spirits, but otherwise in her usual health. My wife went into her room after she was in bed, and told me later on that she had found Edith in hysterics, and could not get her to explain anything. We both talked about taking her to the country without delay. Indeed, our intention was to get off this afternoon."

"Well?" said Vandeleur.

"We had breakfast about half-past nine, and Miss Dallas came down, looking quite in her usual health, and in apparently good spirits. She ate with appetite, and, as it happened, she and my wife were both helped from the same dish. The meal had nearly come to an end when she jumped up from the table, uttered a sharp cry, turned very pale, pressed her hand to her side, and ran out of the room. My wife immediately followed her. She came back again in a minute or two, and said that Edith was in

---

1 Vandeleur shares this characteristic with Sherlock Holmes; according to Dr. Watson in *A Study in Scarlet*, Holmes's chin "had the prominence and squareness which mark the man of determination" (Conan Doyle 15).

violent pain, and begged of me to send for a doctor. Dr. Osborne lives just round the corner. He came at once, but she died almost immediately after his arrival."

"You were in the room?" asked Vandeleur, turning to Osborne.

"Yes," he replied. "She was conscious to the last moment, and died suddenly."

"Did she tell you anything?"

"No, except to assure me that she had not eaten any food that day until she had come down to breakfast. After the death occurred I sent immediately to report the case, locked the door of the room where the poor girl's body is, and saw also that nobody touched anything on this table."

Vandeleur rang the bell and a servant appeared. He gave quick orders. The entire remains of the meal were collected and taken charge of, and then he and the coroner's officer went upstairs.

When we were alone Selby sank into a chair. His face was quite drawn and haggard.

"It is the horrible suddenness of the thing which is so appalling," he cried. "As to Beatrice, I don't believe she will ever be the same again. She was deeply attached to Edith. Edith was nearly ten years her senior, and always acted the part of mother to her. This is a sad beginning to our life. I can scarcely think collectedly."

I remained with him a little longer, and then, as Vandeleur did not return, went back to my own house. There I could settle to nothing, and when Vandeleur rang me up on the telephone about six o'clock I hurried off to his rooms. As soon as I arrived I saw that Selby was with him, and the expression on both their faces told me the truth.

"This is a bad business," said Vandeleur. "Miss Dallas has died from swallowing poison. An exhaustive analysis and examination have been made, and a powerful poison, unknown to European toxicologists, has been found. This is strange enough, but how it has been administered is a puzzle. I confess, at the present moment, we are all nonplussed. It certainly was not in the remains of the breakfast, and we have her dying evidence that she took nothing else. Now, a poison with such appalling potency would take effect quickly. It is evident that she was quite well when she came to breakfast, and that the poison began to work towards the close of the meal. But how did she get it? This question, however, I shall deal with later on. The more immediate point is this. The situation is a serious one in view of the monetary issues and the value of the lady's life. From the aspects of the case, her undoubted sanity and her affection for her sister, we may almost exclude the idea of suicide. We must, therefore, call it murder. This harmless, innocent lady is struck down by the hand of an assassin, and with such devilish cunning that no trace or clue is left behind. For such an act there must have been some very powerful motive, and the person who designed and executed it must be a criminal of the highest order of scientific ability. Mr. Selby has been telling me the exact financial position of the poor lady, and also of his own young wife. The absolute disappearance of the step-brother, in view of his previous character, is in the highest degree strange. Knowing, as we do, that between him and two million sterling there stood two lives—*one is taken!*"

A deadly sensation of cold seized me as Vandeleur uttered these last words. I glanced at Selby. His face was colourless and the pupils of his eyes were contracted, as though he saw something which terrified him.

"What has happened once may happen again," continued Vandeleur. "We are in the presence of a great mystery, and I counsel you, Mr. Selby, to guard your wife with the utmost care."

These words, falling from a man of Vandeleur's position and authority on such matters, were sufficiently shocking for me to hear, but for Selby to be given such a solemn warning about his young and beautiful and newly-married wife, who was all the world to him, was terrible indeed. He leant his head on his hands.

"Mercy on us!" he muttered. "Is this a civilized country when death can walk abroad like this, invisible, not to be avoided? Tell me, Mr. Vandeleur, what I must do."

"You must be guided by me," said Vandeleur, "and, believe me, there is no witchcraft in the world. I shall place a detective in your household immediately. Don't be alarmed; he will come to you in plain clothes and will simply act as a servant. Nevertheless, nothing can be done to your wife without his knowledge. As to you, Druce," he continued, turning to me, "the police are doing all they can to find this man Silva, and I ask you to help them with your big agency, and to begin at once. Leave your friend to me. Wire instantly if you hear news."

"You may rely on me," I said, and a moment later I had left the room.

As I walked rapidly down the street the thought of Madame Sara, her shop and its mysterious background, its surgical instruments, its operating-table, its induction coils, came back to me.

And yet what could Madame Sara have to do with the present strange, inexplicable mystery?

The thought had scarcely crossed my mind before I heard a clatter alongside the kerb, and turning round I saw a smart open carriage, drawn by a pair of horses, standing there. I also heard my own name. I turned. Bending out of the carriage was Madame Sara.

"I saw you going by, Mr. Druce. I have only just heard the news about poor Edith Dallas. I am terribly shocked and upset. I have been to the house, but they would not admit me. Have you heard what was the cause of her death?"

Madame's blue eyes filled with tears as she spoke.

"I am not at liberty to disclose what I have heard, Madame," I answered, "since I am officially connected with the affair."

Her eyes narrowed. The brimming tears dried as though by magic. Her glance became scornful.

"Thank you," she answered; "your reply tells me that she did not die naturally. How very appalling! But I must not keep you. Can I drive you anywhere?"

"No, thank you."

"Good-bye, then."

She made a sign to the coachman, and as the carriage rolled away turned to look back at me. Her face wore the defiant expression I had seen there more than once. Could she be connected with the affair? The thought came upon me with a violence that seemed almost conviction. Yet I had no reason for it—none.

To find Henry Joachim Silva was now my principal thought. Advertisements were widely circulated. My staff had instructions to make every possible inquiry, with large money rewards as incitements. The collateral branches of other agencies throughout Brazil were communicated with by cable, and all the Scotland Yard channels were used. Still there was no result. The newspapers took up the case; there were paragraphs in most of them with regard to the missing step-brother and the mysterious death of Edith Dallas. Then someone got hold of the story of the will, and this was retailed with many additions for the benefit of the public. At the inquest the jury returned the following verdict:—

"We find that Miss Edith Dallas died from taking poison of unknown name, but by whom or how administered there is no evidence to say."

This unsatisfactory state of things was destined to change quite suddenly. On the 6th of August, as I was seated in my office, a note was brought me by a private messenger. It ran as follows:—

"Norfolk Hotel, Strand.

"Dear Sir, —I have just arrived in London from Brazil, and have seen your advertisements. I was about to insert one myself in order to find the whereabouts of my sisters. I am a great invalid and unable to leave my room. Can you come to see me at the earliest possible moment? —Yours,

"Henry Joachim Silva."

In uncontrollable excitement I hastily dispatched two telegrams, one to Selby and the other to Vandeleur, begging of them to be with me, without fail, as soon as possible. So the man had never been in England at all. The situation was more bewildering than ever. One thing, at least, was probable—Edith Dallas's death was not due to her step-brother. Soon after half-past six Selby arrived, and Vandeleur walked in ten minutes later. I told them what had occurred and showed them the letter. In half an hour's time we reached the hotel, and on stating who I was we were shown into a room on the first floor by Silva's private servant. Resting in an arm-chair, as we entered, sat a man; his face was terribly thin. The eyes and cheeks were so sunken that the face had almost the appearance of a skull. He made no effort to rise when we entered, and glanced from one of us to the other with the utmost astonishment. I at once introduced myself and explained who we were. He then waved his hand for his man to retire.

"You have heard the news, of course, Mr. Silva?" I said.

"News! What?" He glanced up to me and seemed to read something in my face. He started back in his chair.

"Good heavens!" he replied. "Do you allude to my sisters? Tell me, quickly, are they alive?"

"Your elder sister died on the 29th of July, and there is every reason to believe that her death was caused by foul play."

As I uttered these words the change that passed over his face was fearful to witness. He did not speak, but remained motionless. His claw-like hands clutched the arms of the chair, his eyes were fixed and staring, as though they would start from their hollow sockets, the colour of his skin was like clay. I heard Selby breathe quickly behind me, and Vandeleur stepped towards the man and laid his hand on his shoulder.

"Tell us what you know of this matter," he said, sharply.

Recovering himself with an effort, the invalid began in a tremulous voice:—

"Listen closely, for you must act quickly. I am indirectly responsible for this fearful thing. My life has been a wild and wasted one, and now I am dying. The doctors tell me I cannot live a month, for I have a large aneurism of the heart. Eighteen months ago I was in Rio. I was living fast and gambled heavily. Among my fellow-gamblers was a man much older than myself. His name was José Aranjo. He was, if anything, a greater gambler than I. One night we played alone. The stakes ran high until they reached a big figure. By daylight I had lost to him nearly £200,000. Though I am a rich man in point of income under my uncle's will, I could not pay a twentieth part of that sum. This man knew my financial position, and, in addition to a sum of £5,000 paid down, I gave him a document. I must have been mad to do so. The document was this—it was duly witnessed and attested by a lawyer—that, in the event of my surviving my two sisters and thus inheriting the whole of my uncle's vast wealth, half a million should go to José Aranjo. I felt I was breaking up at the time, and the chances of my inheriting the money were small. Immediately after the completion of the document this man left Rio, and I then heard a great deal about him that I had not previously known. He was a man of the queerest antecedents, partly Indian, partly Italian. He had spent many years of his life amongst the Indians. I heard also that he was as cruel as he was clever, and possessed some wonderful secrets of poisoning unknown to the West. I thought a great deal about this, for I knew that by signing that document I had placed the lives of my two sisters between him and a fortune. I came to Para six weeks ago, only to learn that one of my sisters was married and that both had gone to England. Ill as I was, I determined to follow them in order to warn them. I also wanted to arrange matters with you, Mr. Selby."

"One moment, sir," I broke in, suddenly. "Do you happen to be aware if this man, José Aranjo, knew a woman calling herself Madame Sara?"

"Knew her?" cried Silva. "Very well indeed, and so, for that matter, did I. Aranjo and Madame Sara were the best friends, and constantly met. She called herself a professional beautifier—was very handsome, and had secrets for the pursuing of her trade unknown even to Aranjo."

"Good heavens!" I cried, "and the woman is now in London. She returned here with Mrs. Selby and Miss Dallas. Edith was very much influenced by her, and was constantly with her. There is no doubt in my mind that she is guilty. I have suspected her for some time, but I could not find a motive. Now the motive appears. You surely can have her arrested?"

Vandeleur made no reply. He gave me a strange look, then he turned to Selby.

"Has your wife also consulted Madame Sara?" he asked, sharply.

"Yes, she went to her once about her teeth, but has not been to the shop since Edith's death. I begged of her not to see the woman, and she promised me faithfully she would not do so."

"Has she any medicines or lotions given to her by Madame Sara—does she follow any line of treatment advised by her?"

"No, I am certain on that point."

"Very well, I will see your wife to-night in order to ask her some questions. You must both leave town at once. Go to your country house and settle there. I am quite serious when I say that Mrs. Selby is in the utmost possible danger until after the death of her brother. We must leave you now, Mr. Silva. All business affairs must wait for the present. It is absolutely necessary that Mrs. Selby should leave London at once. Good-night, sir. I shall give myself the pleasure of calling on you to-morrow morning."

We took leave of the sick man. As soon as we got into the street Vandeleur stopped.

"I must leave it to you, Selby," he said, "to judge how much of this matter you will tell to your wife. Were I you I would explain everything. The time for immediate action has arrived, and she is a brave and sensible woman. From this moment you must watch all the foods and liquids that she takes. She must never be out of your sight or out of the sight of some other trustworthy companion."

"I shall, of course, watch my wife myself," said Selby. "But the thing is enough to drive one mad."

"I will go with you to the country, Selby," I said, suddenly.

"Ah!" cried Vandeleur, "that is the best thing possible, and what I wanted to propose. Go, all of you, by an early train to-morrow."

"Then I will be off home at once, to make arrangements," I said. "I will meet you, Selby, at Waterloo for the first train to Cronsmoor to-morrow."

As I was turning away Vandeleur caught my arm.

"I am glad you are going with them," he said. "I shall write to you to-night *re* instructions. Never be without a loaded revolver. Good-night."

By 6.15 the next morning Selby, his wife, and I were in a reserved, locked, first-class compartment, speeding rapidly west. The servants and Mrs. Selby's own special maid were in a separate carriage. Selby's face showed signs of a sleepless night, and presented a striking contrast to the fair, fresh face of the girl round whom this strange battle raged. Her husband had told her everything, and, though still suffering terribly from the shock and grief of her sister's death, her face was calm and full of repose.

A carriage was waiting for us at Cronsmoor, and by half-past nine we arrived at the old home of the Selbys, nestling amid its oaks and elms. Everything was done to make the home-coming of the bride as cheerful as circumstances would permit, but a gloom, impossible to lift, overshadowed Selby himself. He could scarcely rouse himself to take the slightest interest in anything.

The following morning I received a letter from Vandeleur. It was very short, and once more impressed on me the necessity of caution. He said that two eminent physicians had examined Silva, and the verdict was that he could not live a month. Until his death precautions must be strictly observed.

The day was cloudless, and after breakfast I was just starting out for a stroll when the butler brought me a telegram. I tore it open; it was from Vandeleur.

"Prohibit all food until I arrive. Am coming down," were the words. I hurried into the study and gave it to Selby. He read it and looked up at me.

"Find out the first train and go and meet him, old chap," he said. "Let us hope that this means an end of the hideous affair."

I went into the hall and looked up the trains. The next arrived at Cronsmoor at 10.45. I then strolled round to the stables and ordered a carriage, after which I walked up and down on the drive. There was no doubt that something strange had happened. Vandeleur coming down so suddenly must mean a final clearing up of the mystery. I had just turned round at the lodge gates to wait for the carriage when the sound of wheels and of horses galloping struck on my ears. The gates were swung open, and Vandeleur in an open fly[1] dashed through them. Before I could recover from my surprise he was out of the vehicle and at my side. He carried a small black bag in his hand.

"I came down by special train," he said, speaking quickly. "There is not a moment to lose. Come at once. Is Mrs. Selby all right?"

---

1 A hired carriage usually drawn by one horse; two horses are depicted here and in the accompanying illustration.

"What do you mean?" I replied. "Of course she is. Do you suppose that she is in danger?"

"Deadly," was his answer. "Come."

We dashed up to the house together. Selby, who had heard our steps, came to meet us.

"Mr. Vandeleur!" he cried. "What is it? How did you come?"

"By special train, Mr. Selby. And I want to see your wife at once. It will be necessary to perform a very trifling operation."

"Operation!" he exclaimed.

"Yes; at once."

We made our way through the hall and into the morning-room, where Mrs. Selby was busily engaged reading and answering letters. She started up when she saw Vandeleur and uttered an exclamation of surprise. .

"What has happened?" she asked.

Vandeleur went up to her and took her hand.

"Do not be alarmed," he said, "for I have come to put all your fears to rest. Now, please, listen to me. When you visited Madame Sara with your sister, did you go for medical advice?"

The colour rushed into her face.

"One of my teeth ached," she answered. "I went to her about that. She is, as I suppose you know, a most wonderful dentist. She examined the tooth, found that it required stopping, and got an assistant, a Brazilian, I think, to do it."

"And your tooth has been comfortable ever since?"

"Yes, quite. She had one of Edith's stopped at the same time."

"Will you kindly sit down and show me which was the tooth into which the stopping was put?"

She did so.

"This was the one," she said, pointing with her finger to one in the lower jaw. "What do you mean? Is there anything wrong?"

Vandeleur examined the tooth long and carefully. There was a sudden rapid movement of his hand, and a sharp cry from Mrs. Selby. With the deftness of long practice, and a powerful wrist, he had extracted the tooth with one wrench. The suddenness of the whole thing, startling as it was, was not so strange as his next movement.

"Send Mrs. Selby's maid to her," he said, turning to her husband; "then come, both of you, into the next room."

The maid was summoned. Poor Mrs. Selby had sunk back in her chair, terrified and half fainting. A moment later Selby joined us in the dining-room.

"That's right," said Vandeleur; "close the door, will you?"

He opened his black bag and brought out several instruments. With one he removed the stopping from the tooth. It was quite soft and came away easily. Then from the bag he produced a small guinea-pig, which he requested me to hold. He pressed the sharp instrument into the tooth, and opening the mouth of the little animal placed the point on the tongue. The effect was instantaneous. The little head fell on to one of my hands—the guinea-pig was dead. Vandeleur was white as a sheet. He hurried up to Selby and wrung his hand.

"Thank Heaven!" he said, "I've been in time, but only just. Your wife is safe. This stopping would hardly have held another hour. I have been thinking all night over the mystery of your sister-in-law's death, and over every minute detail of evidence as to how the poison could have been administered. Suddenly the coincidence of both sisters having had their teeth stopped struck me as remarkable. Like a flash the solution came to me. The more I considered it the more I felt that I was right; but by what fiendish cunning such a scheme could have been conceived and executed is still beyond my power to explain. The poison is very like hyoscine,[1] one of the worst toxic-alkaloids known, so violent in its deadly proportions that the amount that would go into a tooth would cause almost instant death. It has been kept in by a gutta-percha[2] stopping, certain to come out within a month, probably earlier, and most probably during mastication of food. The person would die either immediately or after a very few minutes, and no one would connect a visit to the dentist with a death a month afterwards."

What followed can be told in a very few words. Madame Sara was arrested on suspicion. She appeared before the magistrate, looking innocent and beautiful, and managed during her evidence completely to baffle that acute individual. She denied nothing, but declared that the poison must have been put into the tooth by one of the two Brazilians whom she had lately engaged to help her with her dentistry. She had her suspicions with regard to these men soon afterwards, and had dismissed them. She believed that they were in the pay of José Aranjo, but she could not tell anything for certain. Thus Madame escaped conviction. I was certain that she was guilty, but there was not a shadow of real proof. A month later Silva died, and Selby is now a double millionaire.

---

1 A powerful poison found in some plants of the nightshade family.
2 A plastic-like substance made from the latex of a Malaysian tree.

II. —THE BLOOD-RED CROSS. [505–18]

In the month of November in the year 1899 I found myself a guest in the house of one of my oldest friends—George Rowland. His beautiful place in Yorkshire was an ideal holiday resort. It went by the name of Rowland's Folly,[1] and had been built on the site of a former dwelling in the reign of the first George.[2] The house was now replete with every modern luxury. It, however, very nearly cost its first owner, if not the whole of his fortune, yet the most precious heirloom of the family. This was a pearl necklace of almost fabulous value. It had been secured as booty by a certain Geoffrey Rowland at the time of the Battle of Agincourt,[3] and had originally been the property of one of the Dukes of Genoa, and had even for a short time been in the keeping of the Pope. From the moment that Geoffrey Rowland took possession of the necklace there had been several attempts made to deprive him of it. Sword, fire, water, poison, had all been used, but ineffectually. The necklace with its eighty pearls, smooth, symmetrical, pear-shaped, of a translucent white colour and with a subdued iridescent sheen, was still in the possession of the family, and was likely to remain there, as George Rowland told me, until the end of time. Each bride wore the necklace on her wedding-day, after which it was put into the strong-room and, as a rule, never seen again until the next bridal occasion. The pearls were roughly estimated as worth from two to three thousand pounds each, but the historical value of the necklace put the price almost beyond the dreams of avarice.

It was reported that in the autumn of that same year an American millionaire had offered to buy it from the family at their own price, but as no terms would be listened to the negotiations fell through.

George Rowland belonged to the oldest and proudest family in the West Riding,[4] and no man looked a better gentleman or more fit to uphold ancient dignities than he. He was proud to boast that from the earliest days no stain of dishonour had touched his house, that the women of the family were as good as the men, their blood pure, their morals irreproachable, their ideas lofty.

---

1 An overly elaborate or eccentric structure, usually built for decorative purposes.

2 George I reigned from 1714–27.

3 A major English victory (25 October 1415) in the Hundred Years' War between England and France (1337–1453).

4 One of three historic subdivisions of Yorkshire.

I went to Rowland's Folly in November, and found a pleasant, hospitable, and cheerful hostess in Lady Kennedy, Rowland's only sister. Antonia Ripley was, however, the centre of all interest. Rowland was engaged to Antonia, and the history was romantic. Lady Kennedy told me all about it.

"She is a penniless girl without family," remarked the good woman, somewhat snappishly. "I can't imagine what George was thinking of."

"How did your brother meet her?" I asked.

"We were both in Italy last autumn; we were staying in Naples, at the Vesuve.[1] An English lady was staying there of the name of Studley. She died while we were at the hotel. She had under her charge a young girl, the same Antonia who is now engaged to my brother. Before her death she begged of us to befriend her, saying that the child was without money and without friends. All Mrs. Studley's money died with her. We promised, not being able to do otherwise. George fell in love almost at first sight. Little Antonia was provided for by becoming engaged to my brother. I have nothing to say against the girl, but I dislike this sort of match very much. Besides, she is more foreign than English."

"Cannot Miss Ripley tell you anything about her history?"

"Nothing, except that Mrs. Studley adopted her when she was a tiny child. She says, also, that she has a dim recollection of a large building crowded with people, and a man who stretched out his arms to her and was taken forcibly away. That is all. She is quite a nice child, and amiable, with touching ways and a pathetic face; but no one knows what her ancestry was. Ah, there you are, Antonia! What is the matter now?"

The girl tripped across the room. She was like a young fawn; of a smooth, olive complexion—dark of eye and mysteriously beautiful, with the graceful step which is seldom granted to an English girl.

"My lace dress has come," she said. "Markham is unpacking it—but the bodice is made with a low neck."

Lady Kennedy frowned.

"You are too absurd, Antonia," she said. "Why won't you dress like other girls? I assure you that peculiarity of yours of always wearing your dress high in the evening annoys George."

---

1 Vesuvius (French); the hotel is named after the famous volcano located a short distance from Naples. See "At the Edge of the Crater," p. 86.

"Does it?" she answered, and she stepped back and put her hand to her neck just below the throat—a constant habit of hers, as I afterwards had occasion to observe.

"It disturbs him very much," said Lady Kennedy. "He spoke to me about it only yesterday. Please understand, Antonia, that at the ball you cannot possibly wear a dress high to your throat. It cannot be permitted."

"I shall be properly dressed on the night of the ball," replied the girl.

Her face grew crimson, then deadly pale.

"It only wants a fortnight to that time, but I shall be ready."

There was a solemnity about her words. She turned and left the room.

"Antonia is a very trying character," said Lady Kennedy. "Why won't she act like other girls? She makes such a fuss about wearing a proper evening dress that she tries my patience—but she is all crotchets."[1]

"A sweet little girl for all that," was my answer.

"Yes; men like her."

Soon afterwards, as I was strolling on the terrace, I met Miss Ripley. She was sitting in a low chair. I noticed how small, and slim, and young she looked, and how pathetic was the expression of her little face. When she saw me she seemed to hesitate; then she came to my side.

"May I walk with you, Mr. Druce?" she asked.

"I am quite at your service," I answered. "Where shall we go?"

"It doesn't matter. I want to know if you will help me."

"Certainly, if I can, Miss Ripley."

"It is most important. I want to go to London."

"Surely that is not very difficult?"

"They won't allow me to go alone, and they are both very busy. I have just sent a telegram to a friend. I want to see her. I know she will receive me. I want to go to-morrow. May I venture to ask that you should be my escort?"

"My dear Miss Ripley, certainly," I said. "I will help you with pleasure."

"It must be done," she said, in a low voice. "I have put it off too long. When I marry him he shall not be disappointed."

"I do not understand you," I said, "but I will go with you with the greatest willingness."

She smiled; and the next day, much to my own amazement, I

1 Capricious or whimsical.

found myself travelling first-class up to London, with little Miss Ripley as my companion. Neither Rowland nor his sister had approved; but Antonia had her own way, and the fact that I would escort her cleared off some difficulties.

During our journey she bent towards me and said, in a low tone:—

"Have you ever heard of that most wonderful, that great woman, Madame Sara?"

I looked at her intently.

"I have certainly heard of Madame Sara," I said, with emphasis, "but I sincerely trust that you have nothing to do with her."

"I have known her almost all my life," said the girl. "Mrs. Studley knew her also. I love her very much. I trust her. I am going to see her now."

"What do you mean?"

"It was to her I wired yesterday. She will receive me; she will help me. I am returning to the Folly to-night. Will you add to your kindness by escorting me home?"

"Certainly."

At Euston[1] I put my charge into a hansom, arranging to meet her on the departure platform at twenty minutes to six that evening, and then taking another hansom drove as fast as I could to Vandeleur's address. During the latter part of my journey to town a sudden, almost unaccountable, desire to consult Vandeleur had taken possession of me. I was lucky enough to find this busiest of men at home and at leisure. He gave an exclamation of delight when my name was announced, and then came towards me with outstretched hand.

"I was just about to wire to you, Druce," he said. "From where have you sprung?"

"From no less a place than Rowland's Folly," was my answer.

"More and more amazing. Then you have met Miss Ripley, George Rowland's *fiancée*?"

"You have heard of the engagement, Vandeleur?"

"Who has not? What sort is the young lady?"

"I can tell you all you want to know, for I have travelled up to town with her."

"Ah!"

He was silent for a minute, evidently thinking hard; then drawing a chair near mine he seated himself.

"How long have you been at Rowland's Folly?" he asked.

---

1 A major London railway terminus serving the West Midlands, the Northwest, North Wales, and part of Scotland.

"Nearly a week. I am to remain until after the wedding. I consider Rowland a lucky man. He is marrying a sweet little girl."

"You think so? By the way, have you ever noticed any peculiarity about her?"

"Only that she is singularly amiable and attractive."

"But any habit—pray think carefully before you answer me."

"Really, Vandeleur, your questions surprise me. Little Miss Ripley is a person with ideas and is not ashamed to stick to her principles. You know, of course, that in a house like Rowland's Folly it is the custom for the ladies to come to dinner in full dress. Now, Miss Ripley won't accommodate herself to this fashion, but *will* wear her dress high to the throat, however gay and festive the occasion."

"Ah! there doesn't seem to be much in that, does there?"

"I don't quite agree with you. Pressure has been brought to bear on the girl to make her conform to the usual regulations, and Lady Kennedy, a woman old enough to be her mother, is quite disagreeable on the point."

"But the girl sticks to her determination?"

"Absolutely, although she promises to yield and to wear the conventional dress at the ball given in her honour a week before the wedding."

Vandeleur was silent for nearly a minute; then dropping his voice he said, slowly:—

"Did Miss Ripley ever mention in your presence the name of our mutual foe—Madame Sara?"

"How strange that you should ask! On our journey to town to-day she told me that she knew the woman—she has known her for the greater part of her life—poor child, she even loves her. Vandeleur, that young girl is with Madame Sara now."

"Don't be alarmed, Druce; there is no immediate danger; but I may as well tell you that through my secret agents I have made discoveries which show that Madame has another iron in the fire, that once again she is preparing to convulse Society, and that little Miss Ripley is the victim."

"You must be mistaken."

"So sure am I, that I want your help. You are returning to Rowland's Folly?"

"To-night."

"And Miss Ripley?"

"She goes with me. We meet at Euston for the six o'clock train."

"So far, good. By the way, has Rowland spoken to you lately about the pearl necklace?"

"No; why do you ask?"

"Because I understand that it was his intention to have the pearls slightly altered and reset in order to fit Miss Ripley's slender throat; also to have a diamond clasp affixed in place of the somewhat insecure one at present attached to the string of pearls. Messrs. Theodore and Mark, of Bond Street,[1] were to undertake the commission. All was in preparation, and a messenger, accompanied by two detectives, was to go to Rowland's Folly to fetch the treasure, when the whole thing was countermanded, Rowland having changed his mind and having decided that the strong-room at the Folly was the best place in which to keep the necklace."

"He has not mentioned the subject to me," I said. "How do you know?"

"I have my emissaries. One thing is certain—little Miss Ripley is to wear the pearls on her wedding-day—and the Italian family, distant relatives of the present Duke of Genoa, to whom the pearls belonged, and from whom they were stolen shortly before the Battle of Agincourt, are again taking active steps to secure them. You have heard the story of the American millionaire? Well, that was a blind—the necklace was in reality to be delivered into the hands of the old family as soon as he had purchased it. Now, Druce, this is the state of things: Madame Sara is an adventuress, and the cleverest woman in the world—Miss Ripley is very young and ignorant. Miss Ripley is to wear the pearls on her wedding-day—and Madame wants them. You can infer the rest."

"What do you want me to do?" I asked.

"Go back and watch. If you see anything to arouse suspicion, wire to me."

"What about telling Rowland?"

"I would rather not consult him. I want to protect Miss Ripley, and at the same time to get Madame into my power. She managed to elude us last time, but she shall not this. My idea is to inveigle her to her ruin. Why, Druce, the woman is being more trusted and run after and admired day by day. She appeals to the greatest foibles of the world. She knows some valuable secrets, and is an adept in the art of restoring beauty and to a certain extent conquering the ravages of time. She is at present aided by

---

1 One of London's premier shopping streets for luxury goods. Madame Rachel, Sara's real-life counterpart, opened her shop in Bond Street. See Introduction, p. 29.

an Arab, one of the most dangerous men I have ever seen, with the subtlety of a serpent, and legerdemain in every one of his ten fingers. It is not an easy thing to entrap her."

"And yet you mean to do it?"

"Some day—some day. Perhaps now."

His eyes were bright. I had seldom seen him look more excited.

After a short time I left him. Miss Ripley met me at Euston. She was silent and un-responsive and looked depressed. Once I saw her put her hand to her neck.

"Are you in pain?" I asked.

"You might be a doctor, Mr. Druce, from your question."

"But answer me," I said.

She was silent for a minute; then she said, slowly:—

"You are good, and I think I ought to tell you. But will you regard it as a secret? You wonder, perhaps, how it is that I don't wear a low dress in the evening. I will tell you why. On my neck, just below the throat, there grew a wart or mole—large, brown, and ugly. The Italian doctors would not remove it on account of the position. It lies just over what they said was an *aberrant* artery, and the removal might cause very dangerous haemorrhage. One day Madame saw it; she said the doctors were wrong, and that she could easily take it away and leave no mark behind. I hesitated for a long time, but yesterday, when Lady Kennedy spoke to me as she did, I made up my mind. I wired to Madame and went to her to-day. She gave me chloroform and removed the mole. My neck is bandaged up and it smarts a little. I am not to remove the bandage until she sees me again. She is very pleased with the result, and says that my neck will now be beautiful like other women's, and that I can on the night of the ball wear the lovely Brussels lace dress that Lady Kennedy has given me. That is my secret. Will you respect it?"

I promised, and soon afterwards we reached the end of our journey.

A few days went by. One morning at breakfast I noticed that the little signora only played with her food. An open letter lay by her plate. Rowland, by whose side she always sat, turned to her.

"What is the matter, Antonia?" he said. "Have you had an unpleasant letter?"

"It is from——"

"From whom, dear?"

"Madame Sara."

"What did I hear you say?" cried Lady Kennedy.

"I have had a letter from Madame Sara, Lady Kennedy."

"That shocking woman in the Strand—that adventuress? My dear, is it possible that you know her? Her name is in the mouth of everyone. She is quite notorious."

Instantly the room became full of voices, some talking loudly, some gently, but all praising Madame Sara. Even the men took her part; as to the women, they were unanimous about her charms and her genius.

In the midst of the commotion little Antonia burst into a flood of tears and left the room. Rowland followed her. What next occurred I cannot tell, but in the course of the morning I met Lady Kennedy.

"Well," she said, "that child has won, as I knew she would. Madame Sara wishes to come here, and George says that Antonia's friend is to be invited. I shall be glad when the marriage is over and I can get out of this. It is really detestable that in the last days of my reign I should have to give that woman the *entrée* to the house."

She left me, and I wandered into the entrance hall. There I saw Rowland. He had a telegraph form in his hands, on which some words were written.

"Ah, Druce!" he said. "I am just sending a telegram to the station. What! do you want to send one too?"

For I had seated myself by the table which held the telegraph forms.

"If you don't think I am taking too great a liberty, Rowland," I said, suddenly, "I should like to ask a friend of mine here for a day or two."

"Twenty friends, if you like, my dear Druce. What a man you are to apologize about such a trifle! Who is the special friend?"

"No less a person than Eric Vandeleur, the police-surgeon for Westminster."

"What! Vandeleur—the gayest, jolliest man I have ever met! Would he care to come?"

Rowland's eyes were sparkling with excitement.

"I think so; more especially if you will give me leave to say that you would welcome him."

"Tell him he shall have a thousand welcomes, the best room in the house, the best horse. Get him to come by all means, Druce."

Our two telegrams were sent off. In the course of the morning replies in the affirmative came to each.

That evening Madame Sara arrived. She came by the last

train. The brougham[1] was sent to meet her. She entered the house shortly before midnight. I was standing in the hall when she arrived, and I felt a momentary sense of pleasure when I saw her start as her eyes met mine. But she was not a woman to be caught off her guard. She approached me at once with outstretched hand and an eager voice.

"This is charming, Mr. Druce," she said. "I do not think anything pleases me more." Then she added, turning to Rowland, "Mr. Dixon Druce is a very old friend of mine."

Rowland gave me a bewildered glance. Madame turned and began to talk to her hostess. Antonia was standing near one of the open drawing-rooms. She had on a soft dress of pale green silk. I had seldom seen a more graceful little creature. But the expression of her face disturbed me. It wore now the fascinated look of a bird when a snake attracts it. Could Madame Sara be the snake? Was Antonia afraid of this woman?

The next day Lady Kennedy came to me with a confidence.

"I am glad your police friend is coming," she said. "It will be safer."

"Vandeleur arrives at twelve o'clock," was my answer.

"Well, I am pleased. I like that woman less and less. I was amazed when she dared to call you her friend."

"Oh, we have met before on business," I answered, guardedly.

"You won't tell me anything further, Mr. Druce?"

"You must excuse me, Lady Kennedy."

"Her assurance is unbounded," continued the good lady. "She has brought a maid or nurse with her—a most extraordinary-looking woman. That, perhaps, is allowable; but she has also brought her black servant, an Arabian, who goes by the name of Achmed. I must say he is a picturesque creature with his quaint Oriental dress. He was all in flaming yellow this morning, and the embroidery on his jacket was worth a small fortune. But it is the daring of the woman that annoys me. She goes on as though she were somebody."

"She is a very emphatic somebody," I could not help replying. "London Society is at her feet."

"I only hope that Antonia will take her remedies and let her go. The woman has no welcome from me," said the indignant mistress of Rowland's Folly.

I did not see anything of Antonia that morning, and at the

---

1 A one-horse closed carriage with an open seat at the front for the driver.

appointed time I went down to the station to meet Vandeleur. He arrived in high spirits, did not ask a question with regard to Antonia, received the information that Madame Sara was in the house with stolid silence, and seemed intent on the pleasures of the moment.

"Rowland's Folly!" he said, looking round him as we approached one of the finest houses in the whole of Yorkshire. "A folly, truly, and yet a pleasant one, Druce, eh? I fancy," he added, with a slight smile, "that I am going to have a good time here."

"I hope you will disentangle a most tangled skein,"[1] was my reply.

He shrugged his shoulders. Suddenly his manner altered.

"Who is that woman?" he said, with a strain of anxiety quite apparent in his voice.

"Who?" I asked.

"That woman on the terrace in nurse's dress."

"I don't know. She has been brought here by Madame Sara—a sort of maid and nurse as well. I suppose poor little Antonia will be put under her charge."

"Don't let her see me, Druce, that's all. Ah, here is our host."

Vandeleur quickened his movements, and the next instant was shaking hands with Rowland.

The rest of the day passed without adventure. I did not see Antonia. She did not even appear at dinner. Rowland, however, assured me that she was taking necessary rest and would be all right on the morrow. He seemed inclined to be gracious to Madame Sara, and was annoyed at his sister's manner to their guest.

Soon after dinner, as I was standing in one of the smoking-rooms, I felt a light hand on my arm, and, turning, encountered the splendid pose and audacious, bright, defiant glance of Madame herself.

"Mr. Druce," she said, "just one moment. It is quite right that you and I should be plain with each other. I know the reason why you are here. You have come for the express purpose of spying upon me and spoiling what you consider my game. But understand, Mr. Druce, that there is danger to yourself when you interfere with the schemes of one like me. Forewarned is forearmed."

---

1 A loosely coiled bundle of yarn or thread; a complex or confused matter.

Fig. 14. "FOREWARNED IS FOREARMED."

Someone came into the room and Madame left it.

The ball was but a week off, and preparations for the great event were taking place. Attached to the house at the left was a great room built for this purpose.

Rowland and I were walking down this room on a special morning; he was commenting on its architectural merits and telling me what band he intended to have in the musicians' gallery, when Antonia glided into the room.

"How pale you are, little Tonia!" he said.

This was his favourite name for her. He put his hand under her chin, raised her sweet, blushing face, and looked into her eyes.

"Ah, you want my answer. What a persistent little puss it is! You shall have your way, Tonia—yes, certainly. For you I will grant what has never been granted before. All the same, what will my lady say?"

He shrugged his shoulders.

"But you will let me wear them whether she is angry or not?" persisted Antonia.

"Yes, child, I have said it."

She took his hand and raised it to her lips, then, with a curtsy, tripped out of the room.

"A rare, bright little bird," he said, turning to me. "Do you know, I feel that I have done an extraordinarily good thing for myself in securing little Antonia. No troublesome mamma-in-law—no brothers and sisters, not my own and yet emphatically mine to consider—just the child herself. I am very happy and a very lucky fellow. I am glad my little girl has no past history. She is just her dear little, dainty self, no more and no less."

"What did she want with you now?" I asked.

"Little witch," he said, with a laugh. "The pearls—*the* pearls. She insists on wearing the great necklace on the night of the ball. Dear little girl. I can fancy how the baubles will gleam and shine on her fair throat."

I made no answer, but I was certain that little Antonia's request did not emanate from herself. I thought that I would search for Vandeleur and tell him of the circumstance, but the next remark of Rowland's nipped my project in the bud.

"By the way, your friend has promised to be back for dinner. He left here early this morning."

"Vandeleur?" I cried.

"Yes, he has gone to town. What a first-rate fellow he is!"

"He tells a good story," I answered.

"Capital. Who would suspect him of being the greatest criminal expert of the day? But, thank goodness, we have no need of his services at Rowland's Folly."

Late in the evening Vandeleur returned. He entered the house just before dinner. I observed by the brightness of his eyes and the intense gravity of his manner that he was satisfied with himself. This in his case was always a good sign. At dinner he was his brightest self, courteous to everyone, and to Madame Sara in particular.

Late that night, as I was preparing to go to bed, he entered my room without knocking.

"Well, Druce," he said, "it is all right."

"All right!" I cried; "what do you mean?"

"You will soon know. The moment I saw that woman I had my suspicions. I was in town to-day making some very interesting inquiries. I am primed now on every point. Expect a *dénouement* of a startling character very soon, but be sure of one thing—however black appearances may be the little bride is safe, and so are the pearls."

He left me without waiting for my reply.

The next day passed, and the next. I seemed to live on tenter-hooks. Little Antonia was gay and bright like a bird. Madame's invitation had been extended by Lady Kennedy at Rowland's command to the day after the ball—little Antonia skipped when she heard it.

"I love her," said the girl.

More and more guests arrived—the days flew on wings—the evenings were lively. Madame was a power in herself. Vandeleur was another. These two, sworn foes at heart, aided and abetted each other to make things go brilliantly for the rest of the guests. Rowland was in the highest spirits.

At last the evening before the ball came and went. Vandeleur's *grand coup* had not come off. I retired to bed as usual. The night was a stormy one—rain rattled against the window-panes, the wind sighed and shuddered. I had just put out my candle and was about to seek forgetfulness in sleep when once again in his unceremonious fashion Vandeleur burst into my room.

"I want you at once, Druce, in the bed-room of Madame Sara's servant. Get into your clothes as fast as you possibly can and join me there."

He left the room as abruptly as he had entered it. I hastily dressed, and with stealthy steps, in the dead of night, to the accompaniment of the ever-increasing tempest, sought the room in question.

I found it brightly lighted; Vandeleur pacing the floor as though he himself were the very spirit of the storm; and, most astonishing sight of all, the nurse whom Madame Sara had brought to Rowland's Folly, and whose name I had never happened to hear, gagged and bound in a chair drawn into the centre of the room.

"So I think that is all, nurse," said Vandeleur, as I entered. "Pray take a chair, Druce. We quite understand each other, don't we, nurse, and the facts are wonderfully simple. Your name as entered in the archives of crime at Westminster is not as you have given out, Mary Jessop, but Rebecca Curt. You escaped from

Portland prison[1] on the night of November 30th, just a year ago. You could not have managed your escape but for the connivance of the lady in whose service you are now. Your crime was forgery, with a strong and very daring attempt at poisoning. Your victim was a harmless invalid lady. Your knowledge of crime, therefore, is what may be called extensive. There are yet eleven years of your sentence to run. You have doubtless served Madame Sara well—but perhaps you can serve me better. You know the consequence if you refuse, for I explained that to you frankly and clearly before this gentleman came into the room. Druce, will you oblige me—will you lock the door while I remove the gag from the prisoner's mouth?"

I hurried to obey. The woman breathed more freely when the gag was removed. Her face was a swarthy red all over. Her crooked eyes favoured us with many shifty glances.

"Now, then, have the goodness to begin, Rebecca Curt," said Vandeleur. "Tell us everything you can."

She swallowed hard, and said:—

"You have forced me——"

"We won't mind that part," interrupted Vandeleur. "The story, please, Mrs. Curt."

If looks could kill, Rebecca Curt would have killed Vandeleur then. He gave her in return a gentle, bland glance, and she started on her narrative.

"Madame knows a secret about Antonia Ripley."

"Of what nature?"

"It concerns her parentage."

"And that is——?"

The woman hesitated and writhed.

"The names of her parents, please," said Vandeleur, in a voice cold as ice and hard as iron.

"Her father was Italian by birth."

"His name?"

"Count Gioletti. He was unhappily married, and stabbed his English wife in an access of jealousy when Antonia was three years old. He was executed for the crime on the 20th of June, 18—. The child was adopted and taken out of the country by an English lady who was present in court—her name was Mrs. Studley. Madame Sara was also present. She was much interested in the trial, and had an interview afterwards

1 Opened in 1848 on the Isle of Portland on the Dorset coast in southern England.

with Mrs. Studley. It was arranged that Antonia should be called by the surname of Ripley—the name of an old relative of Mrs. Studley's—and that her real name and history were never to be told to her."

"I understand," said Vandeleur, gently. "This is of deep interest, is it not, Druce?"

I nodded, too much absorbed in watching the face of the woman to have time for words.

"But now," continued Vandeleur, "there are reasons why Madame should change her mind with regard to keeping the matter a close secret—is that not so, Mrs. Curt?"

"Yes," said Mrs. Curt.

"You will have the kindness to continue."

"Madame has an object—she blackmails the signora. She wants to get the signora completely into her power."

"Indeed! Is she succeeding?"

"Yes."

"How has she managed? Be very careful what you say, please."

"The mode is subtle—the young lady had a disfiguring mole or wart on her neck, just below the throat. Madame removed the mole."

"Quite a simple process, I doubt not," said Vandeleur, in a careless tone.

"Yes, it was done easily—I was present. The young lady was conducted into a chamber with a red light."

Vandeleur's extraordinary eyes suddenly leapt into fire. He took a chair and drew it so close to Mrs. Curt's that his face was within a foot or two of hers.

"Now, you will be very careful what you say," he remarked. "You know the consequence to yourself unless this narrative is absolutely reliable."

She began to tremble, but continued:—

"I was present at the operation. Not a single ray of ordinary light was allowed to penetrate. The patient was put under chloroform. The mole was removed. Afterwards Madame wrote something on her neck. The words were very small and neatly done—they formed a cross on the young lady's neck. Afterwards I heard what they were."

"Repeat them."

"I can't. You will know in the moment of victory."

"I choose to know now. A detective from my division at Westminster comes here early to-morrow morning—he brings handcuffs—and——"

"I will tell you," interrupted the woman. "The words were these:—

"'I AM THE DAUGHTER OF PAOLO GIOLETTI, WHO WAS EXECUTED FOR THE MURDER OF MY MOTHER, JUNE 20TH, 18—'"

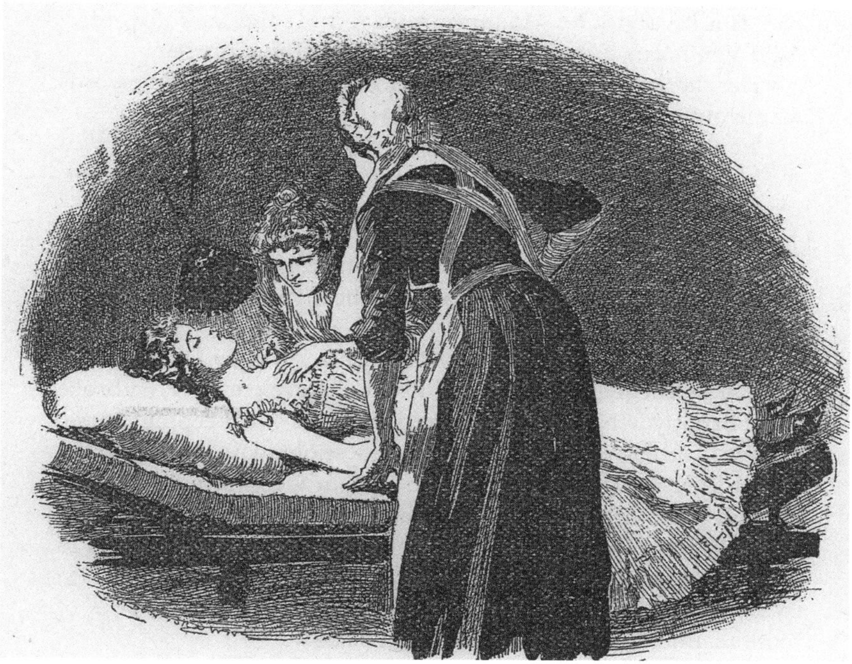

Fig. 15. "MADAME WROTE SOMETHING ON HER NECK."

"How were the words written?"

"With nitrate of silver."

"Fiend!" muttered Vandeleur.

He jumped up and began to pace the room. I had never seen his face so black with ungovernable rage.

"You know what this means?" he said at last to me. "Nitrate of silver eats into the flesh and is permanent. Once exposed to the light the case is hopeless, and the helpless child becomes her own executioner."

The nurse looked up restlessly.

"The operation was performed in a room with a red light," she said, "and up to the present the words have not been seen. Unless the young lady exposes her neck to the blue rays of ordinary light they never will be. In order to give her a chance to keep her deadly secret Madame has had a large carbuncle of the deepest red cut and prepared. It is in the shape of a cross, and is suspended to a fine gold, almost invisible, thread. This the signora is to wear when in full evening dress. It will keep in its place, for the back of the cross will be dusted with gum."

"But it cannot be Madame's aim to hide the fateful words," said Vandeleur. "You are concealing something, nurse."

Her face grew an ugly red. After a pause the following words came out with great reluctance:—

"The young lady wears the carbuncle as a reward."

"Ah," said Vandeleur, "now we are beginning to see daylight. As a reward for what?"

"Madame wants something which the signora can give her. It is a case of exchange; the carbuncle which hides the fatal secret is given in exchange for that which the signora can transfer to Madame."

"I understand at last," said Vandeleur. "Really, Druce, I feel myself privileged to say that of all the malevolent——" he broke off abruptly. "Never mind," he said, "we are keeping nurse. Nurse, you have answered all my questions with praiseworthy exactitude, but before you return to your well-earned slumbers I have one more piece of information to seek from you. Was it entirely by Miss Ripley's desire, or was it in any respect owing to Madame Sara's instigations, that the young lady is permitted to wear the pearl necklace on the night of the dance? You have, of course, nurse, heard of the pearl necklace?"

Rebecca Curt's face showed that she undoubtedly had.

"I see you are acquainted with that most interesting story. Now, answer my question. The request to wear the necklace to-morrow night was suggested by Madame, was it not?"

"Ah, yes—yes!" cried the woman, carried out of herself by sudden excitement. "It was to that point all else tended—all, all!"

"Thank you, that will do. You understand that from this day you are absolutely in my service. As long as you serve me faithfully you are safe."

"I will do my best, sir," she replied, in a modest tone, her eyes seeking the ground.

The moment we were alone Vandeleur turned to me.

"Things are simplifying themselves," he said.

"I fail to understand," was my answer. "I should say that complications, and alarming ones, abound."

"Nevertheless, I see my way clear. Druce, it is not good for you to be so long out of bed, but in order that you may repose soundly when you return to your room I will tell you frankly what my mode of operations will be to-morrow. The simplest plan would be to tell Rowland everything, but for various reasons that does not suit me. I take an interest in the little girl, and if she chooses to conceal her secret (at present, remember, she does not know it, but the poor child will certainly be told everything to-morrow) I don't intend to interfere. In the second place, I am anxious to lay a trap for Madame. Now, two things are evident. Madame Sara's object in coming here is to steal the pearls. Her plan is to terrify the little signora into giving them to her in order that the fiendish words written on the child's neck may not be seen. As the signora must wear a dress with a low neck to-morrow night, she can only hide the words by means of the red carbuncle. Madame will only give her the carbuncle if she, in exchange, gives Madame the pearls. You see?"

"I do," I answered, slowly.

He drew himself up to his slender height, and his eyes became full of suppressed laughter.

"The child's neck has been injured with nitrate of silver. Nevertheless, until it is exposed to the blue rays of light the ominous, fiendish words will not appear on her white throat. Once they do appear they will be indelible. Now, listen! Madame, with all her cunning, forgot something. To the action of nitrate of silver there is an antidote. This is nothing more or less than our old friend cyanide of potassium. To-morrow nurse, under my instructions, will take the little patient into a room carefully prepared with the hateful red light, and will bathe the neck just where the baleful words are written with a solution of cyanide of potassium. The nitrate of silver will then become neutralized and the letters will never come out."

"But the child will not know that. The terror of Madame's cruel story will be upon her, and she will exchange the pearls for the cross."

"I think not, for I shall be there to prevent it. Now, Druce, I have told you all that is necessary. Go to bed and sleep comfortably."

The next morning dawned dull and sullen, but the fierce storm of the night before was over. The ravages which had taken place, however, in the stately old park were very manifest, for trees had been torn up by their roots and some of the stateliest and largest of the oaks had been deprived of their best branches.

Little Miss Ripley did not appear at all that day. I was not surprised at her absence. The time had come when doubtless Madame found it necessary to divulge her awful scheme to the unhappy child. In the midst of that gay houseful of people no one specially missed her; even Rowland was engaged with many necessary matters, and had little time to devote to his future wife. The ballroom, decorated with real flowers, was a beautiful sight.

Vandeleur, our host, and I paced up and down the long room. Rowland was in great excitement, making many suggestions, altering this decoration and the other. The flowers were too profuse in one place, too scanty in another. The lights, too, were not bright enough.

"By all means have the ball-room well lighted," said Vandeleur. "In a room like this, so large, and with so many doors leading into passages and sitting-out rooms, it is well to have the light as brilliant as possible. You will forgive my suggestion, Mr. Rowland, when I say I speak entirely from the point of view of a man who has some acquaintance with the treacherous dealings of crime."

Rowland started.

"Are you afraid that an attempt will be made here to-night to steal the necklace?" he asked, suddenly.

"We won't talk of it," replied Vandeleur. "Act on my suggestion and you have nothing to fear."

Rowland shrugged his shoulders, and crossing the room gave some directions to several men who were putting in the final touches.

Nearly a hundred guests were expected to arrive from the surrounding country, and the house was as full as it could possibly hold. Rowland was to open the ball with little Antonia.

There was no late dinner that day, and as evening approached Vandeleur sought me.

"I say, Druce, dress as early as you can, and come down and meet me in our host's study."

I looked at him in astonishment, but did not question him. I saw that he was intensely excited. His face was cold and stern; it invariably wore that expression when he was most moved.

I hurried into my evening clothes and came down again. Vandeleur was standing in the study talking to Rowland. The guests were beginning to arrive. The musicians were tuning-up in the adjacent ball-room, and signs of hurry and festival pervaded the entire place. Rowland was in high spirits and looked very handsome. He and Vandeleur talked together, and I stood a little apart. Vandeleur was just about to make a light reply to one of our host's questions when we heard the swish of drapery in the passage outside, and little Antonia, dressed for her first ball, entered. She was in soft white lace, and her neck and arms were bare. The effect of her entrance was somewhat startling, and would have arrested attention even were we not all specially interested in her. Her face, neck, and arms were nearly as white as her dress, her dark eyes were much dilated, and her soft black hair surrounded her small face like a shadow. In the midst of the whiteness a large red cross sparkled on her throat like living fire. Rowland uttered an exclamation and then stood still; as for Vandeleur and myself, we held our breath in suspense. What might not the next few minutes reveal?

It was the look on Antonia's face that aroused our fears. What ailed her? She came forward like one blind, or as one who walks in her sleep. One hand was held out slightly in advance, as though she meant to guide herself by the sense of touch. She certainly saw neither Vandeleur nor me, but when she got close to Rowland the blind expression left her eyes. She gave a sudden and exceedingly bitter cry, and ran forward, flinging herself into his arms.

"Kiss me once before we part for ever. Kiss me just once before we part," she said.

"My dear little one," I heard him answer, "what is the meaning of this? You are not well. There, Antonia, cease trembling. Before we part, my dear? But there is no thought of parting. Let me look at you, darling. Ah!"

He held her at arm's length and gazed at her critically.

"No girl could look sweeter, Antonia," he said, "and you have come now for the finishing touch—the beautiful pearls. But what is this, my dear? Why should you spoil your white neck with anything so incongruous? Let me remove it."

She put up her hand to her neck, thus covering the crimson cross. Then her wild eyes met Vandeleur's. She seemed to recognise his presence for the first time.

"You can safely remove it," he said to her, speaking in a semi-whisper.

Rowland gave him an astonished glance. His look seemed to say, "Leave us," but Vandeleur did not move.

"We must see this thing out," he said to me.

Meanwhile Rowland's arm encircled Antonia's neck, and his hand sought for the clasp of the narrow gold thread that held the cross in place.

"One moment," said Antonia. She stepped back a pace; the trembling in her voice left it, it gathered strength, her fear gave way to dignity. This was the hour of her deepest humiliation, and yet she looked noble.

"My dearest," she said, "my kindest and best of friends. I had yielded to temptation, terror made me weak, the dread of losing you unnerved me, but I won't come to you charged with a sin on my conscience; I won't conceal anything from you. I know you won't wish me *now* to become your wife; nevertheless, you shall know the truth."

"What do you mean, Antonia? What do your strange words signify? Are you mad?" said George Rowland.

"No, I wish I were; but I am no mate for you; I cannot bring dishonour to your honour. Madame said it could be hidden, that this"—she touched the cross—"would hide it. For this I was to pay—yes, to pay a shameful price. I consented, for the terror was so cruel. But I—I came here and looked into your face and I could not do it. Madame shall have her blood-red cross back and you shall know all. You shall see."

With a fierce gesture she tore the cross from her neck and flung it on the floor.

"The pearls for this," she cried; "the pearls were the price; but I would rather you knew. Take me up to the brightest light and you will see for yourself."

Rowland's face wore an expression impossible to fathom. The red cross lay on the floor; Antonia's eyes were fixed on his. She was no child to be humoured; she was a woman and despair was driving her wild. When she said, "Take me up to the brightest light," he took her hand without a word and led her to where the full rays of a powerful electric light turned the place into day.

"Look!" cried Antonia, "look! Madame wrote it here—here." She pointed to her throat.

"The words are hidden, but this light will soon cause them to appear. You will see for yourself, you will know the truth. At last you will understand who I really am."

There was silence for a few minutes. Antonia kept pointing to her neck. Rowland's eyes were fixed upon it. After a breathless period of agony Vandeleur stepped forward.

"Miss Antonia," he cried, "you have suffered enough. I am in a position to relieve your terrors. You little guessed, Rowland, that for the last few days I have taken an extreme liberty with regard to you. I have been in your house simply and solely in the exercise of my professional qualities. In the exercise of my manifest duties I came across a ghastly secret. Miss Antonia was to be subjected to a cruel ordeal. Madame Sara, for reasons of her own, had invented one of the most fiendish plots it has ever been my unhappy lot to come across. But I have been in time. Miss Antonia, you need fear nothing. Your neck contains no ghastly secret. Listen! I have saved you. The nurse whom Madame believed to be devoted to her service considered it best for prudential reasons to transfer herself to me. Under my directions she bathed your neck to-day with a preparation of cyanide of potassium. You do not know what that is, but it is a chemical preparation which neutralizes the effect of what that horrible woman has done. You have nothing to fear—your secret lies buried beneath your white skin."

"But what is the mystery?" said Rowland. "Your actions, Antonia, and your words, Vandeleur, are enough to drive a man mad. What is it all about? I will know."

"Miss Ripley can tell you or not, as she pleases," replied Vandeleur. "The unhappy child was to be blackmailed, Madame Sara's object being to secure the pearl necklace worth a King's ransom. The cross was to be given in exchange for the necklace. That was her aim, but she is defeated. Ask me no questions, sir. If this young lady chooses to tell you, well and good, but if not the secret is her own."

Vandeleur bowed and backed towards me.

"The secret is mine," cried Antonia, "but it also shall be yours, George. I will not be your wife with this ghastly thing between us. You may never speak to me again, but you shall know all the truth."

"Upon my word, a brave girl, and I respect her," whispered Vandeleur. "Come, Druce, our work so far as Miss Antonia is concerned is finished."

We left the room.

"Now to see Madame Sara," continued my friend. "We will go to her rooms. Walls have ears in her case; she doubtless knows the whole *dénouement* already; but we will find her at once, she can scarcely have escaped yet."

He flew upstairs. I followed him. We went from one corridor to another. At last we found Madame's apartments. Her bedroom door stood wide open. Rebecca Curt was standing in the middle of the room. Madame herself was nowhere to be seen, but there was every sign of hurried departure.

"Where is Madame Sara?" inquired Vandeleur, in a peremptory voice.

Rebecca Curt shrugged her shoulders.

"Has she gone down? Is she in the ballroom? Speak!" said Vandeleur.

The nurse gave another shrug.

"I only know that Achmed the Arabian rushed in here a few minutes ago," was her answer. "He was excited. He said something to Madame. I think he had been listening—eavesdropping, you call it. Madame was convulsed with rage. She thrust a few things together and she's gone. Perhaps you can catch her."

Vandeleur's face turned white.

"I'll have a try," he said. "Don't keep me, Druce."

He rushed away. I don't know what immediate steps he took, but he did not return to Rowland's Folly. Neither was Madame Sara captured.

But notwithstanding her escape and her meditated crime, notwithstanding little Antonia's hour of terror, the ball went on merrily, and the bride-elect opened it with her future husband. On her fair neck gleamed the pearls, lovely in their soft lustre. What she told Rowland was never known; how he took the news is a secret between Antonia and himself. But one thing is certain: no one was more gallant in his conduct, more ardent in his glances of love, than was the master of Rowland's Folly that night. They were married on the day fixed, and Madame Sara was defeated.

III. —THE FACE OF THE ABBOT. [644–57]

If Madame Sara had one prerogative more than another it was that of taking people unawares. When least expected she would spring a mine at your feet, engulf you in a most horrible danger, stab you in the dark, or injure you through your best friend; in short, this dangerous woman was likely to become the terror of London if steps were not soon taken to place her in such confinement that her genius could no longer assert itself.

Months went by after my last adventure. Once again my fears slumbered. Madame Sara's was not the first name that I thought of when I awoke in the morning, nor the last to visit my dreams at night. Absorbed in my profession, I had little time to waste upon her. After all, I made up my mind, she might have left London; she might have carried her machinations, her cruelties, and her genius elsewhere.

That such was not the case this story quickly shows.

The matter which brought Madame Sara once again to the fore began in the following way.

On the 17th of July, 1900, I received a letter; it ran as follows:—

"23, West Terrace,

"Charlton Road, Putney.

"DEAR MR. DRUCE,—I am in considerable difficulty and am writing to beg for your advice. My father died a fortnight ago at his castle in Portugal, leaving me his heiress. His brother-in-law, who lived there with him, arrived in London yesterday and came to see me, bringing me full details of my father's death. These are in the last degree mysterious and terrifying. There are also a lot of business affairs to arrange. I know little about business and should greatly value your advice on the whole situation. Can you come here and see me to-morrow at three o'clock? Senhor de Castro, my uncle, my mother's brother, will be here, and I should like you to meet him. If you can come I shall be very grateful.—Yours sincerely,

"HELEN SHERWOOD."

I replied to this letter by telegram:—

"Will be with you at three to-morrow."

Helen Sherwood was an old friend of mine; that is, I had known her since she was a child. She was now about twenty-three years of age, and was engaged to a certain Godfrey Despard, one of the best fellows I ever met. Despard was employed in a merchant's office in Shanghai, and the chance of immediate marriage was small. Nevertheless, the young people were determined to be true to each other and to wait that turn in the tide which comes to most people who watch for it.

Helen's life had been a sad one. Her mother, a Portuguese lady of good family, had died at her birth; her father, Henry Sherwood, had gone to Lisbon in 1860 as one of the Under-Secretaries to the Embassy and never cared to return to England. After the death of his wife he had lived as an eccentric recluse. When Helen was three years old he had sent her home, and she had been brought up by a maiden aunt of her father's, who had never understood the impulsive, eager girl, and had treated her with a rare want of sympathy. This woman had died when her young charge was sixteen years of age. She had left no money behind her, and, as her father declined to devote one penny to his daughter's maintenance, Helen had to face the world before her education was finished. But her character was full of spirit and determination. She stayed on at school as pupil teacher,[1] and

1 Pupil teachers were senior students who taught younger children under the supervision of a head teacher. The system favoured students from less affluent backgrounds who wanted to enter the teaching profession.

afterwards supported herself by her attainments. She was a good linguist, a clever musician, and had one of the most charming voices I ever heard in an amateur. When this story opens she was earning a comfortable independence, and was even saving a little money for that distant date when she would marry the man she loved.

Meanwhile Sherwood's career was an extraordinary one. He had an extreme stroke of fortune in drawing the first prize of the Grand Christmas State Lottery in Lisbon, amounting to one hundred and fifty million reis,[1] representing in English money thirty thousand pounds. With this sum he bought an old castle in the Estrella Mountains, and, accompanied by his wife's brother, a certain Petro de Castro, went there to live. He was hated by his fellow-men and, with the exception of De Castro, he had no friends. The old castle was said to be of extraordinary beauty, and was known as Castello Mondego. It was situated some twenty miles beyond the old Portuguese town of Coimbra. The historical accounts of the place were full of interest, and its situation was marvellously romantic, being built on the heights above the Mondego River. The castle dated from the twelfth century, and had seen brave and violent deeds. It was supposed to be haunted by an old monk who was said to have been murdered there, but within living memory no one had seen him. At least, so Helen had informed me.

Punctually at three o'clock on the following day I found myself at West Terrace, and was shown into my young friend's pretty little sitting-room.

"How kind of you to come, Mr. Druce!" she said. "May I introduce you to my uncle, Senhor de Castro?"

The Senhor, a fine-looking man, who spoke English remarkably well, bowed, gave a gracious smile, and immediately entered into conversation. His face had strong features; his beard was iron-grey, so also were his hair and moustache. He was slightly bald about the temples. I imagined him to be a man about forty-five years of age.

"Now," said Helen, after we had talked to each other for a few minutes, "perhaps, Uncle Petro, you will explain to Mr. Druce what has happened."

As she spoke I noticed that her face was very pale and that her lips slightly trembled.

---

1 Plural of *real*, a unit of currency, originally a silver coin in use until 1911.

"It is a painful story," said the Portuguese, "most horrible and inexplicable."

I prepared myself to listen, and he continued:—

"For the last few months my dear friend had been troubled in his mind. The reason appeared to me extraordinary. I knew that Sherwood was eccentric, but he was also matter-of-fact, and I should have thought him the last man who would be likely to be a prey to nervous terrors. Nevertheless, such was the case. The old castle has the reputation of being haunted, and the apparition that is supposed to trouble Mondego is that of a ghastly white face that is now and then seen at night peering out through some of the windows or one of the embrasures of the battlements surrounding the courtyard. It is said to be the shade of an abbot who was foully murdered there by a Castilian nobleman who owned the castle a hundred years ago.

"It was late in April of this year when my brother-in-law first declared that he saw the apparition. I shall never forget his terror. He came to me in my room, woke me, and pointed out the embrasure where he had seen it. He described it as a black figure leaning out of a window, with an appallingly horrible white face, with wide-open eyes apparently staring at nothing. I argued with him and tried to appeal to his common sense, and did everything in my power to bring him to reason, but without avail. The terror grew worse and worse. He could think and talk of nothing else, and, to make matters worse, he collected all the old literature he could find bearing on the legend. This he would read, and repeat the ghastly information to me at meal times. I began to fear that his mind would become affected, and three weeks ago I persuaded him to come away with me for a change to Lisbon. He agreed, but the very night before we were to leave I was awakened in the small hours by hearing an awful cry, followed by another, and then the sound of my own name. I ran out into the courtyard and looked up at the battlements. There I saw, to my horror, my brother-in-law rushing along the edge, screaming as though in extreme terror, and evidently imagining that he was pursued by something. The next moment he dashed headlong down a hundred feet on to the flagstones by my side, dying instantaneously. Now comes the most horrible part. As I glanced up I saw, and I swear it with as much certainty as I am now speaking to you, a black figure leaning out over the battlement exactly at the spot from which he had fallen—a figure with a ghastly white face, which stared straight down at me. The moon was full, and gave the face a clearness that was unmistakable. It was large, round, and smooth, white with a whiteness I had never seen on human face, with eyes widely open, and a fixed stare; the face was rigid and tense; the mouth shut and drawn at the corners. Fleeting as the glance was, for it vanished almost the next moment, I shall never forget it. It is indelibly imprinted on my memory."

He ceased speaking.

From my long and constant contact with men and their affairs, I knew at once that what De Castro had just said instantly raised the whole matter out of the commonplace; true or untrue, real or false, serious issues were at stake.

"Who else was in the castle that night?" I asked.

"No one," was his instant reply. "Not even old Gonsalves, our one man-servant. He had gone to visit his people in the mountains about ten miles off. We were absolutely alone."

"You know Mr. Sherwood's affairs pretty well?" I went on. "On the supposition of trickery, could there be any motive that you know of for anyone to play such a ghastly trick?"

"Absolutely none."

"You never saw the apparition before this occasion?"

"Never."

"And what were your next steps?"

"There was nothing to be done except to carry poor Sherwood indoors. He was buried on the following day. I made every effort to have a systematic inquiry set on foot, but the castle is in a remote spot and the authorities are slow to move. The Portuguese doctor gave his sanction to the burial after a formal inquiry. Deceased was testified as having committed suicide while temporarily insane, but to investigate the apparition they absolutely declined."

"And now," I said, "will you tell me what you can with regard to the disposition of the property?"

"The will is a very remarkable one," replied De Castro. "Senhor Sousa, my brother-in-law's lawyer, holds it. Sherwood died a much richer man than I had any idea of. This was owing to some very successful speculations. The real and personal estate amounts to seventy thousand pounds, but the terms of the will are eccentric. Henry Sherwood's passionate affection for the old castle was quite morbid, and the gist of the conditions of the will is this: Helen is to live on the property, and if she does, and as long as she does, she is to receive the full interest on forty thousand pounds, which is now invested in good English securities. Failing this condition, the property is to be sold, and the said forty thousand pounds is to go to a Portuguese charity in

Lisbon. I also have a personal interest in the will. This I knew from Sherwood himself. He told me that his firm intention was to retain the castle in the family for his daughter, and for her son if she married. He earnestly begged of me to promote his wishes in the event of his dying. I was not to leave a stone unturned to persuade Helen to live at the castle, and in order to ensure my carrying out his wishes he bequeathed to me the sum of ten thousand pounds provided Helen lives at Castello Mondego. If she does not do so I lose the money. Hence my presence here and my own personal anxiety to clear up the mystery of my friend's death, and to see my niece installed as owner of the most lovely and romantic property in the Peninsula. It has, of course, been my duty to give a true account of the mystery surrounding my unhappy brother-in-law's death, and I sincerely trust that a solution to this terrible mystery will be found, and that Helen will enter into her beautiful possessions with all confidence."

"The terms of the will are truly eccentric," I said. Then turning to Helen I added:—

"Surely you can have no fear in living at Castello Mondego when it would be the means of bringing about the desire of your heart?"

"Does that mean that you are engaged to be married, Helen?" asked De Castro.

"It does," she replied. Then she turned to me. "I am only human, and a woman. I could not live at Castello Mondego with this mystery unexplained; but I am willing to take every step—yes, *every* step, to find out the truth."

"Let me think over the case," I said, after a pause. "Perhaps I may be able to devise some plan for clearing up this unaccountable matter. There is no man in the whole of London better fitted to grapple with the mystery than I, for it is, so to speak, my profession."

"You will please see in me your hearty collaborator, Mr. Druce," said Senhor de Castro.

"When do you propose to return to Portugal?" I asked.

"As soon as I possibly can."

"Where are you staying now?"

"At the Cecil."[1]

He stood up as he spoke.

"I am sorry to have to run away," he said. "I promised to meet

1 A grand hotel (built 1890–96, demolished 1930) located between the Thames Embankment and the Strand.

a friend, a lady, in half an hour from now. She is a very busy woman, and I must not keep her waiting."

His words were commonplace enough, but I noticed a queer change in his face. His eyes grew full of eagerness, and yet—was it possible?—a curious fear seemed also to fill them. He shook hands with Helen, bowed to me, and hurriedly left the room.

"I wonder whom he is going to meet," she said, glancing out of the window and watching his figure as he walked down the street. "He told me when he first came that he had an interview pending of a very important character. But, there, I must not keep you, Mr. Druce; you are also a very busy man. Before you go, however, do tell me what you think of the whole thing. I certainly cannot live at the castle while that ghastly face is unexplained; but at the same time I do not wish to give up the property."

"You shall live there, enjoy the property, and be happy," I answered. "I will think over everything; I am certain we shall see a way out of the mystery."

I wrung her hand and hurried away.

During the remainder of the evening this extraordinary case occupied my thoughts to the exclusion of almost everything else. I made up my mind to take it up, to set every inquiry on foot, and, above all things, to ascertain if there was a physical reason for the apparition's appearance; in short, if Mr. Sherwood's awful death was for the benefit of any living person. But I must confess that, think as I would, I could not see the slightest daylight until I remembered the curious expression of De Castro's face when he spoke of his appointment with a lady. The man had undoubtedly his weak point; he had his own private personal fear. What was its nature?

I made a note of the circumstance and determined to speak to Vandeleur about it when I had a chance.

The next morning one of the directors of our agency called. He and I had a long talk over business matters, and when he was leaving he asked me when I wished to take my holiday.

"If you like to go away for a fortnight or three weeks, now is your time," was his final remark.

I answered without a moment's hesitation that I should wish to go to Portugal, and would take advantage of the leave of absence which he offered me.

Now, it had never occurred to me to think of visiting Portugal until that moment; but so strongly did the idea now take possession of me that I went at once to the Cecil and had an interview with De Castro. I told him that I could not fulfil my promise to

Miss Sherwood without being on the spot, and I should therefore accompany him when he returned to Lisbon. His face expressed genuine delight, and before we parted we arranged to meet at Charing Cross on the morning after the morrow. I then hastened to Putney to inform Helen Sherwood of my intention.

To my surprise I saw her busy placing different articles of her wardrobe in a large trunk which occupied the place of honour in the centre of the little sitting-room.

"What are you doing?" I cried.

She coloured.

"You must not scold me," she said. "There is only one thing to do, and I made up my mind this morning to do it. The day after to-morrow I am going to Lisbon. I mean to investigate the mystery for myself."

"You are a good, brave girl," I cried. "But listen, Helen; it is not necessary."

I then told her that I had unexpectedly obtained a few weeks' holiday, and that I intended to devote the time to her service.

"Better and better," she cried. "I go with you. Nothing could have been planned more advantageously for me."

"What put the idea into your head?" I asked.

"It isn't my own," she said. "I spent a dreadful night, and this morning, soon after ten o'clock, I had an unexpected visitor. She is not a stranger to me, although I have never mentioned her name. She is known as Madame Sara, and is——"

"My dear Helen!" I cried. "You don't mean to tell me you know that woman? She is one of the most unscrupulous in the whole of London. You must have nothing to do with her—nothing whatever."

Helen opened her eyes to their widest extent.

"You misjudge Madame Sara," she said. "I have known her for the last few years, and she has been a most kind friend to me. She has got me more than one good post as teacher, and I have always felt a warm admiration for her. She is, beyond doubt, the most unselfish woman I ever met."

I shook my head.

"You will not get me to alter my opinion of her," continued Helen. "Think of her kindness in calling to see me to-day. She drove here this morning just because she happened to see my uncle, Petro de Castro, yesterday. She has known him, too, for some time. She had a talk with him about me, and he told her all about the strange will. She was immensely interested, and said that it was imperative for me to investigate the matter myself. She spoke in the most sensible way, and said finally that she would not leave me until I had promised to go to Portugal to visit the castle, and in my own person to unearth the mystery. I promised her and felt she was right. I am keeping my word."

When Helen had done speaking I remained silent. I could scarcely describe the strange sensation which visited me. Was it possible that the fear which I had seen so strongly depicted on De Castro's face was caused by Madame Sara? Was the mystery in the old Portuguese castle also connected with this terrible woman? If so, what dreadful revelations might not be before us! Helen was not the first innocent girl who believed in Madame, and not the first whose life was threatened.

"Why don't you speak, Mr. Druce?" she asked me at last. "What are you thinking of?"

"I would rather not say what I am thinking of," I answered; "but I am very glad of one thing, and that is that I am going with you."

"You are my kindest, best friend," she said; "and now I will tell you one thing more. Madame said that the fact of your being one of the party put all danger out of the case so far as I was concerned, for she knew you to be the cleverest man she ever met."

"Ah!" I replied, slowly, "there is a cleverer man than I, and his name is Eric Vandeleur. Did she happen to speak of him?"

"No. Who is he? I have never heard of him."

"I will tell you some day," I replied, "but not now."

I rose, bade her a hasty good-bye, and went straight to Vandeleur's rooms.

Whatever happened, I had made up my mind to consult him in the matter. He was out when I called, but I left a note, and he came round to my place in the course of the evening.

In less than a quarter of an hour I put him in possession of all the facts. He received my story in silence.

"Well!" I cried at last. "What do you think?"

"There is but one conclusion, Druce," was his reply. "There is a motive in this mystery—method in this madness. Madame is mixed up in it. That being the case, anything supernatural is out of the question. I am sorry Miss Sherwood is going to Lisbon, but the fact that you are going too may be her protection. Beyond doubt her life is in danger. Well, you must do your best, and forewarned is forearmed. I should like to go with you, but I cannot. Perhaps I may do more good here watching the arch-fiend who is pulling the strings."

De Castro took the information quietly that his niece was about to accompany us.

"Women are strange creatures," he said. "Who would suppose that a delicate girl would subject herself to the nervous terrors she must undergo in the castle? Well, let her come—it may be best, and my friend, the lady about whom I spoke to you, recommended it."

"You mean Madame Sara?" I said.

"Ah!" he answered, with a start. "Do you know her?"

"Slightly," I replied, in a guarded tone. Then I turned the conversation.

Our journey took place without adventure, and when we got to Lisbon we put up at Durrand's Hotel.

On the afternoon of that same day we went to interview Manuel Sousa, the lawyer who had charge of Mr. Sherwood's affairs. His office was in the Rue do Rio Janeiro. He was a short, bright-eyed little man, having every appearance of honesty and ability. He received us affably and looked with much interest at Helen Sherwood, whose calm, brave face and English appearance impressed him favourably.

"So you have come all this long way, Senhora," he said, "to investigate the mystery of your poor father's death? Be assured I will do everything in my power to help you. And now you would all like to see the documents and papers. Here they are at your service."

He opened a tin box and lifted out a pile of papers. Helen went up to one of the windows.

"I don't understand Portuguese," she said. "You will examine them for me, won't you, Uncle Petro, and you also, Mr. Druce?"

I had a sufficient knowledge of Portuguese to be able to read the will, and I quickly discovered that De Castro's account of it was quite correct.

"Is it your intention to go to Castello Mondego?" asked the lawyer, when our interview was coming to an end.

"I can answer for myself that I intend to go," I replied.

"It will give me great pleasure to take Mr. Druce to that romantic spot," said De Castro.

"And I go with you," cried Helen.

"My dear, dear young lady," said the lawyer, a flicker of concern crossing his bright eyes, "is that necessary? You will find the castle very lonely and not prepared for the reception of a lady."

"Even so, I have come all this long way to visit it," replied Helen. "I go with my friend, Mr. Druce, and with my uncle, and so far as I am concerned the sooner we get there the better."

The lawyer held up his hands.

"I wouldn't sleep in that place," he exclaimed, "for twenty contos of reis."[1]

"Then you really believe in the apparition?" I said. "You think it is supernatural?"

He involuntarily crossed himself.

"The tale is an old one," he said. "It has been known for a hundred years that the castle is haunted by a monk who was treacherously murdered there. That is the reason, Miss Sherwood, why your father got it so cheap."

"Supernatural or not, I must get to the bottom of the thing," she said, in a low voice.

De Castro jumped up, an impatient expression crossing his face.

"If you don't want me for the present, Druce," he said, "I have some business of my own that I wish to attend to."

He left the office, and Helen and I were about to follow him when Senhor Sousa suddenly addressed me.

"By the way, Mr. Druce, I am given to understand that you are from the Solvency Inquiry Agency of London. I know that great business well; I presume, therefore, that matters of much interest depend upon this inquiry?"

"The interests are great," I replied, "but are in no way connected with my business. My motive in coming here is due to friendship. This young lady is engaged to be married to a special friend of mine, and I have known her personally from her childhood. If we can clear up the present mystery, Helen Sherwood's marriage can take place at once. If, on the other hand, that terror which hangs over Castello Mondego is so overpowering that Miss Sherwood cannot make up her mind to live there, a long separation awaits the young pair. I have answered your question, Senhor Sousa; will you, on your part, answer mine?"

"Certainly," he replied. His face looked keenly interested, and from time to time he glanced from Helen to me.

"Are you aware of the existence of any motive which would induce someone to personate the apparition and so bring about Mr. Sherwood's death?"

"I know of no such motive, my dear sir. Senhor de Castro will come into ten thousand pounds provided, and only provided, Miss Sherwood takes possession of the property. He is the one

---

1 Twenty million reis, or four thousand English pounds according to contemporary rates (see p. 166, note 1); a conto was a monetary unit equalling a million reis in Portuguese currency.

and only person who benefits under the will, except Miss Sherwood herself."

"We must, of course, exclude Senhor de Castro," I answered. "His conduct has been most honourable in the matter throughout; he might have been tempted to suppress the story of the ghost, which would have been to his obvious advantage. Is there no one else whom you can possibly suspect?"

"No one—absolutely no one."

"Very well; my course is clear. I have come here to get an explanation of the mystery. When it is explained Miss Sherwood will take possession of the castle."

"And should you fail, sir? Ghosts have a way of suppressing themselves when most earnestly desired to put in an appearance."

"I don't anticipate failure, Senhor Sousa, and I mean to go to the castle immediately."

"We are a superstitious race," he replied, "and I would not go there for any money you liked to offer me."

"I am an Englishman, and this lady is English on her father's side. We do not easily abandon a problem when we set to work to solve it."

"What do you think of it all?" asked Helen of me, when we found ourselves soon afterwards in the quaint, old-world streets.

"Think!" I answered. "Our course is clear. We have got to discover the motive. There must be a motive. There was someone who had a grudge against the old man, and who wished to terrify him out of the world. As to believing that the apparition is supernatural, I decline even to allow myself to consider it."

"Heaven grant that you may be right," she answered; "but I must say a strange and most unaccountable terror oppresses me whenever I conjure up that ghastly face."

"And yet you have the courage to go to the castle!"

"It is a case of duty, not of courage, Mr. Druce."

For the rest of that day I thought over the whole problem, looking at it from every point of view, trying to gaze at it with fresh eyes, endeavouring to discover the indiscoverable—the motive. There must be a motive. We should find it at the castle. We would go there on the morrow. But, no; undue haste was unnecessary. It might be well for me, helped as I should be by my own agency, a branch of which was to be found in Lisbon, to discover amongst the late Mr. Sherwood's acquaintances, friends, or relatives the motive that I wanted. My agents set to work for me, but though they did their utmost no discovery of the least value was found, and at the end of a week I told De Castro and Helen that I was ready to start.

"We will go early to-morrow morning," I said. "You must make all your preparations, Helen. It will take us the day to reach Castello Mondego. I hope that our work may be completed there, and that we may be back again in Lisbon within the week."

Helen's face lit up with a smile of genuine delight.

"The inaction of the last week has been terribly trying," she said. "But now that we are really going to get near the thing I feel quite cheerful."

"Your courage fills me with admiration," I could not help saying, and then I went out to make certain purchases. Amongst these were three revolvers—one for Helen, one for De Castro, and one for myself.

Afterwards I had an interview with Sousa, and took him as far as I could into my confidence.

"The danger of the supernatural is not worth considering," I said, "but the danger of treachery, of unknown motives, is considerable. I do not deny this fact for a moment. In case you get no tidings of us, come yourself or send some one to the castle within a week."

"This letter came for you by the last post," said Sousa, and he handed me one from Vandeleur.

I opened it and read as follows:—

"I met Madame Sara a week ago at the house of a friend. I spoke to her about Castello Mondego. She admitted that she was interested in it, that she knew Miss Sherwood, and hoped when she had taken possession to visit her in that romantic spot. I inquired further if she was aware of the contents of the strange will. She said she had heard of it. Her manner was perfectly frank, but I saw that she was uneasy. She took the first opportunity of leaving the house, and on making inquiries I hear that she left London by the first train this morning, *en route* for the Continent. These facts may mean a great deal, and I should advise you to be more than ever on your guard."

I put the letter into my pocket, got Sousa to promise all that was necessary, and went away.

At an early hour the following morning we left Rocio Station for Coimbra, and it was nearly seven in the evening when we finally came to the end of our railway journey and entered a light wagonette drawn by two powerful bay stallions for our twenty-mile drive to the castle.

The scenery as we approached the spurs of the Estrella was magnificent beyond description, and as I gazed up at the great peaks, now bathed in the purples and golds of the sunset, the magic and mystery of our strange mission became tenfold intensified. Presently the steep ascent began along a winding road between high walls that shut out our view, and by the time we reached the castle it was too dark to form any idea of its special features.

De Castro had already sent word of our probable arrival, and when we rang the bell at the old castle a phlegmatic-looking man opened the door for us.

"Ah, Gonsalves," cried De Castro, "here we are! I trust you have provided comfortable beds and a good meal, for we are all as hungry as hawks."

The old man shrugged his shoulders, raised his beetle-brows a trifle, and fixed his eyes on Helen with some astonishment. He muttered, in a Portuguese dialect which I did not in the least comprehend, something to De Castro, who professed himself satisfied. Then he said something further, and I noticed the face of my Portuguese friend turn pale.

"Gonsalves saw the spectre three nights ago," he remarked, turning to me. "It was leaning as usual out of one of the windows of the north-west turret. But, come; we must not terrify ourselves the moment we enter your future home, Niece Helen. You are doubtless hungry. Shall we go to the banqueting-hall?"

The supper prepared for us was not appetizing, consisting of some miserable goat-chops, and in the great hall, dimly lighted by a few candles in silver sconces, we could scarcely see each other's faces. As supper was coming to an end I made a suggestion.

"We have come here," I said, "on a serious matter. We propose to start an investigation of a very grave character. It is well known that ghosts prefer to reveal themselves to one man or woman alone, and not to a company. I propose, therefore, that we three should occupy rooms as far as possible each from the other in the castle, and that the windows of our three bedrooms should command the centre square."

De Castro shrugged his shoulders and a look of dismay spread for a moment over his face; but Helen fixed her great eyes on mine, her lips moved slightly as though she would speak, then she pulled herself together.

"You are right, Mr. Druce," she said. "Having come on this inquiry, we must fear nothing."

"Well, come at once, and we will choose our bedrooms. You as the lady shall have the first choice."

De Castro called Gonsalves, who appeared holding a lantern

in his hand. A few words were said to the man in his own dialect, and he led the way, going up many stone stairs, down many others, and at last he flung open a huge oak door and we found ourselves in a vast chamber with five windows, all mullioned[1] and sunk in deep recesses. On the floor was a heavy carpet. A four-post bedstead with velvet hangings was in a recess. The rest of the furniture was antique and massive, nearly black with age, but relieved by brass mountings, which, strange to say, were bright as though they had recently been rubbed.

"This was poor Sherwood's own bedroom," said De Castro. "Do you mind sleeping here?"

He turned to Helen.

"No, I should like it," she replied, emphatically.

"I am glad that this is your choice," he said, "for I don't believe, although I am a man and you are a woman, that I could myself endure this room. It was here I watched by his dead body. Ah, poor fellow, I loved him well."

"We won't talk of memories to-night," said Helen. "I am very tired, and I believe I shall sleep. Strange as it may sound, I am not afraid. Mr. Druce, where will you locate yourself? I should like, at least, to know what room you will be in."

I smiled at her. Her bravery astonished me. I selected a room at right angles to Helen's. Standing in one of her windows she could, if necessary, get a glimpse of me if I were to stand in one of mine.

De Castro chose a room equally far away from Helen's on the other side. We then both bade the girl good-night.

"I hate to leave her so far from help," I said, glancing at De Castro.

"Nothing will happen," he replied. "I can guarantee that. I am dead tired; the moment I lay my head on my pillow, ghost or no ghost, I shall sleep till morning."

He hurried off to his own room.

The chamber that I had selected was vast, lofty, and might have accommodated twenty people. I must have been more tired even than I knew, for I fell asleep when my head touched the pillow.

When I awoke it was dawn, and, eager to see my surroundings by the light of day, I sprang up, dressed, and went down to the courtyard. Three sides of this court were formed by the castle buildings, but along the fourth ran a low balustrade of stone. I sauntered towards it. I shall never forget the loveliness of the scene that met my eyes. I stood upon what was practically a ter-

1 A mullion is a vertical piece of wood, stone, or metal that divides the units or panes of a window.

race—a mere shelf on the scarping of rock on the side of a dizzy cliff that went down below me a sheer two thousand feet. The Mondego River ran with a swift rushing noise at the foot of the gorge, although at the height at which I stood it looked more like a thread of silver than anything else. Towering straight in front of me, solemnly up into the heavens, stood the great peak of the Serra da Estrella, from which in the rosy sunrise the morning clouds were rolling into gigantic white wreaths. Behind me was the great irregular pile of the castle, with its battlements, turrets, and cupolas, hoar and grey with the weight of centuries, but now transfigured and bathed in the golden light. I had just turned to glance at them when I saw De Castro approaching me.

"Surely," I said, "there never was such a beautiful place in the world before! We can never let it go out of the family. Helen shall live here."

De Castro came close to me; he took my arm, and pointed to a spot on the stone flags.

"On this very spot her father fell from the battlements above," he said, slowly.

I shuddered, and all pleasant thoughts were instantly dispelled by the memory of that hideous tragedy and the work we had still to do. It seemed impossible in this radiant, living sunlight to realize the horror that these walls had contained, and might still contain. At some of these very windows the ghastly face had appeared.

Helen, De Castro, and I spent the whole day exploring the castle. We went from dungeons to turrets, and made elaborate plans for alternate nightly vigils. One of the first things that I insisted on was that Gonsalves should not sleep in the castle at night. This was easily arranged, the old man having friends in the neighbouring village. Thus the only people in the castle after nightfall would be De Castro, Helen, and myself.

After we had locked old Gonsalves out and had raised the portcullis,[1] we again went the complete round of the entire place. Thus we ensured that no one else could be hiding in the precincts. Finally we placed across every entrance thin silken threads, which would be broken if anyone attempted to pass them.

Helen was extremely anxious that the night should be divided into three portions, and that she should share the vigils; but this both De Castro and I prohibited.

---

1 A heavy wooden or iron grating that can be raised or lowered to block a gateway in a fortress or similar structure.

"At least for to-night," I said. "Sleep soundly; trust the matter to us. Believe me, this will be best. All arrangements are made. Your uncle will patrol until one o'clock in the morning, then I will go on duty."

This plan was evidently most repugnant to her, and when De Castro left the room she came up and began to plead with me.

"I have a strange and overpowering sensation of terror," she said. "Fight as I will, I cannot get rid of it. I would much rather be up than in that terrible room. I slept last night because I was too weary to do anything else, but I am wakeful to-night, and I shall not close my eyes. Let me share your watch at least. Let us pace the courtyard side by side."

"No," I answered, "that would not do. If two of us are together the ghost, or whatever human being poses as the ghost, will not dare to put in an appearance. We must abide by our terrible mission, Helen; each must watch alone. You will go to bed now, like a good girl, and to-morrow night, if we have not then discovered anything, you will be allowed to take your share in the night watch."

"Very well," she answered.

She sighed impatiently, and after a moment she said:—

"I have a premonition that something will happen to-night. As a rule my premonitions come right."

I made no answer, but I could not help giving her a startled glance. It is one thing to be devoid of ghostly terrors when living in practical London, surrounded by the world and the ways of men, but it is another thing to be proof against the strange terror which visits all human beings more or less when they are alone, when it is night, when the heart beats low. Then we are apt to have distorted visions, our mental equilibrium is upset, and we fear we know not what.

Helen and I knew that there was something to fear, and as our eyes met we dared not speak of what was uppermost in our thoughts. I could not find De Castro, and presumed that he had taken up his watch without further ado. I therefore retired to my own room and prepared to sleep. But the wakefulness which had seized Helen was also mine, for when the Portuguese entered my bedroom at one o'clock I was wide awake.

"You have seen nothing?" I said to him.

"Nothing," he answered, cheerfully. "The moon is bright, the night is glorious. It is my opinion that the apparition will not appear."

"I will take the precaution to put this in my pocket," I said, and I took up my revolver, which was loaded.

As I stepped out into the courtyard I found that the brilliant moonlight had lit up the north-west wall and the turrets; but the sharp black shadow of the south wall lay diagonally across the yard. Absolute stillness reigned, broken only by the croaking of thousands of frogs from the valley below. I sat down on a stone bench by the balustrade and tried to analyze my feelings. For a time the cheerfulness which I had seen so marked on De Castro's face seemed to have communicated itself to me; my late fears vanished, I was not even nervous, I found it difficult to concentrate my thoughts on the object which had brought me so far from England. My mind wandered back to London and to my work there. But by degrees, as the chill stole over me and the stillness of night began to embrace me, I found myself glancing ever and again at those countless windows and deep embrasures, while a queer, overpowering tension began to be felt, and against my own will a terror, strange and humiliating, overpowered me. I knew that it was stronger than I, and, fight against it as I would, I could not overcome it. The instinctive dread of the unknown that is at the bottom of the bravest man's courage was over me. Each moment it increased, and I felt that if the hideous face were to appear at one of the windows I would not be answerable for my self-control. Suddenly, as I sat motionless, my eyes riveted on the windows of the old castle, I felt, or fancied I felt, that I was not alone. It seemed to me that a shadow moved down in the courtyard and close to me. I looked again; it was coming towards me. It was with difficulty I could suppress the scream which almost rose to my lips. The next instant I was glad that I had not lost my self-control, when the slim, cold hand of Helen Sherwood touched mine.

"Come," she said, softly.

She took my hand and, without a word, led me across the courtyard.

"Look up," she said.

I did look up, and then my heart seemed to stop and every muscle in my body grew rigid as though from extreme cold. At one of the first-floor windows in the north-west tower, there in the moonlight leant the apparition itself: a black, solemn figure—its arms crossed on the sill—a large, round face of waxy whiteness, features immobile and fixed in a hideous, unwinking stare right across the courtyard.

Fig. 16. "THERE IN THE MOONLIGHT LEANT THE APPARITION ITSELF."

My heart gave a stab of terror, then I remained absolutely rigid—I forgot the girl by my side in the wild beating of my pulse. It seemed to me that it must beat itself to death.

"Call my uncle," whispered Helen, and when I heard her voice I knew that the girl was more self-possessed than I was.

"Call him," she said again, "loudly—at once."

I shouted his name:—

"De Castro, De Castro; it is here!"

The figure vanished at my voice.

"Go," said Helen again. "Go; I will wait for you here. Follow it at once."

I rushed up the stairs towards the room where De Castro slept. I burst open his door. The room was empty. The next instant I heard his voice.

"I am here—here," he said. "Come at once—quick!"

In a moment I was at his side.

"This is the very room where it stood," I said.

I ran to the window and looked down. De Castro followed me. Helen had not moved. She was still gazing up—the moonlight fell full on her white face.

"You saw it too?" gasped De Castro.

"Yes," I said, "and so did Helen. It stood by this window."

"I was awake," he said, "and heard your shout. I rushed to my window; I saw the spectre distinctly, and followed it to this room. You swear you saw it? It was the face of the abbot."

My brain was working quickly, my courage was returning. The unfathomable terror of the night scene was leaving me. I took De Castro suddenly by both his arms and turned him round so that the moonlight should fall upon him.

"You and I are alone in this tower. Helen Sherwood is in the courtyard. There is not another living being in the whole castle. Now listen. There are only two possible explanations of what has just occurred. Either you are the spectre, or it is supernatural."

"I?" he cried. "Are you mad?"

"I well might be," I answered, bitterly. "But of this I am certain: you must prove to me whether you are the apparition or not. I make this suggestion now in order to clear you from all possible blame; I make it that we may have absolute evidence that could not be upset before the most searching tribunal. Will you now strip before me?—yes, before you leave the room, and prove that you have no mask hidden anywhere on you. If you do this I shall be satisfied. Pardon my insistence, but in a case like the present there must be no loophole."

"Of course, I understand you," he said. "I will remove my clothes."

In five minutes he had undressed and dressed again. There was no treachery on his part. There was no mask nor any possible means of his simulating that face on his person.

"There is no suspicion about you," I said, almost with bitterness. "By heavens, I wish there were. The awfulness of this thing will drive me mad. Look at that girl standing by herself in the courtyard. I must return to her. Think of the courage of a woman who would stand there alone."

He made no answer. I saw that he was shivering.

"Why do you tremble?" I said, suddenly.

"Because of the nameless fear," he replied. "Remember I saw her father—I saw him with the terror on him—he ran along the battlements; he threw himself over—he died. He was dashed to pieces on the very spot where she is standing. Get her to come in, Druce."

"I will go and speak to her," I said.

I went back to the courtyard. I rejoined Helen, and in a few words told her what had occurred.

"You must come in now," I said. "You will catch your death of cold standing here."

She smiled, a slow, enigmatic sort of smile.

"I have not given up the solution yet," she said, "nor do I mean to."

As she spoke she took her revolver from her belt, and I saw that she was strangely excited. Her manner showed intense excitement, but no fear.

"I suspect foul play," she said. "As I stood here and watched you and Uncle Petro talking to each other by that window I felt convinced—I am more than ever convinced——"

She broke off suddenly.

"Look!—oh, Heaven, look! What is that?"

She had scarcely uttered the words before the same face appeared at another window to the right. Helen gave a sharp cry, and the next instant she covered the awful face with her revolver and fired. A shrill scream rang out on the night air.

"It is human after all," said Helen; "I thought it was. Come."

She rushed up the winding stairs; I followed. The door of the room where we had seen the spectre was open. We both dashed in. Beneath the window lay a dark, huddled heap with the moonlight shining on it, and staring up with the same wide-open eyes was the face of the abbot. Just for a moment neither Helen nor I dared to approach it, but after a time we cautiously drew near the dark mass. The figure never moved. I ran forward and stretched out my hand. Closer and closer I bent until my hand touched the face. It was human flesh and was still warm.

"Helen," I said, turning to the girl, "go at once and find your uncle."

But I had scarcely uttered the words before Helen burst into a low, choking laugh—the most fearful laugh I had ever heard.

"Look, look!" she said.

For before our eyes the face tilted, foreshortened, and vanished. We were both gazing into the countenance of the man whom we knew as Petro de Castro. His face was bathed in blood and convulsed with pain. I lit the lantern, and as I once more approached I saw, lying on the ground by his side, something hairy which for an instant I did not recognise. The next moment I saw what it was—it explained everything. It was a wig. I bent still nearer, and the whole horrible deception became plain as daylight. For, painted upon the back of the man's perfectly bald head, painted with the most consummate skill, giving the startling illusion of depth and relief, and all the hideous expression that had terrified one man at least out of the world, was the face of the abbot. The wig had completely covered it, and so skilfully was it made that the keenest observer would never have suspected it was one, it being itself slightly bald in order to add to the deception.

There in that dim, bare room, in broken sentences, in a voice that failed as his life passed, De Castro faltered out the story of his sin.

"Yes," he said, "I have tried to deceive you, and Gonsalves aided me. I was mad to risk one more appearance. Bend nearer, both of you; I am dying. Listen.

"Upon this estate, not a league across the valley, I found six months ago alluvial gold in great quantities in the bed of the gully. In the 'Bibliotheca Publica'[1] in Lisbon I had years before got accounts of mines worked by the Phoenicians, and was firmly persuaded that some of the gold still remained. I found it, and to get the full benefit of it I devised the ghastly scheme which you have just discovered. I knew that the castle was supposed to be haunted by the face of an old monk. Sherwood with all his peculiarities was superstitious. Very gradually I worked upon his fears, and then, when I thought the time ripe for my experiment, personated the apparition. It was I who flung him from the battlements with my own hand. I knew that the terms of the will would divert all suspicion from me, and had not your shot, Helen, been so true you would never have come here to live. Well, you have avenged your father and saved yourself at the same time. You will find in the safe in a corner of the banqueting-hall plans and maps of the exact spot where the gold is to be found. I could have worked there for years unsuspected. It is true that I should have lost ten thousand pounds, but I should have gained five times the amount. Between four and five months ago I went to see a special friend of mine in London. She is a woman who stands alone as one of the greatest criminals of her day. She promised at once to aid me, and she suggested, devised, and executed the whole scheme. She made the wig herself, with its strangely-bald

1 Public library.

appearance so deceptive to the ordinary eye, and she painted the awful face on my bald skull. When you searched me just now you suspected a mask, but I was safe from your detection. To remove or replace the wig was the work of an instant. The woman who had done all this was to share my spoils."

"Her name?" I cried.

"Sara, the Great, the Invincible," he murmured.

As he spoke the words he died.

L.T. Meade and Robert Eustace, *The Sorceress of the Strand*, *Strand Magazine* 25 (January–June 1903).

IV. —THE TALK OF THE TOWN. [67–80]

There is such a thing as being haunted by an idea or by a personality. About this time Vandeleur and I began to have nightmares with regard to Madame Sara. She visited us in our dreams, and in our waking dreams she was also our companion. We suspected her unseen influence on all occasions. We dreaded to see her visible presence in the street, in the Park, at the play—in short, wherever we went. This sort of thing was bad for both of us. It began to get on our nerves. It takes a great deal to get on the iron nerves of a man like Vandeleur; nevertheless, I began to think that they were seriously shaken when I received, on a certain afternoon in late October, the following note:—

"My Dear Druce,—There are fresh developments in the grand hunt. Come and dine with me to-morrow evening to meet Professor Piozzi. New problems are on foot."

The grand hunt could, of course, only mean one thing. What was up now? What in the name of fortune had Professor Piozzi, the greatest and youngest scientist of the day, to do with Madame Sara? But the chance of meeting him was a strong inducement to accept Vandeleur's invitation. He was our greatest experimental chemist. Six months ago his name had been on everyone's lips as the discoverer of a new artificial lighting agent which, if commercially feasible, would take the place of all other means hitherto used.

Professor Piozzi was not yet thirty years of age. He was an Italian by birth, but spoke English as well as though it were his native tongue.

At the appointed hour I found Vandeleur standing by his hearth. A table in a distant recess was laid for dinner. He greeted me with a gleam of pleasure in his eyes.

"What is the new problem?" I asked. "It goes without saying that it has to do with Madame Sara."

"I am glad you were able to come before Piozzi put in an appearance," was Vandeleur's grave answer.

He paused for an instant, and then he burst out with vehemence:—

"I owe Sara a debt of gratitude. Hunting her as a recreation is as good as hunting a man-eating tiger. I am getting at her now by watching the movements of her victim."

"Who is the victim?" I interrupted.

"No less a person than Professor Piozzi."

"Impossible," I answered.

"Fact, all the same," he replied. "The Professor, notwithstanding his genius, is in many ways credulous, unsuspicious, and easily imposed upon."

"Nevertheless, I fail to understand," I said.

"Have you ever heard of the subtle power of love?"

As Vandeleur spoke he stared hard at me, then burst into an uneasy laugh.

"The Professor is in love," he said. "Madame's last move is truly prompted by genius. She has taken to exploiting one of the most extraordinary-looking girls who have electrified society for many a day. It isn't her mere beauty that draws everyone to Donna Marta; it is her peculiarity. She has all the ways of an unconscious syren,[1] for never was anyone less self-conscious or more apparently indifferent to admiration."

"I have not heard of her," I said.

"Then you have allowed the talk of the town to slip past you, Druce," was Vandeleur's answer. "Donna Marta is the talk of the town. No one knows where she has sprung from; no one can confidently assert that this country or the other has had the honour of her nationality. She belongs to Madame Sara; she accompanies her wherever she goes, and Professor Piozzi is the victim."

"Are you sure?" I asked.

"Certain. He follows them about like a shadow. Madame is keeping more or less in the background for the present. Donna Marta is the lure. We shall next hear of an engagement between our young friend and this girl, whose antecedents no one knows anything about. Madame has an object, of course. She means mischief."

---

1 A dangerously fascinating woman. In Greek mythology, syrens (sirens) were fantastic creatures (half-women, half-birds) whose enchanting songs lured unwary sailors to their deaths.

It was my custom never to interrupt Vandeleur when he was explaining one of his theories, so I sat back in my chair and allowed him to proceed without comment on my part.

"At the present moment," he continued, "I happen to know that the Professor has run to earth another of his amazing discoveries in the carbon compounds. No one but himself knows what it is as yet, not even his assistants. Next week he is going to explode the bomb-shell in the scientific world at a lecture at the Royal Institution. Everyone will flock there on the tip-toe of expectation and curiosity. The thing is at present a dead secret, and the title of the lecture not even mentioned. He means to electrify the world. It is his little amusement to do this, as he did the Ethylene light affair. The man is, of course, a phenomenon, a genius, probably the most brilliant of our times. He is absolutely unsuspicious and absolutely unworldly. I am not going to see him ruin himself if I can help it."

"I perceive that you are in earnest," I said; "but how are you to prevent a man who is his own master from adopting his own methods, even in the subtle cause of love? Supposing your young Professor loves Donna Marta, how are you to stop him?"

"Time will prove how," he remarked; "but stop him I will."

The bell whirred, and the next moment Professor Piozzi entered. I looked at him with keen interest. From his photographs, reproduced freely in the illustrated papers, I had expected to see a young and good-looking man, with a keen, intelligent face; but I was scarcely prepared for his juvenile appearance. He was tall in figure, well made, somewhat slender; his hair was of a fair flaxen shade; his eyes were wide open and of a clear blue. He had a massive forehead, dark eyebrows, and a clean-shaven face. His whole appearance was that of an ordinary, good-looking, everyday sort of young man, and I examined his features with extreme curiosity, endeavouring to detect anywhere a sign of genius. I could not do so. The Professor's whole appearance was everyday; not a doubt of it. He was well dressed and had easy, courteous, manners, and upon a finger of his left hand there gleamed a ring, a Royal gift from the King of his native land.

We sat down to dinner, and the conversation was light, pleasant, and sufficiently witty to cause the moments to fly. No one knew better than Vandeleur how to make a man feel at home in his own house, and I could see that Piozzi was enjoying himself in a boyish way.

It was not until the meal was nearly over that the Professor caused us both to start, and listen with extreme attention. He began to talk of Madame Sara. He spoke of her with enthusiasm. She was the cleverest woman in London, and, with one exception, the most beautiful. Her scientific attainments were marvellous. He considered himself extremely lucky to have made her acquaintance.

"The sort of knowledge you allude to," replied Vandeleur, in a very grave tone, "that scientific knowledge which Madame possesses, and which is not a smattering, but a real thing, makes a woman at times—dangerous."

"I do not follow you," replied the Professor, knitting his brows. "Madame is the reverse of dangerous; she would help a fellow at a pinch. She is as good as she is beautiful."

Vandeleur made no reply. I was about to speak, but I saw by his manner that he would rather turn the conversation.

Once more we chatted on less exciting topics, and it was not until the servants had withdrawn that Vandeleur proceeded to unfold the real business of the evening.

"So you are going to astonish us all next week, Professor, at the Royal Institution? Is it true that you, and you alone, possess the key of the discourse that you are to give us?"

"Quite true," he replied, with a smile. "I cannot help having the dramatic instincts of my race. I love an artistic effect, and I think I can guarantee you English chemists a little thrill on Saturday week. My paper was ready a month ago, and since finishing it I have been having a pleasant time. Until a month ago your London was more or less a closed book to me. Now, Madame Sara and her young companion, Donna Marta, have been taking me round. I have enjoyed myself, not a doubt of it."

He leant back in his chair and smiled.

"That woman does plan things in a most delightful manner," he continued, "and whether she entertains in her own wonderful reception-rooms at the back of her shop in the Strand, or whether I meet her at the houses of mutual friends, or at the play, or the opera, she is always bright, vivacious, charming. Donna Marta, of course, adds her share to the delights. Yes, it is all happiness," continued the young Professor, rubbing his hands together in a boyish manner. "You English," he added, fixing his bright blue eyes on Vandeleur's saturnine face, "are so dull, so—I might add—*triste*.[1] And yet," he added, quickly, "you have your charm. Oh, undoubtedly yes. Your sincerity is so marvellous, so—I ought to add—refreshing. One can rely on it. But Madame has

1 Sad, melancholy (French).

also the sincere air, and yet to her are given the brightness and vivacity which come from living under bluer skies than yours."

The Professor's face was flushed; he looked from Vandeleur to me with eagerness. Vandeleur drew his chair a trifle closer. Then, without warning, as though he could not help himself, he sprang to his feet.

"Professor Piozzi," he said, "you have given our nation, perhaps unwittingly, a rare and valuable tribute. You have just spoken of our sincerity. I trust that we *are* sincere, and I trust also that, so long as England remains England, an Englishman's word will be his bond. The best inheritance an Englishman can receive from his forefathers is the power on all occasions to speak the truth. You are my guest to-night. I have the greatest respect for you; I admire your genius as I never thought to admire the genius of any man. It is most painful to me to have to say a word that may seem discourteous to you, an honoured guest, but my heritage as an Englishman forces me to speak the truth. You know what I am—an official criminal agent of the police. I will be quite candid with you. My invitation to you to-night was not purely the disinterested one of enjoying the honour of your company, but also to give you a warning with regard to Madame Sara and the young girl who accompanies her into society. They are both dangerous. I speak with knowledge. It is true that the girl herself is in all probability only the tool; but the woman——! Professor, I have met that woman before; so has my friend Druce. Our acquaintance with her has not been agreeable. May I proceed?"

The Professor's face had now turned almost crimson; his blue eyes were starting from his head; he kept clenching and unclenching his right hand as though he could scarcely contain himself. Vandeleur's words, however, seemed to force him into an attitude of attention. He listened as though mesmerized.

My friend then proceeded to give a vivid sketch of some of the episodes which had fallen to our share in the life of Madame Sara. He spoke slowly, with great emphasis and precision. He stated his case as though he were addressing a jury in a court of justice, scoring point after point with brevity and brilliance. When at last he ceased to speak the Professor was silent for half a minute, then he rose with a jerk to his feet. He was trembling, and his eyes flashed fire.

"Mr. Vandeleur," he said, "we are acquaintances of only a year's standing; in that time we have had some pleasant interviews. Your business is not an attractive one, even when confined to its official precincts; but to introduce it into private affairs is not to be tolerated. You exceed the limits of propriety in dictating to me as to the choice of the list of my friends. Please understand that from that list I erase your name."

He bowed stiffly, and walking across the room took up his hat and coat and slammed the door behind him.

I glanced at Vandeleur in amazement. His eyes met mine.

"The man must have his fling," he said. "I did what I did for the best, and am not sorry. He is in love with the mysterious girl, who has been brought to England, doubtless, for the express purpose of working his ruin. We must find out all we can about her as quickly as possible. Poor young Professor, I should like to save him, and I will, too, if in the power of man. His powers of research must not be lost to the glories of the scientific world."

"You must admit, Vandeleur," I said, "that you were a trifle harsh in your dealings with him. Granted that he is in love with Donna Marta, can you expect him to take your warning tamely?"

Vandeleur was silent for a minute.

"I do not believe my severe words will do any harm in the long run," he said, then. "The man is a foreigner; he has not an Englishman's knack of keeping his temper under control. He will cool down presently and what I have said will return to him. They will come to him when he is talking to Donna Marta; when Madame Sara is throwing her spells over him. Yes, I am not sorry I have spoken."

"What do you suppose Madame is after?" I interrupted. "What can be her motive? It is not money, for the man is not well off, is he?"

"Not a thousand a year. Bah! and he might be a millionaire if he would only use his ideas commercially. It is the old story—one man finds the brains and a hundred others profit by them. He is a walking test-tube, and doesn't care a sou[1] who profits by his inventions."

"Then you think she is picking his brains?"

"Of course, and she will pick a plum, too, bang it off in England, scoop a million, and we have lost her."

"Good for society if we do lose her," I could not help remarking.

"By no means good for me," replied the detective. "I have staked my reputation on bringing this woman to book. She shall not escape."

1 A French coin worth very little.

Vandeleur and I sat and talked for some little time longer, then I left him and returned to my own rooms. I sat up a long time busy over several matters; but when I retired to rest it was not only to dream of Madame Sara, but of the fascinating young Donna Marta and the boyish-looking Professor.

I dined with Vandeleur on Wednesday evening, and little guessed then how soon events would hurry to a remarkable issue, in which I was to play a somewhat important part.

It is my custom to lunch at the Ship and Turtle, an hour that I always enjoy in the midst of my day's work, for I meet many old friends there, and our meal, as a rule, is a merry one. One of my most constant companions on these occasions is a man of the name of Samuel Pollak, the senior partner in the firm of Pollak and Harman, patent agents, Bishopsgate Street. Pollak is one of those breezy, good-natured individuals who make a pleasant impression wherever they go. He is stout of build and somewhat rubicund of face, an excellent man of business and a firm friend. I have liked him for years, and am always glad when he occupies the same table with me at lunch.

On the Friday following Vandeleur's dinner Pollak and I met as usual. I noticed on his entrance into the lunch-room a particularly merry and pleased expression on his face. He sat down and ordered a quart of the most expensive brand of champagne. He insisted on my joining him in a bumper[1] of the frothy wine, and after drinking his health I could not help exclaiming:—

"You seem pretty jolly this morning, Pollak. A successful flutter in Khakis?"

"Ha, ha, ha!" was the answer. "Better than a flutter, my boy. Certainties nowadays are what I am thinking of, and I have just bagged one, and a fat one."

"Capital. Tell me all about it," I answered. "What is the yarn, Pollak?"

He gave me a somewhat vague smile, which seemed to me to mingle a sort of contempt with amusement, and said, impressively:—

"A roaring commission, the biggest that has been in the market for the last ten years. Patent rights for every country on earth, and a hundred shares allotted gratis when the thing is floated. I tell you, Druce," he added, raising his voice, "if it comes off I retire with as near fifteen thousand a year as I want."

1 A large glass; full to the brim.

"You were born under a lucky star, there's no doubt of that," I answered, somewhat sharply, for Pollak's manner had never impressed me less favourably than it did this morning. He was evidently almost beside himself with excitement.

"I congratulate you, of course," I said, after a moment. "Ask me to the house-warming of your castle in Scotland, whenever that event comes off. But can't you give me a hint with regard to this magnificent affair? I am, as you know, a struggling pauper, and should like to have my share of the pickings if there are any at your disposal to give away."

"My lips are sealed," he answered at once. "I am sorry, for there is no one I should like better to help. But I think I am justified in telling you this—the City will hum when the news is out. It is immense, it is colossal, it is paralyzing."

"You excite my curiosity to a remarkable extent," I could not help saying. "Curiosity has a great deal to do with my trade, as you know."

He finished his glass of champagne and set it down. His eyes, as he fixed them on me, were full of laughter. I almost wondered whether he was amusing himself at my expense; but no, his next words were sane enough.

"There is another little matter I can inform you about, Druce, without breaking any confidence. I happen to know that the fortunate patentee is a friend of yours."

"A friend of mine?" I exclaimed. "An acquaintance, perhaps. I haven't three friends in the world."

"A great friend—an admirer, too," he went on.

"An admirer!" I repeated, staring across at him. "A devoted admirer! Who is he? Come, out with it, Pollak; don't keep me on tenter-hooks."

"Think over your list of admirers," he cried, tantalizingly.

"I will hazard a guess, then; but he isn't an admirer. Vandeleur," I said.

"Ha, ha!" he roared. "Better and better. She admires him, too, I believe."

"She!"

A strange thought seized me. I felt the high spirits which Pollak had infected me with depart as in a flash. I knew that in spite of every effort my face had altered in expression. Pollak gazed at me and said, in a tone of triumph:—

"I see that you guess. The cat is out of the bag."

He chuckled.

"Isn't it superb?" he added.

"Madame Sara!" I ejaculated, when I could find words.

He burst into a fresh roar of delight.

"There's no harm in your knowing that much," he said. "But what's up? You look queer."

The change in my demeanour must have astonished him. I sat almost motionless, staring into his face.

"Nothing," I answered, speaking as quietly as I could. "The admiration you have remarked upon is reciprocal. I am glad that she has done so well."

"She is particularly pleased," continued Pollak, "on account of her young *protégée*, the lovely Donna Marta. The young lady in question is to make a very good match—in a certain sense a brilliant one; and Madame wants to give her a wedding portion. Ah! there are few women so kind, so great, as Madame Sara. She has the wisdom of the ancients and some of their secrets, too."

Fig. 17. "AH! THERE ARE FEW WOMEN SO KIND, SO GREAT, AS MADAME SARA."

I made no reply. The usual thing had happened so far as my good-natured friend was concerned. He was dazzled by the beauty of his client, and had given himself away, a ready victim to her fascinations.

"I see," he added, "that you also are under her spells. Who wouldn't yield to the power of those eyes? The young lady, Donna Marta, is all very well, but give me Madame herself."

With these words he left me. Never was there a more prosperous or happier-looking man. Little did he guess the thoughts that were surging through my brain.

Without returning to my place of business I took a hansom and drove to Vandeleur's office. My heart was full of a nameless fear. Pollak had let out a great deal more than he had any intention of doing. So Donna Marta was engaged. Engaged to whom? Surely not to the poor, infatuated young Professor? Pollak had said that in some respects the proposed match was a brilliant one. That might be a fitting description of a marriage with the young Professor, whose fame was attracting the attention of the greatest scientists in Europe. He was poor, certainly—but then he held a secret. That secret might mean anything—it might even revolutionize the world. Did Madame mean by this subtle trap to lure it from him? It was more than probable. It would explain Pollak's excitement and his attitude. In fact, the scheme was worthy of her colossal brain.

As I entered Vandeleur's room I was surprised to see him pacing up and down with his coat off, his brows knitted in anxious thought. He was evidently in the thick of a problem, and one of no ordinary magnitude. On the table lay a number of beakers, retorts,[1] and test-tubes.

"Sit down," he said, roughly. "Glad you've come. See this?"

He held up a glass tube containing what appeared to be milk.

"Listen," he said. "You will see that my fears were justified with regard to Piozzi. Poor fellow, he is in the toils, if ever a man was. A hurried messenger came from his place to fetch me this morning. I guessed by his face that something serious had happened, and I went to Duke Street at once. I found the Professor in his bedroom, half dressed on his bed, cold, gasping, livid. He had breakfasted half an hour before. He murmured apologies for his treatment of me, but I cut him short and went straight to the case. I made a full investigation, and came to the conclusion that

---

1 Vessels with long downward-bent necks used for distilling liquids by heat.

it is a case of poisoning, the agent used being in all probability cocaine, or some allied alkaloid. By the aid of nitrate of amyl capsules I pulled him round, but was literally only just in time. When I entered the room it was touch and go with the poor fellow. I believe if he had not had immediate assistance he would have been dead in a few minutes. I saved his life. Now, Druce, we have to face a fact. There has been a deliberate attempt at murder on the part of someone. I have baffled the murderer in the moment of victory."

"Who would attempt his life?" I cried.

"Need you ask?" he answered, gravely.

Our eyes met. We were both silent.

"When I was with him this morning he was too bad for me to get any particulars whatever from him; so I know nothing of the motive or details; but I have discovered by means of a careful analysis that there has been introduced into the milk with which he was supplied some poisonous alkaloid of the erythroxylon group. Feeling pretty certain that the poison was conveyed through the food, I took away a portion of his breakfast—in particular I took some of the milk which stood in a jug on his breakfast-table. And here I have the result. I am going back there at once, and you had better come along."

Vandeleur had poured out his words in such a torrent of excitement that he had not noticed how unusual it was for me to visit him at this early hour in the afternoon. Now, however, it seemed to strike him, and he said, abruptly:—

"You look strange yourself. Surely you haven't come here on purpose? You can't possibly have heard of this thing yet?"

"No," I answered. "I have heard nothing. I have come on my own account, and on a pretty big matter too, and, what is more, it relates to our young Professor, unless I am much mistaken. I will tell you what I have to tell in the cab, Vandeleur; it will save time."

A hansom was summoned, and we were soon on our way to Duke Street. As we drove I told Vandeleur in a few words what had occurred between Pollak and myself. He listened with the intentness which always characterized him. He made not a single remark.

As we were entering the house, however, he turned to me and said, with brevity:—

"It is clear that she has tapped him. We must get from him what she knows. This may be a matter of millions."

On arriving at Piozzi's flat in Duke Street we were at once shown into his bedroom by his man-servant. Stretched upon the outside of the bed was the young Professor, wrapped in a loose dressing-gown. His face was ghastly pale, and there was a blue tinge observable round his mouth and under his eyes. He raised himself languidly as we entered.

"Better, I see. Capital!" said Vandeleur, in a cheerful tone.

A very slight colour came into the young man's face. He glanced at me almost in bewilderment.

"You know my friend Druce," said Vandeleur. "He is with me in this case, and has just brought me important information. Lie down again, Professor."

As he spoke he sat on the edge of the bed and laid his hand on the young man's arm.

"I am sorry to have to tell you, Mr. Piozzi, that this is a very serious case. A rapid qualitative analysis of what you took for breakfast has shown me that the milk which was supplied for your use has been poisoned. What the poison is I cannot say. It is very like cocaine in its reactions."

The sick man shuddered, and an expression of horror and amazement crossed his face.

"Who would want to take my life?" he said. "Poisoned milk! I confess I do not understand. The thing must have been accidental," he continued, feverishly, fixing his puzzled eyes on Vandeleur.

Vandeleur shook his head.

"There was no accident in this matter," he said, with emphasis. "It was design. Deadly, too. You would not have been alive now if I had not come to you in the nick of time. It is our duty, Professor, to go carefully into every circumstance in order to insure you against a further attempt on your life."

"But I do no one harm," he answered, irritably. "Who could wish to take my life from me? It is impossible. You are labouring under a wrong impression."

"We will let the motive rest for the present," replied Vandeleur. "That the attempt was made is certain. Our present object is to discover how the poison got into the milk. That is the question that must be answered, and before Druce and I leave this room. Who supplies you with milk, Professor Piozzi?"

Piozzi replied by a languid motion towards the bell.

"My man will tell you," he said. "I know nothing about the matter."

The servant was summoned, and his information was brief and to the point. The Professor's milk was served by the same milkman who supplied all the other members of the mansion.

"It is brought early in the morning, sir," said the man, "and left outside the door of each flat. The housekeeper opens the house door for the purpose. I take it in myself the first thing on rising."

"And the can remains outside your door with the house door open until you take it in?" said Vandeleur.

"Yes, sir, of course."

"Thank you," said Vandeleur. "That will do."

The man left the room.

"You see, Professor," remarked my friend, after the door had closed upon the servant, "how simple the matter is. Anyone could drop poison into the milk—that is, of course, what somebody did. These modern arrangements don't take crime into account when the criminal means business."

The Professor lay still, evidently thinking deeply. I noticed then, for the first time, that a look of age had crept over his face. It improved him, giving stability and power to features too juvenile for the mass of knowledge which that keen brain contained. His eyes were full of trouble; it was evident that his meditations were the reverse of satisfactory.

"I am the last man to pretend not to see when a self-evident fact stares me in the face," he said, at last. "There has been an attempt made to poison me. But by whom? Can you tell me that, Mr. Vandeleur?"

"I could give a very shrewd guess," replied Vandeleur; "but were I to name my suspicions you would be offended."

"Forgive me for my exhibition of rage the other night," he answered, quite humbly. "Speak your mind—I shall respect you whatever you say."

"In my mind's eye," said Vandeleur, slowly, "I see a woman who has before attempted the life of those whom she was pleased to call her friends."

The Professor started to his feet. Notwithstanding his vehement assertion that he would not give way to his emotions, he was trembling all over.

"You cannot mean Madame Sara—you will change your mind—I have something to confide. Between now and last Wednesday I have been affianced to Donna Marta. Yes, we are to marry, and soon. Madame is beside herself with bliss, and Donna Marta herself—— Ah, I have no words to speak what my feelings are with regard to her. Madame of all people would be the last to murder me," he added, wildly, "for she loves Donna Marta."

"I am deeply sorry, Professor, notwithstanding your words and the very important statement you have just made with regard to the young lady who lives with Madame Sara, to have to adhere to my opinion that there is a very deep-laid plot on foot, and that it menaces your life. I still believe that Madame, notwithstanding your word, is head and centre of that plot. Take my statement for what it is worth. It is, I can assure you, the only thing that I can say. And now I must ask you a few questions, and you must have patience with me, great patience, while you reply to them. I beg of you to tell me the truth absolutely and frankly."

"I will," answered the young man. "You move me strangely. I cannot help believing in you, although I hate myself for allowing even one suspicious thought to fall on her."

Vandeleur rose.

"Tell me, Mr. Piozzi," he said, quietly, "have you ever communicated to Madame Sara the nature of your chemical discoveries?"

"Never."

"Has she ever been here?"

"Oh, yes, many times. Last week she and Donna Marta were both here. I had a little reception for them. We enjoyed ourselves; she was delightful."

"You have several rooms in this flat, have you not, Professor?"

"Three reception-rooms," he answered, rather wearily.

"And you and Donna Marta were perhaps alone in one of those rooms while Madame Sara amused herself in another? Is that so?"

"It is," he answered, reddening. "Madame and Donna Marta remained after my other guests had gone. Madame went into my study. She said she would sit by the fire and rest."

"Do you leave your notes locked up or lying about?"

"Always locked up. It is true the notes for my coming lecture were on that occasion on my desk."

"Ah!" interrupted Vandeleur.

"No ordinary person could make anything of them," he continued; "and even," he added, "if Madame could have read them, it surely would not greatly matter that she should know my grand secret before the rest of the world."

"Piozzi," said Vandeleur, very gravely, "I must make another request of you. Whether Madame knows your secret or not I must know it, and at once. Don't hesitate, Professor; your life hangs in the balance. You must tell me that with which you mean to electrify the Royal Institution to-morrow week, now, now at once."

The Professor looked astonished, but Vandeleur was firm.

"I must know it," he said. "I hold myself responsible for your life. Druce," he added, turning to me, "perhaps you can get the Professor to see the necessity of what I ask. Will you tell him that story which you related to me in the cab?"

I did so without a moment's delay. My words were as brief as I could make them. I told him about my interview with Pollak, his excitement, his revelation of the fact that the patentee whose patent was to be secured in all countries all over the world was no less a person than Madame Sara herself. In short, to my infinite delight I managed to convey my suspicions to his mind. His whole attitude altered; he became excited, almost beside himself. His nervousness gave place to unexpected strength. He started to his feet and began to pace the room.

"Heavens!" he exclaimed more than once. "If indeed I have been befooled—made a dupe of—but no, it cannot be. Still, if it is, I will revenge myself on Madame to the last drop of my blood."

"For the present you must only confide in me," said Vandeleur, laying a restraining hand on the young man's arm. "And now for your secret—it is safe with Druce and myself; we must know it."

Piozzi calmed down as suddenly as he had given way to rage. He seated himself on a sofa and began in a quiet voice: "What I have to say is simply this."

Then in terse language he poured out for Vandeleur's benefit an account of some process, interlarded with formulae, equations, and symbols, absolutely beyond my comprehension.

Vandeleur sat and listened intently. Now and then he put a question, which was immediately answered. At last Piozzi had come to the end of his narrative.

"That is it," he said; "the whole thing in a nutshell."

"Upon my word," said Vandeleur, "it is very ingenious and plausible, and may turn out of immense benefit to the world; but at the present juncture I cannot see money in it, and money is what Madame wants and means to have. To be frank with you, Professor, I see no earthly reason in her wanting to patent what you have just told me. But is there nothing else? Are you certain?"

"Absolutely nothing," was his response.

"Well," said Vandeleur, "I am puzzled. I own it. I must think matters over."

He was interrupted by a loud exclamation from the young man.

"You are wrong after all, Mr. Vandeleur," he cried. "Madame

means to patent something else. Why should she not have a great idea in her head quite apart from me and mine? Ah, this relieves me—it makes me happy. True, someone has tried to murder me, but it is not Madame—it is not the lady whom Donna Marta loves."

His eyes blazed with delight. He laughed in feverish excitement.

After soothing him as best we could, and trying to get a half-promise that he would not see either Madame or the young lady until we met again, we left him.

As we were walking from the house Vandeleur turned to me and said:—

"I have been invited to a reception to-night at the house of our mutual friends the Lauderdales. I understand that both Madame and the young lady are to be present. Would you like to come with me? I am allowed to bring a friend."

I eagerly assented. We arranged when and where to meet, and were about to part when he suddenly exclaimed:—

"This is a difficult problem. I shall have no rest until I have solved it. Piozzi's discovery is ingenious and clever, but at present it is unworkable. I do not see daylight, but no loophole is to be despised that may give me what I want. Between now and our meeting this evening I will try to have an interview with Pollak. Give me his address."

I did so, and we parted.

We met again at a late hour that evening at the Lauderdales' beautiful house in Portland Place. Wit and beauty were to be found in the gay throng, also wisdom, and a fair sprinkling of some of the most brilliant brains in London. Men of note came face to face with one in every direction; but both Vandeleur and I were seeking one face, and one alone.

We found her at last, surrounded by a throng of admirers. Madame was looking her most brilliant and, I might add, her youngest self. She was dressed in dazzling white and silver, and whenever she moved light seemed to be reflected at every point. The brilliance of her golden hair was the only distinct colour about her. By her side stood Donna Marta, a tall, pale girl, almost too slender for absolute beauty. Her grace, however, was undeniable, and, although I have seen more lovely faces, this one had a singular power of attraction. When I looked at her once I wanted to look again, and when she slowly raised her luminous eyes and fixed them on my face I owned to a thrill of distinct gratification. I began to understand the possibility of Piozzi's giving himself up absolutely to her charms.

Her presence here to-night, in conjunction with Madame Sara, produced an effect which was as astonishing as it was rare. Each acted as a perfect foil to the other, each seemed to bring out the rare fascination of her companion.

Donna Marta glanced at me again; then I saw her bend towards Madame Sara and whisper something in her ear. A moment later, to my amazement, the great lady and the slender girl were by my side.

"Mr. Druce, this is an unexpected pleasure. May I introduce you to my young cousin, Donna Marta? Is your friend, Mr. Vandeleur, also here to-night?"

"He is; I will find him," I replied.

I darted away, returning in a moment with Vandeleur. He and Madame moved a few paces away and began to chat in pleasant tones, just as though they were the best friends in the world.

Meanwhile Donna Marta lingered near me. I began to talk on indifferent subjects, but she interrupted me abruptly.

"You are a friend of Professor Piozzi's?" she said, in a tentative voice. "Is he not present to-night?"

"No," I replied. It occurred to me that I would test her. "The Professor cannot be present, and I am sorry to have to give a grave reason for his absence, for doubtless Lady Lauderdale expected him to grace her reception."

"She did; he was to be one of the lions," she replied, bending her stately head, with its mass of blue-black hair.

"He is ill," I continued, raising my own eyes now and fixing them on her face.

She gazed at me without alarm and without confusion. Not the most remote emotion did she show, and yet she was engaged to the man.

"He was at death's door," I went on, almost savagely, "but he is better. For the present he is safe."

"I am sorry to hear of his illness," she answered then, softly. "I will—acquaint Madame. She also will be grieved."

The girl turned and glided away from me. I watched her as she went. The brief moment when she fascinated me had come to an end with that callous glance. But who was she? What did it all mean?

In the course of the evening Donna Marta again came up to my side.

"Mr. Druce," she said, abruptly, "you are Professor Piozzi's friend?"

"Certainly," I answered.

"Will you warn him from yourself—not from me—not on any account from me—to keep in the open on Saturday week? You must make the best of my words, for I cannot explain them. Tell the Professor, whatever he does, *to keep in the open*."

"Donna Marta!" called Madame Sara's voice.

The girl sprang away. Her face was like death; but as Madame Sara's eyes met hers I noticed a wave of crimson dye her face and neck.

On my way home I told Vandeleur of the strange words used by Donna Marta. He shrugged his shoulders.

"It is my firm opinion," he said, "that the unfortunate girl moves and speaks in a state of trance. Madame has mesmerized her, I have not a doubt of it."

"You may be right," I said, eagerly. "And the state of trance may have been removed when she said those words to me. That would make a possible solution. But what can she mean by asking the Professor to keep in the open?"

"The girl evidently warns us against Madame Sara," he said, briefly, "and circumstances, all circumstances, seem to point to the same deadly danger. Where Madame goes Death walks abroad. What is to be done? But there, Druce," he added, with petulance, "the Professor's life is not my affair. I must sleep, or I shall lose my senses. Good-night, good-night."

The next few days passed without any special occurrence of interest. I neither saw nor heard anything of Madame and her strange young guest, neither did I hear of the Professor nor did I see Vandeleur. I called on him once, but he was out, and the servant informed me that his master was particularly busy, and in consequence was hardly ever at home.

At last the day dawned which was to see Professor Piozzi in the moment of his glory. I had a line from Vandeleur by the first post, telling me that he had secured tickets for himself and for me for the lecture at the Royal Institution that night. Soon afterwards I found myself at Vandeleur's house. His servant opened the door, and with a look of relief asked me to go up to the sitting-room without delay. I was expected, then, or at least I was wished for.

The first person I saw when I entered the room was my old friend Samuel Pollak, and gazing round in some amazement I also perceived the young Professor, buried in the depths of an arm-chair, his face ghastly and his arm in a sling.

"Ah, Druce," said Vandeleur, "you are heartily welcome. You have come in the nick of time. I was just about to clear up this extraordinary affair in the presence of Mr. Pollak and the Professor. Your advent on the scene makes my audience complete. Now, gentlemen, pray listen. The patent, Mr. Pollak, which you are negotiating for Madame Sara is, as you imagine, a secret. I don't ask you to tell me what it is, for I propose to tell you. But, first, are your operations for securing patent rights complete?"

"I regret to say they are not, sir," replied Pollak.

"I thought as much, and may add that I hoped as much. Now, listen. The key to the specification of the patents is nothing more or less than the astounding discovery of the *chemical synthesis of albuminoids*. In other words, a means of manufacturing artificial foods in a manner which has long been sought by scientific men, but which has so far eluded their researches."

An exclamation of astonishment broke from Pollak, telling us that Vandeleur's guess was correct.

"The other day when you spoke to me, Professor," continued Vandeleur, fixing his eyes on the face of the younger man, "interesting as I thought your discovery, I could not apply it to commercial purposes, nor see why it was so necessary to secure patent rights for its protection. I felt certain, however, that there was such a solution, and it came to me in the small hours this morning. You did not grasp the deduction from your most interesting discovery. I take it to my credit that I have done so, and beyond doubt Madame, whether she be your friend or your foe, perceived the huge financial benefit which would accrue to those who could hold patent rights. It goes without saying that she read your notes, and at a glance saw what you have not grasped at all, and what I have taken days to discover. The attempt on your life is now explained, as is also the queer cab accident in Regent Street[1] which you have just met with. Madame's object is either to murder you or to incapacitate you from giving your lecture to-night. She knows, of course, that when once you publicly proclaim your discovery a clever brain on the watch may deduce the financial value of it. Thus she sees the possibility of being forestalled or rivalled, for Mr. Pollak has just stated that the patent rights are not yet secured. Madame has therefore determined that your lecture shall not take place, nor your idea be given to the world, until she has secured herself by patent rights beyond dispute. I shall take care to guard you, Professor, until you appear before the Royal Society at eight o'clock to-night. And I conclude, Mr. Pollak, that you, knowing at last the true facts of the case, will at

1 A major shopping street for upscale merchandise in London's West End.

once cancel all negotiations with Madame Sara. I presume, sir," he added, bowing to Piozzi, "that you will like him to negotiate the business in your name? A cursory inspection of it must mean an enormous fortune for you, for beyond doubt the chemical synthesis of aliments would prove the solution of many of the difficulties that now present themselves to the human race."

The Professor sat quite silent for a minute or two, then he rose and said, slowly:—

"I follow you, Mr. Vandeleur, and I see that your deduction is the right one as regards the financial importance of my discovery. How I did not see it sooner myself puzzles me. As to Madame Sara, I would rather not mention her name at present."

Vandeleur made no reply to this, and a moment later Pollak took his leave. I rose also to go.

"Come back and dine with us, Druce," said Vandeleur. "If Professor Piozzi declines to talk of Madame Sara, neither will I mention her name. We shall soon know the best or the worst."

The rest of the day passed without adventure. The dinner at Vandeleur's turned out somewhat dull. We were none of us in good spirits, and, without owning it, we were all anxious. As to the Professor, he scarcely spoke a word and hardly touched his food.

About ten minutes to eight o'clock we found ourselves at the Royal Institution. Several leading scientists were there to welcome the distinguished lecturer. I peeped from behind into the hall. It was packed from front to back. The platform was tastefully decorated with palms; one of peculiar grace and size drooped its finger-like fronds over the table at which Piozzi was to stand. As I saw it I heard as distinctly as though the words were again being spoken:—

"Tell him whatever he does to keep in the open. Tell him—from yourself."

I had not done so. A momentary impulse seized me. I would go to Piozzi and ask him to have his table and chair moved to the centre of the platform. Then I reflected that such a proceeding would cause amazement, and that the Professor would probably refuse to comply. Again I looked into the hall, and now I gave a very visible start; for in the front row, in brilliant evening dress, sat Madame Sara and her young cousin. Donna Marta's face, usually so pale, was now relieved by a crimson glow on each cheek. This unusual colour brought out her beauty to a dazzling degree. I noticed further that her eyes had a filmy expression in them. I remembered Vandeleur's words. Beyond doubt Madame had mesmerized her victim. As to what it all meant, I will own that my brain was in a whirl.

A few minutes passed, and then, amid a thunder of applause, Piozzi, pale as ivory, stepped on to the platform and walked straight to the table over which hung the graceful palm.

After a few words in which the young Professor was introduced by the President of the evening, the lecture about which so much curiosity had been felt began. Vandeleur and I stood side by side near one of the entrance doors. From where we stood we could see Piozzi well. Vandeleur's face was rigid as steel.

A quarter of an hour passed, and sentence by sentence, word by word, the young man led up to his crucial point—his great announcement.

"Look!" whispered Vandeleur, grasping my wrist. "What in the world is the matter with him?"

The Professor was still speaking, but his words came in thick and indistinct sentences. Suddenly he took hold of the table with both hands and began to sway to and fro. The next moment he ceased speaking, reeled, made a lunge forward, and, with a loud crash, fell senseless upon the floor. The scene of consternation was indescribable. Vandeleur and I both sprang forward. The unconscious man was taken into one of the ante-rooms, and by the immediate application of restoratives and a great draught of fresh air, caused by the open windows, he came gradually to himself. But that he was still very ill was evident; his brain was confused; he could scarcely speak except in gasps. A doctor who was present offered to see him to his house. We carried him to the first cab we could find. I whispered in his ear that I would call upon him later in the evening, and then I returned to the hall.

Vandeleur was waiting for me. I felt his grip on my arm.

"Come right up on to the platform," he said.

The excitement in his voice was only exceeded by the look on his face. Most of the crowd had dispersed, knowing well that there would be no further lecture that night, but a few people still lingered on the scene. I looked in vain for Madame Sara and Donna Marta; they were neither of them visible.

"You see this," said Vandeleur, pointing to the great palm that towered over the table at which Piozzi had stood. "And you see this," he repeated, seizing one of the branches and shaking it.

The long, tapering, green leaves rattled together with an odd metallic sound.

"Look here!" said Vandeleur, and he pointed to the fine tips of one of the leaves. "This plant never grew. It is made—it is an artificial imitation of the most surprising skill and workmanship. The pot in which it stands has certainly earth at the top"—he swept away a handful—"but there below is a receptacle which is generating carbon monoxide gas."

He bent and broke one of the branches.

"Hollow, you see. Those are the tubes to convey the gas to the leaves, at the extremity of each of which is an orifice. Professor Piozzi was standing beneath a veritable shower-bath of that gas, which is odourless and colourless, and brings insensibility and death. It overwhelmed him, as you saw, and it was impossible for him to finish his lecture. Only one human being could have planned and executed such a contrivance. If we can trace it to her, she spends the night in Bow Street."[1]

Our movements were rapid. The plant was taken to Vandeleur's house. The florist who had supplied the decorations was interviewed. He expressed himself astounded. He denied all complicity—the palm was certainly none of his; he could not tell how it had got into the hall. He had come himself to see if the decorations were carried out according to his directions, and had noticed the palm and remarked on its grace. Someone had said that a lady had brought it, but he really knew nothing definite about it.

Notwithstanding all our inquiries, neither did we ever find out how that palm got mixed up with the others.

We learnt afterwards that Donna Marta left London for the Continent that very night. What her subsequent movements were we could never ascertain. Doubtless, having acted her part in the brief rôle assigned to her, Madame would drop her from her life as she did most of her other victims.

There was, however, one satisfaction—the plot, on which so much hung, had failed. Madame was not successful. Professor Piozzi, his eyes opened at last with regard to this woman, took out his patent without an hour's unnecessary delay.

V. —THE BLOODSTONE. [198–212]

On a certain bright spring morning Violet Sale married Sir John Bouverie, and six months later, when autumn was fast developing into a somewhat rigorous winter, I received an invitation to

1 Associated with policing and law enforcement since the eighteenth century; one of England's most famous magistrates' courts and London's earliest police forces were located in Bow Street.

spend a week or fortnight at their beautiful place, Greylands, in the neighbourhood of Potter's Bar.[1] Violet at the time of her marriage was only nineteen years of age. She and her brother Hubert were my special friends. They were by many years my juniors, but their mother at her death had asked me to show them friendship and to advise them in any troubles that might arise in the circumstances of their lives. They were both charming young people, and having been left complete control of quite a large property were in a somewhat exceptional position. Hubert was remarkably handsome, and Violet had the freshness and charm of a true English girl.

On the evening before my visit to Greylands Vandeleur came to see me. He looked restless and ill at ease.

"So you are going to spend a fortnight at the Bouveries'?" he said.

"Yes," I replied. "I look forward with great pleasure to the visit, Violet being such an old friend of mine."

"It is a curious fact," said Vandeleur, "that Bouverie is an old friend of mine. Did I mention to you that I spent a week with them both in Scotland two months ago? I had then the privilege of prescribing for Lady Bouverie."

"Indeed!" I answered, in some amazement. "I did not know that you gave your medical services except to your own division of police."

He laughed.

"My dear fellow, what is a doctor worth if he doesn't on all occasions and under every circumstance practise when required the healing art? Lady Bouverie was in a very low condition, her nerves out of order—in fact, I never saw anyone such a complete wreck. I prescribed some heroic measures with drugs, and I am given to understand that she is slightly better. I should like you to watch her, Druce, and give me your true opinion, quite frankly."

There was something in his tone which caused me to look at him uneasily.

"Are you keeping anything back?" I asked.

"Yes and no," was his answer. "I don't understand a healthy English girl being shattered by nerves, and"—he sprang to his feet as he spoke—"she is hand and glove with Madame Sara."

"What!" I cried.

"She owns to the fact and glories in it. Madame has cast her accustomed spell over her. I warned Lady Bouverie on no ac-

1 Located in Hertfordshire, a short distance north of London.

count to consult her medically, and she promised. But, there, how far is a woman's word, under given circumstances, to be depended upon?"

"Violet would certainly keep her word," I answered, in a tone almost of indignation.

He shrugged his shoulders.

"Your friend Violet is human," he answered. "She is losing her looks; she gets thinner and older-looking day by day. Under such circumstances any woman who holds the secrets Madame Sara does would compel another to be guided by her advice. At present Sir John has not the slightest idea that Lady Bouverie consulted me, but if you have any reason to fear that Madame is treating her we must tell him the truth at once. I have opened your eyes. You will, I am sure, do what is necessary."

He left me a few minutes later, and I sat by the fire pondering over his words.

Sir John Bouverie was a man of considerable note. He was a great deal older than his young wife, and held a high position in the Foreign Office.

I reached Greylands the next morning soon after breakfast, to find the country bathed in sunshine, the air both crisp and warm, and on the lawn the dew glistening like myriads of sparkling gems.

Sir John gave me a hearty welcome; he told me that Violet had not yet come downstairs, and then hurried me to my room to change and join the day's shooting-party.

We had excellent sport and did not reach home again until five o'clock. Lady Bouverie and several guests were at tea in the library. Although Vandeleur had in a measure prepared me for a great change in her appearance, I was shocked and startled when I saw her. As a girl Violet Sale had been bright, upright, dark of eye, with a vivid colour and an offhand, dashing, joyous sort of manner. A perfect radiance of life seemed to emanate from her. To be in her presence was to be assured of a good time, so merry was her laugh, so contagious her high spirits. Now she looked old, almost haggard, her colour gone, her eyes tired, dull, and sunken. She was scarcely twenty yet, but had anyone spoken of her as a woman past thirty the remark would provoke no denial.

Just for a moment as our eyes met hers brightened, and a vivid, beautiful colour filled her cheeks.

"This is good!" she cried. "I am so glad you have come! It will be like old times to have a long talk with you, Dixon. Come over now to this cosy nook by the fire and let us begin at once."

She crossed the room as she spoke, and I followed her.

"All my guests have had tea, or if they have not they will help themselves," she continued. "Muriel," she added, addressing a pretty girl in a white tea-gown, who stood near, "help everyone, won't you? I am so excited at seeing my old friend, Dixon Druce again. Now then, Dixon, let us step back a few years into the sunny past. Don't you remember——"

She plunged into old recollections, and as she did so the animation in her sweet eyes and the colour in her cheeks removed a good deal of the painful impression which her first appearance had given me. We talked, Lady Bouverie laughed, and all went well until I suddenly made an inquiry with regard to Hubert.

Now, Hubert had been the darling of Violet's early life. He was about three years her senior, and as fascinating and gay and light-hearted a young fellow as I had ever seen. Violet turned distinctly pale when I spoke of him now. She was silent for a few minutes, then she raised her eyes appealingly and said, in a clear, distinct voice:—

"Hubert is quite well, I believe. Of course, you remember that he was obliged to go to Australia on business just before my marriage, but I hear from him constantly."

"I should have thought he would have been back by now," was my answer. "What has he done with the bungalow?"

"Let it to a very special friend. She goes there for week-ends. You must have heard of her—Madame Sara."

"Oh, my dear Violet," I could not help saying, "why did Hubert let the place to her, of all people?"

"Why not?" was her answer. She started up as she spoke. "I am very fond of Madame Sara, Dixon. But do you know her? You look as though you did."

"Too well," I replied.

Her lips pouted.

"I see this is a subject on which we are not likely to agree," she answered. "I love Madame, and, for that matter, so does Hubert. I never met anyone who had such an influence over him. Sometimes I think that if she were a little younger and he a little older—but, there, of course, his devotion to her is not of that kind. She can do anything with him, however. He went to Australia entirely to please her. How strange you look! Have I said too much? But, there, I must not talk to you any more for the present. The fascination of your company has made me forget my other duties."

She left me, and I presently found myself in my own room,

where, seated by the fire, I thought over matters. I did not like the aspect of affairs. The Willows let to Madame Sara; Hubert in Australia and evidently on Madame's business; could Violet's all too manifest trouble have anything to do with Hubert? Her manner by no means deceived me; she was concealing something. How ill she looked; how changed! Those forced spirits, that struggle to be animated, did not for a single moment blind me to the true fact that Violet was unhappy.

At dinner that evening I again noticed young Lady Bouverie's tired and yet excited appearance. Once her dark eyes met mine, but she looked away immediately. She was in distress. What could be wrong?

It was one of Sir John's peculiarities to sit up very late, and that night after the ladies had retired to rest we went into the billiard-room. After indulging in a couple of games I lit a fresh cigar, and, feeling the air of the room somewhat hot, stepped out on to the wide veranda, which happened to be deserted. I had taken one or two turns when I heard the rustle of a dress behind me, and, turning, saw Violet. She was wearing the long, straight, rather heavy, pearl-grey velvet dress which I had admired, and yet thought too old for her, earlier in the evening. She came up eagerly to my side. As I had bidden her good-night a long time ago, I could not help showing my astonishment.

"Don't look at me with those shocked, reproachful eyes, Dixon," she said, in a low voice. "I am lucky to catch you like this. I want to speak to you about something."

"Certainly," I replied. "Shall we go over to those chairs, or will you feel it too cold?"

"Not at all. Yes, let us go over there."

I drew forward one of the chairs at the corner of the veranda, wondering greatly what was coming.

Lady Bouverie looked up at me as I stood by her side, with some of the old, frank expression in her brown eyes.

"Dixon," she said, "I want you to help me and not to question me; whatever your private thoughts may be I want you to keep them to yourself. This is a most private and important matter, and I demand your help to get me through it satisfactorily."

"You have only to command," I replied.

As I spoke I glanced at her anxiously. The moonlight had caught her face, and I saw how deadly white she was. Her lips quivered. Suddenly her eyes filled with tears. She took out a tiny lace handkerchief and wiped them away. In a moment she had recovered her self-control and continued:—

"I am in great trouble just now, and the bitter part of it is that I can confide it to no one. But I want you, as an old friend, to do a little business for me. I can't manage it myself, or I would not ask you. I have not told my husband anything about it, nor do I wish him to know. It is not my duty to tell him, for the affair is my own, not his. You understand?"

"No," I answered, boldly, "I cannot understand any circumstances in which a wife could rightly have a trouble apart from her husband."

"Oh, don't be so goody-goody, Dixon," she said, with some petulance. "If you won't help me without lecturing, you are much changed from the old Dixon Druce who used to give us such jolly times when he called himself our dear old uncle at The Willows. Say at once whether you will go right on with this thing, or whether I shall get someone else to do what I require."

I thought of Madame, who would not scruple to do anything to get this girl into her power.

"Of course I will help you," I said. "We will leave out the goody part and go straight to business. What is it?"

"Now you are nice and like your own old self," she replied. "Please listen attentively. I have in my private box some rupee[1] coupon bonds, payable to bearer. These I inherited among other securities at my mother's death. I want to realize them into cash immediately. I could not do so personally without my husband's knowledge, as I should have to correspond with, or go to see, the family broker in the City. Now, I want you to sell them for me at the best price. I know the price is low owing to the fall in silver, but as they are bearer bonds there will be no transfer deeds to sign, and you can take them to your broker and get the money at once. Can you do this for me tomorrow? I hate asking you, but if you would do it I should be so grateful. The fact is, I must somehow have the money before to-morrow night."

"I will certainly do it," I replied. "I can run up to town to-morrow morning on the plea of urgent business, which will be quite true, and bring you back the money to-morrow afternoon."

Her words had filled me with apprehension, but it was quite impossible, after what she had just said, to attempt to gain her confidence as to the cause of her wish for a sudden supply of cash unknown to her husband. Could she want the money for Hubert? But he was in Australia.

---

1 Standard unit of currency in India.

"Is the amount a large one?" I asked.

"Not very," she answered. "I think the bonds should realize, at the present price, about two thousand six hundred pounds."

"Indeed!" I exclaimed. "That appears to me a large sum."

The amount doubled my anxiety. A sudden impulse seized me.

"We are old friends, Violet," I said, laying my hand on her arm. "You and Hubert and I once swore eternal friendship. Now, because of that old friendship, I will do what you ask, though I don't like to do it, and I would rather your husband knew about it. Since this is not to be, I mean to put to you another question, and I demand, Violet—yes, I demand—a frank answer."

"What is it?" she asked.

"Has Madame Sara anything, directly or indirectly, to do with this affair?"

She glanced at me in astonishment.

"Madame Sara? Absolutely nothing! Why should she?"

"Have you consulted her about it?"

"Well, yes, I have, of course. She is, you see, my very kindest friend."

"And you are doing this by her advice?"

"She did counsel me. She said it would be the only way out."

I was silent. My consternation was too great for me to put into words.

"Violet," I said, after a pause, "I am sorry that Madame has got possession of your dear old home; I am sorry you are friends with her; I am more than sorry you consult her, for I do not like her."

"Then you are in the minority, Dixon. All people praise Madame Sara. She makes friends wherever she goes."

"Ah," I answered, "except with the few who know her as she is. Ask Vandeleur what he thinks of her."

"I admire Mr. Vandeleur very much," said Violet, speaking slowly. "He is a clever and interesting man, but were he to abuse Madame I should hate him. I could even hate you, Dixon, when you speak as you are now doing. It is, of course, because you know Mr. Vandeleur so well. He is a police official, a sort of detective—such people look on all the world with jaundiced eyes. He would be sure to suspect any very clever woman."

"Vandeleur has told me," I said, after a pause, "that you respect and trust him sufficiently to consult him about your health."

"Yes," she answered. "I have not been feeling well. I happened to be alone with him on one occasion, and it seemed a chance not to be thrown away. He did look so clever and so—so trustworthy. He is giving me some medicines—I think I am rather better since I took them."

She gave a deep sigh and rose to her feet.

"Heigh-ho!" she said, "I had no idea it was so late. We must go in. John sits up till all hours. Good-night and a thousand thanks. I will put the parcel of bonds in your room to-morrow morning, in the top left-hand drawer of the chest. You will know where to find them before you go to town."

She pressed my hand, and I noticed that there were tears brimming in her eyes. Her whole attitude puzzled me terribly. It was so unlike the ways of the Violet I used to know. Fearless, bold, daring was that girl. I used to wonder at times could she ever cry; could she ever feel keen anxiety about anyone? Now, only six months after marriage, I found a nervous, almost hypochondriacal, woman instead of the Violet Sale of old.

I thought much of Lady Bouverie's request during the hours of darkness; and in the morning, notwithstanding the fact that in some ways it might be considered a breach of confidence, I resolved to tell Vandeleur. Vandeleur would keep the knowledge to himself; unless, indeed, it was for Lady Bouverie's benefit that he should disclose it. I felt certain that she was in grave danger of some sort, and, knowing Madame Sara as I did, my apprehensions flew to her as the probable cause of the trouble.

After breakfast I made an excuse and went up to town, taking the bonds with me.

Just as I was entering my broker's I observed a man leaning against the railings. He was dressed like an ordinary tramp, and had a slouch hat pushed over his eyes. Those eyes, very bright and watchful, seemed to haunt me. I did not think they looked like the eyes of an Englishman—they were too brilliant, and also too secretive.

My broker gave me an open cheque for two thousand six hundred and forty pounds for the bonds. This I at once took to his bank and cashed in notes. As I was leaving the bank I observed the same man whom I had seen standing outside the broker's office. He did not look at me this time, but sauntered slowly by. I was conscious of a curious, irritated feeling, and had some difficulty in banishing him from my mind. That he was following me I had little doubt, and this fact redoubled my uneasiness.

I got into a cab and drove to Vandeleur's house; when I arrived there was no sign of the man, and, blaming myself for being over-suspicious, I inquired for my friend. He was out, but I was lucky enough to catch him just outside the Court. He was very busy, and could only give me a moment. I told him my news briefly. His face grew grave.

"Bad," was his laconic remark. "I told you I feared there was something going on. I wonder what Lady Bouverie is up to?"

"Nothing dishonourable," I replied, hotly. "Do you think, Vandeleur, she wants the money for her brother?"

"Hubert Sale has plenty of money of his own," was Vandeleur's retort. "Besides, you say he is in Australia—gone on Madame Sara's business. I don't like it, Druce. Believe me, Sara is at the bottom of this. You must watch for all you are worth. You must act the detective. Never mind whether you like the part or not. It is for the sake of that poor girl. She has, beyond doubt, put herself in the clutches of the most dangerous woman in London."

Vandeleur's remarks were certainly not encouraging. I returned to Greylands in low spirits. Lady Bouverie was waiting for me on the lawn; the rest of the party were out. She looked tired; the ravages of some secret grief were more than ever manifest on her face. But when I handed her the parcel of notes she gave me a look of gratitude, and without speaking hurried to her own apartments.

I was just preparing to saunter through the grounds, feeling too restless to go within, when a light hand was laid on my arm. Lady Bouverie had returned.

"I could not wait, Dixon," she cried. "I had to thank you at once. You are good, and you have done better than I dared to hope. Now I shall be quite, quite happy. This must put everything absolutely right. Oh, the relief! I was not meant for anxiety; I believe much of it would kill me."

"I am inclined to agree with you," I answered, looking at her face as I spoke.

"Ah," she answered, "you think me greatly changed?"

"I do."

"You will soon see the happy Violet of old. You have saved me. You are going for a walk. May I accompany you?"

I assured her what pleasure it would give me, and we went together through the beautiful gardens. Her whole manner only strengthened my anxiety. Madame Sara her great and trusted friend; a large sum of money required immediately which her husband was to know nothing about; Hubert Sale at the other side of the world, engaged on Madame Sara's business; Madame in possession of the Sales' old home. Things looked black.

Sir John had asked me to remain at Greylands for a fortnight, and I resolved for Violet's sake to take full advantage of the invitation.

Our party was a gay one, and perhaps I was the only person who really noticed Violet's depression.

Meantime there was great excitement, for a large house-party was expected to arrive, the chief guest being a certain Persian, Mr. Mirza Ali Khan, one of the Shah's favourite courtiers and most trusted emissaries. This great personage had come to England to prepare for his Royal master's visit to this country, the date of which was as yet uncertain. Sir John Bouverie, by virtue of his official position at the Foreign Office, had offered to entertain him for a few days' shooting.

"I do not envy Ali Khan his billet," remarked Sir John to me on the evening before the arrival of our honoured guest. "The Shah is a particular monarch, and if everything is not in apple-pie order on his arrival there is certain to be big trouble for someone. In fact, if the smallest thing goes wrong Mirza Ali Khan is likely to lose his head when he returns to Persia. My guest of to-morrow has a very important commission to execute before the Shah's arrival. Amongst some valuable gems and stones which he is bringing to have cut and set for his monarch is, in especial, the bloodstone."

"What?" I asked.

"The bloodstone. *The* bloodstone, which has never before left Persia. It is the Shah's favourite talisman, and is supposed, among other miraculous properties, to possess the power of rendering the Royal owner invisible at will. Awful thing if he were suddenly to disappear at one of the big Court functions. But, to be serious, the stone is intensely interesting for its great age and history, having been the most treasured possession of the Persian Court for untold centuries. Though I believe it is intrinsically worth very little, its sentimental value is enormous. Were it lost a huge reward would be offered for it. It has never been set, but is to be so now for the first time, and is to be ready for the Shah to wear on his arrival. It will be a great honour to handle and examine a stone with such a history, and Violet has asked the Persian to bring it down here as a special favour, in order that we may all see it."

"It will be most interesting," I replied. Then I added, "Surely there must be an element of risk in the way these Eastern potentates bring their priceless stones and jewels with them when they visit our Western cities, the foci of all the great professional thieves of the world?"

"Very little," he replied. "The Home Office[1] is always specially notified, and they pass the word to Scotland Yard, so that every precaution is taken."

He rose as he spoke, and we both joined the other men in the billiard-room.

On the following day the new guests arrived. They had come by special train, and in time for tea, which was served in the central hall. Among them, of course, was the Persian, Mirza Ali Khan. He was a fine-looking man, handsome, with lustrous dark eyes and clear-cut, high-bred features. His manners were extremely polite, and he abundantly possessed all an Eastern's grace and charm. I had been exchanging a few words with him, and was turning away when, to my absolute surprise and consternation, I found myself face to face with Madame Sara. She was standing close behind me, stirring her tea. She still wore her hat and cloak, as did all the other ladies who had just arrived.

"Ah, Mr. Druce," she cried, a brilliant smile lighting up her face and displaying her dazzling white teeth, "so we meet again. Dear me, you look surprised and—scarcely pleased to see me."

She dropped her voice.

"You have no cause to be alarmed," she continued. "I am not a ghost."

"I did not know you were to be one of Sir John's guest's tonight," I answered.

"In your opinion I ought not to be, ought I? But, you see, dear Lady Bouverie is my special friend. In spite of many professional engagements I determined to give her the pleasure of my society tonight. I wanted to spend a short time with her in her beautiful home, and still more I wished to meet once again that fascinating Persian, Mr. Khan. You won't believe me, I know, Mr. Druce, when I tell you that I knew him well as a

1 Government department responsible for domestic and internal affairs.

boy. I was at Teheran for a time many years ago, and I was a special friend of the late Shah's."

"You knew the late Shah!" I exclaimed, staring at her in undisguised amazement.

"Yes; I spent nearly a year in Persia, and can talk the language quite fluently. Ah!"

She turned away and addressed herself, evidently in his own language, to the Persian. A pleased and delighted smile spread over his dark Oriental features. He extended his hand to her, and the next moment they were exchanging a rapid conversation, much to the surprise of all. Lady Bouverie looked on at this scene. Her eyes were bright with excitement. I noticed that she kept gazing at Madame Sara as though fascinated. Presently she turned to me.

"Is she not wonderful?" she exclaimed. "Think of her adding Persian to her many accomplishments. She is so wonderfully brilliant—she makes everything go well. There certainly is no one like her."

"No one more dangerous," I could not help whispering.

Violet shrugged her pretty shoulders.

"There never was anyone more obstinate and prejudiced than you can be when you like, Dixon," she answered. "Ah, there is Madame calling me. She and I mean to have a cosy hour in my boudoir before dinner."

She flew from my side, and as I stood in the hall I saw the young hostess and Madame Sara going slowly up the wide stairs side by side. I thought how well Violet looked, and began to hope that her trouble was at an end—that the money I had brought her had done what she hoped it would, and that Madame for the time was innocuous.

But I was destined to be quickly undeceived. About an hour later I was standing in one of the corridors when Violet Bouverie ran past me. She pulled herself up the next instant and, turning, came up to me on tip-toe. Her face was so changed that I should scarcely have recognised it.

"The worst has happened," she said, in a whisper.

"What do you mean?" I asked.

"Hubert—I did think I could save him. Oh, I am nearly mad."

"Madame has brought you bad tidings?"

"The worst. What am I to do? I must keep up appearances to-night. Don't take any notice of me; I will tell you to-morrow. But Heaven help me! Heaven help me!" she sobbed.

I watched her as she walked quickly down the corridor. Her

handkerchief was pressed to her face; tears were streaming from her eyes. Hatred even stronger than I had ever before experienced filled me with regard to Madame Sara. My first impulse was to beard the lioness in her den, to demand an interview with the woman, tell her all my suspicions, and dare her to torture Violet Bouverie any further. But reflection showed me the absurdity of this plan. I must wait and watch; ah, yes, I would watch, even as a detective, and would not leave a stone unturned to pursue this terrible woman until her wicked machinations were laid bare.

It was with a sinking heart that I dressed for dinner, but by-and-by, when I found myself at the long table, with its brilliant decorations and its distinguished guests, and glanced round the glittering board, I almost wondered if all that I had felt and all that Violet Bouverie's face had expressed were not parts of a hideous dream; for the party was so gay, the conversation so full of wit and laughter, that surely no horrible tragedy could be lingering in the background.

But as these thoughts came to me I looked again at Violet. At tea-time that evening I had noticed her improved appearance, but now she looked ghastly; her cheeks were hollow, her eyes sunken, her complexion a dull, dead white. Her evening dress revealed hollows in her neck. But it was the tired look, the suppressed anguish on her face, which filled me with apprehension. I could see how bravely she tried to be bright and gay. I also noticed that her eyes avoided mine.

Mirza Ali Khan sat on the right of Lady Bouverie—on his other side sat Madame Sara, and I occupied a chair next to hers. Between Madame and our hostess appeared to-night a most marked and painful contrast. Violet Bouverie was not twenty. Madame Sara, by her own showing, was an old woman, and yet at that moment the old looked young and the young old. Madame's face was brilliant, not a wrinkle was to be observed; her make-up was so perfect that it could not be detected even by the closest observer. Her *tout ensemble*[1] gave her the appearance of a woman who could not be a day more than five-and-twenty. Many a man would have fallen a victim to her wit and brilliancy; but I at least was saved that—I knew her too well. I hated her for that beauty, which effected such havoc in the world.

It was easy to see that Ali Khan was fascinated by her; but

1 Total effect (French).

at table she had the good taste to address him in English. Now and then I noticed that she looked earnestly at our hostess. After one of these glances she turned to me and said, in a low voice:—

"How ill Lady Bouverie is looking! Don't you think so?"

"Yes," I replied, "she is. I feel anxious about her."

"I wish she would consult me," she replied. "I could do her good. But she will not. She is under the impression, Mr. Druce, that I am a quack because I do not hold diplomas—a curious delusion I find among people."

"But a sound one," I answered.

She laughed, and turned again to her other neighbour.

When we joined the ladies after dinner Lady Bouverie crossed over to the Persian and said something to·him.

"Certainly," he answered, and immediately left the room, returning in a few minutes with a despatch-box.[1] We all clustered about him as he placed it on the table and opened it. A little murmur of surprise ran round the group when he lifted the lid and displayed the contents. A mass of gorgeous gems was lying in a bed of white wool. It was a blaze of all the colours of the rainbow. Emeralds, sapphires, diamonds, rubies, pearls, topazes, cats'-eyes, amethysts, and many others whose names I did not know were to be found there. One by one he removed them and passed each round for inspection. As he did so he gave a short description of its virtues, its origin, and value, and then returned it to the box again. Truly the display was wonderful. Madame Sara lingered long and lovingly over some of the gems, declaring that she had seen one or two before, mentioning certain anecdotes about them to the Persian, who nodded and smiled as he replaced, with his pointed fingers, each in its receptacle. He was evidently much pleased with the admiration they excited.

"But surely, Mr. Khan, you have brought the bloodstone to show us?" questioned Lady Bouverie.

"Ah, yes. I kept that supreme treasure for the last."

As he spoke he pushed a spring in the box, and a secret triangular drawer came slowly out. In it, nestling in a bed of red velvet, lay a wonderful stone—a perfectly oval piece of moss-green chalcedony[2] with translucent edges. Here and

---

1 A case for carrying official documents and other valuable items.

2 A precious or semi-precious stone, a form of quartz composed of tiny crystals.

there in irregular pattern shone out in vivid contrast to the dark green a number of blood-red spots, from which the stone derived its name.

"Yes," he said, lifting it out with reverence and laying it on the palm of his hand, "this is the bloodstone. Look closely at it if you will, but I must ask none of you to touch it."

Fig. 18. "LOOK CLOSELY AT IT IF YOU WILL, BUT I MUST ASK NONE OF YOU TO TOUCH IT."

One after another we bent down and peered into its luminous green depths, and doubtless shared some of the fascination that its possessor must feel for it. The stone was wonderful, and yet it was repellent. It seemed to me that there was something sinister in those blood-red spots. The thing inspired me with the same feeling that I often have when regarding some monstrous spotted orchid.

"Yes," said Lady Bouverie, "it is wonderful. Tell us something of its history, Mr. Khan."

"I cannot," he answered, "for the simple reason that no one knows its origin nor when it came into the possession of our Court. I could tell of some of its properties, but the tales would fall unbecomingly on the ears of Western civilization."

He replaced the stone in its drawer and, in spite of our pleading, declined to discuss it further.

It was late that night before I retired to rest. I was sitting with my host in the smoking-room, and we walked together down the corridor which led to my room. Most of the lights in the house were already out, and I fancied as I chatted to Bouverie that I heard a door close softly just ahead of us. The next instant, glancing down, I saw on the dark carpet a piece of paper, open, and bearing traces of having been folded. It was obviously a note.

"Halloa!" cried Bouverie. "What is this?"

He stooped and picked it up. At a glance we both read its contents; they ran as follows:—

"*Bring it to the summer-house exactly at half-past twelve; but make certain first that Dixon Druce has retired. Don't come until he has.*"

Bouverie's eyes met mine. I could not tell what thought flashed into their brown depths; but the rosy hue suddenly left his face, leaving it deadly white.

"Do you understand this?" he said, addressing me briefly.

"Yes and no," I replied.

"For whom was this note intended?" was his next remark.

I was silent.

"Druce," said Bouverie, "are you hiding anything from me?"

"If I were you," I said, after a moment's quick thought, "I would attend that rendezvous. It is now five-and-twenty minutes past twelve"—I glanced at my watch as I spoke—"shall we go together?"

He nodded. I rushed to my room, put on a dark shooting-coat, and joined my host a moment later in the hall.

We slipped out through a side door which stood slightly open. Without a word we crept softly in the shadow of the bushes towards the summer-house at the farther end of the garden, which was clearly visible in the moonlight. Whatever thoughts were coursing through Bouverie's brain there was something about his attitude, a certain forceful determination, which kept him from any words. We both drew into the dark cover of the laurels and waited with what patience we could.

A moment had scarcely gone by when across the grass with a light, quick step came a woman. She was wrapped in a dark cloak. For one instant the moonlight fell on her face and my heart nearly stopped with horror. It was that of Lady Bouverie. At that instant Bouverie's hand clutched my shoulder, and he drew me farther back into the darkest part of the shadow. From where we stood we could see but not be seen. Lady Bouverie was holding a small box in one hand, in the other a handkerchief. Her eyes were streaming with tears. She had scarcely reached the summer-house before a man with a mask over his face approached her. He said a word or two in a whisper, which was only broken by Lady Bouverie's sobs. She gave him the box; he put it into his breast-pocket and vanished.

I wondered that Bouverie did not spring forward, seize the man, and demand an explanation; but whether he was stunned or not I could not say. Before, however, he made the slightest movement Lady Bouverie herself with incredible swiftness disappeared into the darkness.

"Come," I said to Bouverie.

We both rushed to the spot where his wife had stood—something white lay on the ground. I picked it up. It was her handkerchief. Bouverie snatched it from me and looked at the initials by the light of the moon. The handkerchief was sopping wet with her tears. He flung it down again as though it hurt him.

"Great heavens!" he muttered.

I picked up the handkerchief and we both returned to the house.

We had scarcely set foot inside the hall when the sound of many voices upstairs fell on our ears. Amongst them the Persian's accents were clearly distinguishable. Terror rang in every shrill word.

"The bloodstone is gone!—the other jewels are safe, but the bloodstone, the talisman, is gone! What will become of me? My life will be the forfeit."

We both rushed upstairs. The whole thing was perfectly true. The bloodstone, the priceless talisman of the Royal House of Persia, had been stolen. The confusion was appalling, and already someone had gone to fetch the local police.

"I shall lose my life if the stone is not recovered," cried the miserable Persian, despair and terror depicted on his face. "Who has taken it? The other gems are safe, but the secret drawer has been burst open and the bloodstone removed. Who has taken it? Sir John, what is the matter? You look strange."

"I can throw light on this mystery," said Sir John.

I looked around me. Neither Lady Bouverie nor Madame Sara was present. I felt a momentary thankfulness for this latter fact.

"I saw my wife give a package to a stranger in the garden just now," he continued. "I do not wish to conceal anything. This matter must be looked into. When the police come I shall be the first to help in the investigation. Meanwhile I am going to my wife."

He strode away. We all stood and looked at each other. Sir John's revelation was far more terrible to all except the unfortunate Persian than the loss of the bloodstone. In fact, the enormity of the one tragedy paled beside the other.

I thought for a minute. Notwithstanding the lateness of the hour, I would dispatch a telegram to Vandeleur without delay. There was a mystery, and only Vandeleur could clear it up. Black as appearances were against Lady Bouverie, I had no doubt that her innocence could be established. Without a word I hurried out and raced to the post-office. There I knocked up the post-master and soon dispatched three telegrams—one to Vandeleur's house, one to his club, and one to the care of the Westminster police-station. All contained the same words:—

"*Come special or motor immediately. Don't delay.*"

I then returned to Greylands. A hush of surprise had succeeded to the first consternation. A few of the guests had reappeared, startled by the noise and confusion, but many still remained in their rooms. Sir John was with his wife. We assembled in the dining-room, and presently he came down and spoke to us.

"Lady Bouverie denies everything," he said. "She swears she has never left her room. This matter must be thoroughly investigated," he continued, going up to the Persian. "There are times when a man in all honour cannot defend even his own wife."

Meanwhile Madame Sara remained in the library. She was sitting by a table busily writing. When Sir John appeared she came into the room and spoke to him. Her face was full of sympathy.

"Of course Violet is innocent," she said. "I cannot understand your story, Sir John."

He did not reply to her. She then offered to go up to Violet; but he peremptorily forbade her to do so.

On the arrival of the local police a formal inquiry was made. Mirza Ali Khan declared that after showing us the gems he returned the box to his room. On retiring for the night he observed that it had been moved from the position in which he had placed it. He examined it and found that the lock had been tampered with—had, indeed, been ruthlessly burst open, evidently with a blunt instrument. He then touched the spring which revealed the secret drawer—the bloodstone was gone. All the other gems were intact. Knowing that the secret of the drawer was a difficult one to discover, the Persian was convinced that the bloodstone had been stolen by one of the party who assembled round him that evening and who had seen him touch the spring.

"My host, Sir John Bouverie, tells me an incredible story," he said. "I will leave the matter in Sir John's hands, trusting absolutely to his honour."

In a few words Sir John described what he had seen. He handed the note which we had found in the corridor to the police, who examined it with interest. Lady Bouverie was sent for, and pending further investigation the unfortunate girl was placed under arrest.

Half-past one struck, then two, and it was only our earnest appeal to await Vandeleur's arrival that prevented the police from removing Lady Bouverie in custody. Would he never come? If he had started at once on receipt of the wire he would be nearly at Greylands now.

Suddenly I heard a sound and ran breathlessly to the front door, which was open. Stepping from a motor-car, hatless but with the utmost calm, was Vandeleur. I seized his hand.

"Thank Heaven you are here!" I exclaimed. "You must have raced."

"Yes, I shall be summoned to-morrow for fast driving, and I have lost my hat. What's up?"

I hurried him into the dining-room, where a crowd of guests was assembled. It was a wonderful scene, and I shall never forget it. The anxious faces of the visitors; Lady Bouverie standing between two constables, sobbing bitterly; her husband just behind her, his head turned with shame and misery; and then, as though in contrast, the tall, commanding figure of Vandeleur, with his strong features set as though in marble. He was taking in everything, judging in his acute mind the evidence which was poured out to him.

"Have you anything to say?" asked Vandeleur, gently, to Lady Bouverie. "Any explanation to offer?"

"I was not there," was her answer. "I never left my room."

Sir John muttered something under his breath; then he turned brusquely and requested the visitors to leave the room. They did so without a word, even Madame Sara taking herself off, though

I could see that she went unwillingly. Sir John, Vandeleur, myself, the Persian, the two constables, and Lady Bouverie were now alone.

Vandeleur's expression suddenly changed. He was regarding Lady Bouverie with a steady look; he then took up the handkerchief which we had found, examined it carefully, and laid it down again.

"Have you been taking the medicine I ordered you, Lady Bouverie?" was his remark.

"I have," she replied.

"To-day?"

"Yes; three times."

"Will someone give me a large, clean sheet of white paper?"

I found one at once and brought it to him. He carefully rolled the handkerchief in it, drew out his stylograph,[1] and wrote on the package:—

"*Handkerchief found by Sir John Bouverie and Mr. Druce at 12.40 a.m.*"

He then asked Lady Bouverie for the one which she had in her pocket; this was almost as wet as the one I had picked up. He put it in another packet, writing also upon the paper: —

"*Handkerchief given to me by Lady Bouverie at 3.20 a.m.*"

Then, drawing the inspector aside, he whispered a few words to him which brought an exclamation of surprise from that officer.

"Now," he said, turning to Sir John, "I have done my business here for the present. I mean to return to London at once in my motor-car, and I shall take Mr. Druce with me. The inspector here has given me leave to take also these two handkerchiefs, on which I trust important evidence may hang."

He drew out his watch.

"It is now nearly half-past three," he said. "I shall reach my house at 4.30; the examination will take fifteen minutes; the result will be dispatched from Westminster police-station to the station here by telegram. You should receive it, Sir John, by 5.30, and I trust," he added, taking Lady Bouverie's hand, "it will mean your release, for that you are guilty I do not for a moment believe. In the meantime the police will remain here."

He caught my arm, and two minutes later we were rushing through the night towards London.

---

1 A type of fountain pen.

" TWO MINUTES LATER WE WERE RUSHING
THROUGH THE NIGHT TOWARDS LONDON."

Fig. 19. "TWO MINUTES LATER WE WERE RUSHING THROUGH THE NIGHT TOWARDS LONDON."

"My dear fellow," I gasped, "explain yourself, for Heaven's sake. Is Violet innocent?"

"Wonderful luck," was his enigmatical answer. "I fancy Sara has over-acted this piece."

"You can find the bloodstone?"

"That I cannot tell you; my business is to clear Lady Bouverie. Don't talk, or we shall be wrecked."

He did not vouchsafe another remark till we stood together in his room, but he had driven the car like a madman.

He then drew out the two packets containing the handkerchiefs and began to make rapid chemical preparations.

"Now, listen," he said. "You know I am treating Lady Bouverie. The medicine I have been giving her happens to contain large doses of iodide of potassium. You may not be aware of it, but the drug is eliminated very largely by all the mucous membranes, and the lachrymal gland, which secretes the tears, plays a prominent part in this process. The sobbing female whom you are prepared to swear on oath was Lady Bouverie at the rendezvous by the summer-house dropped a handkerchief—this one." He laid his finger on the first of the two packets. "Now, if that woman was really Lady Bouverie, by analysis of the handkerchief I shall find, by means of a delicate test, distinct traces of iodine on it. If, however, it was not Lady Bouverie, but someone disguised with the utmost skill of an actress to represent her, not only physically, but with all the emotions of a distracted and guilty woman, even to the sobs and tears—then we shall not find iodine on the analysis of this handkerchief."

My jaw dropped as the meaning of his words broke upon me.

"Before testing, I will complete my little hypothesis by suggesting that the note, evidently thrown in your way, was to decoy you to be a witness of the scene, and that the handkerchief taken from Lady Bouverie's room and marked with her initials was intended to be the finishing touch in the chain of evidence against her. Now we will come to facts, and for all our sakes let us hope that my little theory is correct."

He set to work rapidly. At the end of some operations lasting several minutes he held up a test tube containing a clear solution.

"Now," he said, opening a bottle containing an opalescent liquid; "guilty or not guilty?"

He added a few drops from the bottle to the test tube. A long, deep chuckle came from his broad chest.

"Not a trace of it," he said. "Now for the handkerchief which I took from Lady Bouverie for a check experiment."

He added a few of the same drops to another tube. A bright violet colour spread through the liquid.

"There's iodine in that, you see. Not guilty, Druce."

A shout burst from my lips.

"Hush, my dear chap!" he pleaded. "Yes, it is very pretty. I am quite proud."

Five minutes later a joyful telegram was speeding on its way to Greylands.

"So it was Sara," I said, by-and-by. "What is your next move?"

He shrugged his shoulders.

"It is one thing to prove that a person is not guilty, but it is another thing to prove that someone else is. Of course, I will try. This is the deepest game I ever struck, and the boldest, and I think the cleverest. Poor Ali Khan, the Shah will certainly cut his head off when he gets back to Persia. Of course, Sara has taken the stone. But whether she has done so simply because she has a fancy to keep it for herself, believing in its power as a talisman, or for the reward which is certain to be offered, who can tell? The reward will be a large one, but she doesn't want money. However, we shall see. Her make-up was good, and she had all her details well worked out."

"But we have not yet found out what Violet's trouble is," I remarked. "There is, I am sure, some mystery attached to Hubert."

"I doubt it," said Vandeleur, brusquely.

He rose and yawned.

"I am tired and must lie down," he said. "You will, of course, return to Greylands later in the morning. Let me know if there are any fresh moves."

By noon that day I found myself back at Greylands. Surely this was a day of wonders, for whom should I see standing on the steps of the old house, talking earnestly to Sir John Bouverie, but my old friend, Hubert Sale. In appearance he was older than when I had last seen him, and his face was bronzed. He did not notice me, but went quickly into the house. Sir John came down the avenue to meet me.

"Ah, Druce," he said, "who would have believed it? Of all the amazing things, your friend Vandeleur's penetration is the greatest. We both saw her with our own eyes, and yet it wasn't my wife. Come into my study," he continued; "I believe I can throw light on this most extraordinary affair. Hubert's unlooked-for return puts the whole thing into a nutshell. I have a strange tale to tell you."

"First, may I ask one question?" I interrupted. "Where is Madame Sara?"

He spread out his hands with a significant gesture.

"Gone," he said. "How, when, and where I do not know. We thought she had retired for the night. She did not appear this morning. She has vanished, leaving no address behind her."

"Just like her," I could not help saying. "Now I will listen to your story."

"I will try to put it in as few words as possible. It is a deep thing, and discloses a plot the malignity of which could scarcely be equalled.

"Violet and Hubert made the acquaintance of Madame Sara a few months before Violet's marriage. You know Madame's power of fascination. She won Violet's affections, and as to Hubert, she had such complete influence over him that he would do anything in the world she wished. We were surprised at his determination to go to Australia before his sister's wedding, but it now turns out that he was forced to go by Madame herself, who assured him that he could be of the utmost assistance to her in a special matter of business. This was explained to Violet and to me fully; but what we were not told was that he took with him Madame's own special servant, an Arabian of the name of Achmed, the cleverest man, Hubert said, he had ever met. In his absence Madame rented his house for at least a year. All this sounds innocent enough; but listen.

"Very shortly after her marriage Violet began to receive letters from Hubert, dated from various stations in Australia, demanding money. These demands were couched in such terms as to terrify the poor child. She sent him what she could from her own supplies, but he was insatiable. At last she spoke to Madame Sara. Madame immediately told her she had learnt that Hubert had made some bad companions, had got into serious scrapes, and that his debts of honour were so enormous that unless she, Violet, helped him he could never set foot in England again. The poor girl was too much ashamed to say a word to me. These letters imploring money came by almost every mail. Madame herself offered to transmit the money, and Violet, with the utmost confidence, placed large sums in her hands.

"At last the crisis arrived. A communication reached my poor girl to the effect that unless she paid between two and three thousand pounds in notes in a couple of days Hubert in his despair would certainly take his life. She was well aware of his somewhat reckless character. Hence her request to you to sell the bonds. Shortly afterwards the Persian arrived here, and Madame, at her own request, came to spend the night. She managed to terrify Violet with a fresh story with regard to Hubert, and the child's nerves were so undermined that she believed everything.

"Well, you know the rest. You know what happened last night. But for Vandeleur's genius, where might poor Violet be now? I must tell you frankly that even I believed her guilty; I could not doubt the evidence of my own senses.

"You can judge of our amazement when Hubert walked in

this morning. He looked well. He said that Madame's business was of a simple character, that he had soon put matters right for her, and after seeing what was to be seen in Australia and New Zealand came home. He was amazed when we spoke of his being in money difficulties; he had never been in any scrape at all. Only one thing he could not understand—why Violet never answered his letters. He wrote to her about every second mail, and, as a rule, gave his letters to the Arabian to post. There is no doubt that Achmed destroyed them and wrote others on his own account.

"Well, Druce, what do you say? The motive? Oh, of course, the motive was the bloodstone. The woman knew probably for months that it was coming to England, and that I, in my official position, would invite the Persian here. She wanted it, goodness knows for what, and was determined to have a long chain of evidence against poor Violet in order to cover her own theft. Druce, we must find that woman. She cannot possibly be at large any longer."

The desire to find Madame was in all our minds, but how to accomplish it was a question which I for one did not dare to answer.

VI. —THE TEETH OF THE WOLF. [279–90]

"I count on your accepting," said Vandeleur.

"But why?" I asked, with some impatience. "I have never heard anything favourable with regard to Mrs. Bensasan. Her cruelties to her animals are well known. Granted that she is the best tamer of wild animals in Europe, I would rather not know her."

"That has nothing to do with the case in point," replied Vandeleur. "Mrs. Bensasan and Madame Sara are working one of Madame's worst plots. I have not the least doubt on the subject. It is my business to solve this mystery, and I want your aid."

"Of course, if you put it in that way I can refuse no longer," was my response. "But what do you mean?"

"Simply this." As Vandeleur spoke he leant back in his chair and drew a long puff from his meerschaum.[1] "I am acting in the interests of Gerald Hiliers. You have, of course, heard of the missing girl?"

---

1 A tobacco pipe made with a clay-like mineral found in the Mediterranean.

"Your enigmas become more and more puzzling," I replied. "I know but little of Gerald Hiliers. And who is the girl?"

"I have rather a pretty story to entertain you with. This is the state of things, as nearly as I can narrate it. Mrs. Bensasan, the owner of Bensasan's Menageries, is in some ways the talk of London. She has dared to do what hardly any other woman has done before her. She runs her shows herself, being always present at important exhibitions. Her lion-taming exploits were remarkable enough to arouse general attention in Paris last year, but now in London she is going on an altered tack. She is devoting herself to the taming of even wilder and more difficult animals to manage—I mean wolves."

"But what about the girl and your friend Hiliers?"

"I will explain. But first let me tell you about Mrs. Bensasan. I must describe her before I go any farther. She is built on a very large scale, being six feet in height. She has strong features, prominent eyes, and a ringing, harsh voice. Her mouth is remarkably large and wide. I understand that Madame Sara has supplied her with a perfect set of false teeth, so well made that they defy detection, but altogether she is disagreeable to look at, although the very essence of strength. Now, this woman is a widow and has one only child of the name of Laura, a girl about nineteen years of age, who is in all respects as unlike the mother as daughter could be, for she is slight, fair, and gentle-looking, with a particularly attractive face. Miss Laura has had the bad taste, according to Mrs. Bensasan, to fall in love with Hiliers, whereas the mother wants her for a very different bridegroom. I have known Hiliers for years, and his father is a friend of mine. He is a nice, gentlemanly fellow, with good commercial prospects. Now, although it is more than probable that Hiliers will be a rich man, Mrs. Bensasan does not wish for the match. She wants Laura to marry a horrible, misshapen little man—a dwarf of the name of Rigby. So far as I can ascertain Rigby is half Jew, half Greek, and he has evidently known Mrs. Bensasan for many years. He lives in expensive lodgings near Cavendish Square,[1] drives a mail phaeton,[2] and has all the externals that belong to a rich man. His face is as repulsive as his body is misshapen. The girl cannot stand him, and what the mother sees in him is the

1 Located in London's West End near the upscale shopping areas of Oxford and Regent Streets.

2 An open four-wheeled carriage with a heavy suspension similar to that used for mail coaches.

most difficult part of the problem which I have got to solve. It may be a case of blackmail. If so, I must prove it. There is not the slightest doubt that this extremely strong and disagreeable woman fears Rigby, although she professes to be a great friend of his.

"In addition, Madame Sara is Mrs. Bensasan's friend. She spends a great deal of her time at Cray Lodge, the pretty little place near Guildford[1] where the Bensasans live. These two women are evidently hand in glove, and both have resolved to give the poor girl to Joseph Rigby; as things are at present Gerald Hiliers stands a poor chance of winning his bride."

"You say the girl is missing?"

"Yes. About a month ago Gerald wrote to Mrs. Bensasan asking her for Laura's hand. He had quite a civil letter in reply, stating that the matter required consideration, and that just at present she would rather he did not pay his addresses to her daughter. Nevertheless, he received an invitation, a few days later, to stay at Cray Lodge.

"He arrived there, was treated with marked kindness, and allowed to see Laura as much as he liked. The poor girl seemed sadly restrained and unhappy. One day when the two found themselves alone she told him that he had better give her up, as she knew there was not the slightest chance of her being allowed to marry him; but she further added that under no circumstances would she marry Rigby. As she uttered the words Mrs. Bensasan came into the room. To all appearance she had heard nothing. Hiliers left Cray Lodge that afternoon.

"Early the next morning he received a letter from Mrs. Bensasan asking him to come to her at once. He hurried to the Lodge; he was received by his hostess, who told him that she had sent Laura from home, and that she did not intend to reveal her whereabouts until she had decided to give her as a bride to Joseph Rigby or to him. She would not say at present which suitor she most favoured; she only reserved to herself the absolute power to choose between them.

"'Laura shall only marry the man I choose her to marry,' was her final announcement, and then she added: 'In order to study your character, Mr. Hiliers, I again invite you to come here on a visit. My friend, Mr. Rigby, will also be a guest.'

"This state of things alone would have made Hiliers anxious, although not greatly alarmed; but Laura's old nurse, who had

---

1 Located in Surrey, 27 miles southwest of central London.

been hiding behind a laurustinus bush[1] in the avenue, rushed up to him as he was returning to the railway-station and thrust a note into his hand. It was written by herself and was very illiterate. In this she managed to inform him that her young lady had been removed from her bed in the middle of the night and been put forcibly into a cab by Mrs. Bensasan and Madame Sara. It was the nurse's impression that the poor girl was about to be subjected to some very cruel treatment.

"Hiliers came to me at once and implored me to help him to find and rescue Miss Bensasan. I must own that I was at first puzzled how to act. It was just then that an extraordinary thing happened. Mrs. Bensasan came to see me. Her ostensible reason was to consult me with regard to some curious robberies which had lately taken place on her premises. Her great fear was that the people who committed the burglaries would try to injure her wolves by throwing poisoned meat to them. She had heard of me and my professional skill from her great friend, Madame Sara, and, in short, she wanted to know if I would take up the matter, assuring me that I should be handsomely paid for my services, and, further, that I might bring my friend, Mr. Dixon Druce, with me.

"'Madame Sara and I would like to have you both staying at Cray Lodge,' she said. 'I hope you will come. Will you, in company with your friend, Mr. Druce, visit me next Monday? We can then go carefully into the matter and you can give me your opinion. It would be a most serious thing for me, more serious than I can give you the least idea of, if my wolves were tampered with. I ask for your presence as a great favour. Will you both come?'"

"And you accepted that sort of invitation?" was my remark.

"I accepted it," replied Vandeleur, gravely, "for us both."

"But why? Your attitude in this matter puzzles me very much. I should imagine that you would not care to darken that woman's doors."

"I suspect," said Vandeleur, slowly, "that the tale of the robberies is a mere blind. I look forward to a very interesting time at Cray Lodge, for I intend to become possessed of the necessary knowledge which will enable me to give Miss Laura to Gerald Hiliers as his bride."

I greatly disliked the idea of going to stay at Cray Lodge. I thought Vandeleur on the wrong track when he entered Mrs.

---

1 A type of evergreen shrub.

Bensasan's house as her guest. There was no help for it, however; he was determined to go, and I, as his special friend, would not fail him in what was extremely likely to be an hour of danger.

On the following Monday accordingly I accompanied Vandeleur to Mrs. Bensasan's house. A smart dog-cart[1] was waiting for us at Guildford, and we drove to the Lodge, a pretty house, situated about three miles out of the town. It stood in its own grounds. There was a pine wood to the left, and I might have thought I was approaching one of the most innocent and lovely homes of England, but for the sinister bay of a wolf that fell upon my ears as we drove up the avenue.

Tea was in full progress in the central hall when we arrived. Mrs. Bensasan wore a gown of tawny velvet, which suited her massive figure and harsh, yet in some ways handsome, face. Her hair was a shade redder in tone than the velvet, and she had it arranged in thick coils round her large head. Her dead-white complexion was unrelieved by any colour. Her reddish eyebrows were thick, and her eyes, large and the colour of agates, gleamed with approval as we entered the hall. She came forward at once to meet us.

"Welcome!" she said, in her harsh voice, and as she spoke she smiled, showing those white, regular teeth which Vandeleur had mentioned as the work of that genius, Madame Sara.

We stood for a moment or two by the fire, and as we did so I watched her face. The brow was low, the eyes very large and very brilliant, but I thought them altogether destitute of humanity. The nose was thick, with wide nostrils, and the mouth was hideous, cut like a slit across her face. Notwithstanding her beautiful teeth, that mouth destroyed all pretence to good looks.

In the presence of one so coarse and colossal Madame Sara, who was standing in the background, appeared at first almost insignificant, but a second glance showed that this woman was the very foil she needed to bring out her remarkable and great attractions. Her slenderness and her young figure, the softness of her blue eyes, the golden sheen of that marvellous hair, which was neither dyed nor artificially curled, but was Nature's pure product, glistening and twining itself into tendrils long, thick, and soft as a girl's, all contrasted well with the heavy appearance of her hostess. Mrs. Bensasan looked almost an old woman; Madame Sara might have been twenty-eight or thirty. She wore a

1 A light horse-drawn vehicle, originally designed to accommodate sportsmen and their dogs.

black dress of cobwebby lace, and nothing could better suit the delicacy of her complexion.

I had just taken my second cup of tea when a voice at my elbow caused me to turn round quickly. Then, indeed, I could not help starting, for one of the most misshapen and altogether horrible-looking men I had ever seen stood before me. His face was all hillocks and excrescences, the forehead bulging forward, the eyes going back very deeply into their sockets; they were small eyes, and seemed ever to glisten with an uneasy and yet watchful movement. The lower part of his face was covered with a thick black moustache and short beard. The nose was small, very *retroussé*,[1] with wide nostrils. Mrs. Bensasan introduced him with a careless nod.

"My friend, Mr. Joseph Rigby—Mr. Druce," she said.

Rigby bowed rather offensively low, and then began to talk.

"I am glad you and Mr. Vandeleur are going to give us the pleasure of your company for a day or two," he said. "Mrs. Bensasan has a very fine scheme for our amusement on Wednesday night. You have, of course, heard of Mrs. Bensasan's wolves? I doubt not she will let you see them if you ask her. She is very proud of these animals, and no wonder. Taganrog,[2] a great Siberian he-wolf, is alone likely to make her famous. It is Mrs. Bensasan's most kind intention to give us an exhibition of her power over Taganrog on Wednesday night."

"Indeed," I answered, "that will be interesting."

Someone called him and he moved away. Tea was over, but there were still a couple of hours of daylight left. Mrs. Bensasan stood a little apart from her other guests. She saw me and came up to my side.

"Should you be afraid if I took you to see my pets?" she said.

"I should like to go very much," I replied.

"You are certain you will not turn coward? Some people dread the special pack I am now training."

I smiled.

"I shall not be afraid," I answered.

A pleased expression crossed her face.

"Then you, Mr. Druce, shall come with me. You alone. Come at once," she added. "This way, please."

1 Turned up (French).

2 A significant port on the Sea of Azov in southern Russia with access to the Black Sea. Taganrog was the birthplace of noted author Anton Chekhov (1860–1904).

We left the house and, crossing the broad avenue, went down a sloping path which led through the pine woods. As we walked I peered through the trees, and just before me, a few hundred yards away, I saw a cluster of low buildings or kennels such as are used to keep foxhounds in. These kennels were, however, very much stronger than those required by the master of a pack of hounds. They were of strong brick on three sides, and in front were placed high iron railings which fenced in a sort of yard. This was further divided into compartments, one compartment for each kennel, and the whole was covered over at the top with an iron penthouse. In short, the arrangements were very much on the scale employed by the Zoological Gardens in London.

"Before I bought Cray Lodge, the late owner kept foxhounds," said Mrs. Bensasan. "I had the old kennels pulled down and built up again to suit my purpose. I have kept all sorts of wild beasts in them. My present fancy is for wolves. Taganrog, my large Siberian wolf, has proved more troublesome than any other animal I have attempted to subdue. I shall, of course, conquer him in the end, but I own that the task is difficult."

We had now reached the kennels. Mrs. Bensasan and I stood together outside the iron bars. The doors of the cages themselves were all open, and the wolves were outside in their yards: some lying down and half asleep, others moving restlessly up and down the narrow confines of their prisons. Mrs. Bensasan walked from one enclosure to the other, looking into each and telling me different stories with regard to the special wolves. At last she came to the enclosure where Taganrog was confined.

"You must watch from there," she said, pointing to a grass mound that stood a few feet away. "I am the only one who ever ventures inside those doors. Taganrog fears me, although he will not as yet submit altogether to my treatment."

As she spoke she took a great key from her girdle and unlocked the gate in the centre of the bars. When she got within she put up her hand in the direction of the iron roof and took down a big stock whip. At the end of the fall of the whip were wires loaded with balls of lead. I now noticed that Taganrog's kennel was closed. I had not yet seen the great wolf.

"What an awful weapon!" I said, pointing to the whip.

Her ugly mouth opened wide and she showed all her glittering white teeth.

"Not more awful than my beautiful Taganrog deserves. He is the grandest creature on earth and the most untameable. But never mind; my heart is set on effecting his moral reformation."

She laughed discordantly. There seemed to be nothing in tune about the woman. Already her personality was getting on my nerves. She gave me a glance, half of contempt, half of amusement.

"Watch me from the grass bank," she said. "You will see what will appear to you an ugly sight; but remember all the time that it is the reformation of the great Siberian wolf Taganrog, and that by-and-by all England, all Europe, will ring with his exploits and mine. It is a strange thing, Mr. Druce, but that great wolf seems part of me. Once, in some primeval age, we must have been akin."

She turned, and before I could utter a word walked to the kennel. The next instant a huge grey wolf sprang into sight. He was a beautiful creature, with long, very thick grey hair, a bushy tail, and a face which at first sight looked gentle as that of a Newfoundland dog. But when he saw Mrs. Bensasan a rapid change came over him. He crouched in one corner, his teeth were bared, he growled audibly, and shivered in every limb. Mrs. Bensasan stood a foot away, holding her loaded whip slightly raised. She said something to the animal. He crouched as though to spring. In another instant the whip descended smartly on his loins. The blood flowed freely from the poor beast's back. A fierce and terrible expression broke from the woman's lips, and raising the whip once again she lashed the animal several times unmercifully. I could not contain myself. I sprang forward to the doors of the cage.

"Don't be so cruel," I said; "this exhibition is too horrible."

She turned at once at the sound of my voice. I noticed that her face was deadly white and covered with perspiration.

"Don't interfere," she said, in a low tone of fierce anger.

Then, fixing her eyes on Taganrog, she raised the whip once more with a menacing attitude and pointed to the kennel. The wolf gave her a cowed look from his bloodshot eyes and slunk in, growling as he disappeared.

Going up to the kennel she shot the bolt and made it fast. Then, returning the whip to its place, she opened the iron gates, passed through, locked them, and faced me.

"When you came so near you were in danger," she said. "You did a mad thing. Taganrog was in the mood to spring at anyone. He fears me, but he would have torn you savagely even through the bars. In his moments of fear and passion, to tear anyone limb from limb would be his delight. You were foolhardy and in danger."

We were walking slowly back to the house, and had gone about twenty yards, when a cry, clear, full, and piercing, rang on the air. It was so terrible and so absolutely unexpected that I stood still and faced Mrs. Bensasan.

"That is the cry of a woman," I said. "What is wrong?"

She smiled, and stood still as though she were listening. The cry was not repeated, but the next instant the howl of many wolves in evident hunger broke on the stillness.

"What was that other cry?" I asked.

"One of the wolves, perhaps," she answered, "or"—she shrugged her shoulders—"the ghost may really exist."

"What ghost? Please speak, Mrs. Bensasan."

Again she shrugged her shoulders.

"There is a story extant in these parts, to which, of course, I give no credence," she replied; "but the country folks say that the old vaults under the kennels are haunted. Those vaults are useless now and out of repair, but they say that a madman once lived in Cray Lodge. He kept foxhounds, and his wife died under mysterious circumstances. The story is that he shut her into the cellars and starved her. I do not know any particulars—the whole thing happened years ago—but the country folks will tell you, if you question them, that now and then her cry comes out on the midnight or evening air. I am rather pleased with the story than otherwise, for it keeps people off the vicinity of my wolves. You know, of course, why I asked you and Mr. Vandeleur here? Not only for the pleasure of your company, but in order that your exceedingly clever friend may discover if there are any people in the neighbourhood who would dare to tamper with my special pets. It would be easy to throw them poisoned meat through the iron bars of their enclosures. A woman in my profession is surrounded by enemies. Ah! how excited my wolves are to-night! Listen to Taganrog; he is expressing his feelings."

A prolonged howl, full of misery, rent the air. We both returned in silence to the house.

"You will find the hall warm and comfortable, Mr. Druce. Ah! there is Madame Sara sitting by the fire; she is always good company. Go and talk to her. You need not begin to prepare for dinner for over an hour."

She left me and I went into the hall. Madame Sara was seated near the fire. The firelight fell on the red gold of her beautiful hair and lit up the soft complexion.

I sat down beside her.

"Will you answer a question?" I said, suddenly. "Where is Miss Bensasan?"

"That secret belongs to her mother."

"But you know—I am certain you know."

"The secret belongs to Mrs. Bensasan," was Madame's reply.

She sat still, gazing into the flames that licked the great logs on the hearth. I watched her. She was as great an enigma to me as ever. Suddenly she spoke in a reflective voice.

"You are, of course, aware that Mr. Hiliers is the son of a very wealthy man?"

"I only know that he is a diamond merchant," I replied.

"And that," she answered, slowly, "is sufficient. I shall have something to do with the elder Mr. Hiliers before long. He has just purchased Orion, the most marvellous diamond that Africa has produced of late years."

"I was not aware of it," I said.

She looked at me again; her blue eyes grew dark, their expression altered, a look of age crept into them—there seemed to be the knowledge of centuries in their depths.

"I have a passion for jewels," she said, slowly, "for articles of vertu,[1] for priceless, unique treasures. I am collecting such. I want Orion. If that gem of gems becomes my fortunate possession it would mean the overthrow of a certain lady, the recovery of an unfortunate girl, and the final extinction of a fiend in human guise."

As she spoke she rose, gave me a slow, inscrutable smile, and walked out of the hall.

By an arrangement which we both considered specially convenient Vandeleur and I had rooms each opening into the other, and when I heard my friend tap at my door just before midnight I felt a sense of relief. I opened it for him and he entered. Crossing the room he flung himself into a deep chair and looked up at me.

"You have something to say, Druce. What is it?"

I replied briefly, giving him a full account of my interviews, first with Mrs. Bensasan and then with Madame Sara.

"You have had all the innings this afternoon," he said, with a smile. "That cry coming from the kennels is certainly ghastly."

The smile faded from his face; it looked sterner than I had ever seen it before. After a pause he said, gravely:—

"This is our worst case. I offer my life willingly at the shrine of

1 Fine art.

this mystery. Things have become intolerable; the end must be at hand. I have resolved to die or conquer in this matter."

As he spoke we both heard the cry of the wolves ringing out on the stillness of the midnight air.

"I shall examine those cellars to-morrow," said Vandeleur. "Good-night. I must be alone to think things over."

I did not detain him, and he left me.

At breakfast the next morning Mrs. Bensasan said:—

"I am glad to be able to tell you, Mr. Druce, that Taganrog is coming to his senses. I gave him a long lesson last night, and he begins to obey. He will be all right to-morrow night. In a fortnight's time he will be as meek as a lamb. He is, I consider, my greatest triumph. Mr. Vandeleur, I have already shown my pet wolf to Mr. Druce; would you like to see him?"

"I should," he answered, gently.

"I shall give Taganrog several lessons to-day," she continued, "and propose to give him his first almost immediately. Will you come with me now or later? He is a great beauty. Mr. Druce admires him immensely. I am proud to feel that I am his conqueror. Although he will always be ferocious to the rest of the world, he will soon be amenable to my least word or look."

Neither of us made any reply, and Rigby, who was present, rose, gave Mrs. Bensasan a peculiar glance, and left the room. I noticed for the first time that with all her fearlessness she seemed to make an exception in his favour. When her eyes met his she did not look altogether at her ease. Fearless and strong as was her nature, was it possible that she was in this man's power?

"Have you told Mr. Vandeleur about that peculiar cry which we both heard yesterday?" continued Mrs. Bensasan, turning to me. "It frightened you, did it not?"

"It certainly did," I replied.

"Knowing so little about wild beasts as you do I am not surprised at that," was her answer. "It is, I assure you, quite a common error to mistake the cry of a brute for that of a human being, for brutes have many tones in their voices, and the wolf in particular has a long gamut of sound in his larynx. Be that as it may, however, I should like you both to be satisfied. Under my kennels are three old disused cellars. Would you not like to go and search them? You will then know for yourselves whether there is any poor creature incarcerated there or not."

Vandeleur rose to his feet.

"I take you at your word, Mrs. Bensasan," he said. "I should like to examine the cellars. Will you come with me, Druce, or shall I go alone?"

"I will go with you," I replied.

"I am going down now to have the wolves locked into their kennels," said Mrs. Bensasan. "Will you follow me in about ten minutes' time?"

We did so. There were no keepers present, but Mrs. Bensasan stood within the enclosure of Taganrog's kennel with a smile on her face and the cruel whip in her hand. She unlocked the iron gates and invited us to enter. To my surprise I noticed that a great flagstone was raised within a couple of feet from the entrance to the enclosure, and we saw a well-like opening in the ground.

"Here is a lantern," said Mrs. Bensasan, handing one to Vandeleur. "I will wait here until you return."

We went down at once in silence. We were both absolutely aware of the danger we ran. It would be easy for Mrs. Bensasan to drop the flagstone over us and to incarcerate us within to starve out our lives. Nevertheless, I do not think we feared.

The air struck damp and chill about us. We heard the cries of the imprisoned wolves over our heads. There were three cellars, each opening into the other, but search as we would we could not see the smallest sign of any human being. Vandeleur stayed some time in the second cellar, examining it most minutely, feeling the walls, and stamping his feet on the ground in order to detect any hollow spot. At last he turned to me and said, slowly:—

"Whoever cried that time yesterday has been removed. There is no use in our staying any longer."

We retraced our steps and soon found ourselves in the open air. Mrs. Bensasan's eyes were shining with intense excitement. There was a small, angry red spot on the centre of each cheek.

"Well, gentlemen," she said, "I hope you are satisfied?"

"Absolutely," replied Vandeleur.

She opened the gate for us and we passed through.

A minute later the excited cry of the released pack broke on our ears.

"Will you walk with me to the railway-station?" asked Vandeleur.

"What!" I cried, in some amazement, "are you going to town?"

"Yes, for a few hours. I have got an idea in my mind. I am haunted by a memory; it goes back a good way, too. I want to have it confirmed; it may bear on this case. If it does I may be able to release Miss Laura, for that she is detained in most undesirable captivity I have not the slightest doubt."

"What about the robberies?" I asked. "Is there anything of the sort going on?"

"As far as I can tell, nothing. We must hurry, Druce, if I am to catch my train."

I saw him off and returned slowly to the house. On my way back I met Gerald Hiliers. He was waiting to see me, and began to talk at once on the subject nearest his heart.

"Taganrog will be in control by to-morrow night," he said. "The exhibition is to take place by electric light, and Mrs. Bensasan is having a small platform raised for us to stand on while she exhibits. She is anxious to accustom the wolves to the flare and light which must be present when she holds her public exhibitions. By the way," he added, suddenly, "I saw Madame Sara this morning, and she told me that she has given you her confidence. She promised to help me, but on an impossible condition. My father will never part with Orion except for a fabulous price. The diamond is watched day and night by two men, and the safe in which it is secured is practically impregnable. There is no help whatever in that direction."

"Have you told Madame Sara yet about your father's view of the matter?" I asked.

"Yes."

"And what did she say?"

"She smiled."

"Then, Hiliers, I counsel you to beware. I like Madame least of all when she smiles."

Vandeleur returned rather late that evening. He informed me briefly that he was satisfied with his investigations, and that it was his intention to force Mrs. Bensasan's hand, by means known only to himself, if she did not soon reveal her daughter's whereabouts.

The next day was Wednesday; that night we were to see Mrs. Bensasan in the hour of her triumph. I awoke with an overpowering sense of restlessness and depression. Vandeleur was seen talking earnestly with Mrs. Bensasan soon after breakfast. Their conversation was evidently of an amicable kind, for when it was over she nodded to him, smiled, and hurried off in the direction of the kennels.

Vandeleur then, with long strides, disappeared up the avenue. I wondered what he was doing and what was the matter. I wanted his confidence, but did not care to press for it.

Shortly before lunch, as I was walking on the borders of the pine wood, I was amazed to see Madame Sara drive up in a dog-cart. She saw me, pulled in the mare which she was driving herself, flung the reins to the groom, and alighted with her usual agility.

"Ah!" she called out, "I am glad to see you. You wonder where I have been."

I made no reply.

"Confess to your curiosity," she continued. "This is an extraordinary day, and my nerves are in a strange state. Much—everything—hangs on the issues of to-night. Mr. Druce, I want to confide in you."

"Don't!" I could not help exclaiming.

"You must listen. This is what has happened. When friends fall out—ah! you know the old proverb—well, friends have fallen out, for Mrs. Bensasan and I have quarrelled; oh, my friend, *such* a quarrel! A point was to be solved. Julia Bensasan wished the solution to take one form, while I was just as resolved that it should take another. She is a powerful woman, both physically and mentally, but she is destitute of tact. She has no reserve of genius in her nature. Now, I——" —she drew herself up—"I am Madame Sara, known to the world for very remarkable abilities. In this conflict I shall win."

"Explain, will you?" I said.

"Ah! you are curious at last. Mr. Druce, it is a very remarkable fact that you and your friend should have been fighting so hard against me for so many months, and in the end be altogether on my side."

"What do you mean?"

"Need you ask?" she replied. "Are not your wishes and mine identical? We want to make a girl happy. We have resolved to give her to the man who loves her and whom she loves. Need I say any more?"

"Madame Sara," I said, "you do nothing without a price. Have you a chance of receiving the diamond?"

"I have a passion," she said, slowly, "for things unique, strange, and priceless. I go far to seek them, still farther to obtain them. Neither life nor death stands in my way. Yes, the stone is mine."

"Impossible!"

"It is true. I went to town this morning. I saw old Mr. Hiliers. He gave me the diamond. I keep it on a condition."

I was speechless from amazement. She looked at me, then said, slowly:—

"I find the lost girl and give her to Gerald Hiliers."

"But why has his father changed his mind? Gerald told me only yesterday how callous he was with regard to the whole matter."

"Ah! he is callous no longer. He and I have both a desire, I for unique treasures and he for unlimited wealth. The love of gold is his passion. I have informed him with regard to some things in connection with Mrs. Bensasan. She is one of the richest women in England; Laura is her only child and heiress. I have done something else for him."

"What is that?"

"Imparted to him a secret by which he can in a measure recover his lost youth. To offer a man both youth and riches presents a temptation impossible for the ordinary man to resist. Mr. Hiliers is quite ordinary; he struggled, but in the end succumbed. I knew he would."

Her eyes sparkled.

"Will you tell me one thing?" I said. "Why does Mrs. Bensasan want her daughter to marry Joseph Rigby? Is he so rich and so desirable?"

She came a step nearer.

"Your friend, Mr. Vandeleur, is on the track of that secret," she said. "I could tell him now, but I delay just for a time. As you know so much you may as well know this. Rigby is greater and more powerful than the richest man or the most beautiful or the greatest on earth. He holds a secret—it is connected with Mrs. Bensasan. Laura is the price of his silence. Ah! have I been overheard?"

She sprang away from me. There was a rustle in the bushes near by. I rushed up to them and tore them asunder. No one was to be seen. But Madame Sara's face had changed. It was full of a curious, most ghastly fear.

"I have been imprudent," she said, in a low voice, "and for the first time in my life. Is it possible that success has turned my brain?"

She did not wait to give me another glance, but hurried to the house.

We dined early that night, as Mrs. Bensasan's exhibition was to take place at eight o'clock. The dinner was gay; the conversation bright; repartee and wit sparkled like champagne. On the face of Mrs. Bensasan, however, there was a fierce, cruel look, which was so dominant that, with all her efforts to appear friendly, sociable—in fact, the perfect hostess—she utterly failed. Once her eyes fixed themselves on Madame Sara's beautiful and charming face, and the expression in their agate depths was far from good to see.

The dinner came to an end. It was too soon to go to the kennels.

"There is still time enough," remarked Mrs. Bensasan, addressing Madame Sara. "Follow me in five minutes. You and I have our work to do first. When we are quite ready for the curtain to rise and the show to begin, my keeper, Keppel, shall announce the fact to the gentlemen."

Mrs. Bensasan went slowly from the room. I had never before been so impressed. Madame Sara beside her hostess looked young, slender, almost childish.

"That woman is the greatest of her age," said Madame. "How great only I who have known her for years can imagine. Mr. Rigby and I both know Mrs. Bensasan well, don't we, sir?"

We none of us spoke, and she went slowly towards the door. Just as she reached it she turned and faced us.

"I have provided against possible mischief," she said.

She thrust her hand into the bosom of her dress and drew out a small revolver. Minute as it was, I knew the sort, and was well aware that it could be used with deadly effect. With a gentle and sweet smile she returned it to its place; then, taking up a cloak which lay on a chair near, she flung it over her evening dress and disappeared into the night.

Four of us were now left in the hall—Rigby, Hiliers, Vandeleur, and myself.

"We shall be summoned in a minute," said Vandeleur. "This is a state of tension quite unpleasant in its strain."

He walked to the house door and threw it open. He had scarcely done so before the sharp crack of a shot sounded from the pine wood below the house. It was followed instantly by another. Fearing we knew not what, we all rushed from the hall and flew down the path through the pine wood. The bright electric light guided us; the howl of many wolves smote savagely on our ears.

In a very short time we had reached the little platform which had been erected in front of the huge cage where Mrs. Bensasan had arranged to give her exhibition. The cage was there, but to my surprise there was no keeper in sight. We instantly crowded on the platform and saw Mrs. Bensasan standing upright in the middle of the cage. She had the stock whip in her hand. A woman lay prostrate at her feet. The woman's fair hair streamed along the floor of the cage; her cloak was torn aside. There was a large and ghastly wound in her throat; blood covered the floor. At a little distance lay Taganrog, shot through the head and motionless. When she saw us approach Mrs. Bensasan turned. Her face was quite calm and her manner quiet. She looked down at the figure of the fallen woman.

Fig. 20. "'THE GREAT MADAME SARA IS DEAD,' SHE SAID."

"Madame Sara, the great Madame Sara, is dead," she said, with slow distinctness. "She ventured into the cage; it was imprudent—I implored her not to come, but she would not heed. Her death is due to Taganrog. He feared me, but the sight of her maddened him. He sprang at her and tore her throat. It was but the work of a second. See, I have shot him. But Madame had also a revolver, and just in the moment of—of—ah! Heavens! Ah!"

She tottered; over her face there came an awful expression, and the next instant she also was lying on the floor of the cage. Long quivers passed over her frame. She was evidently in mortal agony. We all rushed forward, burst open the door of the cage, and entered.

Vandeleur went on his knees and bent over the prostrate woman.

"I die," she said; "I have only a few minutes to live. Listen!"

She tried to press her hand to her side; a great spurt of blood poured from her lips.

"I am shot through the lungs," she said. "Hers was the surest aim in the world. You may know all now. Madame Sara and I arranged this exhibition, and you, Mr. Vandeleur, were to be the victim. Madame got you both down here on purpose. It was she who thought the thing out; we did not believe we could manage the death of you both, but one at least seemed certain. Your methods were more deadly than those of Mr. Druce, therefore you were appointed to be the victim. But when the wicked quarrel—ah! you see for yourselves the result. You shall know all now.

"Joseph Rigby—yes, he is there, but it doesn't matter; he knew a story about me. Madame also knew, but he had the evidence and she had not. He could hang me—it happened years ago—I poisoned my husband."

"I know," said Vandeleur. "I found the particulars yesterday, in the books at Westminster. I meant to speak to you to-morrow—but no matter."

"Bah!" she said, "nothing matters now. I hated that feeble man. I poisoned him with arsenic. Rigby knew, and from that day he blackmailed me heavily. Six months ago he set his heart on securing my pretty, gentle Laura—Laura with her money was to be his price. I did not dare to give her to another. I was determined that she should marry him; I would make her submit. One night Madame and I took her away in a cab. This was to blind the neighbours. Towards morning we brought her back and put her into the cellars below the kennels. When you, Mr. Vandeleur, examined them, you knew nothing of a small dungeon below the second cellar. Laura was put there. She is gagged in the dungeon now. You will find the spot by a jagged cross scratched over the stone above. She is uninjured. She inherits my money. When I die Rigby will be powerless. You can give her to the other man."

Vandeleur placed his hand under her shoulders and slightly raised her head.

"Madame shot me through the lungs," she continued. "My

life is only a matter of minutes. I go to my death unabsolved and unafraid. Madame, at least, is dead. She was cleverer than I and more subtle. Ah! there never was a brain like hers. She arranged to help me; Rigby should obtain Laura, and you, Mr. Vandeleur, should die. All was going well, but avarice got the better of her. For the sake of a stone, a bauble, she gave me up, and I could not brook that. I resolved that the means which were meant to compass your death should compass hers. Revenge became the strongest motive of my life. My intention was, had all succeeded, to lay the blame on Taganrog. It would have been natural, would it not, to suppose that the wolf——But look!"

Her eyes sought the floor, and Vandeleur, bending down, picked up two great sets of steel teeth, fashioned somewhat after the teeth of a wolf. They jangled horribly as he shook them in his hand. The dying eyes gleamed.

"She made them," whispered the exhausted voice. "She made them for me to use in order to take you by surprise, to spring on you and tear your throat out. An excuse was to be made which was to bring you first on the scene to-night. The keepers were to be dismissed beforehand. All the world would suppose that it was an accident and that the wolf had destroyed you. She and I would have known better. I guessed her treachery and followed her to-day, and heard what she said to Mr. Druce. Instantly I changed my tactics. *You should live*, but SHE should die! I sent for her first on purpose. She must have scented my change of front, for she had her revolver. The wolf killed her—I had no need to use those hideous teeth; but before she died she raised that toy instrument and inflicted my death wound. It was I who shot the wolf——"

Her voice faded away into silence. The dimness of death covered her awful, too bright eyes. A minute or two later she breathed her last.

We rescued Laura Bensasan from her terrible prison. We took from that den a distracted and nearly mad girl. We brought her back to the house, and did all that ingenuity and kindness could suggest for her benefit. But one look at Hiliers was better for her than all our sympathy. She flew to him. He took her in his arms. He loved her and she loved him. There was no longer any bar to their happiness and future union.

Appendix A: Contemporary Interviews and Reviews

1. From "Portraits of Celebrities at Different Times of their Lives," *Strand Magazine* 16 (December 1898): 674

[Meade is positioned as the leading celebrity opposite H.G. Wells (1866–1946). "Portraits of Celebrities" was one of the *Strand*'s most popular long-running features.]

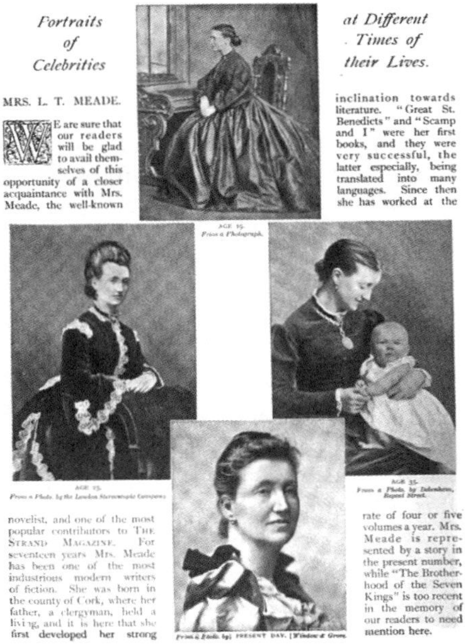

Portraits of Celebrities at Different Times of their Lives.

MRS. L. T. MEADE.

WE are sure that our readers will be glad to avail themselves of this opportunity of a closer acquaintance with Mrs. Meade, the well-known novelist, and one of the most popular contributors to THE STRAND MAGAZINE. For seventeen years Mrs. Meade has been one of the most industrious modern writers of fiction. She was born in the county of Cork, where her father, a clergyman, held a living, and it is here that she first developed her strong inclination towards literature. "Great St. Benedicts" and "Scamp and I" were her first books, and they were very successful, the latter especially, being translated into many languages. Since then she has worked at the rate of four or five volumes a year. Mrs. Meade is represented by a story in the present number, while "The Brotherhood of the Seven Kings" is too recent in the memory of our readers to need mention here.

AGE 15. *From a Photograph.*

AGE 25. *From a Photo. by the London Stereoscopic Company.*

AGE 35. *From a Photo. by Debenham, Regent Street.*

From a Photo. by] PRESENT DAY. [*Window & Grove.*

Fig. 21. "Portraits of Celebrities." *Strand Magazine* 16 (Dec. 1898): 674

2. From L.T. Meade, "How I Began," *Girl's Realm* (November 1900): 57–64

[Meade's autobiographical essay "How I Began" was introduced in the upscale *Girls' Realm* (1898–1915) as "the first of a Series of

Papers which will tell how Women who have made their mark in Literature, Art, Science, and Philanthropy, prepared themselves for their Career; of the Difficulties they encountered, and of the Encouragement they received." In this excerpt, Meade describes her determination to "seek her fortune" in London following the death of her mother in 1874 and recounts her early days working in the Reading Room of the British Museum.]

[O]n a certain November day I came … to London, determined to seek my fortune. My friends at home were very angry with me. One lady in particular said, as I was leaving the country, "Mark my words, L.T. Meade will never make half a sovereign[1] by her writings."

I arrived in London to be greeted by my friend, who came to meet me at Paddington,[2] by the dire information that her husband's house and hers had been burnt to the ground the night before. I was taken to a boarding house, where I had experiences the reverse of pleasant, but which have nothing to do with this story. In process of time my friends were able to receive me, and then I began. I had got to succeed—I had got to prove to my world that I had something in me. I do not think … my ideas were solely those of one who wished to make money. I wanted to prove that I had a gift and that I would use it. But money was also essential, for if I could not add to my income, I could not stay in London, and to come home a failure was impossible!

So I worked. Yes, I worked very hard. I secured a ticket for the reading room of the British Museum, and there I spent my days. Come hail or storm, no matter what the state of the weather, I was always at my desk. My pile of books was placed by my side by an obliging clerk. With a clean pad of blotting paper, pens and ink, all provided by the trustees of the reading room, I did stimulating, and I am inclined to think, good work. I returned to my friends … evening after evening, tired but happy. I would do all that a girl could to prove my right to a niche in the temple of fame. I would earn sufficient money to enable me to live in London until I could do really good work, and so rise above all anxieties.

---

1 A gold coin worth £1 in use until the early twentieth century.

2 Railway terminus in central London providing service to southwest England and Wales.

[Meade's resolve and perseverance were rewarded within a relatively short period of time. With the publication of *Great St. Benedict's* (1876) and *Scamp and I* (1877), her career as a successful professional writer was established. As she told her readers, "from that hour to the present day I may truly affirm that I have always had slightly more work than I knew how to get through. From that day till now I have never been obliged to ask for orders—orders have come to me" (64).]

Fig. 22. "Mrs. Meade in Her Study." *Girl's Realm* 3 (1900-01): 63

3. From Sarah A. Tooley, "Some Women Novelists," *Woman at Home* (1897): 191–93

[Sarah Tooley (1857–1946) was a university-educated professional journalist who specialized in biographical sketches and celebrity interviews. She is best known for her articles on prominent women writers and activists published in *fin-de-siècle* women's papers and magazines such as *Woman at Home*, *Young Woman*, and the feminist *Woman's Signal*.

The Woman at Home (1893–1920) was a glossy middle-class monthly focusing on fashion and domestic subjects, biographies, and fiction. The following essay on Meade appeared in an extended article featuring a number of well-known women writers including Mary Elizabeth Braddon (1837–1915), Frances

Hodgson Burnett (1849–1924), Sarah Grand (1854–1943), and Eliza Lynn Linton (1822–98). The article was embellished with photographs of the authors, facsimiles of their handwriting, and photographs of their homes with interior views of their workspaces and writing desks. Some of the material in the excerpt later appeared in Tooley's article "Some Famous Authors as Girls," published in the *Girl's Realm* in 1899.]

Mrs. L.T. Meade

Mrs. L.T. Meade is one of the most prolific story-writers of the day, and since she published her first book some twenty years ago has produced no less than 100 works of fiction, many of them being specially written for girls. She has a charming suburban house in West Dulwich.[1] Although all her books have been written in London, she is Irish by birth, and was born at Bandon, Co. Cork, her father holding the living of Kilowen near by. He did not approve of her literary proclivities as a child, and refused to supply her with writing paper, upon which she scribbled her stories on the margins of the newspapers. When she was about twelve years old, her father removed to a large rectory near Kinsale, and there indeed was a home fit to stimulate the imagination of the future novelist. It bore the picturesque name of Templetrine (Temple of the Trinity), and was an old-fashioned castle of a house, with curious winding staircases and mysterious passages, and it had ghosts. But although Mrs. Meade has many genuine and blood-curdling ghost stories to relate, she has never, strange to say, put them into fiction; neither has she made the old haunted rectory the scene of any of her stories.

"I find it difficult to write," she said, "of real experiences. Freshness of topic is essential to my work." She has a special aptitude for taking up new subjects, and the more difficult they are the better she likes them! She dictates all her work, and is now so accustomed to that method of composition that she cannot compose so well if she does not hear the words spoken. Mrs. Meade thinks, however, that dictation inclines a writer to be verbose, and when she is particularly anxious to make a scene terse and strong she scribbles it down in pencil and dictates it afterwards.

"I think," she said, "that the demand for short stories is very hard on us poor writers; we have to sacrifice so many plots. I often dictate a short story four times before I can get it to my mind. It is so difficult to make one's points tell in short stories."

1 A district of south London.

Mrs. Meade has done a great deal of work in collaboration with a medical friend, as will be seen in her most popular novel, "The Medicine Lady," and in the "Stories from the Diary of a Doctor."

"I like collaboration," Mrs. Meade said, "for I think the rubbing against another mind is stimulating; but collaborators should always be of the opposite sexes. The union of a man and a woman is a perfect union in the writing of fiction as in other things. Contact with the masculine mind is invigorating, but collaboration with another woman would produce the essence of weakness. And besides," added Mrs. Meade, "a man and a woman are so much more likely to be civil to one another than two of the same sex would be if working together."

Mrs. Meade left her Irish home when a mere girl, after the second marriage of her father, and came to live with some friends in the heart of London.[1] There she had an opportunity for studying the lives of the struggling poor, who have always drawn forth her sympathy. Her first novel, "Great St. Benedict's," dealt with the manner in which out-patients were treated at the London hospitals, and was readily accepted and published. Then came that most pathetic story of child life amongst the London poor, "Scamp and I," a book that went straight to the hearts of the people as it had sprung straight from the heart of the girl writer. She sold the copyright for £30, and has never received anything further for the work. It, however, made her fame as a writer. Shortly after its publication she became connected with Messrs. Tillotson's syndicate,[2] for which she has written ever since. She was also an early contributor to the *Sunday Magazine*, and found in its editor, Mr. Benjamin Waugh, one of her most encouraging friends.[3] Some years ago Mrs. Meade started *Atalanta*, a mag-

1 Meade would have been about 30 when she left Ireland; her mother died in 1874.

2 Also known as "Tillotson's Fiction Bureau" and "Tillotson's Newspaper Literature Syndicate" (1873–1935), founded by William Tillotson, the proprietor of a successful newspaper chain in the north of England. Tillotson bought the serial rights to the works of popular novelists for publication in British and international newspapers.

3 *The Sunday Magazine* (1864–1906) was a six-penny weekly illustrated Evangelical magazine intended as Sunday reading for the middle and lower classes. Reverend Benjamin Waugh (1839–1908) was a social reformer and founder of the National Society for the Prevention of Cruelty to Children.

azine for girls, and it was the insight which, as an editor, she gained into the ignorance of would-be authors, as to methods of work and the demands of the public, which induced her to recently plead for a School of Fiction.[1]

"My critics tell me," she said, "that as we cannot create a genius, a School of Fiction would be useless. It is, however, well known that Schools of Art have not produced one more really great painter than would have come to the fore without their assistance, but they have done something else—they have raised the standard of Art all over the country. So also might a school for the training of our younger novelists do a similar good. The only difficulty that I see in the starting of a School of Fiction is procuring the requisite teachers, as those most qualified to be professors are those who cannot devote time to that work. I believe, however, that sooner or later we shall have our School of Fiction, and," she added, with one of her bright sallies, "a department for critics would be lovely."

Of the many charming children's books which Mrs. Meade has written, she herself likes "Daddy's Boy" [1887] best of all. It is a story of her own boy when very young. There is no class whose struggles appeal more to Mrs. Meade's kind heart than the brave girls who are striving to make their own way in life, and her stories are specially stimulating for them. She sees with pleasure the various means of livelihood now being opened to women, and believes that it is better for every woman to have a career, whether she has money or not. Mrs. Meade does not want women, however, to give up the old beautiful life, but rather to add to it a fuller development and more active usefulness in the world.

---

1 During the last year of her editorship of *Atalanta* (1892), Meade established the "*Atalanta* School of Fiction" to provide encouragement and practical advice to girls interested in literary careers. To this end, Meade recruited a number of well-known writers (including herself) to contribute essays to the magazine on different aspects of writing. Girls could submit their work for critical evaluation (for a fee) and compete for prizes, scholarships, and publishing opportunities in *Atalanta*. Later, as a member of the feminist Pioneer Club, Meade advocated for the establishment of a School of Fiction and in 1897 promoted the idea in a full-length article published in the *New Century Review* (1897–1900), a short-lived monthly journal offering reviews and essays on politics, literature, history, the arts, religion, and social issues.

4. From E.A. Bennett, "The Fiction of Popular Magazines," *Fame and Fiction: An Enquiry into Certain Popularities* (London: Grant Richards, 1901), 133–42

[Like many successful writers, Meade received negative criticism from her competitors. This excerpt from an essay by Arnold Bennett (1867–1931) was originally published anonymously in the *Academy* (1869–1916), a literary journal known for its intellectual tone. The essay is significant not only for its review of Meade's *Brotherhood of the Seven Kings*, but also for its discussion of popular magazine fiction and the mass market. Bennett, a prominent journalist, editor, and novelist, began his career by writing for a number of popular magazines including George Newnes's *Tit-Bits* (1881–1984).]

The large circulations achieved by the three principal sixpenny illustrated magazines[1] are the fruit of the most resolute and business-like attempt ever made to discover and satisfy the popular taste in monthly journalism.... After much research and experiment, the formula for a truly popular magazine has been arrived at; development is accordingly arrested, at any rate, for a time; the sixpenny monthly is stereotyped into a pattern, the chief details of which can be predicted from month to month.

Now the fine flower of every magazine is its fiction, predominant among the other "features" in attractiveness, quality and expense. It is the fiction which first and chiefly engages the editorial care, which has been most the subject of experiment, and which (perhaps for that very reason) is in the result the most strictly prescribed. We shall be justified in believing that the imaginative literature now printed in the popular magazines coincides with the popular taste as precisely as the limitations of human insight and ingenuity will permit. It assumes, of course, varied forms; but we are concerned only with the most characteristic form—that which is to be found equally in each magazine, and which may, therefore, be said to speak the final word of editorial cunning. This form, without doubt, is the connected series of short stories, of five or six thousand words each, in which the same characters, pitted against

1 Although Bennett does not name the magazines, the most popular six-penny illustrated magazines of the day were the *Strand*, *Harmsworth*, and *Pearson's*.

a succession of criminals or adverse fates, pass again and again through situations thrillingly dangerous, and emerge at length into the calm security of ultimate conquest. It may be noted, by the way, that such a form enables the reader to enjoy the linked excitements of a serial tale without binding him to peruse every instalment. Its universal adoption is a striking instance of that obsequious pampering of mental laziness and apathy which marks all the most successful modern journalism. Dr. Conan Doyle invented it, or reinvented it to present uses. The late Grant Allen added to it a scientific subltety somewhat beyond the appreciation of the six-penny public. Mr. Rudyard Kipling[1] has not disdained to modify it to his own ends. But the typical and indispensable practiser of it at the present moment is Mrs. L.T. Meade. The name of Mrs. Meade, who began by writing books for children, is uttered with a special reverence in those places where they buy and sell fiction. She is ever prominent in the contents bills, if not of one magazine, then of another. She has the gift of fertility; but were she twice as fertile she could not easily meet the demand for her stories. With no genius except a natural instinct for pleasing the mass, she has accepted the form from other hands, and shaped it to such a nicety that editors exclaim on beholding her work: *"This is it!"* And they gladly pay her six hundred guineas for a series of ten tales.

In a sequence entitled *The Brotherhood of the Seven Kings*, by Mrs. Meade and Mr. Robert Eustace (it should be stated that Mrs. Meade employs a collaborator who, to use her own words, supplies "all the scientific portion of each story"), the hero is a philosopher and recluse, young, but with a past, and the sinister heroine is a woman of bewitching beauty who controls a secret society. Mrs. Meade has said to an interviewer that her stories "are all crowded with incident, and have enough plot in each to furnish forth a full novel." This is quite true. There is no padding whatever; incident follows incident with the curtness of an official dispatch. In every story the recluse and the beauty come to grips, usually through the medium of some third person whom

1 Born in India but educated in England, Kipling (1865–1936) returned to India in 1882 to begin his literary career as a journalist. While in India, he published numerous poems, stories, and sketches that made him a literary celebrity when he returned to England in 1889. His Indian experiences inspired his best-known works including the *Jungle Books* (1894–95) and *Kim* (1901). Conan Doyle and Grant Allen are discussed in the Introduction, pp. 17–22.

the latter wishes to ruin and the former to save. In nearly every story the main matter is the recital of an attempt by the heroine or her minions to deal out death in a novel and startling manner. Some of these attempts are really ingenious—for example, those by fever germ, tzetze fly, focus tube (through the wall of a house), circlet and ebbing tide, explosive thermometer. Others—such as those involving the poison-scented brougham and the frozen grave—seem a little absurd; and the same is to be said of the beauty's suicide in an oxy-hydrogen flame giving a heat of 2,400 degrees Centigrade. Besides all these mortal commotions, the book teems with minor phenomena in which science is put to the service of melodrama. Thus, after the detective had covered the heroine with his revolver, "the next instant, as if wrenched from his grasp by some unseen power, the weapon leapt from Ford's hands, and dashed itself with terrific force against the poles of an enormous electro-magnet beside him.... Madame must have made the current by pressing a key on the floor with her foot.... 'It is my turn to dictate terms,' she said, in a steady, even voice." But perhaps the marvels of modern science are best illustrated in this succinct and lucid explanation of the destruction of a priceless vase: "It was not till some hours afterwards that the whole Satanic scheme burst upon me. The catastrophe admitted of but one explanation. The dominant repeated in two bars when all the instruments played together in harmony, must have been the note accordant with that of the cup of the goblet, and by the well-known laws of acoustics, when so played it shattered the goblet."

For the rest, the well-tried machinery of coincidences, overheard conversations, and dropped papers is employed to push the action forward. "It is strange how that woman gets to know all one's friends and acquaintances," says the hero of the heroine. And it is strange. The descriptive passages present no novelties. Of a duke it is said: "He was well dressed, and had the indescribable air of good-breeding which proclaims the gentleman." The symptoms of mental uplifting and extreme agitation are set forth in quite the usual manner: "Two hectic spots burned on his pale cheeks, and the glitter in his eyes showed how keen was the excitement which consumed him." On the rare occasions when the hero allows himself to soliloquise for the reader's benefit, his thought and language are conceived on the simple theatrical lines of an address to a jury: "From henceforth my object would be to expose Mme. Kolusky [*sic*]. By so doing my own life would be in danger; nevertheless, my firm determination was not to leave a stone unturned to place this woman and her confederates in the felon's dock of an English criminal court." Lastly, it is to be observed and specially remembered that the "love-interest," so often stated to be indispensable to the literature of the British public, amounts to nothing at all in *The Brotherhood of the Seven Kings*. Certain pretty and amiable girls ... cross the stage from time to time, bringing some odour of an artless passion; but in the dry light of that science which dominates and pervades every theme, these wistful creatures and their adorations are absolutely negligible.

"Wonderful imagination!" exclaims the reader whom the stories are so cleverly designed to allure, echoing the question of the hero's legal friend, Dufrayer: "Who would believe that we were living in the dreary nineteenth century!" Ask this reader what he wants in fiction, and he will reply that he wants something "to take him out of himself." He thinks that he has found that magical something; but he has not found it, nor does he in truth want it. Nothing in a literary sense annoys him more than to be taken out of himself; he always resents the operation. The success of these most typical stories depends largely on the fact that they essay no such perilous feat. In the whole of *The Brotherhood of the Seven Kings* I have discovered not a trace of imagination, no attempt to *realise* a scene, no touch of vehemence nor spark of poetic flame. Nor is there any spirituality or fresh feeling for any sort of beauty. The spirit and the things of the spirit are ignored utterly. That coma of the soul in which nine men out of every ten exist from the cradle to the grave is thus never disturbed as imagination must necessarily disturb it. Imagination arouses imagination, and spurs the most precious of human faculties to an effort corresponding in a degree with the effort of the artist. To enjoy a work of imagination is no pastime, rather a sweet but fatiguing labour. After a play of Shakespeare or a Wagnerian opera repose is needed. Only a madman like Louis of Bavaria[1] could demand *Tristan*[2] twice in one night. The principle of this extreme case is the principle of all cases: effort for effort, and the greater the call the greater the response. The listener, the reader, is compelled by a law of nature to do his share. The point about

1 Ludwig II of Bavaria (1845–86), remembered for his extravagant artistic and architectural projects, most notably his fantastic Neuschwanstein Castle. Ludwig's extravagance and neglect of state affairs prompted allegations of insanity.

2 Richard Wagner's opera *Tristan und Isolde*, first performed in Munich in 1865 and in London in 1882.

a member of the six-penny public is that he coldly declines to do his share. He pays his sixpence; the writer is expected to do the rest, and to do it with discretion. There is to be no changing of the aspect; no invitation to the soul, that poor victim of atrophy, to run upstairs for the good of its health. The man has come home to his wife, his slippers, and his cigar, and shall he be asked to go mountaineering?

What, then, is it in these *gesta*[1] of scoundrels and detectives which suits and soothes him? It is the quality of invention—a quality entirely apart from imagination. To see the facts of life—*his* facts, the trivial, external, vulgar, unimportant facts—taken and woven into new and surprising patterns: this amuses him, while calling for no exertion. He watches the wonderful process (and, of course, it can be made wonderful) as a child watches its Australian uncle perform miracles of architecture with an old familiar block of bricks. But he surpasses the child in simplicity, because he fancies the box of bricks has changed into something else. He fancies he is outside the dull nursery of his own existence, and watching brighter scenes; yet the window-bars were never more secure or the air less free. Pathetic and extraordinary self-deception!

1 Deeds or exploits (Latin).

Appendix B: Degeneration and Crime

1. From Gina Lombroso Ferrero, *Criminal Man According to the Classification of Cesare Lombroso*, introduction by Cesare Lombroso (London: Putnam, 1911), xiv–xv, 135–36

[Italian physician and psychiatrist Cesare Lombroso (1835–1909) is generally considered the founder of criminal anthropology. He is best known for his theory that individuals biologically programmed to commit criminal acts ("born" criminals) exhibit specific physical and psychological anomalies resembling the characteristics of so-called "primitive" people, animals, and even plants. Influenced by Charles Darwin's theory of evolution, Lombroso argued that the most dangerous criminals were atavists or evolutionary "throwbacks." Although he always defended his theory of atavism, he later identified disease and social factors as contributors to criminality.[1]

Lombroso wrote over thirty books and more than a thousand articles for academic journals, popular magazines, and newspapers, but his most significant works were *L'uomo delinquente* (*Criminal Man*), first published in 1876, and *La donna delinquente* (*Criminal Woman*), a companion study published in 1893. His ideas were introduced to English readers through an abbreviated English translation of the latter text (published as *The Female Offender* in 1895) and articles published in British journals in the 1890s. Though his work is now discredited and considered offensive for its representation of groups he considered inferior (women, non-white populations, and certain

1 Although Lombroso and many of his contemporaries frequently used the terms "atavism" and "degeneration" interchangeably when describing criminal behaviour, the terms denoted different conditions. Atavism referred to an innate tendency to revert to an earlier evolutionary stage, while degeneration was thought to result from negative external or social influences such as alcoholism, syphilis, or tuberculosis. According to contemporary theories, degeneration caused a gradual and hereditary weakening of individuals and their descendants (see Introduction to Lombroso's *Criminal Woman* by Rafter and Gibson 20).

ethnic and social groups), his ideas were highly influential because they engaged with *fin-de-siècle* anxieties about crime, degeneration, class, and gender.

Criminal Man appeared in five ever-larger editions by 1897; French, German, Russian, and Spanish translations were published between 1887 and 1899. The first English version appeared as a summary published by Lombroso's daughter Gina Lombroso Ferrero in 1911.]

[Introduction by Cesare Lombroso]
I ... began to study criminals in the Italian prisons, and, amongst others, I made the acquaintance of the famous brigand Vilella.... On his death one cold grey November morning, I was deputed to make the *post-mortem*, and on laying open the skull I found on the occipital part, exactly on the part where a spine is found in the normal skull, a distinct depression which I named *median occipital fossa*, because of its situation precisely in the middle of the occiput as in inferior animals, especially rodents. This depression, as in the case of animals, was correlated with the hypertrophy of the *vermis*, known in birds as the middle cerebellum.

This was not merely an idea, but a revelation. At the sight of that skull, I seemed to see all of a sudden, lighted up as a vast plain under a flaming sky, the problem of the nature of the criminal—an atavistic being who reproduces in his person the ferocious instincts of primitive humanity and the inferior animals. Thus were explained anatomically the enormous jaws, high cheek-bones, prominent superciliary arches, solitary lines in the palms, extreme size of the orbits, handle-shaped or sessile ears found in criminals, savages, and apes, insensibility to pain, extremely acute sight, tattooing, excessive idleness, love of orgies, and the irresistible craving for evil for its own sake, the desire not only to extinguish life in the victim, but to mutilate the corpse, tear its flesh, and drink its blood.

[...]

The criminal is an atavistic being, a relic of a vanished race. This is by no means an uncommon occurrence in nature. Atavism, the reversion to a former state, is the first feeble indication of the reaction opposed by nature to the perturbing causes which seek to alter her delicate mechanism. Under certain unfavourable conditions, cold or poor soil, the common oak will develop characteristics of the oak of the Quaternary period. The dog left to run wild in the forest will in a few generations revert to the type of his original wolf-like progenitor.... Under special conditions produced by alcohol, chloroform, heat, or injuries, ants, dogs, and pigeons become irritable and savage like their wild ancestors.

This tendency to alter under special conditions is common to human beings, in whom hunger, syphilis, trauma, and, still more frequently, morbid conditions inherited from insane, criminal, or diseased progenitors, or the abuse of nerve poisons, such as alcohol, tobacco, or morphine, cause various alterations, of which criminality—that is, a return to the characteristics peculiar to primitive savages—is in reality the least serious, because it represents a less advanced stage than other forms of cerebral alteration.

The aetiology of crime, therefore, mingles with that of all kinds of degeneration: rickets, deafness, monstrosity, hairiness, and cretinism, of which crime is only a variation.

2. From Cesare Lombroso, "Atavism and Evolution," *Contemporary Review* 68 (July 1895): 42

[In the following extract, Lombroso dismisses the common belief that evolution represents a natural progression (one that emphasizes the ascendancy of the "white races") and presents the idea that human societies, no less than individuals, might regress into "lower" forms or disappear altogether (Hurley 56–57). The fear that the evolutionary process might be reversible underlies countless gothic and science-fiction narratives including *The Time Machine* (see Appendix B4 below), one of a number of H.G. Wells's works that scrutinize the idea of humanity's inevitable progress.

The Contemporary Review, founded in 1866, one of the nineteenth century's foremost periodicals, was known for its liberal orientation and its significant articles on religion, philosophy, politics, literature, art, music, science, and social reform.]

It is a prevalent delusion of our times that we are always progressing. We picture progress to ourselves as an endless line leading straight up to heaven, without any turnings, and imagine our own white races at the top of the line, attaining by a continuous rise to immeasurable heights of civilization. But a little calm observation quickly shows how great is the illusion of this view. Progress there certainly is in some nations, not so much in morality—for under certain circumstances they are liable to relapse even into cannibalism—nor even in religion, which is often enough surrounded by fetishism; but unquestionably in the life of intellect and of politics. All the same, an attentive consideration reveals the fact that, even among the most privileged peoples, the line of movement, far from being vertical, is always describing reactionary curves and winding ways; is varied by backward movements, just as in the case of individuals we meet with points of recurrence to atavism.

3. From J. Holt Schooling, "Nature's Danger-Signals. A Study of the Faces of Murderers," *Harmsworth Magazine* 1 (1898–99): 656–60

[John Holt Schooling (1859–1927) was a frequent contributor to the *Strand*, *Windsor*, and *Pearson*'s magazines. Holt specialized in "tit-bits" (short pieces offering accessible information on a variety of subjects)—the defining feature of *Strand*-inspired magazines (see Introduction, pp. 17–18). His contributions include articles on the handwriting of prominent authors and statesmen (*Strand* 1894–97), railway facts, fiscal policy and taxes, the weight of the Earth, British exports, fortune-telling, the population of the world, and "the maddest part of the Kingdom" (*Pearson*'s 1897).

In the following excerpt, Schooling demonstrates how criminal and moral deficiencies might be identified by an analysis of a subject's physical characteristics. The article, which includes 23 photographs taken from models in Madame Tussaud's Waxwork Exhibition, is a popular version of contemporary theories of criminal anthropology derived from Lombroso's influential work. None of the women featured here resemble the clever, glamorous, and highly seductive female criminals created by Meade and other nineteenth-century novelists. The real women described in Schooling's article were, like the majority of nineteenth-century female criminals, poor, scarcely literate, and desperate (Miller, *Framed* 3–4).

The Harmsworth Magazine (1898–1933), later published as the *London Magazine*, was one of the bestselling pictorial magazines of the period. "Nature's Danger-Signals" appears to be Schooling's only contribution to the magazine.]

If you walk along the Strand from Charing Cross to Temple Bar,[1] and back to Charing Cross on the other side of the street, any day at an hour when London hums with life, you probably meet at least one man who has either done a murder or who will do murder before he dies. Perhaps his shoulder rubs yours, or, in the jostle, you kick his heel; perhaps you catch a passing glance from a pair of sinister eyes that somehow causes you to feel a moment's vague uneasiness, or, as is more likely, you walk unconscious of a possible contact with murder—but it's there.

I do not now refer to persons tricked into committing murder by the perfidy of circumstances ... to many of whom a fatal provocation has come at a moment of weakness or of passion, and who, but for that unsought provocation, would have been free from murder; but I do now refer to those men and women who are by nature and inclination callous, scheming, unscrupulous, and insensitive to any pain or injury inflicted by them upon their fellow-creatures, and who are merely human beasts of prey.

The sense of self-preservation possessed by all animals, but not possessed in such a high degree, perhaps, by human beings as it is possessed by many of the lower animals, carries with it an instinctive recognition of approaching danger from some other animal. Nature does in many cases, perhaps in all, hold up to us certain danger-signals, and if we were to let our natural instinct guide us—as dogs and young children are instinctively guided—we might often avoid grave evils that come to us from the human beasts of prey: cunning fraud, no less than actual murder, is not allowed by Nature to walk through the world without tell-tale evidences of its approach that ought to warn us. But, as adults, we usually ignore the finer and more delicate suggestions of our natural instinct, and we are guided much too often by what we think is "reason," or by what we believe to be our "best interests"—and then we are more or less mauled, in our pocket or in our person, by one of the many human beasts of prey, when prompt obedience to our instinct would have saved us.

Look at these [twenty-three] faces. There is not one of them which cannot easily be more or less closely matched as you walk about the streets of a big city, or even, but naturally

1 Located in central London at the junction of the Strand and Fleet Street (long associated with booksellers, publishers, printers, and journalists).

with less frequency, as you notice faces in country districts. There is, of course, no typical murderer's face. But all of these faces are bad faces; they warn you off. In some instances ... the danger-signal is so plain that not even the most casual observer can fail to see it; each of these faces speaks for itself. In other instances, the warning is not so plainly shown, especially as in these photographs you cannot see the colour of the eye and its exact expression; but in no instance does any one of these faces inspire you with sympathy, they all cause a feeling of aversion or of distrust; and we, if we are wise, should not put aside as fanciful that instinct in us which gives to us similar warnings in everyday life....

Fig. 23. "No. 2. Kate Webster, who killed her mistress."[1]

1 Webster, "a tough Irishwoman" who was apparently overly fond of drink, killed her mistress in Richmond in March 1879 by pushing her down the stairs and strangling her. She later cut off her victim's head and boiled it, burned the body in the fireplace, and threw whatever remained into the Thames. Webster was executed in July 1879. She was included in Madame Tussaud's Chamber of Horrors until 1932 and listed in a souvenir pamphlet as late as 1945 (Knelman 198; 299 n. 55).

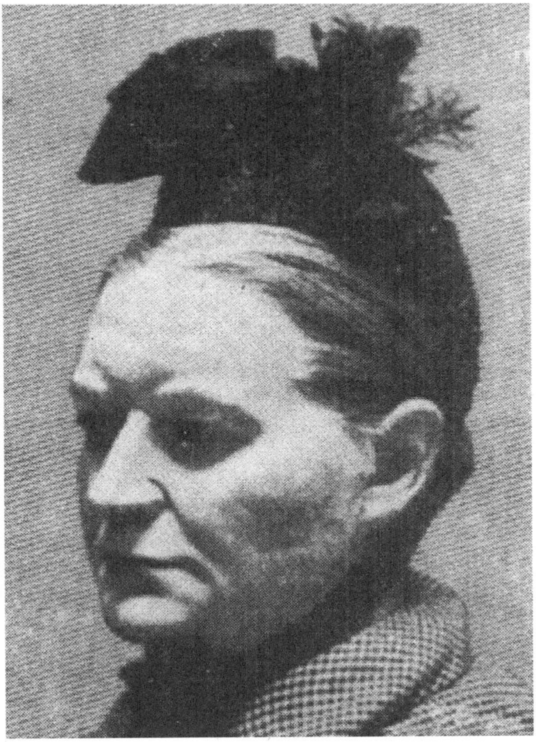

Fig. 24. "No. 6. Mrs. Dyer, the Reading baby farmer and wholesale murderer of infants."[1]

1 Dyer, who worked in Reading outside London, earned her living by baby-farming (taking care of children whose mothers did not want them or could not keep them). Dyer disposed of at least 17 babies over a three-month period in 1896, and as many as 50 over the course of her long career. She was "known in the trade" as a "wholesaler"—one who organized the purchase and distribution of babies to adoptive homes through newspaper ads (Knelman 175). Dyer was executed in June 1896, but her figure remained on display in Madame Tussaud's Chamber of Horrors until 1979 (Knelman 180).

Fig. 25. "No. 11. Mary Ann Cotton, the poisoner."[1]

The danger-signal is shown plainly enough in No. 11. This wretch poisoned a large number of persons for the sake of petty gains with the unconcern of a farm girl who wrings the necks of poultry. She had thick-looking, dark brown eyes, muddy and hard....

1 Cotton used arsenic to murder an estimated 15–20 people in the north of England between 1864 and 1872. Her victims included two husbands (a third husband escaped), numerous children and stepchildren, her mother, a sister-in-law, and a lodger. She is described elsewhere as a "poor, barely literate, unremarkable-looking one-time Sunday school teacher and former nurse in her thirties" (Knelman 74). She was executed in March 1873.

Fig. 26. "No. 13. Wm. Palmer, the Rugeley poisoner."[1]

No. 13 is the face of one of the most cold-blooded poisoners that ever lived. Under the guise of love or friendship he killed his many victims for the sake of gold, coolly smiling at the torture he inflicted, and nicely calculating the effect of each dose of poison. How could anyone have trusted such a face as this? The immense development of the face below the brow, its enormous width between the cheek-bones, the absolute and sickening plausibility of the whole expression, the great lower jaw, the cruel callous mouth (look at this mouth closely), and the peculiarly uncanny light blue eyes, are a collection of danger-signals that are rarely seen in one

1 Palmer (also known as "the Prince of Poisoners") was a medical doctor from Rugeley, Staffordshire excuted in June 1856 for poisoning an acquaintance with strychnine. Palmer was suspected of poisoning as many as 15 victims including seven members of his family.

face. But his victims were probably deceived by this wretch's fat, easy, and bland manner—*they stifled their instinct*, and were duly poisoned....

Fig. 27. "No. 22. Dr. Neill (Cream), the Lambeth poisoner."[1]

One of the worst faces of the lot is No. 22, although the telltale mouth is hidden by hair. The eyes are very bad; they would by themselves give sufficient warning to most of us. Here, again,

1 Cream, an abortionist, blackmailer, and drug addict who poisoned his victims with strychnine, was described as "very good and intelligent looking" in 1880 when he was brought to trial in Chicago for his role in the abortion-related death of a Canadian woman (McLaren 125). He was executed in London in November 1892 for poisoning four prostitutes (a fifth victim escaped to testify against him). Cream has been linked to the notorious Jack the Ripper, who murdered five London prostitutes in 1888. Both men found their victims in London's slum districts; the Ripper's identity remains unknown.

you see the development of cheek-bones and of the lower jaw at the back, which so often goes with a brutal nature, and the eyebrows are very threatening....

There are many men now going about whose entire want of scruple is ... plainly shown in their faces ... but a passable exterior, a plausible manner, seems in many cases to put people quite off their guard. We are, I suppose, so accustomed to regard as sufficient a due attention to social conventions, that we have lost the more primitive sense of self-protection that, in more primitive conditions of society than our own, would be actively used by us for our own protection. Moreover, we have become accustomed to look to the law for protection, and this is, perhaps, another reason why our instinctive recognition of Nature's danger-signals has become dulled, and is now so much less effective than the instinct for danger which some of the lower animals possess in a high degree.

As I have ... suggested, one or more bad signs may often be seen in the faces of persons who are good rather than bad, kind rather than brutal, honourable rather than treacherous. In such instances, the bad point is dominated by the good ones, and it may indeed be converted into a useful quality. For example, the animal brutality of a murderer may become in a good face the resolute energy of the man of action.

But where you see many bad signs collected in one face, and when you feel a certain instinctive aversion for a face, even though your reason or your supposed self-interest gives you no warning, then I say let your instinct have its way, and take the warning that Nature is holding up to you as a danger-signal.

This reliance upon instinct works both ways, moreover. It is equally foolish to distrust all men, as the cynics do, as it is to trust all men, as the imprudent do. In giving these necessarily scanty notes upon faces which contain some of Nature's most obvious danger-signals, my purpose is to warn people off the bad faces, and at the same time to encourage a belief in good faces; but in both instances, I suggest, let instinct be your guide, for in this matter instinct is often a far surer guide than reason.

4. From H.G. Wells, *The Time Machine: An Invention* (New York: Holt, 1895), 107–37

[This excerpt from Wells's famous novel about time travel reflects *fin-de-siècle* fantasies and anxieties about social class and degeneration. In Wells's troubling narrative, the protagonist known as the "Time Traveller" invents a machine that takes him far into the future to the year 802,701, where he is temporarily stranded after his machine mysteriously disappears. Here he learns that man has developed into two species: the beautiful child-like Eloi, decadent vegetarians who inhabit the "overworld," and the sinister Morlocks, subterranean dwellers who maintain the overworlders with what remains of human technology. He later discovers that the Morlocks (who have hidden the time machine for purposes of their own) emerge at night to feed on the helpless Eloi. He eventually recovers his machine and returns to his own time, where he describes his harrowing experiences to a group of professional associates gathered in his home.]

"It was one very hot morning, my fourth morning, I think, as I was seeking a refuge from the heat and glare in a colossal ruin near the great house where I sheltered, that this remarkable incident occurred. Clambering among these heaps of masonry, I found a long narrow gallery, the end and side windows of which were blocked by fallen masses of masonry and which by contrast with the brilliance outside seemed at first impenetrably dark to me.

"I entered it groping, for the change from light to blackness made spots of color swim before me. Suddenly I halted spellbound. A pair of eyes, luminous by reflection against the daylight without, was watching me out of the obscurity!

"The old instinctive dread of wild animals came upon me. I clenched my hands and steadfastly looked into the glaring eyeballs. I feared to turn....

"Overcoming my fear to some extent, I advanced a step, and spoke. I will admit that my voice was hoarse and ill controlled. I put out my hand, and touched something soft.

"At once the eyes darted sideways, and something white ran past me. I turned, with my heart in my mouth, and saw a queer little ape-like figure, with the head held down in a peculiar manner, running across the sunlit space behind me....

"My impression of it was of course very imperfect. It was of a dull white color, and had strange, large, grayish-red eyes. There was some flaxen hair on its head and down its back. But, as I say, it went too fast for me to see distinctly. I cannot even say whether it ran on all fours, or only with its fore arms held very low....

"The thing made me shudder. It was so like a human spider. It was clambering down the wall of the shaft....

"I do not know how long I sat peering down the portentous well. Very slowly could I persuade myself that the thing I had seen was a man. But gradually the real truth dawned upon me; that man had not remained one species, but had differentiated into two distinct animals; that my graceful children of the upperworld were not the only descendants of the men of my generation, but that this bleached, nocturnal thing that had flashed before me, was also heir to our age....

"Evidently this second species of man was subterranean....

"Beneath my feet, then, the earth must be tunneled out to an enormous extent, and in these caverns the new race lived....

"And it was natural to assume that it was in the underworld that the necessary work of the overworld was performed. This was so plausible that I accepted it unhesitatingly. From that I went on to assume how the splitting of the human species came about....

"[S]tarting from the problems of our own age, it seemed as clear as daylight to me that the gradual widening of the present merely temporary and social difference of the capitalist from the laborer was the key to the explanation. No doubt it will seem grotesque enough to you and wildly incredible, and yet even now there are circumstances that point in the way things have gone. There is a tendency plainly enough to utilize underground space for the less ornamental purposes of civilization; there is the Metropolitan Railway in London, for instance, and all these new electric railways; there are subways, and underground workrooms, restaurants, and so forth.[1] Evidently, I thought, this tendency had increased until industry had gradually lost sight of the day, going into larger and larger underground factories, in which the workers would spend an increasing amount of their time. Even now, an East End worker lives in such artificial conditions as practically to be cut off from the natural surface of the earth and the clear sky altogether.[2]

"Then again, the exclusive tendency of richer people, due, no doubt to the increasing refinement of their education and the

---

1 London's Metropolitan Railway, the world's first underground railway, opened in 1863; the city's first electric underground railway opened in 1890. Subways were underground pedestrian walkways.

2 London's East End was notorious for its slums and its cellar sweatshops.

widening gulf between them and the rude violence of the poor, is already leading to the closing of considerable portions of the surface of the country against these latter. About London, for instance, perhaps half the prettier country is shut up from such intrusion. And the same widening gulf, due to the length and expense of the higher educational process and the increased facilities for, and temptation toward, forming refined habits among the rich, will make that frequent exchange between class and class, that promotion and intermarriage which at present retards the splitting of our species along the lines of social stratification, less and less frequent.

"So, in the end, you would have above ground the Haves, pursuing health, comfort, and beauty, and below ground, the Have-nots; the workers, getting continually adapted to their labor.... In the end, if the balance was held permanent, the survivors would become as well adapted to the conditions of their subterranean life as the overworld people were to theirs, and as happy in their way. It seemed to me that the refined beauty of the overworld, and the etiolated[1] pallor of the lower, followed naturally enough....

"My explanation may be absolutely wrong.... But even on this supposition the ... civilization that was at last attained must have long since passed its zenith, and was now far gone in decay. The too perfect security of the overworld had led these [inhabitants] to a slow movement of degeneration at last—to a general dwindling of size, strength, and intelligence. That I already saw clearly enough, but what had happened to the lower world I did not yet suspect. Yet from what I had seen of the Morlocks,—that, by the bye, was the name by which these creatures were called,—I could imagine the modification of the human type was far more profound in the underworld than among the Eloi, the beautiful races that I already knew....

[After recounting further experiences in the future world of the Eloi and the Morlocks, the Time Traveller concludes:]

"Whatever the origin of the existing conditions, I felt pretty sure now that ... [t]he upperworld people might once have been the favored aristocracy of the world, and the Morlocks their mechanical servants, but that state of affairs had passed away long since. The two species that had resulted from the evolution of man were sliding down toward, or had already arrived at, an altogether new relationship. The Eloi, like the

1 Pale or sickly-looking due to lack of light.

Carlovingian kings,[1] had decayed to a mere beautiful futility. They still possessed the earth on sufferance, since the Morlocks, subterranean for innumerable generations, had come at last to find the daylit surface unendurable.... But clearly the old order was already in part reversed. The Nemesis[2] of the delicate ones was creeping on apace. Ages ago, thousands of generations ago, man had thrust his brother man out of the ease and sunlight of life. And now that brother was coming back—changed."

5. From Bram Stoker, *Dracula* (New York: Grossett and Dunlap, 1897), 319–20

[Although Lombroso's theories were controversial, they were widely referenced in literature and popular culture. In the following excerpt, Dr. Van Helsing briefs his fellow vampire hunters about the nature of their foe.]

"To begin, have you ever study the philosophy of crime? ... There is this peculiarity in criminals. It is so constant, in all countries and at all times, that even police, who know not much from philosophy, come to know it empirically, that *it is*. That is to be empiric. The criminal always work at one crime—that is the true criminal who seems predestinate to crime, and who will of none other. This criminal has not full man-brain. He is clever and cunning and resourceful; but he be not of man-stature as to brain. He be of child-brain in much. Now this criminal of ours [Dracula] is predestinate to crime also; he, too, have child-brain....

"The Count is a criminal and of criminal type. Nordau[3] and Lombroso would so classify him, and *qua* criminal he is of an

1 The dynasty founded by the Emperor Charlemagne (742–814), one of the most powerful rulers of Europe after the decline of the Roman Empire. His descendents were remembered for their weakness.

2 Greek goddess of vengeance.

3 Max Nordau (1849–1923), a Hungarian journalist and physician, was one of the most influential cultural critics of the *fin de siècle*. In his most famous work, *Degeneration* (1892; English trans. 1895), Nordau applied Lombroso's theories to nineteenth-century culture and society, arguing that the current period was characterized by fatigue, nervousness, hysteria, egotism, and "depression of vitality" (37). Much of Nordau's discussion focused on cultural degeneration as revealed in *fin-de-siècle* developments in literature and the arts.

imperfectly formed mind. Thus, in a difficulty he has to seek resource in habit. His past is a clue...."

6. From Joseph Conrad, *The Secret Agent* (London: Methuen, 1907), 65

[In this excerpt from Conrad's dynamite narrative, Karl Yundt, a self-described terrorist, states his opinion of Lombroso's ideas during an informal political meeting at double agent Adolf Verloc's London home. Yundt's outburst follows Comrade Ossipon's reference to Verloc's childlike brother-in-law as one of Lombroso's degenerates.]

"Lombroso is an ass.... For him the criminal is the prisoner. Simple, is it not? What about those who shut him up there—forced him in there? Exactly. Forced him in there. And what is crime? Does he know that, this imbecile who has made his way in this world of gorged fools by looking at the ears and teeth of a lot of poor, luckless devils? Teeth and ears mark the criminal? Do they? And what about the law that marks him still better—the pretty branding instrument invented by the overfed to protect themselves against the hungry? Red-hot applications on their vile skins—hey? Can't you smell and hear from here the thick hide of the people burn and sizzle?[1] That's how criminals are made for your Lombrosos to write their silly stuff about."

1 Referring to the treatment of presumed criminals in tsarist Russia.

Appendix C: Female Offenders

1. From "The Probable Retrogression of Women," *Saturday Review* 32 (July 1871): 10–11

[The following essay, written in the context of recent incidents of social and political unrest in France, expresses acute anxiety about growing class and gender conflicts in Britain. The author links the women's movement to widespread social and cultural degeneration, arguing that women's natural duty is to strengthen and nurture the family, the "cornerstone of civilization" and the source of "English safety." Changes in women's place in society would represent a retrogressive evolution—"a relapse into savagery" and barbarism.

The Saturday Review (1855–1935) was a conservative upper-middle-class journal. It published many of Eliza Lynn Linton's antifeminist essays, including her sensational "Girl of the Period" series (1868). See Appendix C2.]

Here and there the cracks in our social edifice yawn so significantly that we feverishly try to plaster them up, but the passion of the day for every variety of reform is more a sign of conscious disorganization than of healthy energy. And the alterations clamoured for in the position of women, the quack cures suggested for the miseries of their present struggle with circumstance, are among the ugliest symptoms of serious social disorder. Their restlessness, though happily not as yet general, is, we take it, a mark of their deterioration. Not advance but retrogression is indicated by their assumption of men's work and their boast of masculine power. We acknowledge the isolation and uselessness of thousands among them, but this is no argument for further disruption of home and wresting of the feminine faculties. That women should suffer as they do comes of complicated causes, some evident and some obscure. Thousands of families are out of gear; wives are beaten by drunken husbands, daughters are sold or driven out of their fathers' houses. Starvation or vice, baby-farming or other unlegalized professions, seem the necessary prospect of the undomesticated women who prowl in our byways. Victims of commercial pressure, ignorance, and in some cases of a lying literature, their religious instincts crushed by the dense atheism of those who form their society, they are the saddest sight and most puzzling problem of our world. But what will be gained by further unsexing them, and encouraging their less muscular frames and smaller brains to a competition with men, which the Society for preventing cruelty[1] should really interfere to stop? Certainly some women are superior to many men, but there is abundant work for such exceptional persons in the better fulfilment of those duties by which women have so largely contributed to the development of mankind. If, in search of pastures new, capable women abandon the field in which they have hitherto, and successfully, worked, who shall prophesy the result? Slight checks may seriously affect the prospects of a race in the severe struggle of humanity, and if our better halves alter the conditions which have raised us from the condition of orang-outangs [*sic*], a relapse into savagery is quite possible. It is true that the fair sex will enjoy that equality of labour, if not that excess of it, which will quickly remove from it the reproach of fairness. We do not think, however, that enfranchisement in manners will secure personal respect, nor have the late events in Paris[2] given us hope that women will attain even ephemeral independence by throwing off the restraints of primeval custom. In vain, even for momentary license, can women agree in weakening the marriage tie and in denial of the family, which, until we fall back to the twilight of arboreal existence, remains the true unit of life and the condition of progress among men. When the plant is injured at the root the flowers droop first, and the earliest consequence of social disorder is the suffering of women....

Far from undervaluing the part played by women in the history of our race, we think them more powerful than men to disturb the deeper foundations of order, as they have probably been more powerful to insinuate custom and to mould the first impressions of the young. It has been said that our more recent development has tended to reduce the inequalities of the sexes and to confuse their several duties. So much the more should we react against this tendency if it be also true that hitherto the advance of our race has been marked by an increasing diversity between men and women, which makes one, not the contradiction, but the complement of the other.

---

1 The Society for the Prevention of Cruelty to Animals, founded in London in 1824.

2 Women took an active role in the establishment of the Paris Commune, a socialist-inspired revolutionary government that controlled Paris for three months beginning in March 1871. A feminist faction within the Commune sought social, economic, and legal rights for women, including the right of divorce. The Commune was suppressed by the French government.

The lower we go among savage tribes, the less of this diversity there would seem to be; so that it appears to be a direct retrogression to assimilate the work of the highly-developed woman to that of her mate; and if perfection is to be the aim of our efforts, it will be best advanced by further divergence of male and female characteristics. It would appear, then, to be rash to labour in another direction, however plausible the immediate object. The agitation for women's so-called emancipation should be strenuously resisted, lest we come to see such disintegration of family life, such reversal of women's right action, as shall leave us, to quote eloquent words, a population of "unattached individuals, the fine dust of a social desert, incapable of being built into anything, and the prey of whirlwinds"[1]....

By their support, conscious or unconscious, of the fifth commandment,[2] women largely promote the observance of the others; and the whole order of the family, which, as we have seen, is specially an object of socialist attack, is contained in the precept to honour father and mother. Highly developed women are the most numerous, if not the chief, exemplars of that courage to endure and obey, that enthusiasm which finds expression in unselfish and patient love, that hereditary and almost instinctive repugnance to evil which is so valuable a counterpoise to the hereditary vice of our dangerous classes. They are teachers of subordination, and to secure the desired insubordination of mankind their influence must be undermined by International[3] and like Societies. Probably the most rapid way to disable her whose mission it is to crush the serpent's head[4] is the attempt to unsex her which we see being urged in all "advanced" communities....

It may not be long before women will need even more than

---

1 Paraphrased from one of Charles Loyson's Advent sermons on the family and the Church given at Notre Dame Cathedral in Paris in December 1866. Loyson (1827–1912), also known as Father Hyacinthe, was a Roman Catholic preacher and theologian famous for his eloquence. His Advent sermons (1865–69) were popular events, but his attempts to reconcile Catholicism with modern ideas led to his excommunication in 1869. See Leonard Woolsey Bacon, ed., *The Family and the Church. Advent Conferences of Notre-Dame, Paris, 1866–7, 1868–9, by the Reverend Father Hyacinthe* (New York: Putnam, 1870), 65–66.

2 Honour thy father and thy mother, the fifth of the ten laws given by God to Moses as recorded in the Old Testament of the Bible.

3 The First International, an international association founded in London in 1864 to bring together a variety of socialist, communist, and anarchist political groups and trade-union organizations.

4 In the Judeo-Christian tradition, the serpent symbolizes evil, temptation, deceit, and Satan himself. Christ's mother is often shown trampling a serpent.

now all their womanliness to help in the reconstruction of society in Western Europe; but as it is, there is [a] pressing call for all their energies. The attack on marriage, the isolation and division that our system of trade tends to produce in families, misapprehension of justice and liberty, and the incitements of a press interested in social disturbance, have weakened women's confidence in themselves. The pressure of existence is especially severe on them just now, and to thousands it seems a mockery to talk of home or family. Pauperism, the use of lodging-houses, and many like causes, have taken from the unmarried the resource of domestic work; but will help be found in further dislocation of family relations? They become impossible if women will not take their place in the group which is the corner-stone of civilization, the natural school of duty, and the fountain of law. To shelter it from the friction of the times, to strengthen its influence, should be the aim of all who are interested in English safety; and ... it would be well if right-thinking women gave all the help they can to those who are wounded and borne down in the battle of womanhood. Meantime, whether women turn traitors to their cause or not, no outcries from unemployed spinsters or tormented wives should tempt us to meddle with what revelation, science, and experience declare to be a necessary condition of the prosperity of mankind. To discourage subordination in women, to countenance their competition in masculine careers by way of their enfranchisement, is probably among the shortest methods of barbarizing our race.

2. From Eliza Lynn Linton, "The Wild Women as Social Insurgents," *Nineteenth Century* 30 (October 1891): 596–605

[Eliza Lynn Linton (1822–98) was one of the most prominent and controversial women writers of the nineteenth century. Linton's defence of female subservience, opposition to the expansion of women's roles in society, and strident attacks on the New Woman contrasted sharply with her own independent lifestyle as a professional writer. Though she promoted the idea that a woman's place was in the home, she separated from her husband and stepchildren in order to pursue her literary career.

Linton's skills were well suited to popular journalism, where she excelled at creating clever caricatures, exploiting stereotypes, and making the most of the period's social and cultural anxieties.

Her antifeminist essays brought her fame and financial stability. In 1896, she became one of the first women elected to a seat on the governing council of the influential Society of Authors.

"The Wild Women as Social Insurgents" was the second of three "Wild Women" essays[1] that Linton published in the *Nineteenth Century* (1877–1901), a distinguished monthly known for its contributions by many of the most prominent intellectuals and social critics of the day. The excerpt begins after a description of notable women who distinguished themselves by acts of devotion, bravery, and self-sacrifice.]

For the '*tacens et placens uxor*'[2] of old-time dreams we must acknowledge now as our Lady of Desire the masterful *domina*[3] of real life—that loud and dictatorial person, insurgent and something more, who suffers no one's opinion to influence her mind, no venerable law hallowed by time, nor custom consecrated by experience, to control her actions. Mistress of herself, the Wild Woman as a social insurgent preaches the 'lesson of liberty' broadened into lawlessness and licence. Unconsciously she exemplifies how beauty can degenerate into ugliness, and shows how the once fragrant flower, run to seed, is good for neither food nor ornament.

Her ideal of life for herself is absolute personal independence coupled with supreme power over men. She repudiates the doctrine of individual conformity for the sake of the general good; holding the self-restraint involved as an act of slavishness of which no woman worth her salt would be guilty. She makes between the sexes no distinctions moral or aesthetic, nor even personal; but holds that what is lawful to the one is permissible to the other. Why should the world have parceled out qualities or habits into two different sections, leaving only a few common to both alike? Why, for instance, should men have the fee-simple[4] of courage, and women that of modesty? to men be given the right of the initiative—to women only that of selection? to men the freer indulgence of the senses—to women the chaster discipline of self-denial? The Wild Woman of modern life asks why; and she answers the question in her own way.....

1 See also "The Wild Women as Politicians" and "The Partisans of the Wild Women" (1891–92).

2 Silent and pleasing wife (Latin).

3 Mistress or lady (Latin).

4 Complete and unconditional ownership of a property or title.

Nothing is forbidden to the Wild Woman as a social insurgent; for the one word that she cannot spell is, Fitness. Devoid of this sense of fitness, she does all manner of things which she thinks bestow on her the power, together with the privileges, of a man; not thinking that in obliterating the finer distinctions of sex she is obliterating the finer traits of civilisation, and that every step made towards identity of habits is a step downwards in refinement and delicacy—wherein lies the essential core of civilisation. She smokes after dinner with the men; in railway carriages; in public rooms—when she is allowed. She thinks she is thereby vindicating her independence and honouring her emancipated womanhood. Heaven bless her! Down in the North-country villages, and elsewhere, she will find her prototypes calmly smoking their black cutty-pipes,[1] with no sense of shame about them. Why should they not? These ancient dames with 'whiskin' beards about their mou's,'[2] withered and unsightly, worn out, and no longer women in desirableness or beauty—why should they not take to the habits of men? They do not disgust, because they no longer charm; but even in these places you do not find the younger women with cutty-pipes between their lips. Perhaps in the coal districts, where women work like men and with men, and are dressed as men, you will see pipes as well as hear blasphemies; but that is surely not an admirable state of things, and one can hardly say that the pit-brow women,[3] excellent persons and good workers as they are in their own way, are exactly the glasses in which our fine ladies find in their loveliest fashions—the moulds wherein they would do well to run their own forms. And when, after dinner, our young married women and husbandless girls, despising the old distinctions and trampling under foot the time-honoured conventions of former generations, 'light up' with the men, they are simply assimilating themselves to this old Sally and that ancient Betty down in the dales and mountain hamlets; or to the stalwart cohort of pit-brow women for whom sex has no aesthetic distinctions....

Free-traders in all that relates to sex, the Wild Women allow men no monopoly in sports, in games, in responsibilities. Beginning by 'walking with the guns,' they end by shooting with them;

---

1 Short tobacco-pipes.

2 From Robert Burns, "Willie's Wife" (1792).

3 Women who worked above ground sorting and shovelling coal. The women generally rolled their skirts above their waists and worked in men's trousers.

and some have made the moor a good training-ground for the jungle. As life is constituted, it is necessary to have butchers and sportsmen. The hunter's instinct keeps down the wild beasts, and those who go after big game do as much good to the world as those who slaughter home-bred beasts for the market. But in neither instance do we care to see a woman's hand. It may be merely a sentiment, and ridiculous at that; still, sentiment has its influence, legitimate enough when not too widely extended; and we confess that the image of a 'butching' woman, nursing her infant child with hands red with the blood of an ox she has just poleaxed or of a lamb whose throat she has this instant cut, is one of unmitigated horror and moral incongruity. Precisely as horrible, as incongruous, is the image of a well-bred sportswoman whose bullet has crashed along the spine of a leopardess, who has knocked over a rabbit or brought down a partridge. The one may be a hard-fisted woman of the people, who had no inherent sensitiveness to overcome—a woman born and bred among the shambles[1] and accustomed to the whole thing from childhood. The other may be a dainty-featured aristocrat, whose later development belies her early training; but the result is the same in both cases—the possession of an absolutely unwomanly instinct, an absolutely unwomanly indifference to death and suffering; which certain of the Wild Women of the present day cultivate as one of their protests against the limitations of sex. The viragoes[2] of all times have always had this same instinct, this same indifference. For nothing of all this is new in substance. What is new is the translation into the cultured classes of certain qualities and practices hitherto confined to the uncultured and—savages.

This desire to assimilate their lives to those of men runs through the whole day's work of the Wild Women. Not content with croquet and lawn tennis, the one of which affords ample opportunities for flirting—for the Wild Women are not always above that little pastime—and the other for exercise even more violent than is good for the average woman, they have taken to golf and cricket, where they are hindrances for the one part, and make themselves 'sights' for the other..... The prettiest woman in the world loses her beauty when at these violent exercises. Hot and damp, mopping her flushed and streaming face with her handkerchief, she has lost that sense of repose, that delicate

1 Slaughterhouse(s); meat or fish market.

2 Women displaying masculine strength or spirit; female warriors (Latin *vir*, man).

self-restraint, which belongs to the ideal woman. She is no longer dainty. She has thrown off her grace and abandoned all that makes her lovely for the uncomely roughness of pastimes wherein she cannot excel, and of which it was never intended that she should be a partaker.

We have not yet heard of women polo-players; but that will come. In the absurd endeavour to be like men, these modern *homasses*[1] will leave nothing untried; and polo-playing, tent-pegging, and tilting at the quintain[2] are all sure to come in time. When weeds once begin to grow, no limits can be put to their extent unless they are stubbed up betimes.

The Wild Women, in their character of social insurgents, are bound by none of the conventions which once regulated society. In them we see the odd social phenomenon of the voluntary descent of the higher to the lower forms of ways and works. 'Unladylike' is a term that has ceased to be significant. Where 'unwomanly' has died out we could scarcely expect this other to survive. The special must needs go with the generic; and we find it so with a vengeance! With other queer inversions the frantic desire of making money has invaded the whole class of Wild Woman; and it does not mitigate their desire that, as things are, they have enough for all reasonable wants. Women who, a few years ago, would not have shaken hands with a dressmaker, still less have sat down to table with her, now open shops and set up in business on their own account—not because they are poor, which would be an honourable and sufficing reason enough, but because they are restless, dissatisfied, insurgent, and like nothing so much as to shock established prejudices and make the folk stare. It is such a satire on their inheritance of class distinction, on their superior education—perhaps very superior, stretching out to academical proportions! It is just the kind of topsy-turveydom that pleases them. They, with their long descent, grand name, and right to a coat-of-arms which represents past ages of renown,—they to come down to the market-place, shouldering out the meaner fry, who must work to live—taking from the legitimate traders the pick of their custom, and making their way by dint of social standing and personal influence—they to sell bonnets in place of buying them—to make money instead of spending it—what fun! What a grand idea it was to conceive, and grander still to execute! In this insurgent playing at shopkeeping by those who do not

1 Mannish or masculine women (French).

2 Target used in jousting exercises.

need to do so we see nothing grand nor beautiful, but much that is thoughtless and mean. Born of restlessness and idleness, these spasmodic make-believes after serious work are simply pastimes to the Wild Women who undertake them. There is nothing really solid in them, no more than there was of philanthropy in the fashionable craze for slumming[1] which broke out like a fever a winter or two ago. Shopkeeping and slumming, and some other things too, are just the expression of that restlessness which makes of the modern Wild Woman a second Io,[2] driving her afield in search of strange pleasures and novel occupations, and leading her to drink of the muddiest waters so long as they are in new channels cut off from the old fountains. Nothing daunts this modern Io. No barriers restrain, no obstacles prevent. She appears on the public stage and executes dances which one would not like one's daughter to see, still less perform. She herself knows no shame in showing her skill—and her legs. Why should she? What free and independent spirit, in these later days, is willing to be bound by those musty principles of modesty which did well enough for our stupid old great-grandmothers—but for us? Other times, other manners; and womanly reticence is not of these last!....

[Linton criticizes Wild Women as actresses, artists, authors, philanthropists, adventuresses, and globetrotters before beginning a lengthy diatribe against Wild Women as missionaries.]

Ranged side by side with ... vagrant Wild Women, globetrotting for the sake of a subsequent book of travels, and the *kudos*

---

1 Slumming—visiting urban slums—was a popular form of tourism in the late nineteenth century. London guidebooks described excursions to philanthropic institutions in notorious slum neighbourhoods including London's Whitechapel (the location of the Ripper murders) and Shoreditch (featured in Arthur Morrison's slum novel *A Child of the Jago* [1896] and Meade's *A Princess of the Gutter* [1895]). In 1884 the popular satirical journal *Punch* (1841–2002) mocked the fashion for omnibus tours through London slums with a cartoon titled "In Slummibus," featuring a well-dressed clergyman ushering two fashionable women through a squalid street crowded with slum "types" (ragged street children, men and women in various stages of degradation, and a dead cat). See Koven 1–22.

2 According to Greek mythology, Zeus changed Io into a white heifer to protect her from his jealous wife Hera. But Hera became suspicious and sent a gadfly to torment Io. Io fled wildly through the world until she reached Egypt, where Zeus restored her to her human form (and impregnated her).

with the pence accruing, are those who spread themselves abroad as missionaries, and those—a small minority, certainly—who do not see why the army and the navy should be sealed against the sex. Among these female missionaries are some who are good, devoted, pure-hearted, self-sacrificing—all that women should be, all that the best women are, and ever have been, and ever will be. But also among them are the Wild Women—creatures impatient of restraint, bound by no law, insurgent to their finger-tips, and desirous of making all other women as restless and discontented as themselves. Ignorant and unreasonable, they would carry into the sun-laden East the social conditions born of the icy winds of the North. They would introduce into the zenana[1] the circumstances of a Yorkshire home. In a country where jealousy is as strong as death, and stronger than love, they would incite the women to revolt against the rule of seclusion, which has been the law of the land for centuries before we were a nation at all. That rule has worked well for the country, inasmuch as the chastity of Hindu women and the purity of family life are notoriously intact. But our Wild Women swarm over into India as zenana missionaries, trying to make the Hindus as discontented, as restless, as unruly as themselves....

When we have taught the Hindu women to hunt and drive, play golf and cricket, dance the cancan on a public stage, make speeches in Parliament, cherish 'dear boys' at five-o'clock tea, and do all that our Wild Women do, shall we have advanced matters very far? Shall we have made the home happier, the family purer, the women themselves more modest, more chaste? Had we not better cease to pull at ropes which move machinery of which we know neither the force nor the possible action? Why all this interference with others? Why not let the various peoples of the earth manage their domestic matters as they think fit? Are our Wild Women the ideal of female perfection? Heaven forbid! But to this distorted likeness they and their backers are doing their best to reduce all others.

Aggressive, disturbing, officious, unquiet, rebellious to authority and tyrannous to those whom they can subdue, we say emphatically that they are about the most unlovely specimens the sex has yet produced, and between the 'purdah-woman'[2] and

1 Secluded quarters for women and girls in some Hindu and Muslim households.

2 Purdah is the custom of secluding women from public (particularly male) view.

the modern *homasses* we, for our own parts, prefer the former. At least the purdah-woman knows how to love. At least she has not forgotten the traditions of modesty as she has been taught them. But what about our half-naked girls and young wives, smoking and drinking with the men? our ramping platform orators? our unabashed self-advertisers? our betting women? our horse-breeders? our advocates of free love, and our contemners of maternal life and domestic duties?

The mind goes back over certain passages in history, and the imagination fastens on certain names which stand as types of womanly loveliness and love-worthiness. Side by side with them were the *homasses* of their day.... [Then] as now we have certain sweet and lovely women who honour their womanhood and fulfil its noblest ideals, and these Wild Women of blare and bluster, who are neither man nor woman—wanting in the well-knit power of the first and in the fragrant sweetness of the last.

Excrescences of the times, products of peace and idleness, of prosperity and over-population—would things be better if a great national disaster pruned our superfluities and left us nearer to the essential core of facts? Who knows! Storms shake off the nobler fruit but do not always beat down the ramping weeds. Still, human nature has the trick of pulling itself right in times of stress and strain. Perhaps, if called upon, even our Wild Women would cast off their ugly travesty and become what modesty and virtue designed them to be; and perhaps their male adorers would go back to the ranks of masculine self-respect, and leave off this base subservience to folly which now disfigures and unmans them. *Chi lo sa?*[1] It does no one harm to hope. This hope, then, let us cherish while we can and may.

3. From Cesare Lombroso and William Ferrero, *The Female Offender* (1895; New York: Appleton, 1898), 147–91

[Lombroso discussed female criminals in his various editions of *Criminal Man*, but in 1893 he brought his research together in a separate volume that focused on the criminal woman, the prostitute, and the normal woman (*La donna delinquente, la prostituta e la donna normale*). Much of Lombroso's discussion of prostitutes and normal women was omitted from an abbreviated English translation published in 1895 as *The Female Offender.*

---

1 Who knows? (Italian).

Some of Lombroso's more interesting claims about female criminals include the idea that although there are fewer female born criminals than male, female criminals tend to be more depraved and monstrous. He also claimed that female criminals display masculine characteristics and that women "are more numerous among political criminals than among criminals in general" (*Criminal Man*, trans. Gibson and Rafter, 313).]

Chapter XII. The Born Criminal.

.... "No possible punishments," wrote Corrado Celto,[1] an author of the fifteenth century, "can deter women from heaping up crime upon crime. Their perversity of mind is more fertile in new crimes than the imagination of a judge in new punishments."

"Feminine criminality," writes Rykère, "is more cynical, more depraved, and more terrible than the criminality of the male."[2]

"Rarely is a woman wicked, but when she is she surpasses the man" (Italian Proverb).....

Another terrible point of superiority in the female born criminal over the male lies in the refined, diabolical cruelty with which she accomplishes her crime....

[W]e may assert that if female born criminals are fewer in number than the males, they are often much more ferocious....

We [have seen] that women have many traits in common with children; that their moral sense is deficient; that they are revengeful, jealous, inclined to vengeances of a refined cruelty.

In ordinary cases these defects are neutralized by piety, maternity, want of passion, sexual coldness, by weakness and an undeveloped intelligence. But when a morbid activity of the psychical centres intensifies the bad qualities of women, and induces them to seek relief in evil deeds; when piety and maternal sentiments are wanting, and in their place are strong passions and intensely erotic tendencies, much muscular strength and a superior intelligence for the conception and execution of evil, it is clear that the innocuous and semi-criminal present in the normal woman must be transformed into a born criminal more terrible than any man.

What terrific criminals would children be if they had strong passions, muscular strength, and sufficient intelligence; and

---

1 Conradus Celtis (1459–1508) was a German humanist scholar and Latin lyric poet.

2 Raymond de Rykère, *"La criminalité féminine,"* published in Lombroso's *Archivio di antropologia criminale* (1891).

if, moreover, their evil tendencies were exasperated by a morbid psychical activity! And women are big children; their evil tendencies are more numerous and more varied than men's but generally remain latent. When they are awakened and excited they produce results proportionately greater.

Moreover, the born female criminal is, so to speak, doubly exceptional, as a woman and as a criminal. For criminals are an exception among civilised people, and women are an exception among criminals, the natural form of retrogression in women being prostitution and not crime. The primitive woman was impure rather than criminal.

As a double exception, the criminal woman is consequently a monster....

A strong proof of degeneration in many born [female] criminals is the want of maternal affection....

This want of maternal feeling becomes comprehensible when we reflect on the one hand upon the union of masculine qualities which prevent the female criminal from being more than half a woman, and on the other, upon that love of dissipation in her which is necessarily antagonistic to the constant sacrifices demanded of a mother. Her maternal sense is weak because psychologically and anthropologically she belongs more to the male than to the female sex. Her exaggerated sexuality so opposed to maternity would alone suffice to make her a bad mother....

In general the moral physiognomy of the born female criminal approximates strongly to that of the male. The atavistic diminution of secondary sexual characters which is to be observed in the anthropology of the subject, shows itself once again in the psychology of the female criminal, who is excessively erotic, weak in maternal feeling, inclined to dissipation, astute and audacious, and dominates weaker beings sometimes by suggestion, at others by muscular force; while her love of violent exercise, her vices, and even her dress, increase her resemblance to the sterner sex. Added to these vile characteristics are often the worst qualities of woman: namely, an excessive desire for revenge, cunning, cruelty, love of dress, and untruthfulness, forming a combination of evil tendencies which often results in a type of extraordinary wickedness. Needless to say these different characteristics are not found in the same proportion in everybody. A criminal ... will be deficient in intelligence, but possessed of great physical strength; while another ... who is weak physically, triumphs over this obstacle by the ability with which she lays her plans. But when by an unfortunate chance muscular strength and intellectual force meet in the same individual, we have a female delinquent of a terrible type indeed. A typical example of these extraordinary women is presented by Bell-Star, the female brigand,[1] who a few years ago terrorized all Texas. Her education had been of the sort to develop her natural qualities; for being the daughter of a guerilla chief who had fought on the side of the South in the war of 1861-65, she had grown up in the midst of fighting, and when only ten years old, already used the lasso, the revolver, the carbine, and the bowie-knife in a way to excite the enthusiasm of her ferocious companions. She was as strong and bold as a man, and loved to ride untamed horses which the boldest of the brigands dared not mount. One day at Oakland she twice won a race, dressed once as a man and once as a woman, changing her dress so rapidly that her ruse remained unsuspected. She was extremely dissolute, and had more than one lover at a time.... At the age of eighteen she became head of the band, and ruled her associates partly through her superior intelligence, partly through her courage, and to a certain degree through her personal charm as a woman. She organized attacks of the most daring description on populous cities, and fought against government troops.... She wrote her memoirs, recording in them her desire to die in her boots. This wish was granted, for she fell in a battle against the government troops, directing the fire to her latest breath.

Another Napoleon in petticoats similar to Bell-Star was Zélie, a Frenchwoman by birth. She was extremely intelligent, spoke three languages perfectly, had extraordinary personal fascination, and even from childhood showed herself perfidious and profligate. Her adventures having carried her to the brigand

---

1 Myra Maybelle Shirley Reed Starr (1848–89), better known as Belle Starr, was associated with numerous outlaws including the notorious Jesse James (1847–82) and his gang. She was known in Texas and Oklahoma where most of her criminal activities took place, but her name and exploits gained wider fame with the publication of *Bella Starr, the Bandit Queen, or the Female Jesse James. A Full and Authentic History of the Dashing Female Highwayman, with Copious Extracts from her Journal* (1889), a sensational "dime" (cheap) novel by Richard K. Fox, editor and publisher of the *National Police Gazette* (1845–1977). She died from gunshot wounds received during an ambush by an unknown assailant (not in a battle against government troops). Starr has since become a popular character in film and television as well as the subject of novels, songs, and manga.

country of North America, she became the leader of a band of malefactors. With a bold and audacious air, and her revolver in her hand, she was always the first to face danger, and when quarrels arose among her companions she would throw herself into the midst of them and make them lay down their arms. Laughing, she crossed perilous mountain-paths where others feared to follow her: neither epidemics, earthquakes, nor war availed to cow her. She eventually died in a lunatic asylum in France, a prey to hysteria.

M. R. ... was a thief, a prostitute, a corrupter of youth, a blackmailer, and all this at the age of 17.... [W]hen only 16 she organized a vast system of prostitution, by which she provided young girls of 12 and 15 for wealthy men, from whom she exacted large sums, of which only a few sous went to the victims. And by threats of exposure she managed to levy costly blackmail on her clients, one of whom, a highly-placed functionary, was dismissed from his post in consequence of her revelations....

It would be difficult to find greater wickedness at the service of a vindictive disposition and an unbridled greed. We may regard M. R. as an instance in which the two poles of depravity were united. That is to say, she was sanguinary (for she went about always with a dagger in her pocket, and stabbed anybody who offended her in the least) and at the same time inclined to commit the more cautious and insidious crimes, such as poisoning, blackmail, &c. And we consequently find in her an example of the law we have already laid down, to the effect that the female born criminal, when a complete type, is more terrible than the male.

4. "We Want the Vote" (1909). Colour Postcard

[This postcard satirizing the votes-for-women campaign reflects the common accusation that those campaigning for the vote were neglecting their traditional domestic duties of wife and mother. Like other anti-suffrage posters and postcards, "We Want the Vote" depicts the suffragette as hysterical, dangerous, and unwomanly, but this card is particularly significant for the way in which it draws on common stereotypes from criminal anthropology. The suffragette shows signs of "atavistic degeneracy" (according to Lombrosian taxonomy), as indicated by her facial features, skin colour, cross-eyes, and small forehead. The subject's large mouth and pointed teeth suggest both vampirism and racial otherness (Stott 202). The card was sent to women's activist Christabel Pankhurst (1880–1958) with the message, "Don't you think you had better sew a button on my shirt?".]

Fig. 28. "We Want the Vote." © Museum of London

5. From Bram Stoker, *The Lair of the White Worm* (London: William Rider, 1911), chs. 25–26

[Although Bram Stoker (1847–1912) is now best remembered for his vampire narrative *Dracula* (1897), he had a productive career as the author of thirteen novels, two biographies, a play, and numerous short stories and lectures. *The Lair of the White Worm*, his last novel, was published five months before his death. Though moderately popular in its day, the novel was later dismissed as confused and rambling. Subsequent editions of the work were significantly abridged, amended, and rewritten in an attempt to make it more coherent. Like *Dracula*, the work expresses *fin-de-siècle* anxieties about gender, race, crime, and degeneration. Both novels depict honourable men leagued against transgressive, sexually aggressive women represented as grotesque vampiric creatures. In *The Lair of the White Worm*, Sir Nathaniel de Salis, an elderly historian, and Adam Salton, a young Australian-born heir to an English estate, combat a monstrous primordial female worm (serpent) that appears in human form as the beautiful but predatory Lady Arabella March.[1] In this excerpt, de Salis and Salton discuss the creature's history and crimes, linking her to the prostitute and the suffragette, women frequently represented in *fin-de-siècle* literature and popular culture as examples of atavism and degenerate criminal femininity (elsewhere in the text, Lady Arabella is associated with the New Woman).[2] The protagonists fear that the female worm has become more dangerous over the centuries because she has developed an intellect.]

"In the past, in the early days of the world [Adam stated], there were monsters who were so vast that they could exist thousands of years. Some of them must have overlapped the Christian era. They may have progressed intellectually in process of time. If they had in any way so progressed, or got even the most rudimentary form of brain, they would be the most dangerous things that ever were in the world. Tradition says that one of these monsters lived in the Marsh of the East and came up to a cave in Diana's Grove[3] which was also called the Lair of the White Worm. Such creatures may have grown down (small) as well as up (long). They *may* have grown into, or something like, human beings. Lady Arabella March is of snake nature. She has committed crimes to our knowledge. She retains something of the vast strength of her primal being—can see in the dark—has eyes of a snake.... [S]he is intent on evil....

---

1 Lady Arabella's initials (LAM) associate her with Lamia, a fabulous snake-like woman in Greek and Roman mythology. In other lore, lamiae, serpent-like spirits or demons, were said to suck the blood and vital essences of human children and unfortunate lovers.

2 Stoker's description of Lady Arabella resembles a caricature of the New Woman published in the *Cornhill Magazine* in 1894. The former is described as "tall and exceedingly thin," clad in a "close-fitting" white fur cap and a garment of "some kind of soft white stuff, which clung close to her form, showing to the full every movement of her sinuous figure" (*Lair* ch. 4), while the New Woman is similarly depicted in "close-fitting garments" and a "close-fitting" hairstyle: "She wears her elbows well away from her side [which] serves to diminish the apparent size of the waist.... It certainly adds to a somewhat aggressive air of independence...." ("Character Note" 365). See Hebblethwaite 397 n. 5.

3 The site of a Roman temple dedicated to Diana, virgin huntress and goddess of the moon, now the location of Lady Arabella's house.

"It seems ... that we are in an exceedingly tight place. Our first difficulty is to know where to begin. Our opponent has pretty well all the trumps. I never thought this fighting an antediluvian monster was such a complicated job. This one is a woman, with all a woman's wisdom and wit, combined with the heartlessness of a *cocotte*[1] and the want of principle of a suffragette. She has the reserved strength and impregnability of a diplodocus.[2] We may be sure that in the fight that is before us there will be no semblance of fair-play...."

Sir Nathaniel commented on this:

"That is so. But being of feminine species, she probably will over-reach herself. That is much more likely—more in woman's way. Now ... it strikes me that, as we have to protect ourselves and others against feminine nature, our strong game will be to play our masculine against her feminine. Men can wait better than women."

He laughed a mirthless laugh that was all from the brain and had no heart at all, and went on:

"You must remember that this female has had thousands of years' experience in waiting. As she stands, she will beat us at that game."

For answer Adam began preparing his revolver....

[Lady Arabella is eventually destroyed during a violent electrical storm when she returns to her lair carrying a cable attached to an enormous kite flying above the neighbouring castle. The kite is struck by lightning, causing an electrical current to pass down the cable and into her lair, where de Salis and Salton have hidden a large quantity of dynamite.]

1 A prostitute or promiscuous woman (French).

2 A giant herbivorous dinosaur with four legs and a very long neck and tail.

Appendix D: Anarchism and Terrorism

1. From "Dynamite Outrages," *The Times* (26 January 1885): 10

[The following excerpt predates Meade's "The Seventh Step" (1895) and "A Little Smoke" (1901), but it is included here as an example of the detailed reporting of dynamite incidents in the press in the late nineteenth century. The "dynamite outrages" described here were recalled a decade later in "Dynamite and Dynamiters," the first in an illustrated series on crime and criminals published in the *Strand* in February 1894. The *Strand* article includes photographs of the destruction at the Tower of London in 1885 in addition to photographs of the damage caused at other significant sites during the previous decade (Victoria Station, Scotland Yard, and a number of public and private buildings in Britain and Ireland) and examples of "infernal machines" and explosive devices—including a baby's bottle and explosive cigars—used in actual attacks. Through the 1880s and 1890s, the press regularly published details of dynamite outrages at home and abroad, interviews with anarchists, police statements, and diagrams of explosives and detonators. These reports naturally fanned public anxiety, but the details were a boon to a host of writers, including Henry James (1834–1916), Grant Allen (1848–99), Isabel Meredith (Helen [1879–1969] and Olivia [1875–1960] Rossetti), Joseph Conrad (1857–1924), and Meade herself.]

Dynamite Outrages.

Attempts on the House of Commons, Westminster Hall, and the Tower of London.

The "Dynamite War," as it is termed by the disloyal Irish and the Irish-American outrage-mongers, was continued in London on Saturday with some degree of success to the perpetrators. Accepting the privilege accorded to all comers to view the Houses of Parliament and the Tower of London, they cunningly placed charged machines of dynamite in the

Crypt leading out of Westminster Hall, in the House of Commons Chamber itself, and caused, almost at the same time, an explosion in the Tower of London. In all three cases the material damage was comparatively slight. The public buildings are as far as ever from being blown down; but the cowardly miscreants have achieved the success of damaging the most cherished monuments of London, and have injured some of the policemen who were on duty within Westminster Hall, as well as some of the public.

The two explosions at Westminster and the one at the Tower were evidently timed to occur at 2 o'clock in the day, a time when visitors would be likely to be gathered in great numbers. As a fact the explosion at the Tower of London was some minutes before those at the Houses of Parliament, but the manner of the perpetration of the outrages shows that there is not the slightest reason to doubt their being due to the notion of the same plotters, and evidence is furnished sufficient to show that the plotters are more numerous than the band under Gallagher,[1] who, with three others, is undergoing penal servitude for life for complicity in a like plot.

The first explosion at Westminster was in the Hall itself, near the entrance to the Crypt, on the stairs leading to St. Stephen's Hall, and occurred a few minutes after 2 o'clock. It was clearly intended that this explosion should occur in the Crypt itself, and the fact that it did not was owing to a remarkable circumstance. Some visitors were passing through the passage of the Crypt when one noticed a parcel on the ground. It is described as the usual "black bag," and, it is important to add, it was surrounded by a woman's or child's dress; and the visitor called her brother's attention to it, remarking, too, that "it smoked." Her brother at once seemed to surmise that the parcel contained explosive, for he uttered the word "Dynamite!" and hurried his sister away, calling the attention of the policeman on duty to the fact that a parcel was in the place.

---

1 Glasgow-born Dr. Thomas Gallagher (born 1850), an Irish physician, was one of the best-known Fenian (Irish Republican) dynamiters of the 1880s. In 1883, Gallagher and a group of militants travelled from New York intending to detonate explosives at a number of symbolic buildings and national monuments in Britain. They were arrested before they could execute their plans. Gallagher was eventually released to an insane asylum where he spent his final years.

The nearest police constable, Cole by name, picked up the smoking parcel, and brought it to the entrance to the Crypt, where from its heat, or from some other cause, he dropped it. It was fortunate for him that he did so, for in an instant a terrific explosion burst from the parcel. The explosion was so violent that it was felt on Westminster-bridge and in the streets adjoining, and the vast Hall was filled with a dense fog of dust and vapour. The constables and other persons were thrown down, and, indeed, the policeman Cole was very seriously injured. The stone of the flooring was shattered and the rails round the Crypt were somewhat twisted by the immediate blow of the explosion. Its secondary effect was to break some of the windows, and to shake down from the vast beams of Irish oak forming the roof the accumulated dust of ages, and it was this dust with the vapour from the explosive, which together formed the fog. There had not been time to recover from the alarm which this unexpected event would naturally cause to all who experienced it, when a second explosion seemed to shake the building, and it was soon found that the Chamber of the House of Commons had been wrecked by a parcel of dynamite which had evidently been placed near the cross benches under the Peers' Gallery....

The explosion at the Tower of London was the most serious in its effects of the three, for several persons were injured, some damage was done to the building, and a fire ensued, lasting an hour. The means by which this outrage was carried out are similar to those adopted in the other cases. The public, it is well known, are admitted to view the Tower, and, moreover, as there are many people who do not care to be hurried from place to place in the historic building by the guide, some latitude has been allowed to those who have preferred to wander or linger behind. The criminal or criminals took advantage of the liberty thus allowed to lay the dangerous mine in the armoury in such a manner as to explode when there was a goodly number of the humbler class of visitors present, and many of these were injured.... The explosive was placed between the stands of arms in the ancient banqueting room of the Tower, and its vivid and instantaneous explosion injured, not only this room, but also the Council chamber. The cries of the wounded and alarmed people, women and children mostly, were most distressing, and when the shock had passed away many of them were found holding their heads, apparently stunned by the shock. The first measures taken by the authorities were to speedily stop all egress from the Tower, to attend to the wounded, and to bring the fire-extinguishing appliances into work, for the White Tower was in flames....

The police have in custody, and still detain on grave suspicion of being concerned in these outrages, an Irish-American....

[The article continues with descriptions of previous dynamite outrages and attacks in London beginning in 1883 involving government buildings, four railway stations, private clubs and residences, and the Nelson Column in Trafalgar Square. According to later reports, the numbers of "important dynamatic efforts" in Britain between 1881 and 1892 totaled 86. So-called "minor explosions" were not included in the yearly count ("Dynamite and Dynamiters" 120).]

2. From "Explosion in Greenwich Park," *The Times* (16 February 1894): 5

[The following report inspired similar accounts in Isabel Meredith's *A Girl among the Anarchists* (1903) and Joseph Conrad's *The Secret Agent* (1907).]

Explosion in Greenwich Park.[1]

Last evening an explosion was heard by a keeper of Greenwich Park on the hill close to the Royal Observatory. Proceeding thither he found a respectably-dressed man, in a kneeling posture, terribly mutilated.

One hand was blown off and the body was open. The injured man was only able to say, "Take me home," and was unable to reply to a question as to where his home was. He was taken to the Seamen's Hospital on an ambulance, and died in less than half an hour.

A bottle, in many pieces, which had apparently contained an explosive substance, was found near the spot where the explosion took place, and it is conjectured that the deceased man fell and caused its contents to explode.

The deceased, who was not known in Greenwich, is a young

1 Greenwich is a Royal Borough located on the south side of the Thames River. It is the site of the Greenwich Meridian (0° longitude) and iconic buildings and monuments associated with the nation's maritime history.

man of about 30, supposed to be a foreigner. The only evidence of identification was a card bearing the name "Bourbon."[1] Several letters, which the police have taken possession of, were found upon him, and it is stated that his hands were covered with a black substance, which cannot be got off.

The *Central News* says:— The London police have discovered an Anarchist conspiracy. These facts, among others, are beyond dispute—that the inquiries of the detectives, although cautiously made, frightened the plotters, that the gang hurriedly scattered, and that its chief met with his death last evening when endeavouring to carry away to some place the explosives which were to have been used against society either in this country or in France.

3. From "The Were-Wolf of Anarchy," *Punch* 105 (23 December 1893): 290

[The werewolf—part human, part wolf—has appeared as a powerful symbol of transformation in world myth and folklore since ancient times. Though common in English literature during the Middle Ages, the werewolf virtually disappeared in literature until the nineteenth century. The revival of interest in the werewolf was associated with the popularity of new forms of gothic literature and a growing interest in folklore in Britain and Europe. But as Alexis Easley and Shannon Scott demonstrate in *Terrifying Transformations*, the werewolf was also used to represent a range of contemporary anxieties about social change, Darwinism, imperialism, class, gender, and sexuality. In the following illustration taken from the middle-class satirical journal *Punch* (1841–2002), the werewolf is used to symbolize middle-class fear of social and political anarchy in a period marked by labour unrest and terrorist threats at home and abroad.]

1 The deceased was identified in a subsequent *Times* report as Martial Bourdin, an unemployed tailor originally from Tours, France.

Fig. 29. "The Were-Wolf of Anarchy." *Punch* 105 (23 December 1893): 290

Appendix E: Crime Fiction

[Many *fin-de-siècle* critics lamented the increase in crime fiction, seeing in its proliferation evidence of cultural degeneration. According to Arnold Smith, author of "The Ethics of Sensational Fiction" (*Westminster Review* 1904), "The increasing mass of sensational literature which appears daily is a serious symptom of mental debility in the country at large" (190). Smith's complaint echoed social critic Max Nordau's controversial claim that modern literature (including sensation fiction and works by such diverse writers as John Ruskin [1819–1900], Leo Tolstoy [1828–1910], Henrik Ibsen [1828–1906], Friedrich Nietzsche [1844–1900], and Émile Zola [1840–1902]) contributed to "a severe mental epidemic" and a "black death of degeneration and hysteria" (*Degeneration* 537).[1] For his part, Smith blamed the demand for sensational fiction on the "nerve-shattering conditions of modern life," the "ceaseless strain and worry which must be escaped from somehow, if only for an hour," and the "jaded state of the mind which craves a stimulus" (190). Novelists who regularly gathered their material from sensational reports in the press were frequently criticized for their role in encouraging the public's fascination with crime and criminals and for failing to bring criminals to account. The following excerpts from *Blackwood's Edinburgh Magazine* and the *Westminster Review* are examples of the contemporary discussion.

Blackwood's Edinburgh Magazine (1817–1980) was a highly regarded literary journal known for its critical essays and quality fiction by prominent authors such as George Eliot (1819–80), Anthony Trollope (1815–82), Margaret Oliphant (1828–97), and Joseph Conrad (1857–1924). *The Westminster Review* (1824–1914), one of the most significant periodicals of the nineteenth century, published essays on history, literature, politics, religion, philosophy, and science by leading writers including Eliot, William Thackeray (1811–63), Harriet Martineau (1802–76), and Thomas Huxley (1825–95).]

1. From "Crime in Fiction," *Blackwood's Edinburgh Magazine* 148 (August 1890): 172–89

Soporifics[2] are very well in their way, but on the whole the patrons of

1 See Appendix B5, p. 276, note 3.

2 Sleep-inducing substances. See "At the Edge of the Crater," p. 92.

the circulating libraries[1] prefer to be excited and interested. Hence the popularity of the sensational novel, taking horrors for its subjects and criminals for its heroes, and leading the reader onwards from surprise to the dramatic *dénouement* which should be enveloped in mystery. The range of the criminal romance is wide enough in all conscience. At the best it may be the subtle masterpiece of the analytical genius of a Balzac;[2] at the lowest, though not invariably at the worst, it may be dashed off in blood and thunder for the "penny dreadfuls" and the "shilling shockers."[3] Much depends, of course, on the public for whom the romance is intended; and the blood-besmeared story which has a grand success in the New Cut[4] would possibly not go down in Belgravian[5] drawing-rooms. Yet we venture to affirm that the criminal romance pure and simple ... has one unfailing characteristic—it leaves an unpleasant and unwholesome flavour behind.... [A]fter a tale of crime, however talented it may be, some taint of the disreputable company we have been keeping clings to us: we feel as if we had been conniving at their guilt, if not actually accomplices in it.... It is asserted, and we daresay with some truth, that novels like Ainsworth's 'Jack Sheppard,'[6] and illustrated sheets like the 'Police News,' have largely recruited the ranks of the thieves and the burglars. There the seed had fallen in kindly soil prepared by circumstances and hereditary depravity. The mass of

1 Private libraries that supplied books and periodicals to customers for a subscription fee.

2 French novelist and playwright Honoré de Balzac (1799–1850) was known for his detailed representation of French society.

3 Penny dreadfuls, also called "bloods," and shilling shockers were a form of cheap sensational fiction focusing on violent crime, adventure, and various gory subjects.

4 Extending from Waterloo Road into Blackfriars Road in Lambeth, the New Cut was the site of one of the largest of London's weekly street markets catering to working-class Londoners.

5 Belgravia is a fashionable and expensive residential district in London.

6 William Harrison Ainsworth (1805–82), a prolific author and editor, is best known for *Jack Sheppard* (1839), his enormously successful historical romance about a criminal executed in 1724 after a series of remarkable escapes from London's Newgate prison. The novel, which prompted numerous theatrical adaptations and cheap plagiarized versions, was particularly popular with working-class boys. Ainsworth's portrayal of his criminal protagonist as a hero and a dashing rogue caused considerable moral outrage through the 1840s. Concerns that the novel would encourage crime seemed founded when a young servant charged with murdering his master testified that he had been inspired to commit the deed after reading *Jack Sheppard*.

amateurs of the horrible in the upper or middle classes are more prosaically minded or less romantically disposed. At all events, they seldom dream of translating thought into action, and taking the short but dangerous cuts to their crimes which come so naturally to their favourite heroes and heroines. They are content to admire, to gape, and to swallow; to shrink delightfully at the rustle of the stealthy poisoner's nightdress and to shudder at the heavy thud of the hired ruffian's bludgeon as it lights upon some respectable head. Criminal fiction does little direct harm, in the sense of shortening inconvenient lives or tampering with important deeds. But it steadily demoralizes the palate for anything milder and more delicately flavoured: the habitual dram-drinker will have his stimulants stronger and stronger, and you cannot expect him to turn with satisfaction from spirits above proof, fresh from the distillery, to the choicest of Schloss Johannisberg or Château Yquem.....

2. From Arnold Smith, "The Ethics of Sensational Fiction," *Westminster Review* 162.2 (August 1904): 188–94

[Smith comments on the popularity of detective fiction featuring "doctors and men of science," a direct reference to medical mysteries, a subgenre that Meade apparently invented with her medical collaborators Edgar Beaumont ("Clifford Halifax") and Robert Barton ("Robert Eustace"). Smith takes modern writers of sensational fiction to task for frequently ignoring the "conventional morality" of bringing criminals to justice.]

The increasing mass of sensational literature which appears daily is a serious symptom of mental debility in the country at large. The cause of the demand for this fiction is not far to seek. It lies in the nerve-shattering conditions of modern life; in the ceaseless strain and worry which must be escaped from somehow, if only for an hour; in the jaded state of the mind which craves a stimulus. In a certain class of society a man seeks forgetfulness in a drink; in another he seeks it in the sensational novel; it may be doubted which anodyne[1] is the more dangerous. Both inevitably sap the intellect and destroy the mental powers; but the latter, thanks to free and circulating libraries, is the cheaper. Only the other day a case occurred in our law courts of a man who allowed his wife and children to starve while he read novels,

1 Something that soothes, comforts, or relaxes.

his mind apparently being so enfeebled with this modern drug that he was incapable of making an effort to procure work. We are not, however, concerned here with the benefits and evils of novel-reading itself, but with the ethics which find favour among certain modern novelists....

It is clear from the flood of detective stories with which we are deluged that the situation which interests, more than any other, a large section of the public, is that of the criminal fleeing from justice. The doings of the scientific murderer surpass in popularity even illustrated interviews with eminent personages. The ingenuity of these doctors and men of science with a *penchant* for poisoning people is perfectly amazing: many of the suggestions made by our writers must be of considerable use to the fraternity of rogues. It is probably by no means a cynical exaggeration to suggest that the callousness of modern sensational fiction is only a reflection of the callousness of its readers. We are too apt to assume that we are always progressing, and that humanitarian principles are the peculiar possession of our own time. The fact is that the fast-dwindling humanitarianism of to-day is a heritage from the first half of the nineteenth century; and this change, like every other symptom of public morality is to be noted in the novel: compare the *Frankenstein* of Mary Shelley[1] with the Frankensteins of to-day. It is becoming infrequent for the novelist to make the traditional concession to conventional morality of bringing his criminal to justice; when he does so the punishment is miserably out of proportion to the man's crimes. This rubbish which fills our magazines and lies on every railway bookstall is a very morbid indication of the mental health of the public. It is a direct incentive to vice and it panders to the lowest taste....

It is safe to say that all the evil tendencies of the time in which we live are magnified and disseminated by a class of sensational fiction which excites the passions and dulls the reasoning powers, is directly antagonistic to morality, and in its ever-increasing bulk threatens to overwhelm all other forms of literature.

1 *Frankenstein, or the Modern Prometheus* (1818) by Mary Wollstonecraft Shelly (1797–1851).

Works Cited and Recommended Reading

Adrian, Jack, ed. *Detective Stories from the Strand.* Oxford: Oxford UP, 1991.

——. *Strange Tales from the Strand.* Oxford: Oxford UP, 1991.

Agathocleus, Tanya. Introduction. *The Secret Agent.* By Joseph Conrad. 1907. Peterborough, ON: Broadview P, 2009.

Arata, Stephen. *Fictions of Loss in the Victorian Fin de Siècle.* Cambridge: Cambridge UP, 1996.

——. "The Occidental Tourist: *Dracula* and the Anxiety of Reverse Colonization." *Victorian Studies* 33.4 (1990): 621–45.

Bennett, E.A. "The Fiction of Popular Magazines." *Fame and Fiction: An Enquiry into Certain Popularities.* London: Grant Richards, 1901. 133–42.

Black, Helen C. "Mrs. L.T. Meade." *Pen, Pencil, Baton and Mask: Biographical Sketches.* London: Spottiswoode, 1896. 222–29.

Boase, George C. "Madame Rachel." *Notes and Queries* 8th ser. 6 (27 October 1894): 322–24.

Boothby, Guy. "A Service to the State." *A Prince of Swindlers. Pearson's Magazine* 3 (March 1897): 425–41.

Braddon, Mary Elizabeth. *Lady Audley's Secret.* 1862. Ed. Natalie M. Houston. Peterborough, ON: Broadview P, 2003.

Carnell, Jennifer, ed. *The Black Band; or, The Mysteries of Midnight.* By Mary Elizabeth Braddon. 1861–62. Hastings: Sensation P, 1998.

"Character Note. The New Woman." *Cornhill Magazine* 23 (October 1894): 365–68.

Chesney, Kellow. *The Victorian Underworld.* Harmondsworth, UK: Penguin, 1976.

Clarke, Clare. "Imperial Rogues: Reverse Colonization Fears in Guy Boothby's *A Prince of Swindlers* and Late-Victorian Detective Fiction." *Victorian Literature and Culture* 41.3 (2013): 527–45.

Collins, Wilkie. *Armadale.* 1866. Oxford: Oxford UP, 1991.

Conrad, Joseph. *The Secret Agent.* London: Methuen, 1907.

"Crime in Fiction." *Blackwood's Edinburgh Magazine* 148 (August 1890): 172–89.

Dawson, Janis. "'Not for girls alone, but for anyone who can relish really good literature': L.T. Meade, *Atalanta*, and the Family Literary Magazine." *Victorian Periodicals Review* 46.4 (2013): 475–98.

——. "'Write a little bit every day': L.T. Meade, Self-Representation, and the Professional Woman Writer." *Victorian Review* 35.1 (2009): 132–52.

Doyle, Arthur Conan. *A Study in Scarlet*. 1887. *The Original Illustrated 'Strand' Sherlock Holmes*. Ware, UK: Wordsworth, 1989. 11–63.

"Dynamite and Dynamiters." First article in series "Crime and Criminals." *Strand Magazine* 7 (February 1894): 119–32.

"Dynamite Outrages. Attempts on the House of Commons, Westminster Hall, and the Tower of London." *Times* 26 January 1885: 10.

Easley, Alexis, and Shannon Scott. *Terrifying Transformations. An Anthology of Victorian Werewolf Literature*. Kansas City: Valancourt, 2013.

"Explosion in Greenwich Park." *Times* 16 February 1894: 5.

The Extraordinary Life and Trial of Madame Rachel at the Central Criminal Court, Old Bailey, London, On the 22, 23, 24, and 25 September, 1868: The Report Copied Verbatim from the Times. London, 1868.

Ferrero, Gina Lombroso. *Criminal Man According to the Classification of Cesare Lombroso*. Intro. Cesare Lombroso. London: Putnam, 1911.

Greene, Douglas G. Introduction. *The Detections of Miss Cusack*. By L.T. Meade and Robert Eustace. 1899–1901. Shelburne, ON: Battered Silicon Dispatch Box, 1998. vii–xiii.

Hall, Trevor H. *Dorothy L. Sayers: Nine Literary Studies*. London: Duckworth, 1980.

Halloran, Jennifer A. "The Ideology behind *The Sorceress of the Strand*: Gender, Race, and Criminal Witchcraft." *English Literature in Transition* 45.2 (2002): 176–94.

Harkness, Margaret. *In Darkest London*. 1889. Cambridge, UK: Black Apollo P, 2009.

Harris, P.R. *The Reading Room*. London: British Library, 1986.

Hebblethwaite, Kate, ed. *Dracula's Guest and Other Weird Stories with The Lair of the White Worm*. By Bram Stoker. 1914 and 1911. London: Penguin, 2006.

"How I Write My Books. An Interview with Mrs. L.T. Meade." *Young Woman* 1 (1892–93): 122–23.

Hughes, Linda. "A Club of Their Own: The 'Literary Ladies,' New Woman Writers, and *Fin-de-Siècle* Authorship." *Victorian Literature and Culture* 35.1 (2007): 233–60.
Hurley, Kelly. *The Gothic Body: Sexuality, Materialism, and Degeneration at the Fin de Siècle*. Cambridge, UK: Cambridge UP, 2004.
Knelman, Judith. *Twisting in the Wind. The Murderess and the English Press*. Toronto: U of Toronto P, 1998.
Koven, Seth. *Slumming: Sexual and Social Politics in Victorian London*. Princeton, NJ: Princeton UP, 2004.
Linton, Eliza Lynn. "The Wild Women as Social Insurgents." *Nineteenth Century* 30 (October 1891): 596–605.
Lombroso, Cesare. "Atavism and Evolution." *Contemporary Review* 68 (July 1895): 42–49.
——. *Criminal Man*. 1876–97. Trans. Mary Gibson and Nicole Hahn Rafter. Durham, NC: Duke UP, 2006.
——, and Guglielmo Ferrero. *Criminal Woman, the Prostitute, and the Normal Woman*. 1893. Trans. Nicole Hahn Rafter and Mary Gibson. Durham, NC: Duke UP, 2004.
——, and William Ferrero. *The Female Offender*. 1895. New York: Appleton, 1898.
Luckhurst, Roger. "Trance-Gothic, 1882–1897." *Victorian Gothic: Literary and Cultural Manifestations in the Nineteenth Century*. Ed. Ruth Robbins and Julian Wolfreys. Basingstoke, UK: Palgrave, 2000. 148–67.
McDonnell, Maude. "The Wonderland of the Pacific." *Girl's Own Paper* 4 (July 1883): 645.
McLaren, Angus. *A Prescription for Murder: The Victorian Serial Killings of Dr. Thomas Neill Cream*. Chicago: U of Chicago P, 1995.
Meade, L.T. "How I Began." *Girl's Realm* (1900–01): 57–64.
——. "A School of Fiction." *New Century Review* 1 (1897): 220–31.
——, and Robert Eustace. *The Brotherhood of the Seven Kings*. *Strand Magazine* 15 (January–June 1898).
——, and Robert Eustace. *The Brotherhood of the Seven Kings*. *Strand Magazine* 16 (July–December 1898).
——, and Robert Eustace. *The Heart of a Mystery*. *Windsor Magazine* 14 (June–November 1901).
——, and Robert Eustace. *The Sorceress of the Strand*. *Strand Magazine* 24 (July–December 1902).
——, and Robert Eustace. *The Sorceress of the Strand*. *Strand Magazine* 25 (January–June 1903).

——, and Clifford Halifax. *Stories from the Diary of a Doctor. Strand Magazine* 6 (July–December 1893).
——, and Clifford Halifax. *Stories from the Diary of a Doctor. Strand Magazine* 7 (January–June 1894).
——, and Clifford Halifax. *Stories from the Diary of a Doctor.* Second Series. *Strand Magazine* 9 (January–June 1895).
——, and Clifford Halifax. *Stories from the Diary of a Doctor.* Second Series. *Strand Magazine* 10 (July–December 1895).
Melchiori, Barbara Arnett. *Terrorism in the Late Victorian Novel.* London: Croom Helm, 1985.
Miller, Elizabeth Carolyn. *Framed. The New Woman Criminal in British Culture at the Fin de Siècle.* Ann Arbor: U of Michigan P, 2008.
——. "'Shrewd Women of Business': Madame Rachel, Victorian Consumerism, and L.T. Meade's *The Sorceress of the Strand.*" *Victorian Literature and Culture* 34 (2006): 311–32.
Mitchell, Sally. "Elizabeth Thomasina Meade." *Oxford Dictionary of National Biography.* Oxford: Oxford UP, 2004. 643.
——. *The New Girl. Girls' Culture in England, 1880–1915.* New York: Columbia UP, 1995.
Nordau, Max. *Degeneration.* 1895. Lincoln: U of Nebraska P, 1993.
Parrett, Aaron. "The Medical Detective and the Victorian Fear of Degeneration." *Formal Investigations: Aesthetic Style in Late Victorian and Edwardian Detective Fiction.* Stuttgart: Ibidem, 2007.
Pittard, Christopher. *Purity and Contamination in Late Victorian Detective Fiction.* Farnham, UK: Ashgate, 2011.
——. "Victorian Detective Fiction—An Introduction." *Crimeculture.* Web. 24 July 2015. [1–8].
"Portraits of Celebrities at Different Times of their Lives. Mrs. L.T. Meade." *Strand Magazine* 16 (December 1898): 674.
Pound, Reginald. *Mirror of the Century: The Strand Magazine, 1891–1950.* New York: Barnes, 1966.
"The Probable Retrogression of Women." *Saturday Review* 32 (July 1871): 10–11.
Rappaport, Helen. *Beautiful For Ever. Madame Rachel of Bond Street.* London: Vintage, 2012.
Reimer, Mavis. "L.T. Meade." *Dictionary of Literary Biography, Volume 141: British Children's Writers, 1880–1914.* Ed. Laura M. Zaidman and Caroline Hunt. Columbia, SC: Bruccoli Clark Layman, 1994. 186–98. Web. 7 Sept. 2007. [1–15].
Rev. of *Lettie's Last Home*, by L.T. Meade. *Aunt Judy's Magazine* 16 (1878): 59–60.

Ridenhour, Jamieson, ed. *Carmilla*. By Sheridan Le Fanu. 1872. Kansas City: Valancourt, 2009.

Schooling, J. Holt. "Nature's Danger-Signals. A Study of the Faces of Murderers," *Harmsworth Magazine* 1 (1898–99): 656–60.

Showalter, Elaine. *Sexual Anarchy: Gender and Culture at the Fin de Siècle*. New York: Penguin, 1990.

Sims, Sue, and Hilary Clare. *The Encyclopaedia of Girls' School Stories*. Aldershot, UK: Ashgate, 2000.

"The Six Most Popular Living Writers for Girls." *Girl's Realm* 1 (1898–99): 431.

Smith, Arnold. "The Ethics of Sensational Fiction." *Westminster Review* 162.2 (August 1904): 188–94.

Standlee, Whitney. *"Power to Observe": Irish Women Novelists in Britain, 1890–1916*. Bern: Peter Lang, 2015.

Stoker, Bram. *Dracula*. 1897. Ed. Glennis Byron. Peterborough, ON: Broadview P, 1998.

Stott, Rebecca. *The Fabrication of the Late-Victorian Femme Fatale: The Kiss of Death*. London: Palgrave Macmillan, 1992.

Sutherland, John. *The Stanford Companion to Victorian Fiction*. Stanford, CA: Stanford UP, 1989.

Sweet, Matthew, ed. *The Woman in White*. By Wilkie Collins. 1860. London: Penguin, 2003.

Thomas, Ronald R. "The Fingerprint of the Foreigner: Colonizing the Criminal Body in 1890s Detective Fiction and Criminal Anthropology." *English Literary History* 61.3 (1994): 655–83.

Tooley, Sarah A. "Some Women Novelists." *Woman at Home* (1897): 161–211.

Tracy, Robert, ed. *In a Glass Darkly*. By Sheridan Le Fanu. 1872. Oxford: Oxford UP, 2008.

Wells, H.G. *The Time Machine: An Invention*. New York: Holt, 1895.

——. *The War of the Worlds*. 1898. London: Penguin, 2005.

Willis, Chris. "The Female Moriarty: The Arch-Villainess in Victorian Popular Fiction." *The Devil Himself: Villainy in Detective Fiction and Film*. Ed. Stacy Gillis and Philippa Gates. Westport, CT: Greenwood, 2002. 57–68.

Wolfreys, Julian, ed. *The Beetle*. By Richard Marsh. 1897. Peterborough, ON: Broadview P, 2004.

From the Publisher

A name never says it all, but the word "Broadview" expresses a good deal of the philosophy behind our company. We are open to a broad range of academic approaches and political viewpoints. We pay attention to the broad impact book publishing and book printing has in the wider world; we began using recycled stock more than a decade ago, and for some years now we have used 100% recycled paper for most titles. Our publishing program is internationally oriented and broad-ranging. Our individual titles often appeal to a broad readership too; many are of interest as much to general readers as to academics and students.

Founded in 1985, Broadview remains a fully independent company owned by its shareholders—not an imprint or subsidiary of a larger multinational.

For the most accurate information on our books (including information on pricing, editions, and formats) please visit our website at www.broadviewpress.com. Our print books and ebooks are also available for sale on our site.

On the Broadview website we also offer several goods that are not books—among them the Broadview coffee mug, the Broadview beer stein (inscribed with a line from Geoffrey Chaucer's *Canterbury Tales*), the Broadview fridge magnets (your choice of philosophical or literary), and a range of T-shirts (made from combinations of hemp, bamboo, and/or high-quality pima cotton, with no child labor, sweatshop labor, or environmental degradation involved in their manufacture).

All these goods are available through the "merchandise" section of the Broadview website. When you buy Broadview goods you can support other goods too.